THE Left Hand IS THE Dreamer

BY NANCY WILSON ROSS

Fiction

THE LEFT HAND IS THE DREAMER

TAKE THE LIGHTNING

Non-Fiction

FARTHEST REACH

THE WAVES: *The Story of the Girls in Blue*

WESTWARD THE WOMEN

NANCY WILSON ROSS

THE Left Hand is THE Dreamer

WILLIAM SLOANE ASSOCIATES, INC.
Publishers   New York

Published by William Sloane Associates, Inc.

Manufactured in the United States of America

For

S. Y.

THE Left Hand IS THE Dreamer

Chapter One

SINCE BREAKFAST THE MOURNING doves had been reminding Fredericka Perry that it was time to cut forsythia. Hearing them now plainly from the stair landing, where someone had left the window ajar, she stopped on her way to her bedroom to look out at the March garden. Her eyes sought the bushes beside the brick wall. There, yearly, ever since she was a child—for twenty-five springs, or was it nearer thirty?—she had taken cuttings to force into early blossom. The bushes still looked stripped and dry, yet the purling doves assured her that close at hand she would find cocoons of bloom along the brittle twigs.

April, promised the doves, April, April. Fredericka allowed the gentle half circles of sound to cast a spell on her body until, forgetting what had brought her upstairs, she leaned against the window frame breathing in the fragrance of the new season.

When she heard a step in the hall below, she turned from the window and saw Aunt Palm moving about under the cast-iron lantern. She was looking for something in the teakwood cabinet that stood in the perpetual twilight of the stained-glass window. With a little pang of sadness Fredericka observed the old-lady droop at the back of her aunt's neck, a laxness in the lean body that had always been so quick. Aunt Palm was growing old. Her brown eyes were still warm and deep, but her dark eyebrows had turned gray to match the two bands of white hair moving away from her temples like wings.

Although she was wearing the usual bottle-green work smock over a black bouclé dress, her slight figure under the great lantern seemed foreign and unfamiliar. It must be the angle of my vision, Fredericka thought, staring down at her; she looks from here like a lonely lady of large affairs in another era, bound now on some strange errand—giving a prince a lesson on the lute, or putting poison in a pearl.

Or did these fanciful ideas spring from the family's new attitude on Aunt Palm? Dimly, obscurely, some shadow was falling over her mind and spirit—or so they all said. Her own son Christopher, who was Fredericka's husband, said so in particular, and all the rest of them whispered that lately Aunt Palm appeared to be a little touched in the head.

Fredericka resented these whispers. They also made her afraid. She could not bear to admit any change in this person whom she loved most in all the world, to whom her life had been bound since earliest childhood. She would argue: What more was there to the apparent change in Aunt Palm than merely her years—a blurring of the mind alternating with a sudden acuteness of perception, as though she received information from some special source? Hadn't Aunt Palm always found it difficult to distinguish clearly between what was true and what imagined?

"That's because she's an artist." Fredericka, just the day before, had defended his mother to Christopher. "All artists are like that."

"What do you know about artists?" Christopher had asked.

Fredericka started to answer, "Because I"—but she did not finish. In all the family it was only Aunt Palm who would have understood her reply. Instead she went on—trying to talk herself out of her vague apprehensions. "I think your mother has always been just the way she is now, only not so bold—or so careless—about showing it."

Christopher had made no answer. . . .

Aunt Palm, having found what she was looking for in a shoe box full of oddments, now returned the box to the interior of the wooden cabinet and started toward the stairs. From the way she moved it was plain there was something definite on her mind. Her small feet in the black pointed oxfords that had been the style several years before—she never wore out shoes—came decisively up the stairs to Fredericka by the window on the landing.

"The doves," Fredericka said, inclining her head, meaning, Listen!

Aunt Palm did not stop. She smiled faintly, nodded, and went past down the hall murmuring to herself lines Fredericka knew and so could recognize, even spoken as they were now, almost below the breath: *Shade is on the brightest wing and dust forbids the bird to sing.*

It was not unusual for Aunt Palm to reply with a line or two of poetry—all the Woodward family were great quoters —but this morning it made Fredericka uneasy. They were melancholy lines and the doves underscored them mournfully. Aunt Palm is in one of her dark moods! A shadowy fear, irrational, barely perceptible, brushed across Fredericka's mind. This will make it almost impossible to tell her about Christopher, she thought.

Christopher was going to war; volunteering, of his own free will, after weeks, months even, of "Shall I? Shan't I?" (For it was unlikely he would ever be drafted.) Surely to announce this decision to his mother was commonplace enough, when so many were going. Though Aunt Palm was never one for making undue fuss or protest, neither Fredericka nor Christopher had been able to gather the courage to break the news. Only that morning Christopher had said a little crustily: "I do wish you'd tell Mother about me. You're better with her than I am. I'll be going to Washington to see Charlie Goodrich in two days. It's high time she was told."

"I'll tell her while you're gone," Fredericka had promised, outlining her mouth with lipstick; and, as she did so, hearing Bridgie saying, "You should use a brush, Freddy. You've a mouth like Hedy Lamarr." Hedy Lamarr, indeed! Was it true? She had bent a little toward the mirror. True or not it was certainly like Bridgie, who forgot half the time to use any lipstick at all, to want her sister to appear bewitching.

"Why not tell her today?" Christopher had interrupted Fredericka's critical observation of her mouth. His question was reasonable enough but his voice had an edge.

"All right, today then," she said hastily, busy with the black velvet band for her long pale bob.

"She will probably be difficult," he had continued, using the angular tone in which he so frequently spoke of his mother.

Fredericka half turned. "Why should she be?"

"No reason—except, coming so soon after Father's death . . ."

Christopher did not finish what he was saying. He was reknotting his tie for the third time. Fredericka watched him, suddenly taking in his casual good looks, the double-breasted gray flannel, the dark-blue tie, the modified crew haircut. He really didn't look thirty-seven. There was something boyish in him still—soft now, but still boyish. . . .

"What is it?" he asked half irritably, returning her stare. "Is something wrong? Don't you like the tie?"

"The tie?" She was startled. "Oh, yes, of course." She added, "I gave it to you."

"Did you?" He was mollified. "That's right. I'd forgotten." He carefully put a fresh handkerchief in the breast pocket of his suit, adjusted his cuffs.

For a small-town man, she thought, living among people who wouldn't know a pin stripe from a hounds-tooth check, he does have a lot of fussy mannerisms.

"Mother worries me," he said. "She's not acting herself."

"Perhaps she was never more herself," Fredericka could not help suggesting, as she gave her hair a last quick brush.

Christopher set his mouth, a habit he had when crossed in conversation. It went back a long way, that habit. She could remember it when they were children playing together. She knew all his habits—as he must know hers—intimately. Not only had they grown up together like brother and sister, they had been married for fourteen years. Yet they could still say to each other, and frequently did, "I don't understand you."

That was the special thing about Aunt Palm—she had always understood. From the day Fredericka as an infant had come to live permanently—because of her mother's illness—in the Perry household, Aunt Palm had been more like a mother than her own mother. Between them from the first there had been a natural bond. But lately, no matter how Fredericka denied it to the family, something was wrong. She could no longer move as freely in and out of her aunt's mind and moods. There was some subtle blockage, making it necessary to think of special ways to reach her. Now, for instance, to keep the promise to break Christopher's news, she would have to devise means of capturing Aunt Palm's attention. Otherwise, Aunt Palm might pretend later not to have been told at all.

Fredericka looked out again at the garden. Something imaginative, she thought—something perverse—it would take to do it. She looked again at the doves. Two of them on the garden wall were pecking viciously at each other's throats.

Birds! Birds would do it! Birds seen as monsters—with their shrill dartings, impersonal cold eyes, quick vicious claws, and beaks designed for cruelty: the worm-seeking robin on the spring lawn, all angry appetite, irascibly demanding more rain to make his murderous life easier; snip, snip, snap, the jay shreds the wings of the gentle yellow moth. . . . Her memory quickened. She saw medieval paintings of underworld punishment by Bosch and Grünewald, where winged creatures, with birds' legs, heads, and wings, tortured man through a presumable eternity.

This fancy about birds as creatures of cruelty would probably delight Aunt Palm. It might even bring back memories of the lively days of the aviary at Wrenkill.

Years before, Aunt Palm had built an aviary off the dining room, the time Uncle Caleb went all the way to Chicago. She had deliberately planned it during his absence and it was quite obviously done to spite him, to interfere with his mealtime monologues, or to compete with the homely aphorisms, hearty predictions of doom, and general overexpansiveness that were characteristic of Uncle Caleb at the dining table.

Fredericka remembered the afternoon—she couldn't have been more than seven—when Otto Schultz, painting the aviary walls the special green he and Aunt Palm had spent the morning mixing, fell off the stepladder on overhearing that the Old Man was already in Utica on his way home a week early.

It was sheer fear of Uncle Caleb that dropped Otto five feet onto the hard stone floor. The stepladder fell with a clatter and the twenty birds—waiting in the dining room for the completion of their home—protested at once at the top of their operatic voices. . . . That was all Fredericka recalled of this particular scene, but the splintery arias of the Harz Mountain canaries ran through her childhood, and melted, at last, into a composite tonal memory of meals with Aunt Palm, Uncle Caleb, and the three boys—Robert, resistant; Sprague, furtive; Christopher, detached; and herself, the pet, with Uncle Caleb's boom roaring around the dark-oak walls in vain rivalry with Aunt Palm's flock of shrill competitors.

The canaries had been gone for years. They had succumbed, finally, to a mass disease of mysterious origin, and were buried in the birch grove back of the house under a single headstone. Fredericka could hardly remember their names now: Ella, Prunella, Trixie, Dixie, Wahltraub—the other Valkyries. . . . Even the careful headstone carving, done by Sprague's scout knife, was disappearing in the weather. *Dust forbids the bird to sing.* Sprague gone too—dead at fifteen—dying as swiftly, as meaninglessly, as the canaries. No longer missed even, Sprague; remembered only dimly like a character in a book.

And now Uncle Caleb was gone. But he would be remembered, for he had lived long and violently enough to leave his own legend. These old high-ceilinged rooms with their flowered wallpapers and their hand-carved cornices had echoed to his shouting and his stomping, making the very draperies tremble, tinkling the distant parlor sconces as he passed. Uncle Caleb! Uncle Caleb throwing cobs of corn on the dining room carpet if it came in overcooked, emptying lukewarm coffee into the centerpiece as he bellowed for Eunice on a gloomy Monday morning, relieving his bladder from the upstairs side balcony in summer moonlight when he chose to, no matter who happened to be in the front garden at the time. Uncle Caleb was a Perry, and for over one hundred and fifty years no Perry had had to give a damn for anybody along the New York stretch of the Susquehanna or the Delaware River. This had remained the only world that Uncle Caleb had ever found of any consequence.

And Aunt Palm, thought Fredericka, as she lingered listening to the cool buttery phrasing of the doves, Aunt Palm found no world of any importance. Yet for all her seeming indifference down the years she had put Caleb Perry in his place for his Perry arrogance and mock theatrics. Upon occasion she spoke of him as a "rural Barrymore." His frequent "Hah!" and "Bah!" his clenched jaw, the toss of his wild hair, left her unmoved. She observed his repertoire of poses with analytical eyes.

But Fredericka as a child had never managed to become indifferent to Uncle Caleb. Every gesture he made had been memorable, like that of an unpredictable and wholly wonderful giant. She could still see him cracking chicken bones with his big strong teeth to extract the marrow. Always he had kept a small oyster fork and a walnut pick beside his plate with which to dig out the succulent lining of the tender bones. Sometimes he would reach over to Aunt Palm's plate—or perhaps, terrifyingly, to Fredericka's—and remark, "Wasting the best part of it!" Then he would proceed to split the bone with a quick snapping sound of his cigar-stained teeth, the sight of which had frightened Fredericka as a baby every time the mouth under the thick mustache opened in a prodigious roar of mirth or rage.

Whenever Uncle Caleb reached for the bones on her plate Aunt Palm, sitting back from her own half-touched dinner, she left the window and went to regard her reflection long and deliberately in the hall mirror. She observed, with some appreciation, the clear dark gray of her eyes, the fine black brows and lashes, the pale ash-blond hair, the oval of her face. Why in childhood had she been given the strange nickname of Flea? No one any longer knew.

"You might have been a beauty," she murmured, half aloud, appraising the face with a painter's detachment.

Might have been? Why not are? Why not could be? she demanded immediately, a little nettled; and almost at once supplied her own answer: Because it takes effort. Too much effort. And she avoided effort. She frankly admitted that she did not possess the juice and ginger of Aunt Palm. Even her painting—the thing she would have said she cared most about of anything in life (more about, in a way, than her two children)—was shamefully neglected. The days went by, the weeks, the months—and, although the thought of the passing of time and her half-done canvases filled her with despair, it never filled her with energy.

We've all lost what Uncle Caleb called "git-up-and-git," she went on thinking. Uncle Caleb considered "git-up-and-git" an exclusive Perry trait—but of course it wasn't, for there was that fearless mythical river giant, Philander Decatur Gleason, lurking in the background of the less spectacular Woodward line. "Philander Decatur, give me strength!" murmured Fredericka, crossing her fingers and uttering the old charm she remembered using in childhood to ward off fears in the dark.

Strength for what? To give up Christopher? This was not going to take strength, it was merely going to demand some minor readjustments in the pattern of her life, a pattern fixed almost to the point of ritual. To give up Christopher was not would comment in the flat, high-pitched, and artificial voice she reserved for such occasions: "The saber-toothed tiger consumes his prey in one swift bite," or, "The jaws of the sulphur-bottomed whale measure two hundred feet across."

No one ever bothered to question Aunt Palm's zoological data, no one, that is, except her brother, Philander Decatur Woodward. Uncle Philander was an amateur naturalist, ornithologist, geologist, and zoologist. He knew—and had given Fredericka occasion to remember—the name and nature of every animal, bird, twig, leaf, root, weed, moss, and pebble in all upstate New York. For that matter his knowledge, according to his own estimate, extended also west and east of the Rocky Mountains into a strip that included the Black Hills of Dakota, parts of Montana and Wyoming, and a portion of the Great American Desert.

"In referring to the sulphur-bottomed whale, Palmy Days," Philander would begin, addressing his sister in a leisurely but deadly professional tone, stroking his red beard with careful rhythmic gestures like a fakir taming a snake.

But Aunt Palm always cut him short. Making no gestures —for she had few mannerisms—she would remark: "I was not referring to the sulphur-bottomed whale as such. I was referring to Caleb's zoo table manners."

In spite of the barbed comments Aunt Palm directed at Uncle Caleb, Fredericka knew quite well that some way, somehow, he had commanded her respect—even her love, or a bond very like it. What was it she had said of him? That he was a "man." It had been her last and final measure of her husband as he lay dying.

Still staring out dreamily at the awakening garden, Fredericka asked herself: What quality did the older generation have that we have lost? As though hoping to find the answer, going to demand a garnering of her forces. Surely she could admit this much without feeling guilty.

Christopher had never caused her pangs or torture, heart-burning or anxiety. He had not lost all his money in the Crash and then tried to open his veins or inhale monoxide gas as two men of his class at Princeton had done. He did not drink heavily, like Charlie Jones, or make up to other women, like Clifford Keynes. He was not quarrelsome, he was not vulgar, he was, as a matter of fact, very like her father, who was the least intense and eccentric of the Woodwards, a man of even temperament whom no one disliked and no one adored—except perhaps her sister, Bridgie. Christopher should have been her father's son, she thought, and Louis Aunt Palm's. For Aunt Palm was the only one in the family who understood Louis, the family wanderer; Louis who had been home only once in twelve years, who had had the courage to take what he wanted. Freedom? Was that it? But what was freedom? Perpetual movement? Six times around the globe in as many years, an authority on the politics of small confused countries like Hungary, Albania, Czechoslovakia? . . .

Though Aunt Palm had abetted Louis in his escape years ago, she had never been anywhere herself. Uncle Caleb would not travel. The very notion upset him. "Caleb won't go where he can't stamp his foot and get attention" was Aunt Palm's explanation. It was true. Uncle Caleb was not at ease in any environment that he could not dominate. Once he did get as far as buying tickets for Europe, but a week before their sailing date he fell ill with a baffling malady and took to his bed. The symptoms did not yield readily to medical diagnosis but after the boat had left the New York pier without them his temperature dropped perceptibly and he took a renewed interest in food. Soon he was on his feet again and, not long after, he and Aunt Palm were able to go away to Saranac Lake, a resort Aunt Palm heartily loathed.

So Aunt Palm had never seen Europe. But Fredericka had, on her honeymoon. Everyone she knew had done Europe then. The world was flowing with money. She and Christopher set off for six weeks of the breathless tourists' tour. They did it all, and Fredericka came home worn out. For while Christopher slept until noon recovering from the bars and night clubs where they went to meet his Princeton friends and their brides, she was up and out early trying to look at Paris, London, Rome with Aunt Palm's eyes, hearing her distant voice . . . "Take a good look at the Mona Lisa, lovie. I've often wondered if it wasn't overrated. And do try to get to the Zwinger—it will be worth it to you. That's in Dresden. You might as well give up Lake Geneva. There's only the view. Remember the glass at Chartres. I'd go to The Hague in your shoes . . ."

"You should be going yourself, darling," Fredericka had cried, pained and ashamed to be given an opportunity that she accepted so calmly.

Aunt Palm had dismissed the remark with, "Not in this life, I'm afraid."

Fredericka took Europe in such a large dose that it was only a shapeless mass in her memory. She had a hundred colored prints she had bought. She had the Georgian silver teapot from London, purchased with Uncle Caleb's check. That was about all. As for Christopher, he had brought back some small talk about the French oysters and the way they cooked sole at Prunier's, and the roast beef at Simpson's and —and this was funny!—a gesture, now characteristic, of pushing down his thick blond mustache like a guardsman they had dined opposite one day at Claridge's. So much for culture!

Oh, culture, culture, culture,
It's on us like a vulture . . .

as Uncle Philander always sang when Bridgie spoke of her Current Events Group in Thermopylae. But he shouldn't laugh at Bridgie, Fredericka thought, smiling, for Bridgie's intentions were of the best. Bridgie said she didn't want to "get behind on things." Her husband, Owen, felt the same. She, Fredericka, got behind—and with no excuse. Christopher too. He read *Time* spasmodically and depended on it for his views of world events. He knew less about national and international affairs than Nathan Frisch, the local barber, who read all the current periodicals in the Wrenkill library from eight to nine three evenings a week.

"We're a dull lot," Fredericka told herself out loud. "A dull lot!" she repeated, listening to her voice echo dismally in the empty hall. She saw herself and Christopher, their friends—the Barretts, the Terrys, the Keyneses, the Joneses—like single-dimensioned figures cut from paper. What one of us is capable of Aunt Palm's surrealism, Uncle Philander's flamboyance, Uncle Caleb's theatrics? We aren't characters, she thought, we are just pale people with tics: Christopher chainsmokes, rubs the pages of books with his fingers as he reads; Joe Barrett bites his nails; Charlie Jones drinks too much; Cliff Keynes ogles girls; Owen is always sucking on his pipestem as he talks; even serene and placid Bridgie has a furtive way of pinching her flanks in inactive moments as though in compensation for the double helping of cream pie. . . . Mild aberrations, yes, but not the stuff of drama.

And what is your tic—if you have one? she asked herself abruptly. The question drew her up short. Like the queen in the fairy tale, Fredericka consulted the mirror for the second time. If she had any nervous habits the mirror did not reveal them. The face that looked back at her was calm, controlled. Yet Christopher found her tense. "What are you so tense about?" he frequently asked. "Tense? Am I tense?" Nothing she could think of indicated it, except, perhaps, the way her shoulder blades sometimes took on a look of tightness. She dropped them now deliberately, thinking, "String, string, unwinding string!" which a gymnasium instructor had once told her was a technique for relaxing.

Tense I may be, she admitted, but of my worst fault, my most fatal weakness, no one has ever accused me. Yet how well I know it myself! My aversion to change and disruption. My dreamy procrastination. Right now, because of this flaw in my character, I am postponing going down the hall to break the news to my aunt that her son, my husband, is going to war. Also I am unable to face the fact that he is going not out of nobility, but out of boredom.

Why had she said that? Christopher had not admitted his boredom to her. Perhaps, she thought, he does not even know it, yet now she was sure that this was the underlying reason for his wish to go to war. For one thing, Christopher was too old to fight—though his health was good, with the exception of infrequent bouts of stomach disorder invariably diagnosed by him as imminent ulcers, but by Dr. Payne as "dyspepsia" or "nervous stomach." Why was he bored? Was it because of some failure of hers? Or was it the business? It couldn't be the business. Apparently the bank and the family real estate had, up to now, occupied him just enough, not too much. He was his own master and could go and come as he chose. Yet he seldom went anywhere—not even to New York. They talked every autumn about going down for the winter, but they never did. When winter arrived a sort of apathy came over them. The days flowed past with easy and familiar monotony and soon it was spring again with everything as before.

They saw the same friends year in and year out, the handful the countryside afforded, who had had the same advantages and possessed relatively the same outlook and income: the heads of the chemical plant at Spartanville, the two gentlemen farmers, the local insurance man. But Christopher had always appeared satisfied with these companions for fishing, duck shooting, deer hunting, Saturday afternoon gatherings with highballs when they listened to football games played in distant stadiums they no longer visited.

Now this life would be over. The routine would be broken. Christopher was going away. A surprising feeling of release rushed through Fredericka. All sorts of shapeless plans and ideas sprang into her mind, all of them leading away from Wrenkill.

She began to think of her children. She tried to estimate their reactions to their father's departure. It would be hard to tell about Leslie and Forrest. They were very self-contained— "frighteningly poised," Bridgie had once said of them. "Dutch genes," Uncle Philander had muttered in reply. They were beautiful children—long-boned, blond, with wide blue eyes. The painter in Fredericka never saw them without a little lift of pride and the wish to capture them again on canvas. She had painted or sketched them every other year.

They were away at school now, and had been since Uncle Caleb's lingering illness made it seem wise to send them. She had expected to be lonely without them, but actually, after the first weeks, she had missed them very little. There were times when she was really glad they were gone. Am I unnatural? she asked herself. She thought at once of her sister —of Bridgie's single-pointed concentration on family life:

stamps, butterflies, paper dolls with her children; pressed glass and hardy perennials with her father; genealogy with her husband; herb cookbooks, baskets of knitting, Christmas cookies. . . . Bridgie would never feel the way I do, Fredericka thought. She had never confessed to Bridgie her true opinion of domesticity. She had talked freely only with Aunt Palm. She remembered now how she had questioned Aunt Palm about her unending fatigue when the children were little. Even with the help she had had then she had been distracted and exhausted by the constant attention, the unflagging questions, the fixed routine. Until the children came she had worked every day at her painting. Afterwards she could never seem to get back to a work schedule.

"Energy," Aunt Palm had said, explaining the weariness. "It's where your energy is. Bridgie's is in her body."

"In her body?" Fredericka had asked in some astonishment.

"Yes, in her body," Aunt Palm said, a touch irritably, as though finding her half-witted.

Fredericka did not continue with the next question: But where would it be if not in her body? Dimly she understood what Aunt Palm meant. Aunt Palm herself was frail in her bones, but strong in her spirit, tireless when doing what she wanted to do—sitting on a hillside painting, looking at books on art. . . .

Strength came into Fredericka at the thought of her aunt's powers of concentration and absorption. But under this feeling lay also the familiar ache of realization that her aunt's life had been wasted. Wasted? Could she say that? It was a very strong word, a word that, at this moment, both arrested her attention and frightened her.

She turned abruptly and walked down the hall to Aunt Palm's room.

Chapter Two

WHEN, AFTER KNOCKING, FREDericka opened the door of Aunt Palm's "studio" she found her seated at the oak table that ran almost the length of the room. The handsome, high-nosed old lady did not look up or speak when her daughter-in-law entered. Her long thin hands, with their prominent knuckles, were busy with a paste pot and shears. She was at work on her baseball scrapbook.

Fredericka walked over to the table and looked down. Aunt Palm was pasting in a large picture, clipped from the sports page of a newspaper, entitled SCORING AND FAILING TO SCORE IN ST. LOUIS YESTERDAY. Under the picture the caption read:

Stephens of the Browns doubled, sending Epps (15 left) home, but McQuinn failed in his attempt to tally as Richards, Detroit catcher, tagged him out on this play in the fourth inning. Moore (15 right) is the next batter and Stewart is the umpire. Both Epps and Moore wore shirts with the number 15.

"Beautiful," Aunt Palm murmured.

She had been working on the newspaper photograph with red and blue crayons. It had become an abstraction of triangles, rectangles, half circles, and arcs built around the rising and falling, sprawling and bending forms of Stephens, Epps, McQuinn, Moore, and Stewart.

As long as Fredericka could remember she had heard Aunt Palm murmuring "Beautiful," "Exceptional," "Very interesting," over the sports pages of newspapers. Aunt Palm knew nothing at all about baseball—or for that matter any other sport. She did not know one league from the other and, if anyone turned on the radio to hear a game, she was annoyed and left the room. But baseball photographs interested her passionately. There were, she said, in all modern life few pleasures as great as observing in photographic form the rhythmic abstractions created quite unconsciously by batters, runners, umpires, and basemen.

She had well over a thousand photographs that she had collected and "abstracted" with her colored crayons. Fredericka knew that she had left the collection in her will to the Art Department at Attica Center. In the front of each volume she had written: *Presented in the hope of opening the unawakened American eye.*

Obviously not trusting even the eye of instructors in art, however, these scrapbooks conveyed hints on how she meant the pictures to be seen. Above a study in moving triangles entitled FURTHER PROOF THAT STEALING BASES DOESN'T PAY Aunt Palm had pasted a slip reading: "See *Michelangelo's Entombment of Christ (a rhythmic triangular dance). Also Perugino's The Combat of Love and Chastity.*"

Aunt Palm's knowledge of art was encyclopedic, her opinions arbitrary and highly personal, based as they were almost exclusively on reproductions cut out of magazines or purchased by mail.

The most ordinary conversation with Aunt Palm had always led around to art, to painting, painters. . . . "Here, lovie, let me crimp your hair so tomorrow it will look like curly moss. . . . Green hair would be nice. We might dye it in a vat of elm leaves at the dark of the moon. There was a painter once who painted his models' hair green. No, come to think of it— it was their faces. Faces green as moldy Cheddar. Lovely! Like the bread at the lake in August. This man was a noble- man, and a dwarf . . ."

And so on and on, a tale spun of fact and fancy until the young Fredericka no longer felt the pull on her skull as her hair was braided. For she was wearing the velvet beret and the long full velvet smock with the flowing bow tie and the round collar, while in her left hand, extended rather self-consciously but proudly, like an amateur's sword en garde, she carried a brand-new shiny painter's palette. She was dressed like her favorite photograph of Aunt Palm in the heavy leather album with the gold clasps, the one opposite the artificial snow scene showing her aunt with Uncle Caleb in a sleigh, a little ermine muff held to her laughing face. . . .

"Do you know what I'm remembering?" Fredericka asked, still looking over her aunt's shoulder. Without waiting for a reply: "I'm remembering a day when I was about fourteen years old. We walked up Hungry Hollow road to the old Grayson place and sat down on a big flat rock."

Aunt Palm was listening. You could tell it by the way she held her head.

"We had our sketch pads," Fredericka went on. "You said, Look, the bull is a rectangle. I looked over into the fields on the side hill and I saw that it was. Then you said, The hay- mow is a circle and the poplars in the wind are whirling green tops. Put in a bit of the fence rail down at one side like ribbons, you said, and make the grass like green confetti and you'll have a painting."

"I remember that day." Aunt Palm stirred her paste pot with the wooden end of a paint brush. "Some days you remember for no special reason. Or else the reason doesn't seem special at the time."

Fredericka dropped down by the fire on a stool. She held her hands out to the warmth. "I think I remember it so clearly because it was the first time I understood something about form." There was a silence stirred only by Aunt Palm's scissors whispering through the newspapers.

"What's on your mind?" Aunt Palm asked suddenly. She lifted her dark eyes to her niece's face for one brief instant.

Fredericka, startled, pulled back her hands from the fire. "What makes you think there's anything on it?"

"It's all too plain," Aunt Palm said dryly.

"Only to witches, I'm sure." Fredericka gave a little nervous laugh, took a full breath and came out with it. "Christopher is going to enlist."

Aunt Palm did not look up or even stop cutting. Her scissors moved steadily through the newspaper on the table.

"Right away," Fredericka went on, "as soon as he can. He thinks he can make the Air Corps, with a little help. He's too old to fly, of course, but he hopes he can get some ground work. Air Ordnance, maybe. Charlie Goodrich is going to help him. He's a colonel already."

"And what if he is too old for the Air Corps?" Her aunt's voice was perfectly matter-of-fact.

"Then I think he'll try to get into Military Government. They train men for it somewhere in Virginia, I believe."

"I thought he would be going off before long," Aunt Palm said calmly. "What will you do?"

What had she been afraid of? Fredericka asked herself. The whole thing was natural, simple, and easy. "Well, I thought I might go to Attica Center this spring and take a course or two at the college. Try to peel the rust off my brain."

"Courses in what?"

"I thought of getting back into my painting." She stumbled a little as she explained. "Farrell is still there. The man I studied with before. He has New York shows regularly now. He's quite successful."

Aunt Palm was still listening.

"I even thought of taking some other courses," Fredericka ventured. "World history—something like that."

"That's sound common sense," Aunt Palm remarked.

Fredericka was flooded with relief.

Aunt Palm began to run her shears expertly around another clipping. "Exceptionally interesting," she murmured, pausing to study it.

Fredericka came to look over her shoulder again. HANK GREENBERG HOMES ON A FLY read the caption. Her aunt's delicate nose—the nose that was supposed to be pure d'Abbeville—bent nearer the scrapbook. The glasses she should wear, and would not, lay beside her on the table, perilously near the edge. It was deliberate, though apparently unconscious, carelessness. That her eyes were failing she could not bear to admit, because her eyes had given her the unqualified pleasures of her life.

Fredericka, restless, went to look out the window in the thin sunlight. "I'm going to pick some forsythia today. I'm sure it's ready to bring indoors. We'll have blooms in ten days."

Aunt Palm wiped her fingertips openly on her bottle-green smock. "Forget the forsythia. You do it every year."

"Well, why not?" Fredericka asked, a little defensively. "Spring comes every year, doesn't it?"

Aunt Palm did not choose to make any direct reply to this manifestly absurd question. After a moment, "Christopher wants to escape," she said. "He's bored. The war means nothing to him, but escape does."

Fredericka waited tensely for the rest of it.

"He wouldn't break the news himself because he knew I'd tell him what I thought, and he doesn't want to hear it."

Still Fredericka said nothing.

"The truth is," concluded Aunt Palm, "the old nag is dead."

"Now what do you mean by that?" Fredericka demanded.

> "Trot, trot, to Boston
> To buy a loaf of bread,
> Trot, trot, home again
> The old nag's dead."

The old woman repeated the nursery rhyme quite flatly, without emphasis or humor. There were certainly no dramatic gestures, no Witch of Endor cackling, and yet she managed to convey an uncomfortable impression of dark prophecy. For the hundredth time in the year just past Fredericka asked herself: Is Aunt Palm changing or am I? Has she always been like this? How mad is she? Is she really mad at all?

"Remember I'm one of the less imaginative Woodwards," Fredericka said, after a pause. "Put it another way if you can."

"Your home is breaking up."

At these words Fredericka's heart jumped violently. Here it was! The thing she had been fearing, the thing Aunt Palm was going to say to her that she could not bear to hear.

"What do you mean?" she forced herself to repeat indifferently.

"A general breakup," Aunt Palm went on, calmly applying glue to Hank Greenberg homing on a fly. "It's the beginning of a general breakup. Everywhere! War always does it. The pieces never get put together in the same way. New forms have to emerge."

"What new forms?"

"How should I know? I'm not a prophet."

"You certainly sound like one." Fredericka glanced nervously at her aunt's calm averted face. Her attitude is as detached as though she were diagramming our lives like her baseball pictures, she thought. A feeling very like panic swept through her.

"Perhaps I shouldn't do it—go to school, I mean. Perhaps I should do something more toward the war effort. Be a nurse's aide like Bridgie."

"Rubbish," said Aunt Palm, slapping the paste onto the page. Her tone became for a moment almost personal. "Aid yourself! You need it!"

This time Fredericka did not ask her what she meant. She was afraid to hear the answer. "Then you approve—I mean about going to Attica Center?"

"I approve." She nodded once sharply. "You aren't more than ten years late."

When Aunt Palm was in this state of mind you did not press her. You were apt to hear quite enough without asking for it. Today Fredericka felt she had taken all she could.

"I'm driving over to Thermopylae to see Daddy and Bridgie this afternoon," she said, rising. "I want to tell them about Chris . . . Will you come along?"

"Not today, lovie." Her aunt's tone was again remote, but gentle. "I've started this now and I want to finish it." She pointed the scissors at the basket of clippings. "Most of these are last year's. The new season will be here before you know it and I'll be swamped again. I saw by the papers that the Red Sox—or was it the Indians?—were warming up somewhere in Florida."

Aunt Palm bent her nose again over the yellowed clippings.

She departed as definitely as though she had left the room. The absorbed, averted face filled Fredericka with a terrible loneliness. She had the impulse to cry out, "Aunt Palm, come back! Where are you? I need you!" She waited a moment longer, hoping her aunt would speak. When she said nothing Fredericka went out and closed the door quietly behind her.

Chapter Three

IT WAS TWO IN THE AFTERNOON WHEN Fredericka drove her car from under the porte-cochere of the Perry Mansion—as Uncle Caleb's house, inherited from his father, was known in the town of Wrenkill. Viewed from the front the house was tall and gaunt; from the sides it was spacious but shapeless. It had turrets, pillars, and gables. It had bay windows, dormer windows, and an oriel window with stained glass. It had a watchtower occupied of late years by the squirrels, and any number of unused porches with fancy wooden eyelet embroidery, like the lace edging on an old-fashioned pillow sham. Although it was an architectural monstrosity, Fredericka had always loved it. Yet today, somehow, she could not bear it. As ugly as the rest of the town, she thought to herself, giving it a fleeting glance from the turn in the drive.

Winding on down the hill she looked critically over the familiar grounds, and they too wore for her an air jaded to the point of shabbiness. She made an effort to correct the feeling, summoning the mood of hot July afternoons in the garden near the imitation antique well, with the heavy lazy scent of roses promising an evening storm. She tried next the silence of December snow in the birch grove with the gently creaking pine woods just beyond, the band of cold bright sky seen above the icy slope. She put on rubber boots and squished through the spring mud of the farm immediately adjoining, where Emmet Burns of the cleft palate raised chickens, pigs, and vegetables for the Perry table. Fluffs of peeping chicks, squeal of curly-tailed pigs, the trusting stupid eyes of newborn calves—none of it made any appeal.

At once, having admitted this, she was ashamed. She reminded herself quickly that she was privileged and should be grateful; that she had always been privileged, even long before this turbulent moment in history when homeless people —people like herself, Christopher, and their two children— were everywhere plodding hopelessly on springtime roads, with hands as empty as their eyes. She tried to imagine Wren-kill as a heap of rubble—the whole time-worn town—no longer sagging, but smashed flat. She saw herself alone walking the river road, one of a few survivors. Where would she go? What road could she take? . . . the bridges out, the meadows mined, the sky a great enemy eye . . .

The triple honk of Jake Blunden's car brought her up sharply. Jake was the postman; the honk was his greeting to all villagers. She honked back, and Jake repeated the signal and rattled on. She noticed that his car appeared to be noisier and junkier than she remembered. Was this another proof of the sharpening of her critical sense? Ever since Christopher had broken the news of his wish to go to war she had observed a change in herself. She saw things about her with a fresh eye; it was almost the eye of one who is saying goodbye to familiar objects for a long time.

If it is farewell I should feel more tender, she thought, indulging her aimless fancies. She looked toward the rolling hills that moved off along the river. She saw, nearer at hand, how magnificent the elms were in the front yards. No, in all fairness, she rebuked herself, one could not say that Wrenkill was a completely ugly town, though it lacked the atmosphere of many upstate New York communities where Greek revival and colonial architecture had happily escaped the Victorian blight. Wrenkill had enjoyed a wave of railroad prosperity at the wrong time. During the boom period most of the owners of semiclassical houses had seen fit to add, on a scale at once cramped and ornate, tower rooms, hand-carved porches, and those characteristic and useless upstairs excrescences barely large enough to admit a single chair where a resident might perch amidst the smothering green leafage of an upstate midsummer. A few Wrenkill houses, like the chaste Presbyterian manse which had not been able to afford redecoration, stood as monumental rebukes to transient taste.

The Perry mansion, resting majestically on its hill, set the community's architectural tone. In spite of its annual coat of paint it too breathed the local miasma of decay. As for the houses she was passing now, within her lifetime Fredericka had seen almost all of the ones larger than six rooms given over either to corpses or to tourists—the Oakes Funeral Home, the Twin Elms Tourist Rest. The main street, she thought, parking her car near the family bank, might be a stage-set for a rural Hollywood comedy—almost, not quite. It was a little too down-at-the-heel and weather-stained.

As she got out of the car she saw in the window of the Citizens Bank and Trust Company the old shined-up hurricane lantern that Cyrus Perry, in the days before electricity, had kept burning nightly for fifty years inside the bank's front door. The sight of the lantern made Fredericka feel distinctly queasy—it always did, though why she could not have said until today. Now the explanation began to stir dimly in the depths of her mind as she crossed the street to the drugstore.

During the depression Christopher had found the old lantern in a vault and had persuaded his father to put it in the window as a sort of symbol, something steady to point to that had endured down the years—like the Perry name. "The Light That Never Failed," wrote the Wrenkill *Bee*, and published a little story on the Perry and Woodward families. The papers in Utica and Binghamton—and even as far away as Syracuse and Rochester—took it up and reprinted it. Christopher had been very pleased with himself.

The lantern, Fredericka decided, was depressing precisely because of the aura that clung to it—an aura of stale tradition, of name and place that no longer stood for anything positive in the changing modern world, kept alive like the town's three-legged dog coming down the street now, hopping as always behind his red-faced master, his swollen body stretched into his skin like a gigantic sausage. The owner, having decided to let his pet live after the injury, was fondly feeding him to death, making his movements every day more difficult.

Fredericka never saw this mutilated creature without a wave of mysterious discomfort. She hurried into the drugstore. Taking out her list she began to read: dental floss, milk of magnesia, aspirin . . . Pinned to the list was the sheet from Christopher's reminder pad. "Please," heavily underlined, "don't forget to tell . . . to look up . . . to write . . . to ask . . ." Christopher never trusted his own or anyone else's memory.

Standing by the salted nuts case waiting for someone to attend to her wants, she listened idly to the talk. An alarming world disorder, anti-Semitism, was being aired by Mr. Blodgett of the Ladies Emporium. He slouched his great bulk on one of the spindly-legged stools of the soda fountain, eying with furtive interest the bursting pink sweater of the girl who was making his milkshake. Seeing Fredericka, he raised his voice, first nodding to her and briefly lifting his large posterior a fraction of an inch from the stool as a gesture of respect to a Perry.

"Jew prices," he was saying. "$11.29. $1.49. See what I mean? Prices that act as though they're givin' you something. But what the hell're they givin' you, I ask you? Never could abide it. *Two* scoops, Mabel."

Mabel, having put in the double scoop of chocolate, placed the metal container under the mixer, and began languidly to wipe the counter with a cloth. Under her plucked brows her sullen eyes were dreaming of the embraces of Robert Taylor. Robert Taylor being unavailable, she was accepting the services of Guy Crandall at the filling station. The whole town knew it. It was a public scandal. Mrs. Crandall was now having her sixth. The Baptist Ladies had threatened to have their husbands boycott Guy's filling station, but its handy location —plus the growing gas problems which made it wise to stick to your former sources of supply—worked against them. These details Fredericka knew because Eunice, the downstairs maid, with the license permitted by her service of twenty-five years, insisted on regaling local gossip no matter how cold its reception.

Although Mabel's attention was obviously elsewhere and Fredericka was not even looking at him, Mr. Blodgett drove on relentlessly with the development of his favorite theme. Fredericka fastened her eyes on the nuts moving in their little heated house. Ronald Case, the druggist, made a specialty of his salted nuts. Did keeping them in movement really attract the purchaser? Fredericka wondered. It was the kind of advertising question Christopher's friend Joe Barrett would enjoy discussing after dinner.

She could not help hearing Mr. Blodgett.

"Take a suit, for instance—$39.94. What's the matter with a good straight forty dollars? What're you goin' to do with the six cents your generous-hearted friend just gave you? That's what I ask 'em!"

When he turned his swollen, rubbery face toward her Fredericka could not avoid meeting his eye. She averted her head quickly and moved away. At once she was afraid her disdain had been too apparent. She reminded herself that his remarks were not greatly unlike some she had heard recently from a number of their friends, and from her brother-in-law, Robert. Just a little more veiled and suave, those others— that was the only difference.

She had now come within earshot of the other conversation in the drugstore. This one had to do with allergies. It was Ronald Case's favorite topic of discussion. Wrenkill was in the center of a hayfever zone and Ronald annually made a tidy income from his assortment of respiratory remedies, all of which—with cunning psychology—he deprecated as "useless . . . complete waste of money . . . try it if you like but I can't recommend it." He was now going on to some stranger in the aggressively cheerful voice with which he customarily spoke of afflictions and calamities:

"Worse every year! Worse and worse! More people affected . . ."

Ronald Case came from an old family that had "gone to seed," as they said in Wrenkill. The last of his father's estate had been used to send him to Harvard, fifty years before. Traces of his experience were left in his well-bred, rather mincing voice. He was an ardent bird lover and used to trouble Aunt Palm with frequent telephone calls about the first swallow, the last thrush—until she finally told him one day, somewhat shortly, that she had given up the observation of birds. They bored her, she told him. He had never quite recovered from the shock of this desertion. It was one more contribution to the local legend of Palm Perry's growing madness.

Over Bridgie's protest Owen would sometimes do an imitation of Ronald Case in his Famous Program of Bird Calls, Featuring in Particular the Mating Call of the Double-billed Duckbill. "Now don't!" Bridgie would cry. "The children love him." In Bridgie's opinion that forgave Ronald for everything. When the spring herbariums were displayed for the annual prize at the Thermopylae Public Library (of which Bridgie was the most active board member) Ronald Case was always invited to perform. He gave his bird calls; Uncle Philander displayed his collection of local rocks . . .

"Hello, Fredericka," Ronald interrupted to say now. "Be with you in a moment!"

He went on with his monologue to the stranger, who was obviously a salesman and so at Ronald's mercy. "No, thank Heaven! I have never been allergic, not to any stinging shrub or insect either—poison ivy, for instance, or spider bites. No, sir, the only thing I'm allergic to is redheads. They do something terrible to me. Got a redhead for a wife. Yes, sir, that's a fact."

Suddenly Ronald Case's unrelieved banality, Mr. Blodgett's now audible enjoyment of the double scoop of chocolate, Mabel's bursting sweater, the revolving disk of salted nuts took on, for Fredericka, the aspects of a nightmare. She could not go on standing at the counter, waiting to read aloud her list . . . dental floss, aspirin . . . She saw herself as meaningless, as impersonal, as the nuts in their glass case, revolved slowly by a hidden mechanism. . . . Murmuring something vague to no one in particular she hurried out of the store, aware as she did so that her going would probably be put down to irritation at having had to wait. "Who does she think she is? Those high and mighty Perrys!" Then in time she supposed it would be: "Oh, well—all the Perrys are crazy. So are the Woodwards. Old Mrs. Caleb Perry—she was really daft. Her niece took after her . . ."

Seeing Nate Frisch in his barbershop window was like a sudden brief breath of sanity. Nate's nearsighted eyes were bent over the boxes of green plants that would later become his tomatoes, lettuce, cabbages, and broccoli. Nate's windows caught the full morning sun and he always had the first garden in town. He had grown vegetables there for so many years that only strangers to Wrenkill commented on the incongruity of vegetable frames in a barbershop.

Nate had the face of a kindly scholar, with furrowed brow, warm thoughtful eyes behind heavy lenses, and a full humorous mouth that also wore a look of hidden suffering. He and Fredericka had been friends since the days when he cut the children's hair. She knew him better, she often thought, than many of the people with whom she sat down to dinner. They had more in common, though she had to admit that she was his intellectual inferior.

Uncle Caleb had always used Nate Frisch as an example of how little practical value there is in pure knowledge—knowledge for knowledge's sake. Nate could discuss, if you were interested, religion, politics, history, sociology as he cut your hair, and still he had never climbed higher than the Wrenkill barbershop. It was a mystery that seemed to baffle everybody but Nate. He called himself a philosophical anarchist. Apparently that explained it all. There was no meanness in his nature. He had followed a dream to the New World from a little German town, and when the dream remained a dream he simply transferred it to the future of his grandchildren and went his way without bitterness.

Catching sight of Fredericka, Nate lifted his hand in greeting and beckoned to her. She opened the door of the empty barbershop and stepped inside. She was always a little embarrassed to be seen talking with him. This, she supposed, went back to the dicta of Uncle Caleb, who had been a great believer in people's keeping their places. Frequently very hearty himself with his economic inferiors, he did not invite remarks beyond the state of the weather from those who contributed little if anything to the nation's taxes. Christopher shared his father's viewpoint though he did not know the people of the town. He had never had much to do with them. During his father's last illness he stepped into his place, but to Wrenkill residents he would always be simply "running the Old Man's bank."

"I just heard Mr. Christopher's going to war," Nate said, his kindly voice as interested, Fredericka thought to herself, as though he really cared.

"If they'll have him. . . . I want a jar of that special ointment of yours for him to take along," she added, to explain what she was doing inside, if questioned later.

"I think that's mighty fine of him," Nate continued, reaching for the ointment. "With all his responsibilities. My boy joined up just before Pearl Harbor. He said he saw it coming." He put the ointment in a paper bag.

"I remember. Where is he now?"

"Just got his wings. Passed high. He's a lieutenant now." He spoke with a mixture of pride and sadness.

"I just can't realize that your boy is old enough," Fredericka said, pausing at the door. "I'm afraid I haven't come to grips with the idea of the war at all. We seem so cut off here."

"Never mind," Nate said solemnly. "It'll reach us. Bound to! In time it'll touch all the houses in Wrenkill one way or another."

His face was the same kindly face Fredericka had always known, but his words seemed ominous, and somehow unlike him.

Opening the door and saying goodbye she realized suddenly that Nate was German by birth. In the last war his windows had been broken by hoodlums. What if in this war someone should scrawl JEW across the cheap glass of his shop windows? She could imagine it: the ugly word—ugly only by implication—sprawling over the pane, hiding the new green plants in the window boxes, concealing the shining overhead light, the two worn leather barber chairs, and the shelf of homemade ointments.

Back in her car she drove slowly down the familiar side streets to Mrs. Jessup's house. Mrs. Jessup washed the Perrys' Sunday damask tablecloths and all their sweaters. She lived in the part of town where women made spring housecleaning a ritual. Because of the unexpected warmth, they were already scrubbing their porches, airing the cushions of the porch swing, dusting the rigid rockers. In the evenings, very soon now, these same women would be pointing up the quiet green twilight with the creak and squeak of swing and rocker, their work-twisted hands folded comfortably on their laps. Sometimes as children Fredericka, Christopher, and Robert had been permitted to come down into the town to roller-skate here with their school friends. Now this remembered squeak-creak, squeak-creak seemed to Fredericka the very sound of time itself.

Mrs. Jessup began to talk before she had the door open.

She led the way into the parlor where she tied up the package. She never had it ready. Intentionally so. Not for anything would she deprive herself of this weekly chat. "As I was sayin' to Miz Perry," she would be telling her neighbors for days to come—a conversational opening sure to command attention.

While Mrs. Jessup packed the laundry, nodding her frizzed white bob in constant affirmation of her own remarks—uttered at the top of a nasal pitch—Fredericka, who had learned to practice a technique of even-paced murmurs, stood looking at the plants that crowded the bay window. Every week as she studied these hyperthyroid growths Fredericka questioned how Mrs. Jessup, a chronic pessimist, whose touch on everything seemed that of frost, drought, taint, and death, could produce such phenomenal greens. The cascading ferns fell from the ceiling of the narrow room with all the powerful sweep of the cataracts of the Nile. There were hen-and-chicken plants that multiplied from pot to pot, like the miracle of the loaves and fishes. On stand, shelf, taboret, and ledge was a dense thicket of nameless plants which never appeared to bloom but did produce bloody and acned leaves, as colorful as a mad painter's sunset.

Could this welter of unnatural vegetation be painted, Fredericka found herself wondering, painted in all its sickness and greed?—for it was like some monstrous evil consuming the light and air in the dark, unventilated parlor, over which Mrs. Jessup's muscular purse-lipped mother and limp haggard father brooded in chromo unreality.

". . . It's all in the Bible," Mrs. Jessup was shrilling, placing the sweaters carefully in the same worn box from Saks Fifth Avenue.

She had Fredericka's attention at last. "What is?"

Mrs. Jessup stared in feigned surprise. (She suspected Mrs. Perry of not listening.) "What I was just sayin'." Her voice rose half an octave. "The prophecies!" She almost shrieked the menacing word. "About what's happenin' now in the world," she added, dropping her voice to a more normal level.

"Oh," Fredericka murmured, and then sensing the inadequacy of her response, "Which prophecies?" She knew at once that this question was a serious mistake. She could already hear Mrs. Jessup speaking to her neighbors about young Mrs. Perry's lack of Biblical knowledge.

"Revelations!" Mrs. Jessup rounded her lips and shot the word at Fredericka as though her mouth were a pea shooter. "Revelations! Just you read the Bible, Miz Perry. It's all there. Why, only last night in Daniel I was reading aloud to Dad and I said, If this isn't it, Dad, I said, Listen to this: *In the same hour came forth fingers of a man's hand, and wrote over against the candlestick upon the plaister of the wall . . . MENE, MENE, TEKEL UPHARSIN. . . . God hath numbered thy kingdom, and finished it. . . . Thou art weighed in the balances, and art found wanting.*"

"But which kingdom is finished, Mrs. Jessup?" Fredericka pressed, this time with genuine interest.

Mrs. Jessup looked up from winding the rest of the string onto a cardboard cone, her face rigid with a fanatic's hatred. "Why, the Japanese, of course. Those heathen! Attacking our good Christian boys! I wouldn't trust a one of them. That Saito now. I wouldn't buy a vegetable from him if I was to starve. They're all spies!"

"Oh, come now," Fredericka said in mild protest. "Saito? He's a harmless little man. What would he be spying on around here?"

"The chemical plant," whispered Mrs. Jessup, thrusting her loose chin forward like a turkey reaching into a trough.

"But that's absurd," Fredericka said. "Saito isn't anywhere near any of the roads that lead to Spartanville. And anyway, he works too hard in his garden to have time for spying."

Mrs. Jessup drew in her mouth until it disappeared. Through the incision she spoke haughtily. "Well, you'll see!"

Fredericka, timid about creating ill will, tried now to placate her. "What about Germany?" she asked, beginning to move toward the hall where the "Stag at Bay" stood etched forever in the glass pane of the door. "I mean in the prophecies."

"Oh, Germany too, of course," Mrs. Jessup agreed with cool haughtiness. "But still you can't quite feel the same way about the Germans. They're too much like us, I'd say."

"I wonder," Fredericka said, and in the instant that Mrs. Jessup paused to ponder this cryptic phrase, Fredericka slipped past her and got outside.

Putting the bundle of laundry on the back seat, "Coward!" she said to herself grimly. Sliding in behind the wheel she repeated it. "Coward!" Why, she asked herself, didn't you really put Mrs. Jessup in her place about Saito? For that matter, why didn't you tell Mr. Blodgett in the drugstore that his prejudices are precisely what we're at war about? She thought of her brother Louis. Louis would have told them both off. He would have made a public scene if necessary. She remembered Louis's scorn of the smug and sheltered existence of Wrenkill residents the last time he came home with his blonde Hungarian wife. He and Hedi, on their historic visit, conducted themselves like characters in a Russian novel of the nineteenth century, arguing violently over everything from politics to wine temperatures, slapping each other at double solitaire, embracing each other with frank fervor in the sitting room, breaking the antique four-poster in the guest room. . . . Yes, Louis would certainly have challenged Mr. Blodgett, Mrs. Jessup—would have rebuked them, set them straight, silenced them at least temporarily.

But, for that matter, so would Owen, her brother-in-law, rebuke Blodgett, defend Saito. Using the Thermopylae *Clarion* as his mouthpiece Owen stood for local justice and for both ill-timed and well-timed interference in civic matters. She could imagine what he would say when she told him about Blodgett on the soda-fountain stool. She reminded herself that she was on her way to Thermopylae to see Owen and Bridgie and, coming to the crossroads, she took the turn along a branch of the river.

She had not gone more than half a mile when she passed the house where Saito, the Japanese vegetable man, lived. With a distinct shock she saw that the little house was abandoned. She stopped the car and got out to look. He was gone, gone without a trace—and he had been here only a week ago. The house was stripped. The sheds empty. . . . Nate was right. The war was beginning to affect even Wrenkill. Months after the wave of "alien" exclusion had swept the Pacific Coast, the far-flung spume of its fury was reaching these hidden sleepy backwaters.

When she maneuvered the car out of Saito's muddy roadway she turned it around toward home. She had decided that she did not want to see Owen or Bridgie, did not want to listen to their cheerful, admirable civic talk. She wanted only to go back to the garden and cut the forsythia before the afternoon turned too chilly.

Chapter Four

BACK IN WRENKILL, FREDERICKA picked up Christopher at the bank and brought him up the hill. He was acting abstracted and remote, like a man with a lot on his mind.

"Everyone thinks you're wonderful to do what you're doing," she told him.

"Everyone? Who's everyone?"

"Well, people in town . . . Nate Frisch . . ."

He grunted.

"I'll bet Owen gets the jitters soon. He hates to miss anything."

Fredericka was silent.

As they drove under the maples he asked, "Do you know where the oil coupons are kept?"

"You mean the furnace coupons?"

"Yes."

"Of course," she said. "In the same place. The top right-hand drawer in my room upstairs."

"I want to go over all that stuff," he said vaguely. "Oil coupons, gas coupons, the state income tax . . . I've got a heavy two days ahead of me. Thank God, I've got Rusty to leave in the bank. I'll have to raise his salary some way or other—though technically he's frozen. . . ."

Aunt Palm was standing on the porch as they drove up.

She was wrapped in an old tweed coat and she carried her knotted walking stick.

Opening the door of the car, Aunt Palm said to Fredericka, "Emmet says he heard a hermit thrush this afternoon, down by the spring. He'll be singing again about now. Want to come?"

"I'll meet you there."

She and Christopher went together into the hall. Kicking off her pumps and pulling on some boots, Fredericka told him that she had broken the news of his departure to his mother that morning.

Christopher came immediately to attention. "How did she take it?"

"Perfectly calmly."

"Really?"

"Yes."

"Well, I'm damned!" he said.

Fredericka took a leather jacket from the closet and went out into the early twilight. She ran across the garden to Aunt Palm.

Dinner that night was difficult. Christopher was irritable. He had discovered, just before they ate, that there was no more Noilly Prat for Martinis, and none to be bought now in all America. He decided to use the dinner hour to go over with his mother some details of his father's estate. This, Fredericka knew, was because Aunt Palm had come in from the walk, and the hermit thrush's evening concert, more cheerful than she had been in some time. But she resisted Christopher's attempts to interest her in business details. She lapsed into monosyllables and crumbed up her roll with gestures of repressed annoyance.

"Don't fuss so," she said finally. "It's all of no consequence."

Christopher set his mouth in the familiar hard line. "Unfortunately, Mother, not everyone can adopt that cavalier attitude."

"You should read *Superman*," Aunt Palm suggested, cracking walnuts of which she was perversely making a belated meal. "It's all so easy. Put your heels together and zoom off. They say the Atlanteans could do it. *Vril*, they called it. Presumably it's the power that built the pyramids, too. Knowledge of the atom. Wendy could do it, too. How well I remember Maude Adams in *Peter Pan*. No one like her. I wonder why she dropped out of the theater."

"Did you ever seriously face the idea of the poorhouse, Mother?" Christopher asked. He was not usually so sharp.

"No," Aunt Palm said, calmly. "Why should I? If you didn't have me to worry about, what would you worry about? You have used your brain so exclusively for worrying, my son, that you could not force it to function in any other way. I'm delighted you're going to the army. There's always someone above you or below you to whom you can pass the responsibility. This should prove relaxing."

"Speaking of passing on," said Fredericka, hastening to come between them, "Forrest writes that he has to have a dinner jacket. Do you think he could use yours cut down?"

"Use mine?" Christopher looked astounded. "What will I do for one?"

"Well, I thought the war . . ." Fredericka dropped it uncertainly.

"They may be cutting dinner jackets like the new pajamas by the time this war is over," Aunt Palm said. "You wouldn't want to be out of fashion, would you?"

"Forrest can buy his own—out of his allowance," Christopher suggested grimly.

Fredericka laughed. "He should have one by the time he graduates from Yale then. That gives him around seven years to buy it—if he gives up Coca-Cola."

"Well, you buy him one," Christopher said. "Don't bother me with it. I've enough on my mind."

After dinner Joe Barrett came in to go over insurance details with Christopher. Joe, according to Christopher's estimate, was "one of the smartest insurance men in the state." Christopher often said that he trusted Joe's judgment implicitly and that he was willing to confide in him any and all matters. He was a small man, a little older than Christopher, growing faintly rotund. He wore shell-rimmed glasses and walked with a cocky rolling gait that had always amused Aunt Palm. He and Christopher had been friends from boyhood, and Fredericka had played many a game of Pilgrims-and-Indians and hide-and-seek with Joe in the Perry woods and on the adjoining farm. Joe had been one of her regular playmates until the boys reached the baseball stage and Fredericka passed from such close association with her male cousins and their friends.

The two men retired at once to Uncle Caleb's den, taking Fredericka with them to answer possible questions.

The night was cool enough for a fire and she lit it and sat down in the hard leather wing chair beside it to wait until she could be useful. The den had remained an unfamiliar room to her. During Uncle Caleb's lifetime it had been sacrosanct, set foot in only by invitation. Tremblingly, at irregular intervals, Eunice had entered with a duster, always expecting, and always receiving later, the accusation of having disturbed some of Uncle Caleb's precious papers. His huge old-fashioned square desk had been piled high with a miscellaneous disarray of written matter which he wished to attend to personally without any interference from vinegary and competent Miss Harvey at the bank. It also held, buried under dead correspondence, boxes of his favorite candied ginger, discarded cigars, fur earmuffs; his own first button boots preserved in bronze, holding well-sharpened pencils; Christmas cards, birth and death notices, photographs, as well as buried neckties, cuff links, and suspenders that he had discarded in a flurry of concentrated work.

Now the room, with Christopher occupying it, was conspicuously, coldly tidy. Christopher used it only when listening to the radio programs no one else wanted to hear, and for holding his Saturday night poker games.

Sitting with a magazine in her lap, idly flipping through it, Fredericka dimly heard the two men moving from Life to Education, from Education to Fire and Theft. Her mind went back to the morning's conversation with Aunt Palm. . . . *Trot, trot home again the old nag's dead . . . Shade is on the brightest wing and dust forbids the bird to sing . . . Nonsense, aid yourself . . .*

She suddenly became aware that a question had been addressed to her by Joe. She flushed. "I'm sorry. I was woolgathering."

"I was asking what you thought your aunt's paintings would be worth—if anything."

"Yours too, for that matter." Christopher was making nervous marks on a sheet of paper. Fredericka observed that he was looking embarrassed and slightly ill at ease. Joe's expression was carefully blank.

"I don't know," she began uncertainly.

"You see now why I wanted an inventory," Christopher said pointedly.

"Do you mean you want me to list all her paintings—and mine?"

"Is it such a job?" Joe asked. He grinned. "I've heard your mother has an atticful of her work."

"Hundreds," Christopher said grimly.

"Well, the canvases themselves must be worth something," Joe continued, "whether what's on them has any value or not."

Fredericka found his tone offensively smug and superior. It reduced Aunt Palm to an elderly eccentric with means enough to indulge her crazy whims. What it makes of me, who also paint, I don't know, she thought. Her face must have reflected her feelings, for Joe hastened to add:

"Mind you, I don't know a damn thing about painting . . . only what I like, as the fellow said. Wrenkill may be harboring a genius for all I know. Two geniuses," he added with easy heartiness.

"I've no idea what value to place on them," Fredericka said coldly. "I'd say no value—and include mine."

"But the canvases," Joe began. "I mean the stuff itself. Theoretically, can't the other side be used?"

"No," Fredericka said firmly.

She got up and went out of the room. Annoyed at herself for betraying her feelings, she decided to pretend that she had merely gone to the pantry for the liquor tray. Standing for a moment between the dining room and the kitchen, breathing in the familiar smells, the ghosts of many good dinners, the cool nostalgic scent from the bowl of fruit that always waited here, the jar of raisin and oatmeal cookies, never empty since childhood—How foolish you are, Fredericka! Why should you care? Anyway, you deserve it. Every bit of it. You've never made your painting stand for anything, so why should Joe or Christopher respect it? Why should anyone? But her heart burned again at the thought of their open indifference, their veiled contempt for her aunt's work.

When she reappeared in the den with the liquor tray Joe looked up and gave her his most beamish glance through his shell-rimmed glasses, exposing at the same time his little sharp glistening squirrel teeth.

"Good girl!" he said approvingly.

She put down the tray.

"One and a half or two?" she asked, holding the jigger in her hand.

"Make it two. That's a very becoming dress, Freddy."

"Thank you."

"Green's your color, I think. Suits your hair."

"I'm glad you like it."

"I don't believe your hair has altered a shade," he went on, "since you were a kid. Gosh, I remember those long blond pigtails. Quite a temptation, weren't they, Chris?"

Christopher, with his back turned, murmured distantly.

She poured their drinks. "You won't need me any more, will you?"

Christopher looked up from the papers on the desk. "Stick around a little longer, if you can. Something might come up that only you can answer."

"I doubt that." But she sat down again.

The two men went on with their talk.

It was boring, but at least Joe had not brought Merry, his wife, to spend the evening, she thought gratefully. Meredith Barrett was a pleasant enough girl, a great friend of Bridgie's because they both believed in community activities like garden clubs, book clubs, and current events clubs. Between them they had organized the whole countryside into little knots of earnest women who met regularly to read aloud, over mending, the latest best seller, to discuss the situation in South America, to give prizes for the most striking autumn arrangement of cattails, sumac, and china mallard ducks.

Fredericka approved of these activities in theory but she had never been able to give herself to them. "But aren't you *lonely?*" Bridgie cried frequently. "No," Fredericka always replied. "Why should I be?" But she supposed the question was reasonable enough. She had no close friends. Perhaps, viewed in a certain light, it was an alarming condition. The truth was that she had lived in such a communion of interests with her aunt in her growing years that she had never needed or wanted outside companionship. Even at college she had formed no bonds intimate enough to last. There was indeed only one vivid memory from that time—but this was a memory she did not allow herself ever to entertain.

No, she said quickly, turning her mind away from this disturbing thought with a smoothness born of long practice. She had needed no one but Aunt Palm. Her eyes, her ears had been enough. For Aunt Palm was always stopping as she walked, pointing, crying "Look," to a red leaf, to a roof with snow on it; whispering "Listen" to the first whippoorwill, to a fish splashing, to the drip of icicles in a sudden thaw, or the churn and chink of water under a float. She was forever stooping, scraping, picking up, examining the delicate secret life of the hidden world close to the earth. She had taught Fredericka a kind of simple ecstasy that was easily fed out of a country environment. It was a pleasure that really endured, ever changing, yet ever constant; it could be counted on to soothe pain, banish unrest, appear to be, finally, an end in itself. And this, she supposed, might be considered its danger. For in time, grown slack and lazy with the years and with no challenge on any hand, you found satisfaction enough just to observe, to feel, to let the sharp sweet trickle of painful joy rush into the heart, with no related necessity to express the mood, the light, the scent and form in your own way. Yet you knew, experiencing it as you did, that you were supposed to give something back—a gift you offered freely to life, with no strings attached, a tacit give-and-take not to be ignored without payment of a heavy price. It was this tacit demand that she had failed, was failing. She knew it. Aunt Palm knew it. It had become something of which they could no longer speak—her neglected painting.

When around midnight Joe had said his final cheery good night, Christopher returned from the front door with a lowering face.

"What was the matter with you tonight?" he demanded abruptly.

"What do you mean—what was the matter?"

"The way you picked up old Joe on that remark about canvases. What hit you?"

"I'd rather not try to discuss it," Fredericka said. She knew these scenes. They were not frequent but they did occur often enough to leave a clear pattern in her memory. After one of them she always felt afresh the sense of her inadequacy in explaining herself to Christopher.

"But I want to get at the bottom of it," Christopher continued belligerently. He was tired, overwrought. His imminent departure, with the flood of last-minute details, was making him nervous. Fredericka understood the symptoms. She determined not to speak. But when he went on, "What's the matter with you lately, anyway? You and Mother are both acting absolutely bats," she turned and looked at him directly.

"Christopher, have you ever been really bored?"

"Bored?" he cried. "Do you mean fed up? Hell, yes, all the time. Who isn't?"

"Do you suppose Joe and Merry and the Joneses and the Terrys and everybody we see feels the way we do? I exclude Owen and Bridgie . . ."

"Why ask me?" he inquired grittily. He was annoyed at the turn the conversation had taken, but felt that he could not get back to his main grievance without seeming boorish.

"I think it's an awful thought," Fredericka continued, poking at the fire. "Don't you?"

"Why?" He was stubbing out a half-smoked cigarette and reaching automatically for a fresh one as he did so.

"It makes everything seem utterly useless. What are we bored about?"

"I don't know what you're bored about," Christopher said, stepping grimly into the opening she had provided for him, "unless from having nothing to do. But I know what I'm bored with. I'm bored with that damned routine of the bank, the real estate, the factory, directors' meetings—day after day. God! Who wouldn't be fed up?"

"Then why do you do it?" she asked.

"Why do I . . .?" he began irascibly. He dropped his voice to cold dispassion. "Why do I do it!" he repeated flatly. "You and Mother! You make about as much sense as a pair of asylum inmates. If I didn't, who would?"

"You're going to war and someone's doing it for you—for us," she reminded him, "so there must be a way out if you want it."

"That's different," he said quickly. "A hell of a lot different. And you know it."

"No, I don't." She was not often this stubborn. She usually stopped arguing first, not finding it worth the effort or the energy. But tonight was not the same. Aunt Palm's morning remarks had jolted her from her accustomed groove.

"Way out," Christopher repeated, going back to her remark. "What do you mean by way out? Way out to *what?*"

"That's what I wonder," Fredericka said. "This certainly isn't all of it, is it?" She made a gesture that took in the two of them, the whisky tray, the room, Wrenkill.

"All of what?"

"Well," she stumbled. "Life," she said defiantly. "I mean—this isn't all there is to life, is it?"

"What more do you want?" he demanded inconsistently. "What more could anyone want? A good home, an easy life, two fine children, no overwhelming responsibilities or troubles . . ."

"I know." Fredericka poured some soda water slowly into a glass. "I know," she repeated. "It does make one ashamed. But . . ." She fell silent.

"I don't see myself why you don't get more out of the kids," Christopher remarked abruptly.

"How can I? They're away at school. And it was you who wanted them to go," she reminded him, pricked to defend herself. She was invariably defensive about the children and her relationship to them.

"I don't think you ever wanted them," he said, with sudden cruelty.

"That's not true," she cried. "How can you say that?"

He was ashamed. "I don't know. I've just thought it some-times."

"What attention do you really pay the children yourself?" Fredericka demanded, anger stirring in her. "Now that Forrest is old enough to go fishing, learn to shoot, share sports with you, you take more interest, but when he was younger you didn't."

"I don't know what you're talking about," Christopher said with spirit. "I saw a lot of the kids."

"In a very stop-start, dot-dash style," Fredericka assured him. "And when they were little it was your daughter who was your pet, and now it's plainly Forrest and that's probably why Leslie wants to be a veterinarian," she ended, with un-expected probity. "It's a man's job."

"I don't know what you mean."

He plainly spoke the truth. Fredericka wasn't sure what she meant herself. It was only that as she talked she saw in a very subtle series of changes, of scenes flashed on and off her con-sciousness with lightninglike brilliance and swiftness, the emer-gence of the cool, deep-voiced, competitive, detached child Leslie, who could ride better than her brother and hit a target equally well.

What have we done to our children? she asked—but not aloud. The thought was too painful, too unexpected and singular. It had not entered her mind in this way before, but now that it was there she had the uneasy feeling that she might never again be rid of it.

A coldness began to settle over Fredericka—the sensation that this moment was stretching on interminably. Far, far away on a long track reaching into the future she saw herself still sitting opposite Christopher in a warm firelit room, feeling the chill of the grave, and time as an insupportable weight on the heart.

"I don't think our lives make any sense," she cried. "Because, probably, they make too much sense," she added. "We're so sensible, and careful, and conventional and—and dull. Bound and dull," she finished.

Her vehemence astonished Christopher. He was looking bewildered and a little shocked. Fredericka's brow puckered, the salt sting of tears drained into her throat. Why am I so emotional today? she wondered, angry at herself, wanting to be sane and balanced and for once to "talk it out."

"Well," he said finally, "I don't understand you. But I must say it doesn't give me a very secure feeling—going off with you in this state."

"Never mind." Her head was turned from him. "It won't last." She spoke almost bitterly.

After a moment, "I'll tell you why I was short with Joe tonight," she said, turning to face him. "I was really being short with myself. Because I realize I've never done anything with my painting—and I had talent—I really did—I still have it—but I don't work. I don't work half as hard as Aunt Palm, actually. Something has sapped my energy. What is it? Something has made me feel that it isn't important whether I paint or not . . ."

"And you blame that on your life—on life in Wrenkill?"

"Yes," she said, "I believe I do."

"Listen," he said, growing annoyed again. "I don't know a damn thing about being an artist . . ."

"Oh, why will you and Joe boast about it?" Fredericka cried. "There's nothing so admirable in the admission."

"Will you let me finish my sentences?" he demanded coldly.

"I beg your pardon. Go on."

"As I was saying, I don't know a damn thing about the life of the artist, but I'm pretty sure if you've got the stuff you can turn it out under any conditions."

"You mean the genius in the attic," Fredericka said. "I know. And I'm willing to believe the attic might bring it out, but not—not this kind of an existence."

"I'm sorry." Christopher rose, his face drawn and hard. "I'm tired and I've got a lot to do. I can't stay up all night discussing why you don't paint more than you do. It seems to me that you do quite a lot of it."

The last was intentionally a barb, she realized, listening to his firm tread on the stairs and thinking of Uncle Caleb's stomping. There was never any release in a scene with Christopher. It ended with a prick, a sting, not with a thunderclap, a cataclysm, as Uncle Caleb's scenes with Aunt Palm had invariably ended—with Aunt Palm bursting out laughing, or walking away coldly, or perhaps pushing over the andirons with a quick gesture to startle him into silence. All the drama will soon be gone from this place, Fredericka thought, all the color and the violence—Uncle Caleb gone, Uncle Philander aging . . . When Aunt Palm goes there will be no one left to shake up the atmosphere of this old musty house, and then truly it will be a ruin, long before it falls apart and settles into dust.

Do I wish Christopher were more forceful? Would I even wish him more violent? Maybe I would, she admitted.

Without warning, the face of Greg Davie rose before her, turned from her laughing, turned from her angry.

But you don't like violence, she whispered in the room that was growing colder. You didn't like violence. Remember?

She began to remember. She tried to stop. Rising, she put a log on the fire. As she bent over she felt for a moment unexpectedly dizzy, as though she might be going to faint. She reached for the mantel, held it firmly for a moment before leaning over again to push the log farther onto the still glowing coals.

Pulling up her chair to the fender she tried to remind herself that the whole day was unreal. She thought "glands," did hasty calculations. No, not that. Then tiredness, perhaps, just plain tiredness. People did get tired for no reason . . . the end-of-winter malaise . . . April, the doves, the forsythia, Aunt Palm's growing detachment, Christopher's departure. . . . She began to make a Chagall painting of all these whirling elements: doves above the roof, the forsythia growing out of Christopher's modified crew haircut, Aunt Palm snipping at it with her scrapbook scissors. She went on playing with the fanciful scene until Aunt Palm's wrist grew the hand of McGregor Davie, with a surgeon's scalpel in its lean, quick, and steady fingers.

Then Fredericka firmly dismissed the picture and began to watch instead, behind her lids, the curious waves of abstract form and color, like water folding in over an object dropped in a whirlpool. "It has a simple explanation," Greg Davie had told her (his favorite phrase), beginning once long ago to explain those mysterious kaleidoscopic shapes and figures that appear to the rear of vision when one rubs one's eyes after long reading, or comes in out of the sun, or jumps too quickly from a hot bath. She couldn't remember what he'd said now, but she could hear him talking in that blunt, rough-edged, warm voice he had. . . .

Chapter Five

THEY HAPPENED TO SIT BESIDE each other the first day in Henley Hall, her freshman year at Attica Center. Room Twenty-one. English Composition I. They walked out together into the hazy gold of the September afternoon, each already aware of the other, having caught eyes and smiled twice during the lecture.

"He's a stinker, isn't he?" His brown eyes were laughing; his fresh eager face was looking warmly and inquisitively into hers.

"Professor Norton? I don't know yet."

"I can tell you. It's my third round with him."

"You mean you've had this course twice already?"

"Yep." His eyes laughed harder and his mouth opened in a grin exposing very white, faintly irregular teeth.

"You don't look stupid."

"Thanks. I'm not. But he is."

She laughed, and immediately a wonderful excitement rose in her. She felt, for the first time since she had arrived, a part of the vivid gay swarming activity blowing past her on the campus walks. Life is beginning! she thought with a brief upswing of joy and exhilaration. She saw herself walking beside this unknown boy with his beguiling grin, she looking trim and alluring in her shell-pink sweater and her gray flannel skirt. "What's your name?" she asked with unaccustomed directness.

"Davie."

"You mean David?"

"No, I mean Davie."

"What's your last name?"

"That's it."

"*Davie?*" She didn't believe it.

"Yes. It's Scotch!" He was prepared to be belligerent about it.

"Well, then, what's your first name?"

"McGregor."

She laughed again and he had to laugh too. "They were certainly rubbing it in," she said.

"You can call me Greg," he told her. "Everyone does. But you needn't act so superior. You haven't much to say about names."

"Do you know mine?" She was astonished.

"Yes. I asked."

"Fredericka Woodward!" She considered it. "It is a little heavy," she conceded. "All the names in our family are pretty fierce. My mother is Penelope, my aunt is Palm—because she was born on a Palm Sunday—I have an Uncle Philander, and I live in Wrenkill. Where do you live?"

"I was born in Buffalo," he said darkly, "but I don't live anywhere. I mean I haven't a real home. I'm an orphan."

"Oh." She could feel her face melting.

At once he made her appear ridiculous. "Don't cry," he said. "This isn't Oliver Twist you're walking with, or Jo the Street Boy."

"What do you mean? she asked, with an attempt at hauteur that could not have been very convincing since he grinned at her as he answered:

"I mean I wasn't black-snaked by a sadistic matron, or

anything like that. I had a grandmother to look out for me who was all right as grandmothers go."

His tone was so indifferent that she could not refrain from asking, "What do you mean—as grandmothers go?"

"Don't you have any?"

"They died when I was pretty young—I don't remember them really."

"Well, I mean church twice on Sunday, the goodness and mercy of God, and all that bunkum."

"You mean you don't believe in any of that?"

"Certainly not," he said firmly. "And don't tell me you do, either."

"I don't believe I've thought much about it," she said uncertainly.

"Then you're Episcopalian. They don't let religion bother them. They just keep up the front. I'm northern Irish, Scotch-Irish, and we're the fellows who struggle with our lower natures—at least that's what I've gathered watching some of my relatives."

"You're very observant, aren't you?"

"I have to be. I'm studying medicine. I'm going into diagnosis . . . What are you doing here?"

"I'm majoring in art."

"I mean, what brought you here?"

"To Attica Center? Why not?"

"Girls like you are not usually coeds, and you know it, so don't pretend . . ."

"I hate that silly notion," Fredericka declared earnestly. "It does the college harm."

"Sure," he said. "It's snobbish. You have to bring a boarding-school girl to a club dance or she'll be frozen out. Coeds aren't accepted socially—never have been. Pretty silly, isn't it? That's what made me ask you why you came here."

His speech annoyed her intensely, partly because it was an echo of the arguments that had gone on in the family when she announced her intention of entering the college at Attica Center. Christopher and Robert had both accused her of wanting to martyr herself—called her a Girl Scout, asked her if she thought she could singlehanded change the status of coeds. Their criticism had only stiffened her in her intention. Actually she wanted to go to Attica Center for the simple reason that she did not want to go to a college where she saw only girls all week long. Aunt Palm said she understood. Her father had at least pretended to be gratified at her choice, since he was a trustee and took a warm interest in the university he had also attended.

She replied now to this arrogant, bad-mannered boy with as superior an air as she could muster, "I'm not here to go to club dances." It sounded terribly priggish. She went on hastily, making it worse with every word. "I'm studying art—seriously. And besides, my father is a trustee."

"Now we have it!" he said annoyingly. "The family wanted it."

"Don't be silly," she said. "They opposed it. I have a mind of my own."

"Have you?"

It was really absurd how easily he could rouse her anger.

They began to quarrel at once, from the first day, but they had to see each other anyway. They established the habit of spending the half hour immediately after English class together. She had a free period then and he stole the time from his heavy schedule of study and work. They always went to the same drugstore, just off the campus, and tried always to get the same booth.

Their school lives could hardly have been further apart. With the exception of the English class, in which they had only met by chance and because of Greg's failure to pass, they went entirely different ways. Fredericka was taking all the art and literature she could cram into a rather shapeless program of studies that was leading to no specific job, as Greg regularly pointed out to her. He was hurrying as fast as possible through a medical education on borrowed money.

She had never known anyone like him—outspoken, domineering, unexpectedly tender, full of Irish good humor balanced by dark periods of Scotch glowering. He made everyone else—with the exception of Aunt Palm—seem dull by comparison. Uncle Caleb was unpredictable, but his unpredictability was all on the unpleasant side. With Greg you never knew when he was going to bite your head off at the first word you spoke in the drugstore booth, or when he would arrive in the front hall of the sorority house carrying the first lilacs, stolen after dark from over a stranger's wall.

For all the differences between them they had one thing in common—a curiosity about life. Greg was the leader—he wanted to be. He never enjoyed the things she was first to show him half as much as he enjoyed showing her first. It was one of the sore points between them. She sometimes accused him of bad spirit, for he was a thorough contradiction in all respects. He blamed this inner war on his mixed blood.

There was, for instance, his attitude on astrology. He said he didn't believe a word of it and yet he knew a lot about it. He knew he was Scorpio and that she was Aquarius. "And you'll always be dampening me down," he said dishearteningly.

His landlady, who was also a local seamstress, did astrological charts in a back room of her musty house. Greg suggested they have theirs done—"just for a laugh. She's strictly bats." "Madame Trumpet Trance," he called her because she went every summer to Lily Dale to the spiritualists' colony. The first time he took Fredericka to the house he showed her on the walls—during the landlady's absence—pictures of mysteriously bearded men in turbans who were said to be the alphabetically designated Masters—K, H, M, and so on—who secretly ran the universe and revealed themselves only to the chosen. The landlady had never spoken of these magnet-eyed gentlemen but Greg had picked up the information about them somewhere.

He scoffed regularly at astrology, palmistry, second sight, intuition, prophecy, until someone in his presence attacked these phenomena. Immediately he turned fervent defender—on the strength of "all the other mysteries," he declared. Pressed, he would explain: the thumb print, unique in everyone; the eyeballs also; the snowflakes, each different; the faces of hornets, every one individual. He talked passionately, irrationally, and convincingly, for these were ideas that caught his Irish fancy.

"This palm business now," he cried heatedly. "How can you assert there's nothing in it?"

He frightened into silence one night at Sunday supper poor Terry Lawrence, the assistant in the drama department, who had flattered Fredericka by inviting her to his apartment with the suggestion that she bring a friend.

"I really don't know a thing about it," Terry had protested, fluttering over the coffee. But Greg gave him no quarter.

"Do you know how many nerve fibers there are to the

square inch on the palm? Twenty-eight hundred! And by comparison, in the thigh, for instance? Well, there are only eight. Isn't it possible that everybody's nerve fibers could make a different pattern, a revealing pattern if you knew how to read it? When a baby gives his first cry his hand comes open with a jerk—he's breathing then, he's human, he's begun to feel, to live, and his hands will register it . . . Isn't that plausible?"

Walking back to the sorority house in the soft dusk later, "You were wonderful with Terry," Fredericka had breathed —Terry whose information on such subjects as Paul Morand, George Gershwin, *transition* had up till now kept her in a state of intense awe.

But Greg wouldn't have her admiration. "Oh, nuts!" he said rudely. "I didn't really believe a word of what I was saying. I was just shooting off my mouth to make that guy uncomfortable. That stuff's all irrational, Fredericka. There's just the body. And it's mysterious enough, God knows. You don't have to assign some special prophecy or plan to it."

She began to protest feebly in her bewilderment, but he rode her down.

"No! No!" he said firmly. "Cut up a cat, a dog, a guinea pig, or a cadaver—where's the soul? Can't be found. All alike—dead matter."

"You don't convince me," she said.

He liked that. He seized her arm and held it warmly for a moment, laughing. "I'm glad."

"I'm going to bring you a book." They laughed together. It had become one of her most common phrases: "I'm going to bring you a book." "I'm going to show you."

It was a book of Death Masks. She got it from the Art Library because she wanted particularly to show him the picture of the girl suicide of the Seine, with her serene madonna smile.

He took the book and looked at it. They were in his room where, breaking a number of rules, she frequently went late in the afternoon before he had to go to the hospital for his night job as orderly. He examined the picture and shook his head.

"People don't die smiling," he said sternly. "It's a lie. If they seem to, it's just a contraction of the lips. Quite often it's just the last puff of inner gases. Try to be rational, Fredericka. As to this girl, she probably died hopped-up."

She hit him with the book. It was her first act of violence. It seemed natural and did not shock her. The book fell on the floor. Trying hard not to laugh, he calmly picked it up, open, unfortunately, at the death mask of Beethoven.

"Now here's a happy fellow!" he cried. "Beethoven, one of the few important men the world has ever produced. Looks the picture of joy, doesn't he?"

"Give me the book!" Fredericka cried, struggling with him. "Beethoven was stone deaf—and besides, he had an awful life."

"Just what I keep telling you," he went on, holding her at arm's length and retaining the book. "That kind, lovable God who takes such good care to hide his plans from the creature he has so thoughtfully made in his own image, so that the torture can be more subtle . . ."

She was so angry she began unexpectedly to cry. At once he handed her the book.

"What is it? Don't, Fredericka, please don't! Look, kid, I didn't mean to push it so far. Come on now, stop it!"

Nothing had ever felt as comforting as his arms around her—strong, warm, protecting, and cherishing.

"God, you're a funny girl!"

She was too young then to understand that it was his will to believe which led him to shout out his opinions with apparent anger. He was always asking questions impossible to answer, like: What were the desert deities of long-bearded Bedouins doing among the Nordics anyway? What were Abraham, Joseph, Moses to us? Why did we work so hard to make an Old Testament monster with his inconsistencies, his petty rages, and his cheap revenges suit our way of life, our notions of justice and intelligence? . . .

After one of these outbursts she said to him, "You'll make a terrible doctor." She was so sincere that the charge shook him. He took his career very seriously.

"Why?" He grew quiet.

"Because no one wants a hardhearted cynic at a bedside. I wouldn't myself."

"You needn't be a cynic to be realistic."

"Maybe not, but you have to make people think you believe in life, or they won't—they won't be able to stand dying."

He looked at her a long time soberly. "But I do believe in life," he said earnestly. "Honestly, Fredericka, you say the damnedest things." He became morose and moody. She had really upset him and he left under a cloud.

She went to her room and cried. The next day after class she brought along Stephen Benét's *Tiger Joy* and read him the satirical poem on King David. This was to make amends. He liked it and she made a copy for him. He memorized most of it and from time to time would recite ironically:

> "The justice of God is honey and balm,
> I will soothe her heart with a little psalm."

This was for her, when she was on what he called "the peck."

He also enjoyed declaiming in a stage voice, at the high point of subsequent arguments over the Christian religion (in which up to this time Fredericka had taken no interest whatsoever), the lines:

> "Break mine enemy's jaw, O Lord!
> For the Lord is King above all gods."

Yes, Greg had a proper respect for words. He enjoyed them when they were artfully put together to create simple sensory reactions. He always declared he would enjoy reading if it hadn't been forced on him in the wrong way. He would scornfully hold up to ridicule the works on which he said his mind had been "nourished" in high school—*Ivanhoe*, *The Mill on the Floss*, *Silas Marner*.

He did not, however, care for the word and the form so intensely as Terry Lawrence, whom Greg in part despised, because he said he walked like a ballet dancer, and in part admired, because he had such a fund of far-flung information. There was never any chance of Greg's telephoning Fredericka in the middle of the night like Terry, crying in his thin high-pitched voice, "Darling, wake up and listen to this. You've got to listen to this . . ." It was from Hart Crane, and years later she came on it marked with three parallel lines in a book from those dead days:

> *your hands within my hands are deeds;*
> *my tongue upon your throat—singing*
> *arms close; eyes wide, undoubtful*
> > *dark*
> > > *drink the dawn—*
> *a forest shudders in your hair!*

She had tried the Crane on Greg. He didn't like it. He finally admitted that it gave him an acute feeling more nearly like embarrassment than any other word he could think of. He had tried to explain. "If you do it you don't talk about it —not like that anyway. That's why fairies are always so wordy."

"Don't be intolerant," she said. "They can't help it."

"I'm not intolerant," he cried. "God knows I'm not intolerant about that sort of thing anyway. *You're* the intolerant one. You just think you aren't because you don't know anything about any of it."

Out on this limb she had learned, very early in their friendship, not to climb. His answers were always too direct. She was beginning a little to understand him—so she thought. If he had just cut up a cat and studied its visceral convolutions with a knowing eye he would arrive whistling. "Oh, the beauty of the cat!" he would cry. "If only you could see it for yourself—the pearly gray beauty of the intestines of a cat." If something like this had happened—something to intensify his sense of the mystery and importance of medicine —he would be wise and gentle; would bridge the gulf that occasionally stretched between them with one big sweet laugh or one touch of his sure and sensitive hands.

"You all talk so damned much," he would say, catching at her fingers—meaning her group of special friends from the art and drama departments. But he was really entertained by the things she brought him to read, and the reproductions she gave him to pin up and look at as he shaved—Monet's haystack, Sung ladies preparing silk. "They certainly beat 'The Horse Fair' and 'Sir Galahad.' That was my art education." If she hadn't been so priggish, so insistent and prissy, he would surely have accepted more.

"That's the fellow for me," he said once about the Toulouse-Lautrec reproductions wrapped in cerise blotting paper
that a friend had given her for a valentine. "But I suppose if
'd given them to you you'd have been insulted."

"Why is he the fellow for you?" she asked. For some reason she felt vaguely disturbed; a sensation like the pain of
jealousy shot through her.

He was willing to analyze. "They're real," he said, looking at Toulouse-Lautrec's women; the lifted leg in the can-
can, the shrewd, still humorous but cynical face under the red
wig, the cold and measuring eyes beneath a black pompa-
dour. "Hard and real. Honest. They're whores. They know
the score."

"What do you mean—the score?" she pressed.

"They know why women wear black lace stockings, high
heels, and big hats."

"Why do they?" she demanded.

"You know."

"I don't know," she insisted.

"Oh, yes, you do. You're full of it."

"Full of what?" She was beginning to be angry again.

"Talk."

He had her in his power now and so he could laugh, for
she had revealed something to him that amused him, made him
want to tease her. She was jealous. It was the way she got
when he talked of the local hospital where he was working
as an orderly—of surgeries, laboratories, doctors, and nurses.
Mostly nurses. Girls of a special knowing breed who, she
imagined, knew all about the only world he thought of as
real: how women look bearing babies; about birth control,
blood transfusions, death throes, pessaries; and where to buy
ergot.

Suddenly she was all humble and female. "Why do you love me?" For by this time he had admitted it.

"I have my reasons." And then repeating, "You talk too much," he would bring all talk to an end with the reach of his arms and his strong full mouth that held hers with an intensity she could neither withstand nor evade.

The strange thing, the really unbelievable thing, viewed from the vantage point of more than fourteen years, was the fact that they had never lived out to the fullest their attachment for each other. And it was Greg who decided it that way, after the first resistance and fear on her part. They went days, even weeks at a time, without any love-making —arguing, talking, skating on the icy lake, canoeing in the soft darkness of early fall and late spring. Now, of course, looking back, Fredericka understood it. She was unawakened. He was taken care of elsewhere. She realized now that he had had a certain principle about it, a principle that was ridiculous and romantic, born half of Scotch Calvinism, half of Irish mysticism. She was the girl he intended to marry. Therefore she was special. Once he had made up his mind to this fact he wanted to keep her so. It led them after three years of the most intense life together—a life more intense than fourteen years of sharing bed and board with Christopher— to a break as violent as an explosion.

She knew all along that Greg saw other girls. He was quite frank in admitting it. Her life was more strictly supervised than his and she too had, of necessity, to see other boys— boys from the side of the university in which Greg had no time to take part, boys who were athletes, headed committees, ran things. Sorority life too presented a great many activities that she had halfheartedly to perform—in part because her father's position in the school hierarchy demanded cooperation of his daughter, lent the use of her name a certain value. . . . The days, weeks, months went past with bright monotony. Greg remained the one intense point of feeling that ever dipped below the glazed surface.

Chapter Six

IT WAS IN THE SPRING OF THE THIRD year that Fredericka began to sense a change in Greg. His natural moodiness seemed to her intensified. Alternately he was more irritable and more gentle. She tried to explain to herself that he was working too hard carrying his job at the hospital, a heavier schedule of studies. Fredericka also had more demands made on her than in the previous year. For one thing, her mother's invalidism was now chronic. Fredericka had gone to Thermopylae every other weekend during the winter for at least a day, since she was within easy distance of home while Bridgie was as far away as Bryn Mawr. And in this period her bond with Aunt Palm grew weaker, for she did not see her so often.

One afternoon in early spring Fredericka was downtown in a bookshop in Attica Center, and she raised her eyes from the magazine rack just in time to see Greg pause before the window with a girl. They stood looking in at a display of photographs—snow scenes—and something about the ease of their standing together struck Fredericka with peculiar force. Their relatedness was unmistakable. It was relaxed and intimate.

The girl was not pretty but she had a charming face, full-mouthed, with wide green eyes and short, tight curls of red-gold hair. She pointed at something, looking up to Greg as she spoke. Greg looked down, their look caught and held, hers brimming with feeling, his warm but also—and how well Fredericka knew the look—faintly abstracted, not happy in the depths, thinking there, questioning. He turned away and the girl turned with him quickly, too quickly, not to let him escape, to placate him for she knew not what, even as Fredericka had so often done. The intimacy of her immediately shared feeling with the girl was an added pang.

They crossed the street together, the girl moving with a quick birdlike walk—something a little tense and nervous in it. Halfway across the street Fredericka, watching from the magazine rack, saw two things: Greg's hand, as though to make amends, to quiet her unexpressed unease, folding itself lightly, warmly around her elbow; that she saw, and the girl's feet—her shoes, white, sturdy with sensible heels on the end of trim little ankles—nurse's shoes. She was a nurse!

Fredericka's insides, which had been suspended in space while the two stood at the window, began now to descend through endless layers of time like an elevator melting slowly as it fell in hot arcs of liquid pain. She couldn't remember leaving the store or how she got home, but once there she did force herself to wait until evening before she called Greg. She had a date but she broke it. At six she rang Greg's house. He was out. She asked the landlady to have him call the moment he got in. It was nine before he rang her. She said she had to see him at once and her voice, which she tried to make matter-of-fact, was so unnatural that he asked her at once what was up. She managed to say, "Nothing."

They met at the usual drugstore in half an hour. Hidden in their favorite booth in the rear she felt such relief at being opposite him, as easily, as quickly as this, that she had to struggle not to cry. She looked at his hands—square, strong and wide, with their incongruously pointed, delicate fingers. Their shape, the way they held the straw of his milkshake, the scrubbed nails, the fine dust of hairs on their backs, made her weak.

"Greg," she said huskily, "I do love you."

Her earnestness astonished him. He was pleased, but uneasy; sorry, she could see, that she had to make such a declaration in the booth of a drugstore.

"Good," he said awkwardly. "I hope you do."

"Oh, I do," she said fervently. "I wanted to see you—to ask you—can you come home with me this weekend?"

"Well, I'm not sure . . ." he began.

"Oh, please," she said, with nervous intensity. "Please. I want you to so much. You've always said you would when I thought the time was right."

"It's just that my weekends are bad. You know it. But I'll try. Maybe Jack Wright could handle my Saturday morning job for me. It's just two hours."

"We could go after you're through," Fredericka said quickly. "In the afternoon. That would be time enough. It will be awfully dull for you anyway—but I do want you to."

"All right," he said. "I'll come. You act as though it's now or never."

"I hate that phrase." Fredericka shivered. "Now or never! I don't think things are really like that—do you?"

"Like what?"

"So final, so—so fatalistic. Now or never!"

"Well, if you don't think so, why does it frighten you?" he asked her reasonably.

The trip home went off well enough the first day. This was the only time in her life that she confided first in her father

ather than in Aunt Palm. She got up early Sunday morning to catch him alone at breakfast to tell him that Greg Davie was the boy she meant to marry.

Her father seemed only mildly astonished. He did ask immediately about Greg's family. She spoke of the Buffalo grandmother, realizing as she did so that she did not know whether the old lady was dead or alive. Her father said he thought that he would like to meet her, and perhaps Greg could arrange it. Fredericka's heart sank. She was afraid to present the subject for fear he would accuse them all of being snobs.

Then her father asked her if she had told her aunt yet. She had to admit that she had not, and, although she did not say so, with the admission came the realization that she was avoiding it.

Why had she brought Greg first to Thermopylae rather than to Wrenkill? Why had she so carefully concealed from Aunt Palm for almost three years the place Greg had come to occupy in her life? Whenever she tried to find the answer to these questions she felt wretched. The outlines of the answer grew fuzzy and blurred the harder she pressed for it. It was almost as though there were some obscure guilt connected with it—as though she were failing Aunt Palm, that it would wound her aunt to discover how close she and Greg had grown.

Particularly would it hurt because she did not share with Greg what she and Aunt Palm shared: the sensations on a blowy day in early April walking up Hungry Hollow to look at the first catkins, or sitting in silence together watching sunset at the lake, with the last heat rising from the gray rocks patterned with the yellow-green-pink medallions and rosettes of lichen, the running sound-scallops of golden light where the water traced the small sandy beach and cast its reflected line of liquid movement onto the birch trunks, and the russet huckleberry.

No, Greg would never know the unspoken binding questions that she and Aunt Palm shared. How can one paint loon cry, pine scent, water song under a log, log rot, tree sough, huckleberry taste? This was their own world. The doors to it were not locked—there were no doors—but no one else entered because no one else lived where they lived.

On Sunday, with an inner tremble that she could neither understand nor shake off, Fredericka drove over to Wrenkill from Thermopylae taking Greg to meet Aunt Palm and Uncle Caleb.

If Aunt Palm was surprised that Fredericka should visit her father first with a strange young man she concealed it. She acted natural and easy, detached but perfectly friendly with Greg. Unhappily her son Christopher was home from Princeton with his annual attack of poison ivy. He was just recovering, and he was painted like a clown with a whitish liquid. His disposition was at its worst. He was in one of his lolling and lofty moods that brought out all Greg's defensiveness. He sat on the end of his spine—Christopher—and spoke in monosyllables. In reply Greg spoke too loudly. Fredericka, torn with mingled emotions—anger at Christopher, annoyance with Greg for obviously disliking him, unease about Aunt Palm—retreated into a shell of coldness for her own protection. She let Greg take the bus back to Attica Center that evening without her, although the moment he was gone she regretted it and began to worry about their next meeting.

Aunt Palm made no reference at all to the visitor after he had left. Fredericka gave Christopher no chance to comment, excused herself from supper, and went upstairs to bed where she cried for an hour.

On Monday night, back in Attica Center, she and Greg had their first big quarrel. This time he was very angry. He called Christopher a snobbish ape, her Uncle Caleb a tyrannical bastard, Aunt Palm an eccentric, and her a cold bitch. She cried. She came and knelt beside him and said she was confused and wanted to admit it. He was already ashamed of himself. He buried his head in her shoulder. They embraced long and passionately. It was he who terminated it though she did not want him to.

"No," she said, "Greg, I—I want to stay with you. Please let me."

But he wouldn't have it, though he was white and trembling. He said it was a Monday night and she would be expelled if she stayed out. He walked her home, hardly speaking. They were both exhausted but somehow Fredericka felt closer to him than she ever had before, and certain that he too was happier in spite of the strain of the weekend and the quarrel.

The only one of her relatives who made an enduring impression on Greg seemed to be Aunt Palm. "She mystifies me," he said a number of times in the next weeks.

"Why?"

"She's a strange woman."

"What's strange about her?"

"I don't know what she wants."

"Wants? What do you mean *wants*? What makes you think she wants anything?"

"Because everybody wants something." He was quite positive about it.

This interested her. "What do I want?"

He grew silent, speculative. "Damned if I know. That's why you're puzzling. And that's why you're like your aunt too. Either you were born like her, or else you've learned to be like her from association. I don't know which. One thing I do know, though—you'll have to get away from her before you'll ever find out."

"Find out what?"

"Who you are and what you want."

Get away from Aunt Palm! The suggestion rang ominously. She could not imagine being unable to share with Aunt Palm. The "Relief at Lung-Mēn," for instance. She could remember vividly the day she turned the page and saw it in a book on Chinese art. It was during her sophomore year. She got excused and took a bus to Wrenkill that very afternoon to show it to Aunt Palm—the Wei relief of serene gentlemen in long robes with no bodies underneath, wearing high-crowned hats, carrying banners like fern fronds so that you thought at once of all filigrees of moss, lichen, watermark, and snail track seen in the edge of woodlots and on old rail fences.

Until Aunt Palm saw the picture of the "Relief at Lung-Mēn," Fredericka would not know herself what she had seen. Aunt Palm made clear Fredericka's own half-formed perceptions: the Wei donors—bringing no one knew any longer what gifts to what forgotten and nameless potentate of China in 400 B.C.—had achieved with centuries the final classic detachment of nature, creating pattern without reference to any possible observer. What world had they come from, these formal figures of unearthly dignity with their stone smiles forever elusive, serene, and secret? . . . "The Gothic look," said Aunt Palm, "the Wei smile—scholars' tags. Snail track, stone turned by water, lichen embroidery on a careless pebble—mysteries beyond the naming . . ."

Here was the joy that surpassed definition, the world where Fredericka was not required to write down any explanation for a mid-term grade, or analyze the finding for the skeptical mind of a medical student . . . Oh, Aunt Palm, I cannot live without you! I cannot, I dare not, shed this sweet cocoon!

Spring that third year at Attica Center came early. May was oppressively hot and sultry with almost tropically lush damp nights, heavy with the scent of mock orange, peony, iris, lily of the valley, and balm trees. Restlessness took hold of Fredericka. Her life and everything in it seemed unreal unless she was with Greg, and, although ever since their quarrel she had known they were nearer each other, she also knew, partly because of the new intimacy and understanding between them, that there was a compartment in him which he kept carefully locked.

She tried subtly, carefully, to draw him out about his life. It was the first time she had ever taken an interest in human beings as such. Up to now it had been only in things—the fall of light, the turn of forms—and a few ideas. Greg had often accused her of knowing more about "Coptic ornament" than about the girls with whom she lived. This had come up apropos of the threatened "unpinning" of a sorority sister for unmaidenly acts that led to the girl's expulsion. Fredericka's astonishment at her friend's hidden life had amazed and annoyed Greg.

"It's the way you were brought up. That rarefied atmosphere!"

"Rarefied! With Uncle Caleb? Why, he's a barbarian most of the time."

"That's just his way of getting even for what your aunt does to him."

"What does she do to him?"

"Humiliates him."

"How?"

"By knowing more than he does about a lot of things he can't quite dismiss as unimportant—that's why he's not really a barbarian. He just acts the way he does to keep your aunt in line, remind her that males are not to be trifled with."

"Either you're very wise or you're very silly," she had said, trying to make light of it because in her heart she felt that he was uttering truths that sank down deep into her memory and might eventually change her way of thinking.

"I'm wise," he said, "and someday you'll know it." Such arrogance. Still she could not deny it.

"*Someday! Now or never!* Those phrases!" she cried. "How I dislike them!"

"You're afraid of life," he taunted her. "It's the price you have to pay for being protected since you were born."

"Well, I can't help it. I wish I had been on my own always, like you."

"Oh, no, you don't!" he said quickly, a little harshly, and then checking himself, "Anyway, whether you do or not, *I* don't. I like you the way you are. You're a special kind of girl."

"What was it like, working in the cannery?" she asked him, longing to share the memories of his difficult adolescence.

"Like? The cannery? Well, it was like any other hot stinking place where you don't want to be and have to be. . . . No, not quite that bad. The people were all right."

If he was in a good mood he might describe them to her. He had almost the writer's perception, so that he began to open her eyes to people seen casually in shops, on buses, or street corners, until behind their faces she could imagine districts, houses, the pattern of strangers' lives. . . . Two girls, sisters or cousins—she would always remember them—as seen in the bus station one time with Greg. The significant matter of money—a quarter—passed back and forth, each girl pressing it on the other, the awkwardness of mutual relinquishment perfectly timed so that the coin finally fell between them on the wooden seat with a loud clatter. Who would reach for it? Fredericka could not bear to look. She averted her gaze for a safe interval. When she looked back they were both still flushed rosy-red. Their lips were created full and sensuous, but they were slack with unfulfillment. Their hair grew in length, not strength, falling back languidly instead of springing with vigor from the scalp. The heavy lenses of their glasses hid their timid guarded eyes, used to the damp gloom of the sagging house on the back street where ivy rotted the porch and the wooden frame breathed out endless dust as it settled slowly on its foundation. There must be, Greg said, an invalid in one of the rooms—a querulous old man or old woman, forever demanding the bedpan, the lowered shade, the killing of the fly, the sweetening of the custard. . . .

These things Greg taught her to see, and if she had not been afraid of his quick scorn she would have told him how she longed to make up to him for his early years of struggle, for not having had parents, for never having known a real home. Even though she knew he would laugh only because he would otherwise choke up she still could not say it to him. But she did begin to plan with him how she would come to New York and take art classes half a day and keep house for him while he went on studying medicine. They would be married, naturally, and perhaps her father or Uncle Caleb could give her a little extra allowance so that they would have it easier. Oh, of course they would eventually pay back every penny. Or, if he would rather, she might teach half a day—art to children maybe.

He was always a little uneasy about these plans. Once he said: "If I were really wise I'd never marry you until I was on the staff of a big New York hospital with the years of struggle well behind me. Then we could swing it without danger."

"Danger?" She protested the word.

"Yes, danger. But don't worry, I'm not going to wait!"

The thought of the summer holidays when she would not see him, except furtively if she managed to get down to New York where he was to be working, began to weigh on her spirits. Somewhere she felt unsure of him, vaguely uneasy, so that she even said to him that she wished they could be married right away. He had laughed gently at this, looking at her with a new look, running his hand up the back of her head and tightening his fingers hard on the top of her skull.

But the more she thought of it the sounder the idea seemed. She wanted to marry him before she went back to Wrenkill. Without talking to Aunt Palm, without asking permission, she wanted to run away and be married. The idea became an obsession and one afternoon when she had been lying alone on the sleeping porch of the sorority house, pretending to study but actually dreaming about Greg, she got up and went to his room to wait for him.

As she walked through the hot afternoon, languorous with the heavy green boughs and rich scents of early summer, an excitement rose in her that was a new experience. It took complete possession of her, set her pulse to drumming, her heart to thumping, carrying away the blood from her head so that it felt as light as a flower on her shoulders. She would not leave his room until he agreed to elope; and the thought of not leaving, of staying with him and proving once and for all that she was no longer afraid of anything, quickened her steps.

The landlady seemed uneasy about admitting her. Fredericka attributed it to the state his room was in. Sometimes Greg wouldn't let Madame Trumpet Trance set foot across his threshold for days on end because he said she messed up his papers and invited her friends in to look at the more horrible pictures in his medical books.

"If you'll take the responsibility," the landlady said nervously, "about going in, I mean, I'll just take the opportunity to water my geraniums." And she hurried out and came back with a pitcher for the wilted plants on the sill.

Fredericka sat down on the unmade bed-couch to wait. She decided not to touch the room, not to set it to rights in any way for fear it might annoy him when he got back and they would be off to a bad start. She picked up a copy of a magazine and pulled up the pillow to rest it behind her head. Under it lay a note that slid off now onto the floor. Fredericka reached for it and without a second thought read it through:

> What made you get up and leave me? I was awake and heard you go. At first I thought you'd gone into the bathroom. When you didn't come back I turned on the light and saw that your clothes were gone. This is the third time. Greg, why do you act this way? Do I deserve it?

Fredericka put the note carefully back under the pillow. She lay very still for a moment and then she began to tremble.

She began to tremble so violently that she had to stand up and walk around. I must get myself in hand, she thought, as she moved about the room. I mustn't show a thing when he comes in. She sat down again rigidly on the side of his bed. Shall I say I read the note? Shall I leave before he gets here—leave and refuse to see him again? Shall I face him with it the moment he enters and watch him lie out of it?

When she heard him on the stairs she was still unsure of what she would do. When he opened the door she was quite calm. "Hello," he said, with a rising *o;* he was surprised, pleased to see her. Her hello in reply committed her to nothing. She was still not sure what the Fredericka that had now split off from her familiar self (and was definitely going to take things over) would do.

"You're getting awfully attentive," he said, grinning.

The grin was the signal, like a flash of red, like a raised hand, like the command to fire:

"Am I!" Her voice was not yet the volley, but it was the hand on the gun. The feel of metal was in it, the deadly weapon with which the deed would be done.

"What's the matter?" His look had abruptly changed; it was on guard, puzzled.

"What do you mean what's the matter?" (There's no hurry; you've got him with his back to the wall, he can't possibly escape.)

"You look funny—as though you were going to be sick. Has something happened?"

"No." And now, calm as you please, hard as flint, cold as death, she took aim and fired. "I've just read an interesting letter from the girl you sleep with."

Had she wounded him? Who could tell?—for immediately

he was encased from head to foot in impenetrable armor; and she knew he would drop like the Spartan boy before he would let her know if he had been struck, or where. She also knew too late, in a flash of insight deep and final, that they could never in all their lives return to the two people they had been the other side of this moment.

"You must come on many interesting items reading other people's mail." His voice was light and detached.

Hers also. "Well, this is one of the best bits." It was all happening in a play, Somerset Maugham's perhaps, between the coffee table and the expensive chintz of the sofa, the tea things spread, entrance rear down a famous staircase commanding a full view of the room and its occupants. "But then, of course, I was particularly interested in this one."

He shrugged, took up a pipe indifferently, filled it, lit it, dropped down and picked up the nearest newspaper. It was a week old, Fredericka's split-off self observed.

"Aren't you going to make any explanations?" after a long minute the familiar Fredericka demanded furiously.

"No. Why should I?" (Obviously the gun had misfired. He was remote, collected.)

"Why *should* you? How can you ask such a thing? Why *should* you! Wouldn't you ask for an explanation from me?"

And now he had her. "I wouldn't read your mail in the first place, so I can't say what I'd do if I did."

The gun was in his hand now. He was always too quick for her. She began to tremble again. How to find her way back to the moment before she had spoken? Was it all a mistake? Could it be? How could it be? Three o'clock . . . bathroom . . . third time . . . do I deserve it . . .

"Greg," she began, "please, I . . ."

"I suggest you get out of my room," he cried, his eyes suddenly as hard as marbles. "Nobody invited you here in the first place. People who come to snoop usually regret it."

"How dare you?" she cried, jumping up. "How dare you say that to me?"

"How dare you read my letters?" he shouted, also springing to his feet. "Don't talk to me about daring. Just get the hell out of here and leave me alone."

He too was trembling. His eyes were moist as though he were about to cry. The scene became suddenly so sordid, so anguished, so hopeless, that Fredericka turned and ran from the room leaving the door open. She ran down the stairs and out into the May sunlight, and she heard herself moaning down somewhere in her stomach as she hurried away.

Fredericka did not see Greg again. Not even at a distance. There were just two weeks until school was out. Then she was home in Wrenkill lying in the upstairs back porch swing, moving it gently, listening. She could hear a bee very near at hand in the roses sawing on his little golden saw, while far away, very far, half a mile at least, another kind of saw, a steel saw for cutting wood, grown drowsy with distance, was dividing the afternoon into little blocks of thin, sweet sound. The door to the old playroom stood open and through her half-closed eyes she could catch a glimpse of the bookcase with the elaborate carving on the sides and the books that the carelessness of young hands had turned to a uniform toneless color. She knew them all. They were the books of her childhood. *The Prodigious Hickey, Tom Sawyer, Huckleberry Finn, Pilgrim's Progress, David Copperfield, The Bow of Orange Ribbon, The Trail of the Lonesome Pine*—all faded, smelly, and familiar.

The dampness of the winter was rising from the straw matting in the warm sun and something was baking in the kitchen—spicy, oniony. The bee . . . the saw . . . and now the cutout of a truck far away on a distant road, very far away so that it did not break the drowsy peace but only intensified it. It was all the summers of her childhood rolled into one, this moment, and she pulled it more tightly around her, held it wrapped around her like a warm comforter—the very word for it, comforter. If the bee would only go on humming, the truck stay in the distance, the smell of early supper and straw matting in the sun float over the roses, then nothing could ever reach her, touch her, hurt her—and life would be one long June afternoon.

But even as she thought this the bee flew away, the saw ceased, the sound of the motor drew nearer. Greg, Greg, and up gushed the black juice so bitter and so rancid, the taste in the throat that nothing could relieve.

She heard a car come sliding down the gravel on the road below and she knew it was her cousin Christopher because he always came in the back road, took the car out of gear at the mailbox and slid on down. She sat up with relief and brushed back her hair.

"Hi!" she said, leaning over the railing when the car had stopped under the porte-cochère.

He looked up. "Hi!" Beginning to take the packages from the car, "Come on down and help me with these, will you?"

She went down to the drive and let him load the packages into her arms.

"Enough for an army."

"Father's on a buying bust today. Where's Mother?"

"Lying down, I guess. She said she didn't feel very well."

He looked momentarily worried and she was pleased at the

little shade that passed over his face at her words. Christopher is kind, she interpreted the shadow, Christopher would worry. Or would he? For now he was saying:

"Hell! She'll probably be in a mood and Father's asked the Drummonds for dinner. Let's clear out right afterwards. . . . Go to a movie."

"Why don't we clear out before?" Fredericka suggested. "We could pick up a sandwich on the road."

"That's an idea! Let's go right this minute before anybody stops us."

There was a movie they both wanted to see. It was a double bill. They got out late. The moon was up, the air warm and faintly misty.

"Let's have a drink," Christopher said. A year ago he would never have suggested such a thing. Now he was a Princeton graduate—a grown man. He seemed suddenly a stranger, very mature, to Fredericka. He knew where. It was just another place on the highway, with crepe paper decorations and dark stained-wood booths with dim lights burning as though undersea, but after the second drink it began to frighten Fredericka. It made her think of Greg and the places he went to that she never saw and only imagined—up back stairs, down cellars, knocks on doors, mysterious rings, Joe sent me, Nora told me . . .

"Let's get out of here!"

"God, you're jumpy lately," Christopher said.

"Am I? I'm sorry."

They got into the car and started off, farther away from town. At once Fredericka began to cry. Christopher was genuinely upset. Fredericka had never been given to easy tears.

"What in hell is it, Flea?" The old childhood name.

"Don't mind me," Fredericka murmured into her handkerchief. "I'm just tired, I guess."

"Tired from what?"

"I don't know," she wailed. "Oh, Chris, God! I do feel so miserable, or—or scared, or something."

They were along the lake road now and he turned into a driveway and stopped the car. "Hey!" he said. "Pull yourself together, kid."

He put his arm around her and she leaned against him and cried harder. He didn't say anything, just sat there holding her. Her longing for Greg swept up in her for a moment so strongly that she thought of asking Christopher to drive to Attica Center on the faint chance that he might be there. And then in a sudden panic, lest she give way to her impulse, she flung her arms around him crying, "Oh, Chris, please, please . . ."

"Please what?" he asked huskily.

"I don't know." She was trembling. She lifted her face to his in the summer moonlight. He bent swiftly toward her. They kissed tremulously, then hotly, wildly. She pressed herself against him. He returned the pressure with force and direction. The drinks they had had, the moon shimmering on the treetops—their warm young bodies fused together. After a while, "Let's go to the lake," Christopher said thickly.

He started the car and they drove fast in silence, trembling, expectant. As they turned off onto the lonely road that led to the closed house at the lake, the headlights picking up boughs and leaves and darkening the farther shadows made Fredericka shiver. But she did not suggest turning back.

They dived into the lake just once and came out shocked and tingling. Christopher had a bottle. She didn't ask him where he got it. They gulped the raw liquor in the moonlight. Quickly, before their pulses steadied, they lay down together inside the boathouse in the old flat-bottomed fishing boat under Christopher's topcoat. Fredericka felt no fear at all. It was only Christopher, Christopher her cousin who was almost like a part of herself, like a brother—only not a brother, that was important; Christopher, with whom she had been bathed in the same tub as a baby, punished with for peeping at one another behind the square-cut box tree long long ago in another June. . . .

Two weeks later the letter from Greg came.

I've been through Hell. I can't take any more of it. I want to talk to you about the whole thing. I hope I can make you understand. If I can we can have a good life together, if I can't you'll never be able to make me out and I'll never be able to trust you and we'll make one another miserable. Please let me know when, where, and how I can see you.

Her first feeling was one of triumph—lovely, rich and warming triumph—that Greg would write her like this! Humbly almost. Admitting he was suffering. But not too humbly, of course. For lurking in these few lines she imagined she could read that old double-standard argument that he was so fond of—right there, the old argument.

Well, it was too late. He could no longer reach her. She was not going to open the door and let in the troop of black devils again, just as she had them all boxed up nicely and neatly. No, she was going to stay right where she was, in the sun, near the beloved and familiar haunts, with Christopher and Aunt Palm. Inside her something shrank back in fear and distaste from McGregor Davie, a dark-browed stranger with wild ways, with a heart alternately too soft and too hard, an irrational nature tied to a rational mind, worshiping Science and behaving like Neanderthal man.

Acting on impulse, as he had so often asked her not to do, she ran upstairs to her room and wrote a hasty note, by hand with a scratchy pen that made little dramatic black accents on every other letter:

> It's no use. It would never work. I think you're a sadist. You think I'm silly. What's the use? Anyway, I am going to marry Christopher. It is all settled and everyone is pleased.

And they were pleased.

"Well, well," Uncle Caleb had said. "So we don't lose you after all." But he had looked startled, and he gave Christopher a sharp glance which Christopher carefully did not meet.

"Oh, my dearie," Aunt Palm said, clasping her tight in her arms. "I was wondering how I would ever give you up . . ." But then almost immediately, "No!" she cried, unclasping her arms, taking Fredericka by the elbows and looking into her face. "Are you sure, lovie, are you sure?"

"Yes, Aunt Palm, I'm sure."

Yet for a brief moment Fredericka had been tempted to ask Christopher, "Are you sure? Are *we* sure?" But she didn't. The relief was too great. "It is all settled," she had written Greg. What a load off her mind! She sealed the envelope, stamped it, ran to the kitchen to give it to Eunice, whose day off it was. She wanted it on its way. But that night she couldn't sleep. She had another crying spell after dinner, refused to go out driving with Christopher. The whole place seemed hateful, its very familiarity a prison into which she was now forever entering. No escape from the circular pavilion, useless and ugly under the weeping willow; no escape from the two porch swings, the petunia beds, the graveled road, the fading books in the yellow bookcase, the vine against the window that began turning red with death in mid-July just when everything was greenest.

A week later the second note came:

Please let me see you.

That was all. She tore it up.

She heard once more from him. This letter she read with her mind half closed, because it was long and thoughtful and she was afraid to take it in too fully for fear the words would really upset her:

I know now that you mean not to see me again. I cannot let it go at that. I swallow my pride to try to reach you. You know enough about my stiff-necked Davie pride to know what that means. (I only put this in because I can imagine you frozen and unfeeling and I want to get in behind that guard.)

Listen to me, Fredericka. Please listen!

You must get away from home. I think you should even get away from your wonderful aunt whom you love so much. I don't know why. I just feel it. I think you are too much alike. As long as you stay with her you will never know who you are yourself—as I told you one day. You know you can't marry Christopher. What would it mean? You don't love him. It's just easy. He's like a brother. Lots of brothers and sisters think they're in love. If they're honest they'll admit it. It's propinquity and maybe something deeper—since it's a blood bond. And there is a blood bond with Christopher, but it's not a real one. A real bond is a fresh one, new made, that would lead you out into life where you need to go, Fredericka. Please believe me! I know your aunt encourages your painting. I know you think I don't know anything about it—but this I promise you: I'll help you all I can. I'll try to understand. I'll never interfere. And this also I tell you: In the end you'll paint more and you'll paint better by coming with me even if you have to be poor for a while, poorer than you'll be if you stay where you are.

As to what you discovered that day in my room, I know someday you'll understand it. It may always hurt, because there is something half instinct, half ego, in jealousy that you can't shake off by being superior about it. But it is not grounds for throwing me over without a chance to see you and talk. Freddy, I beg of you, write me and tell me I can see you just once more. You are the only true woman for me and always have been since the first day I saw you. You always will be no matter what happens. Somewhere inside you, you know this is true. Someday maybe you'll know what it is not to be able to explain!

She did not answer. She never saw him again. She did not have today the slightest idea what had become of him.

Chapter Seven

THE DAY AFTER CHRISTOPHER LEFT for Washington to try for the Air Corps, Fredericka, at three o'clock in the afternoon, entered Room 21, Henley Hall, in Attica Center, and slid quietly into the nearest chair. The lecture had already begun. Before her was the man whom her father's old friend, Dr. Cooper, had recommended as a stimulating instructor in world history.

He was a thin man, handsome in a grave way, with dark skin, dark hair noticeably gray at the temples, and eyes concealed behind heavy-rimmed glasses. An Austrian, Dr. Cooper had told her. His name was Franz Allers. His hands, as he spoke, were clasped behind him, his head thrust forward, turning now toward his class, now away from it, as he paced the platform. He spoke clearly but with a pronounced foreign accent.

Studying him in those first moments Fredericka saw that he was serious about his lectures. There was a tenseness in his long, thin frame. The way he stood, it looked almost as if he hoped, by concentrating his muscles, by sheer physical force, to draw up from the well of his being the thoughts he now offered his students.

"And so," he was saying in a voice that managed, in spite of his posture, to be casual, "as I told you at the beginning of this course, from time to time we shall digress and talk a little about man as he exists outside the present history books. For this is a class in history—but what is history?"

He stopped and looked hopefully at his students as though expecting some sudden illumination to break upon them. The girl seated beside Fredericka took advantage of this interval to draw out a pocket mirror, blow on it, look at herself critically, lick her lips, and return the mirror to her pocket, after which she hastily scribbled on a fresh page in her notebook: HISTORY; *what is it?* and then added her own name in large letters at the top.

"History," Dr. Allers repeated, pacing again. "What is history? Is it events, dates of statesmen and battles? Is it William of Orange, the Council of Trent, the years 1492 and 1776? Or is it cave paintings, test tubes, the visions of saints? Is it the quantum theory, the last words of Socrates, the martyrdom of Freud, Elizabethan lyrics? Is it Roman laws? . . ."

He paused again. Was he actually waiting for them to answer? No one spoke. Looking around her nervously, with the feeling that the class must not fail the earnest man before them, Fredericka could see that the students were used to this type of rhetorical question from Dr. Franz Allers. They took it calmly, almost indifferently. Their pencils waited, like that of the girl beside her, poised in readiness for the ponderable fact.

Fredericka began to think of her scene with Dr. Cooper just the hour before, and of what he had said about the lecturer in world history—Dr. Cooper under the well-remembered sepia print of the Roman Coliseum, making the careful tents of his hands, bringing his index fingers to his nostrils to inhale them delicately, abstractedly; breaking up the tents, snapping his fingers into his palms: "I think Dr.

Allers is the man for you. Definitely out of the usual academic groove. Former medical man, Viennese . . ." and he had gone on with the details about Franz Allers. How it was a great feather in Attica's cap to acquire him; how Princeton and Harvard had put in bids; how Dr. Cooper's great friend, Frank Dibble, had run into Allers at Cambridge—or was it Oxford—a half-broken man trying to come back . . .

"Half-broken?" Fredericka had interrupted.

"I understand he was very ill. Almost a complete breakdown; some years of wandering around Europe—working in the Underground, following the murder of his wife."

"The what!" Fredericka had literally jumped.

Dr. Cooper found her reaction gratifying. He did not often have as responsive an audience for his mumbling monologues. His eye brightened perceptibly.

"Yes, murdered," he repeated, enjoying the use of the word in intimate talk. "A political murder, I understand. Dr. Allers never speaks of it. In fact, no one sees much of him. He's still something of a recluse. Takes little part in faculty life . . ."

Fredericka looked again at the grave thin man on the platform, thinking to herself how little any face, viewed casually, ever reveals. Perhaps the eyes will show what this human creature has experienced—the tragedy, the shock, the horror, the suffering. . . . Do any of his students suspect how deeply alien he is to them as he walks back and forth, watching their idle note-taking?

"Today," he was now saying, "we go on a little journey with a postage stamp and a penny, thanks to the suggestion of Sir James Jeans."

Franz Allers took a penny and a stamp in either hand and held them up to the class to view. "With these we set out to climb Cleopatra's Needle where we lay the penny flat, with the postage stamp on top."

Fredericka observed for the first time on the blackboard a sketch of the Needle, beside a mountain drawn to scale. Allers half turned and nodded at the board.

"The height of this obelisk we are taking to represent the time that has elapsed since the earth was born. The thickness of the postage stamp represents the time man has been civilized. The penny represents the time man lived in an uncivilized state."

"Now we take postage stamp number two, and we lay it on top of the first. It now represents the next five thousand years of civilization. Then we just keep on sticking postage stamps on top of one another—which unfortunately I do not have—until we have built a pile as high as Mont Blanc." Again he nodded toward the drawings on the board.

"Even when the postage stamps reach the height of that great mountain, we are not near the length of the future which astronomy leads us to expect civilized humanity will enjoy. The penny and stamp together represent the time man has lived on earth. Postage stamp number one was the past of civilization. Postage stamp number two is the next five thousand years. The column of stamps higher than Mont Blanc is humanity's future."

He stopped, measuring their response, then went on: "Or, to put it another way, the first postage stamp is man's achievement so far; the pile higher than Mont Blanc represents what he may achieve if his future development is proportional to the time he presumably has on earth."

The pencils were flying automatically over the notebooks.

"Don't try to write this down," he said rather sternly as he looked over his glasses at the class. "It's all on the board. You can copy it down word for word later. Just relax!" He grinned suddenly. "Relax and think!"

His grin was young, Fredericka decided. The front view, with the black shock of hair, was ten years the junior of the graying profile.

"I merely want to jolt you a little, if possible," he said, "into seeing your responsibility. I also want to give you hope —if you need hope."

Did they need hope? The jaws in front of Fredericka were moving rhythmically with gum. The hair of the girls was hidden under similar kerchiefs of bright color, their raincoats all the same cut and make. The girls were dressed with a monotonous uniformity and with a certain sloppy ease more pronounced than she remembered costumes from her own student days. . . . There were also more men than she had expected to find in a war year. 4Fs, she supposed, though there was a sprinkling of boys in uniform who must be taking the course by special permission, for surely there was nothing here to help them in manning a PT boat, firing a machine gun, or making a beachhead over coral.

During her interview with Dr. Cooper, Fredericka had discovered that he was troubled by the preponderance of women now on the campus. He saw that it was inevitable but he deplored it. He had implied that professors lost interest in teaching women only. Don't let this upset you! Fredericka had said firmly to herself. What does it matter? She had tried to remain quite passive throughout her interview with him, noting, almost with amusement, how indifferent he was to her ambition to take up painting again with her former teacher. "Ah, Farrell!" he said, dismissing him by tilting back in his swivel chair. Fredericka mentioned Farrell's recent New York successes, but Dr. Cooper did not alter his expression. It was plain that he found it impossible to imagine painting as an occupation for an adult.

She left the interview depressed. What am I doing here anyway? she asked herself, as she breasted the tide of uniformed young men streaming across the campus, the free-swinging, glance-conscious girls. I'm old! I'm out of it! The notes from the bell tower sounding the hour deepened her depression. What am I looking for? What do I expect to find? Something to spur me on to paint?

As she walked she realized that she had never been related to this place. Even as a student she had felt herself living in a dream, moving behind a veil. Only Greg Davie had pierced this opacity, rousing her to passion—from which she had turned away—causing her to know shame, humiliation, wild anger, deep regret, all of which she had buried successfully. Successfully? The question darted at her like an adder as she passed Henley Hall, and since it was the hour for Allers' class, and since she was passing the door, she had turned in, hurriedly, wishing to escape, to divert her mind.

So here she was! And the grave dark foreigner whose wife had been murdered and who had gone to pieces and put himself together again was saying, "Yes, man is a dust speck measured against space and time." He stopped, while with his thumb and middle finger he measured man, the dust speck.

"A dust speck!" he repeated. "Yet when man sees this to be true, his faith and self-respect must increase, considering what he has achieved in only a breath of world time."

As he said the last words his voice dropped a little and he paused. He seemed to be running his mind over the achievements of man. Fredericka tried to summon her own list of human attainments. She saw the Sistine Chapel, sulfa drugs, the wheel, the arch, and a stratosphere plane . . . It was not a very convincing assemblage and she was about to try again when Franz Allers continued abruptly:

"But man, Western man, is what you Americans call a 'nervous wreck.' This is a danger signal. It is not just an outgrowth of war, this increasing tension. It was here well before the last two wars. It is a danger signal because it arises in part from man's placing the sensations of his own ego at the center of the universe. Perhaps we should try a displacement of some kind—old Chinese style, perhaps, where man is small against nature."

Up came the puzzled faces. The pencils hung again poised. *Chinese style: Nature vs. man*, wrote Fredericka's neighbor. She added a large firm question mark.

Dr. Allers dismissed his example of the Chinese with a quick impatient gesture, a gesture which had in it all his awareness of the gaps in his audience's knowledge.

"No matter," he said almost sharply, signifying, Don't, for God's sake, make a note of it! Don't question me later! . . . "No matter!" he repeated. "Forget the Chinese for now."

He took a paper from the desk and began to read aloud:

" 'Man is the intermediary between the great world and the small world. On one hand he can observe the planets, on the other the atoms. In time, without question, man will know the control of the atom, and even perhaps visit other planets. Your funny-paper heroes, your comic-strip dreams, your magazines of pseudo science on cheap paper are the prophets of these things to come. Man as observer brings into focus and meaning things as far apart as atoms and planets. In a sense he unites them in his own person because of the wonderful instruments of perception that he possesses with which to observe and evaluate them.' "

He put down the paper and stared straight at the class. "Instruments of perception . . ."

Fredericka's attention wandered once more. The way he was leaning now on the desk reminded her of something—of Dr. Hendricks in the pulpit at home when as a child she had gone to the Unitarian church with Aunt Palm. Dr. Hendricks had talked this way, like one friend talking with others—merely a wiser friend . . . Why had they stopped going to the Unitarian church? Was it Uncle Caleb who insisted? A phrase of his came back to her: "Bad for business." It was one of Uncle Caleb's famous clichés. He applied it to everything from Aunt Palm's sketching in the graveyard to the gray flannel knee pants—cut English style—that she had bought once for her sons. An odd phrase, "Bad for business," considering how Uncle Caleb indulged his own eccentricities. Perhaps he considered his on the reassuring side, rural and primitive, whereas Aunt Palm's were . . .

But what was it about Dr. Hendricks that came back to her now with Dr. Allers' easy pose? Had Dr. Hendricks been bad for business? Or had the Unitarian faith been bad for business—this suspect, semi-intellectual denomination, New England in origin, that denied Christ's divinity? Dr. Hendricks had an invalid wife. At one time, when Fredericka was young, he came frequently to the house. Aunt Palm and the one woman friend she had ever had, a Miss Flora Tolley from the library, and Dr. Hendricks used to read aloud—Emerson, as Fredericka remembered it. Then suddenly they weren't doing it any more and Dr. Hendricks was seldom seen and Aunt Palm stopped attending church altogether. These clues were so simple that it astounded Fredericka to think she had never given them full value before. Surely Dr.

Hendricks—though in memory he seemed a gray, frail, and elderly man—had represented something emotional to Aunt Palm in her isolated life. . . .

She brought herself firmly back to the man on the platform before her. She had apparently lost some important link while her thoughts dipped into the past, for he was saying: "The East, the Orient, has one great thing to teach us—that logic does not apply to life itself. The East can accept contradictions, or what we Westerners call contradictions, without even recognizing that that is what it does. It can, for instance, accept holy men who have miraculous powers of healing and prophecy and who yet live lives of nonmorality by our standards. To the East this is not necessarily a contradiction. To us in the West it is very baffling.

"Yes, it is baffling." His voice, his half-grin, recognized the bafflement on the faces before him. "Very baffling!" he repeated.

He went on to say how the West wants things cut and dried: the good are good, the bad are bad; Hitler is the Antichrist while every Allied soldier is an expression of the highest virtue. "Yet Hitler too is a man—one of us." He paused, faced the class, let it sink in. "From what did he spring? From us! And the Allied soldier, he too is what all men are—he is man, halfway between ape and angel."

Surely this is dangerous talk, Fredericka thought, startled —dangerous talk for a foreign professor in wartime. It is always unwise in America to look in two directions at once in public; in wartime it could be downright hazardous. Someone should warn him. He thinks he has come to the land of free speech—but it is not that free, not free enough for philosophical appraisals of the Enemy in a classroom. She felt absurdly that she must save him from a danger of which she magined he was unaware. For he is a good man, she thought, nd a man who has suffered a great deal, so that he says to imself in all likelihood: What does it matter? I must speak s I feel! And so no warning would reach him.

"Man—halfway between ape and angel," he repeated.

He paused, a long pause, standing behind his desk, cupping ne fist in the palm of the other hand, repeating the motion half dozen times slowly, as though deciding whether to continue. Then abruptly, his tone stronger:

"If I were to read to you psychiatric reports about soldiers who have broken in battle, you would find human creatures —shocked into unconsciousness, into loss of memory by days of strafing without shelter, by too many scenes of horror— ceasing to act like men, in some cases reverting to an apelike state, the walk simian, shoulders down, arms hanging long and loose, wide shuffling gait. I have seen them."

Briefly he moved like an ape to illustrate. It was not humorous. No one laughed. It might have struck them as funny, but it didn't. The man was too earnest.

"Also they lose the power of speech." He was leaning on the desk now. (The preacher, Fredericka thought again.) "Fear and horror," he was saying, "have projected them back that small space of world time to the state of an apelike ancestor. Also, frequently, a traumatized soldier—shell-shocked, as we used to say—returns to infancy. He drools, blubbers, slobbers, loses control of his sphincter muscles, soils himself . . ."

He had now, at last, his class's full attention. This was something dramatic, a picture they could all understand, something that reached into all their lives—the effect of battle on a human being. The silence in the room was impressive.

"These examples," Allers continued—and now his accent

was more marked, his placing of words a little foreign, though the deeper he felt the less control he had of his speech —"do you know what they to me say? They say that this creature, this so-called animal, is in reality a being of the greatest delicacy and sensitivity. War is not natural to him, always we are being told it is. Normal man has an essential deep recoil from the act of murder. One proof—if proof you wish—is this: soldiers have been known to lose the entire use of the hand and arm with which they have killed another man. Yes, an enemy, to be sure, but still *another man*, at close range, looking into his frightened, equally reluctant eyes . . ."

His voice had grown thick. He stopped. There was a long pause. He had the class on his side now. Fredericka could sense it. But he did not let emotion mount. He resumed his former unimpassioned tone. His accent improved as he said quietly:

"Of course I hope I do not need to stress that there are times when man must fight. Obviously! We have not yet progressed beyond it. If we do not see danger in time to prevent the purchase of the gun, then we must strike when the gun is drawn on us."

He walked back to the desk, looked down for a moment at the papers in a nearsighted, abstracted way as though trying to remember where he had digressed.

"Logic, I have said, does not apply to life itself. Life is something else again."

He took off his glasses and held them out in front of him, revealing remarkable eyes, intense, remote, yet full of a desperate question: How can I say it, any of it, any of what I know so terribly to be true?

"It is here," he said aloud in a slow deliberate voice, "that an faces his greatest paradox—one of the great riddles. For the human mind has a passion for unification, for getting things neatly tagged and named, classified, filed away for andy reference under certain large simple labels. Nature, on the other hand, exhibits an equally ardent passion for multiplication, novelty, uniqueness, surprises, inconsistencies. . . . So, man, the poor devil . . ."

It's too much for me, Fredericka said to herself. It's like concentrated food offered suddenly to a starving man. Now I realize how shut-off, how vacuumlike, my life has become. She looked around the class. The other students did not seem to find Franz Allers' remarks too much to swallow. Their minds, hitched to their pencils, moved along easily over what was to her totally unfamiliar and challenging material. Were their minds, being younger, more plastic, more agile? Or was it that, like all young people, ideas were just ideas to them and none seemed more important, more illuminating than any other?—whereas Fredericka knew she could ponder a single one of these fragmentary statements for days: "Logic does not apply to life. . . . Life is something else again. . . . Accept contradictions . . ."

The ideas she had heard in the past hour began to go round in her head with uncomfortable dizzying speed.

I'm too old to begin this kind of course, she thought. It will exhaust me. I feel tired already. Why should I bother at my age? She deliberately closed her eyes and ears and rested.

When she listened again Franz Allers was winding to a finish, preparing to give the students something to take away that would not too greatly trouble or perplex them. She opened her eyes swiftly when he cried:

"Here one is!"

"Here one is!" he was saying, throwing out his arms, staring down at his legs in their dark trousers as though they were separate objects. "Here am I!" he cried, holding up his foot until the class laughed. "A human being! A marvelously subtle and intricate mechanism with blood stream and lungs, cells and nerves, a face, hands, arms, ten toes and fingers, and all the rest of it, and we do not shout with amazement at the sight and thought of it. Instead we sit down with the thing and grow heavy and die thirty years before we are buried.

"I am alive," he said solemnly. "You are alive. No, do not laugh. It is a sober thought. It carries grave responsibility. It is also a wonderful thought. To some of us—Europeans—it is a thought of the greatest mystery and wonder. I am still alive! It makes us at once supremely elated and supremely sad. . . . Class is dismissed."

He broke off abruptly, and turning his back began to wipe some marks off the blackboard. Without glancing around he tapped the middle section with the eraser. "I'll leave this for anyone who wants to copy it."

As the class filed out, Fredericka, acting on an impulse that she did not stop to analyze, moved up front until she stood before Franz Allers' desk. Here she waited while he gathered his papers.

"Yes?" he said, after a moment, looking at her through his glasses. He was not cold, he was not indifferent, he was just waiting for whatever she had to say.

"I want to enter your class—if you will give me permission." As soon as she said it Fredericka wished she had not spoken. She was sure that she did not want to come here twice a week and try to make her rusty mind struggle again with weighty questions.

"I believe it is not my permission that you have to get," Mr. Allers began quietly.

Here was her way out, but she did not use it.

"I have already seen Dr. Cooper. He said I should ask you." She knew that she was speaking like a timid schoolgirl and wanted to add, Never mind. I don't really mean any of this.

It was plain that Franz Allers did not care one way or another about her entering the class. "If you have permission," he said, "and if you wish to . . ." He trailed off.

Fredericka felt that she owed him some explanation.

"Naturally I'm coming as a special. I mean I'm not a regular student. My husband has gone to war—is going—and I—I feel the need to get back into—into the world of ideas."

She had never felt more banal and inept. As though he caught her confusion and embarrassment Franz Allers asked kindly, "You live in Attica Center?"

"No. I live quite near, in a town called Wrenkill."

She saw the word register on him. He was pulling the zipper on his brief case and there was the faintest hesitation in his movement. "Wrenkill," he repeated. That was all.

"Do you know someone there?" she asked him.

"It has a familiar sound," he said, after a little pause. He seemed almost to be struggling with something in his thoughts. "What is your name?" he asked, lifting the brief case, looking at her as though studying her for some possible resemblance.

"Fredericka Perry."

He came down the steps of the platform and they began to move together up the center aisle.

"I know your brother, Louis Woodward," he said quietly.

"Louis! You know Louis?" She could not have been more astonished. "How amazing!" she cried. "Where?"

"I knew him in—in Europe," he went on in the same quiet voice.

"But this is really extraordinary!" Fredericka exclaimed. It seemed to her amazing beyond words, but she could see that Dr. Allers did not share her astonishment.

"Is it?" He did not say it to contradict her, but as though he would like to understand if it really was as strange as all that. "Today the whole world is moving," he said. "Europeans to America, Americans to Europe—the great migrations, east to west, north to south. . . ."

"I suppose so," Fredericka said. "But my world is still very small and—and unsurprising, so something like this seems very astonishing to me."

She was going on to ask how he had linked her name so quickly with Louis, when he said, "As a matter of fact I have a letter for you—a note of introduction from your brother. You must forgive me for not presenting it. I have been living a hermit's life since I came here."

His tone seemed to indicate that this life was not at all an unpleasant one, but Fredericka, again acting quite unlike her usual self, heard her voice insisting: "You must come to Wrenkill! We would all like it so much—to see someone who has seen Louis recently, who can tell us something about him."

"It has been over two years," he said in his detached way. "Much can happen in two years to men like Louis."

Did he imply something special? She could not make out. "But my aunt and my father would be so happy . . ." She left it there.

"Louis spoke particularly of your aunt." Allers half smiled as though remembering something amusing. "She must be a most remarkable woman."

"She is. . . . If you come to Wrenkill you can see for your-self."

He smiled again faintly. How insistent I'm being, Fredericka thought.

They had come to the doorway through the noisy hall. They emerged into the soft air.

"Spring!" It was as if he were making a discovery. His face lifted.

"Wrenkill is beautiful now—our garden anyway," Fredericka said, offering it like a bribe. She forgot her morning's distaste for the local scene. "It's just beginning to emerge from winter. I do hope you can come."

"Of course," he said, and then as though determined to finish it properly: "Do you wish me to say when now?"

"If you can—if you like."

He hesitated.

"What about this coming Sunday?" she suggested. "I wish I could offer to come and pick you up, but our gas is rationed now . . ." The sense of the unimportance of the gas ration-ing laid against political murder, trauma from war shock, the progress of man civilized only to the thickness of a postage stamp, swept immediately over her.

"Americans are terribly spoiled," she remarked, with what appeared to be irrelevance.

But he had followed her, and when she said it he looked amused and gave her his first direct personal glance.

"Americans are young." He smiled.

At his smile, which was free and open, Fredericka felt able to press the invitation to a specific date.

"Do make it Sunday. There's a morning bus that gets in around noon."

He hesitated only a moment. "I should like to."

They began to walk together down the path.

"It was really a wonderful lecture." Again what a school-girlish phrase. She blushed.

But he took it simply. "You are very kind. I'm afraid it was two things—over their heads in part and, when it was not, too emotional."

"That's why they'll remember it," Fredericka said positively. "All their lives."

For the second time he looked directly at her, and this time when his face lighted up his eyes lighted also. "I'd like to think that, but I'm afraid I only believe that they'll remember the emotion they felt and not the words that aroused it."

"I shall never forget what you said, anyway." She almost added, I feel it has changed my whole life, but something stopped her. They had shaken hands, spoken again of Sunday, and she was once more in her car backing out of the place where she had parked—but what was it she would never forget? Only with the utmost concentration and will could she reproduce Franz Allers' words that afternoon. And how, she asked herself, turning the car out the campus gates, could she ever explain to Christopher, to Aunt Palm, to Bridgie and her father what had come over her, meeting a man once and asking him to Wrenkill for a family Sunday dinner? Not that there was anything remarkable in such a simple act, except that it was entirely unlike her. If only, she thought, he will send Louis's note in advance! That will help make it seem a natural impulse. But she knew that from her point of view her action had been quite unreasonable, even quixotic.

Winding up the hill she looked down on the lake of her school days, the lake on which, in her memory, it was always spring—though she had skated here often. It was a small lake, tree enclosed, intimate, romantic. Freshmen were not supposed to go near it without permission. It cast a spell, haunted sleep in after years, for it was the embodiment of all the budding mystery of the awakened emotional life of boys and girls, moving side by side through the campus dream. Here she had gone canoeing with Greg in those buried years. Here they had first embraced and she had withdrawn, full of tremors of fear and longing. . . . The masked and guarded face of Franz Allers rose before her. He too is dead, she said to herself, but something more terrible killed him. . . . Heavy boots in the night, a body in a gunny sack, a train derails near Lyons, factory machinery falls apart, bread shipments disappear—the more lurid European stories in the Sunday magazine sections came alive to Fredericka for a moment on the rolling cement highway leading through the peaceful farmland of New York State.

I have again asked a man to Wrenkill for dinner, she thought, and she poked deliberately into the cold ashes of the once-burning memory of that other Sunday years ago—Greg's loud aggressive voice; Christopher, painted for his poison ivy, speaking in repressed and clipped tones . . .

I've come around a circle, she thought; a circle is completed; and quite unreasonably she felt happy and mysteriously relieved.

. . . She was turning up the driveway toward the house in Wrenkill before she realized that she had not gone near Farrell to ask about working with him again on her painting. This was definitely upsetting. How can I be so easily diverted from my purpose? she asked herself hopelessly. She saw the light burning in Aunt Palm's studio as she came around the last curve and the sight of it gave her an added stab of self-reproach.

Chapter Eight

FRANZ ALLERS' EYE FELL UPON HIS right hand with a sudden focusing of attention. The hand was idle. Between its forefinger and middle finger was a well-sharpened pencil, yellow with a red end, held as though in readiness to make a mark. It had lain thus, ready and waiting, for many minutes. "Ach!" he cried in exasperation. He flung the pencil down on the desktop, and it rolled off onto the floor losing its beautiful sharp tip. With another impatient exclamation he swung his swivel chair away from his desk. For a long time he stared out the windows without seeing anything beyond the pane. Only gradually did he become aware of what it was that had stayed the yellow pencil.

He was annoyed—annoyed because his carefully guarded privacy was at last open to assault. He had let down the bars, taken the first step. He could no longer say, But I don't go out, I simply go nowhere, for he had promised Louis Woodward's sister to come to Wrenkill. Here he would spend his Sunday, that one precious day on which he need not go to his campus office to be available to his students.

Although he had implied to Fredericka Perry that he did not think it strange they should have met, he realized, thinking about it now, that it was strange. It was simply because there seemed almost an element of fate in the meeting that he had yielded against his judgment to this impulse, had said that he knew who she was, and that he had a letter of introduction from her brother.

He rose impatiently and walked to the window. He had a view, and he was thankful for it, though the view was not extensive nor even very inspiring. It was a meadow—or so he liked to think of it, as "meadow" was one of his favorite English words. Actually it was, he supposed, only a back lot that someone was holding for a high price, a lot on which a fraternity group, or a retired professor, might be expected to raise one of the pseudo-Tudor houses the architects of this community seemed to favor above all other styles.

In this meadow during the past year, he had watched the multiple forms of nameless life close to the earth, the subtle shift and swing of the seasons from a soiled and tired yellow through all the greens, shrill and serene, and back again. The crescendo of the greens was beginning to rise to its full tonal range and, believing as he did that man is affected by the appearance of nature, he felt grateful to be facing the upbeat rather than the downbeat of change.

For he was again in one of his recurrent periods of black dreams. Night after night he would start up out of unconsciousness, his heart beating with jagged strokes, his body torn between an impulse to spring, strike, run, and that other impulse—worse by far—to cower, to wait, trying not to whimper. Minutes would pass with the timelessness of deep terror and finally he would dare to touch the light by the bed with his cold fingers . . . Bright glare! Emptiness! No one is here . . . And here—where is here? What is it really like here? . . . He would stiffen his body cautiously as, with infinite care, he tested the atmosphere, sniffing it, weighing it on imponderable scales of delicate awareness. Still not moving he would decide: Here it seems safe, unfamiliar but safe—yet still he could not place himself. And so he would wait. Finally he would begin to count. Five hundred. Five hundred slow counts—the ear alert, every fiber of his being stiff with attention and suspense, the eye strained to bursting in its socket, the blood pumping, veins throbbing in wrist and head. Five hundred at last! If by then there was no alien sound, nothing to frighten him further, he would cautiously raise himself in his bed, and in raising his head from the pillow he was always able immediately to name the place. Attica Center. The country, America. The hour, past midnight. The house indifferent and so—safe.

Yet now that he had found himself again in space and time he could feel only the cold, the terrible cold of a prison cell. Rising he would light newspapers, one after another, watching them roar up the chimney to give him instantaneous brief warmth. When his blood thawed a little, he could rest again. Worn out as though with a physical struggle, his body would lie back brokenly in the fireside chair of the dentist's wife, his landlady. Finally he was really "here." His name was Franz Allers. He even knew his street address, if anyone cared to have it. Since he was "here," who, then, was the man he had seen behind the fingers pressed hard against his eyes, the man stumbling up a ruined street, searching wildly in the rubble, standing mute with shock? . . . Bones, hair, and a remembered dress with small spring flowers on it; the keyboard of a piano, the charred remnants of a manuscript, the dust of Etruscan glass and a child's toy . . . images, ideas, objects, dreams and flesh, all one, all rubble. He is not this man, and yet he is this man. He is this man because he is a European.

It is gone. All of it. He is alone. He must make a new life. Of what shall he build it having seen that all is finally rubble? He must pretend to forget. He must try once more to forget.

"Get out more, see more people; no matter how boring, how trivial, it will help you!" That had been the advice of his friend, the New York psychiatrist, Carl Reuter. Reuter would be pleased if he knew that he was making the great effort to take a bus trip to a neighboring town to see the relatives of a newspaperman whose only claim to exacting this act of extreme self-sacrifice was—his own sacrifice. And at this thought Franz felt ashamed of himself, remembering Louis's great kindness, his wild, ridiculous courage, his wit, his shrewdness, his fear of showing sentiment. . . . If it would please Louis to have him meet his aunt, visit his sister—well, it was little enough! He owed Louis a good deal!

But he could have wished that it had not happened—this meeting with Fredericka Perry. Next autumn would have been soon enough to present the letter, with some plausible explanation for the delay. He still did not feel that he had the energy for anything more than his lectures, his reading . . . Besides, his sleeping took so much time. For he slept a great deal, particularly in the daytime. Fatigue would rise in him like a quick-acting poison, fell him as he sat working at his desk. While the light was around him he could sleep. Only the night was bad for sleeping. . . .

Looking out now in the afternoon light at the willow bush bending gently in the wind, with the lower branches tapping out a dancer's code on the ground, Franz suddenly saw, as he so often did, Vania, his dead wife, going down the walk that last day. He saw her glancing back to reassure him— the sun strong on her bright hair—lifting her hand before she opened the gate, closing it and looking up once more at him in his study window, this time with a long look in which there was, he now knew, everything—her sense of danger, her love and concern for him, her wish to reassure him, her fear of worrying him, her plea with him to be strong. . . .

Why, he asked himself for the thousandth time, the agony rising in him, draining his energy as it rose, did I let her go that day alone? For something had told him, as it told her, that she was in danger. Yet he had let her go. He had only waved his hand for the second time and turned away. As he turned away he had glanced in the large wall mirror and seen that she was blowing him another kiss—one that she did not know he could see—and there came into his mind, seemingly from nowhere, the words "der Kuss im Spiegel."

He could not make any association with the phrase but a cold premonition shot through him and for a moment he had, even more consciously, the impulse to rush to the window, lift it and cry out, Wait, Vania, wait! Don't go! . . . But why? she would have asked him, reasonably enough. And he would not have been able to explain. Yet somehow he believed that if he could have explained about her reflection in the glass and the cold shock in the associated words, "the kiss in the mirror," she might have stopped and turned back. Even in that moment of indecision he had known this dimly. But, as he struggled to dredge up the lost association, Vania turned the corner—and was gone.

Gone around the brick wall and so gone forever! It had become a familiar nightmare, one from which he always woke sweating and trembling. Vania turns the corner and as she turns he sees her disappear into the air like something in an enchantment. And in the dream he struggles to prevent its happening. He tries to wind back the reel of the film: the diver can return to the springboard, the horse to the goalpost, the plane to the hangar, surely then if he turns quickly enough, knowingly enough, the reel will come back to its start and Vania will again be at the gate and he can open the window and prevent her going.

"But what for?" the voice of the dream always asks him. "What for?"

"To die with her," he cries, "for I am dead anyway."

And the voice laughs; laughs horribly, laughs gently, laughs sardonically and knowingly and says, "Ah, no. Make no mistake! You are alive. *You* are alive!"

And he struggles up from the pillow and it is bitterly and desperately true. He is a living man who must try to pretend that he cares to be alive.

Franz had not let himself worry about Vania for the first hours after she disappeared. Frequently she was gone overnight. With the transportation problems of Vienna what they were, she sometimes remained near her patient if the case was serious. But when by noon of the next day she had not reappeared he called the clinic where she worked and a voice said to him in surprise, "Why, Dr. Allers has not been here for several days. She said she was going away to Budapest for a week."

Several days! But he had seen her only yesterday. . . . It was then his heart began to knock against the wall of his chest like a hammer in the hand of an imprisoned giant.

Whom to call next? At once he knew—the formidably ugly woman doctor who had once or twice accompanied Vania home for the night to sleep on the couch in the sitting room. Dr. Anna Weissberg.

He found her number and called it. It rang six times and then there was a very official voice:

"Whom are you calling?"

"I am calling Dr. Anna Weissberg."

"Are you a friend of hers?"

"I know Dr. Weissberg slightly. She is a colleague of my wife's."

"Ah, yes. Well, I am sorry to say that Dr. Weissberg is not in and will not be for some time. Who is calling, please?"

He had given his name.

"Thank you," said the voice.

The receiver was returned to the hook.

The police came that afternoon to make a search of the apartment just as he was leaving to go to them for help. He had called the Bureau twice already about Vania, and the very quality of the response over the telephone told him that something had changed. The police of Vienna were no longer there to serve the people; they were there to spy, to suppress, to frighten and deny. All this he had heard before. All this he had already known. And yet he did not actually know it until he himself had come face to face with the reality and all that it implied.

The police apparently found nothing in their search—though they did not say what they were after. They went through all the papers, including Franz's manuscript and notebooks. They put them back precisely where they found them, but he knew, as he stood watching them, that he would have to get his work out of the country as soon as possible. It too was suddenly suspect.

The officers carefully put stress on his honorary titles: *Herr Professor, Herr Doktor*. It seemed servile rather than polite. They gave no explanation, no satisfaction. "Your wife has been detained." That was all. Where, why, how . . . this they would not say. They were suave, they were bland, they were politely inhuman.

Then began the days and nights of growing horror. He lost all track of time. It was hard to remember now what he had done. He knew that he had gone to every friend who had influence. He dimly remembered visiting government buildings, waiting interminably in outer offices—he, unaccustomed to waiting—sitting, sick with helplessness and fear, in inner rooms, searching everywhere he thought she might have been in those last days and realizing desperately, as he walked hatless and haggard through the streets, that he knew nothing of Vania's real life.

Once they had shared every waking thought. It began when they went away together, two months before they were married, over a June holiday to the Tyrol. He was already practicing medicine. She was still a student. "Piccolo" he called her—the name of the apprentice boys in Tyrolean inns. They wandered all day in the high summer pastures, a lunch in their pockets. In that magic upper realm of the earth, bemused with tinkling bell and fir scent, with the sound of a distant zither through the early mist, they had lain together locked in the enchantment of their new love.

And the enchantment had lasted. He would swear to it. Can a man be sure? No, never to that extent—and yet he was. When he decided to begin his long arduous work of research he had talked solemnly with Vania, had told her what it meant to him, but how it would inevitably change the pattern of their closely knit lives. She had understood, had urged him on to his solitary labors; yet it had often given him a feeling of guilt, particularly the fact that on so many mornings as he went to bed from a night of work (for he could concentrate only in the nights) she was rising to go to her clinic, or to a patient.

"On the other side of this gestation of mine," he would say, stopping to kiss her, to hold her slender strong body for a moment in his arms, "we will be really together again, Piccolo, my darling."

"But we are together now," she would protest. "I understand completely. You must do it. That I know."

"Then you don't think I've cut myself off from life?"

"But of course not. The man in the study alone is as important as anyone else in the world."

"You really believe this?"

"How can you doubt it? I know your temperament. You are the scholar and the teacher—far more than merely the doctor. But as for me, I am a doer. I must do it with my hands. I must see it done—the milk down the baby's throat, the cyst opened, the room aired, the woman put to bed with a sedative."

"This book," he had repeated, "it is really a gestation for me. And when the brain child is delivered we shall go off again to the Tyrol."

But the child of his brain was still not delivered, now might never be. The manuscript had not been touched since Vania failed to come back around the brick wall. Once, since coming here to Attica Center, he had taken it out and spread it on his desk. He had read to the bottom of the second page. He could go no farther. His stomach had turned over. He had had to lie down in order to meet with his class some hours later.

The willow outside his window tapped the ground again, turned, twisted, created another shape, the shape of the man with the broken jaw, the limp, the mangled hand with the gold ring lying flat on its callused palm, the palm of the hunted visitor who rang the bell softly at midnight and came to deliver a plain gold band that broke forever the reel on which the film of Vania was wound.

Franz could still remember his calm at this meeting, the calm of someone who can no longer feel anything.

"Tell me," he had said, taking the ring and looking at it curiously as though he had never seen it before. "Vania—my wife—what was it she really did?"

And he would never forget, would see all his life long—rising out of the pages of a book, out of the coals of a fire, out of the dance of leaves or the play of sun on grass—the man's eyes at his question. They were eyes gone blank with what they had seen, and determined eternally to remember. Yet a peculiar expression flickered across their dark glazed surface. In another man it would have been surprise.

"You do not know?" The voice flattened. There was a pause. "She had been helping to mimeograph a paper," it said tonelessly.

"A paper?"

"A paper with excerpts from foreign broadcasts."

"But where did she go to hear a foreign radio?"

The stranger was silent.

"I do not know," he said finally.

Franz realized then that he was not trusted. He asked nothing more.

"Anna was with her," the visitor added through his broken teeth, "to the end. They took your wife first. I thought you would want to know."

"Yes, of course. Thank you."

The control and formality of his own voice horrified him. Yet he could not speak in any other way.

"Go on," he added, and then suddenly, "*Anna?*"

"Dr. Anna Weissberg."

"Ah, yes, of course."

The man would not stay, not to sleep, or even to rest. He would not wait for coffee. He refused the schnapps. "It would be too strong." He accepted a small piece of wurst and the end of a loaf of bread and was gone again into the darkness as mysteriously as he had emerged from it.

Then up and down, back and forth all night Franz walked the apartment smoking and trying to feel something—anything. Toward morning he went into the bathroom. Hanging on the nail of the bathroom door was her blue robe. He put out his hand and touched it. He began to gather its folds into his fists, to clutch it with his hands as he buried his face in its soft texture, and then suddenly the teeth and claws of his controlled agony began to tear at his frozen bowels.

In the morning the servant found him delirious in his study chair. It was weeks before he was again able to take up the threads of his life, the new life that he had now to make for himself, darting for cover, listening, watching—foe or brother? —the life of a man who is not sure whether he is marked or not, but must act like the hunted, and thus becomes the hunted.

Chapter Nine

WHEN THE DELIRIUM OF HIS first illness cleared while he was still in Vienna, Franz's mind had gone back, straight as an arrow to a target, to the time the Gemeindehäuser were first fired on by soldiers. (It was as though his memory had been patiently waiting for his mind to clarify in order to present him with a clue to Vania's end.) The Heimwehr, without warning, had attacked the modern workers' apartments. One part of the body of Vienna had turned upon another to destroy it. "Cancer," he had said to Vania at the time, "cancer in the body of a people; as unconscious, as significant a self-destruction as the growth of malignant cells within a human organism." He often spoke of men and society in medical terms. It was part of a point of view that he had been slowly forming since the days when, still little more than a boy, he had served in World War I.

When he spoke as he did about cancer in the body politic, Vania had nodded in agreement, but her nod was abstracted, her face remote. He saw that she was upset about the political situation in Austria in a different way. She took it all more personally, while he could view it as existing apart from himself, with the essential detachment of a doctor studying a patient. To be sure, it troubled him, this growing sense of national conflict and tension; yet when he retired to his study with the fire burning, the door closed on intruders, his books and papers spread about, he could forget it. The shooting of innocent workmen, who had demanded only the simplest human decencies, did not stab as vitally into his consciousness as his own work problems.

He was trying at the time to analyze certain findings on the conditioning of animals. He was attempting to assemble and state in readable lay language the facts and the questions having to do with the development of neurosis in sheep:

Sheep fed to the ticking of a metronome at 120 degrees and *not* fed when the beat is 50 learn to distinguish between the two rates of the beat. They soon ignore the metronome when the measure is 50. If, however, the metronome is changed to 80 and 100, making the distinction more difficult so that they begin to make frequent mistakes in going to the feedbox, it is not long before they have developed states of tension, irritability, nerves. They even develop eczema!

Good! This much is established about the docile, simple sheep. Well, then, may we not infer:

Small wonder that man—a creature of far more complex nervous structure, unable in the modern world to distinguish positive from negative conditionings, the right from the wrong, the helpful from the harmful—develops all the unhappy characteristics of indecision, hypertension, cynicism, and exhaustion of which we today see him the victim?

Careful! he had warned himself. Take it easy! Not too fast! Keep on that hypothetical fence where you may enlighten the laity without being accused by your fellow scientists of turning cheap popularizer. For those who guard the mysteries must keep them mysterious, must adhere rigidly to their own special formalized vocabulary, a vocabulary the ordinary human being is never taught and has little chance to learn, so that the priests of medicine, chanting the esoteric language of their cult, are never understood by those who come to them for healing. . . .

At the time the Gemeindehäuser were fired upon and workmen died unattended before their own doors, Franz had been deep in the study of conditioned reflexes—Schilder, Pavlov; in the analysis of the development of cardiovascular manifestations in tricked and baffled animals. His concentration on this material—working by night and sleeping by day —gave his infrequent talks with Vania the unreality of dreams.

Thus, on the morning that his wife spoke about the killing of the workmen, only half his mind had taken in what she was describing. Vania told him that she had visited, against strict police orders, two suspected men who were in hiding—badly wounded, innocent workers, she said. It seemed right to him that she, a doctor, should have gone to them, but he did warn her to be careful. Yet as he half listened, and sounded his mild warning, the deeper part of his mind was still pondering the night's problem:

Why does the sheep left free in the pasture and taught to run a maze with more food at the end of it never develop a neurosis when tricked? Why does the pasture sheep, when things get difficult and the problem is beyond him, simply lie down, or quietly graze, and try again later? Is it the laboratory sheep's loss of freedom that contributes to his frenzy? Dare I compare this to the human being who develops neurotic behavior because he has had to submit his personal instincts to the pressures of a restrictive society?

. . . Vania was speaking . . . "I was allowed in for half an hour."

"In?" He had not been following her, had not heard her last words.

"Into the courtyard where the shooting was. Men died there without knowing they were dying. And some of them bled to death and no one dared to help them. Some of them are still bleeding to death, for no one is allowed to enter now. It's verboten."

She broke a roll in half and dipped it into her coffee, her eyes far away, her hands thoughtful with the bread. "I noticed the last picture that was shown in the workers' cinema. It was *Der Kuss im Spiegel*."

So that was where the words had come from! But what did they mean—"the kiss in the mirror"? He had returned over and over again, with a bitter compulsion in the months that followed, to the memory of that breakfast table, forcing himself to recall each word, each movement. . . .

Vania had dipped her bread again, her eyes still remote. "For some reason that title seems—it seems like an evil omen, like something in a fairy tale, a witch's tale I'd almost forgotten . . ." She had tapered off, uncertainly.

But she had his full attention by then. "You are being fanciful, darling. You're tired out."

"Yes," she had agreed at once, making her tone lighter. "Yes, I'm being fanciful. Only, when I read those words a terrible shudder went all through me—as though I'd seen something prophetic."

So there it was! And what was it? A title of five words: *The Kiss in the Mirror*. One thing it told him—so it *was* a clue of sorts—it told him when the change in Vania occurred. As he looked back on it, it seemed to him that from the day she uttered the words of that last title in the abandoned cinema to the day she blew him her last kiss, caught fleetingly in the wall mirror of his study, she had lived apart from him. Those words, that breakfast table scene, were the beginning of a long farewell, the first step in a chain of events that ended in a specter's kiss. For he was sure that the destruction of the Gemeindehäuser brought about a new purpose in Vania, led her into activities which had finally deprived her of her life.

As for him, during the period that led directly to her terrible death, he had gone deeper and deeper into a particularly trying phase of his work, in an attempt to sum up, to rephrase near the layman's level of understanding, the psychogenic factors in heart disease. And as always, when he came to his summations, he was impaled once more on the old dilemma of the psyche and the body—the unity, and the seeming split. He longed to be in Budapest with Horvath, his old master, discussing it before the coal grate in Horvath's shabby, smoke-filled room. But he had been to Budapest only a month before, and he could hardly keep running off to claim this, his most sympathetic and critical audience.

To Vania at this time he did not turn for discussion of his work. Afterwards this too seemed significant, for they had always shared ideas. He had never failed to have her responsive attention. And yet somehow, then, he had sensed he would not have her deepest interest. She was too involved with heart and hands to give her mind fully to problems of research and speculation.

It was two or three nights after his breakfast conversation with Vania about the dying men in the workers' courtyard. He had made a fresh summary and it had, temporarily at least, suited him:

There is never merely a physical disease, never merely a psychical one, but only a living event taking place in a living organism which is itself alive only because of the simultaneous coexistence in it of the physical and the psychical. Psyche and soma; these two are but aspects of a single unity.

He wrote the few lines on his pad and went to bed around midnight, earlier than usual. He slept heavily for several hours. In the gray light of early moning he woke abruptly, sure that he had heard voices. He got up at once and went down the hall to the kitchen wing of their apartment. Opening the door he found Vania sitting at the oilcloth-covered table with a strange woman. The room was filled with the pleasant fumes of coffee and the pot was beginning to bubble on the gas flame.

In the white overhead light his doctor's eye noticed at once how strained and exhausted Vania appeared.

She came to him at once. "Franzi, we have disturbed you. I'm so sorry. This is Dr. Anna Weissberg. We've been to the prison together, delivering a baby."

He greeted the woman seated at the table and she nodded with no change of expression. In this his first view of her, she seemed almost grotesquely ugly. Her shoulders were built wide like a wrestler's. She had good clear brown eyes but her oily skin had surely never been powdered, and above her lips that were full, but more gross than sensual, there was a wisp of small black mustache. Exhaustion heightened the unattractiveness of her face, for it was swollen with hours of denied sleep. Her body sagged with a weariness she made no attempt to conceal. The very openness of her fatigue embarrassed Franz. He felt soft and pampered coming into the cold kitchen fresh from sleep, wrapped in his warm robe.

"Vania," he said tenderly turning to his wife, "you need sleep, my dear. Do come and get some rest soon."

"Soon," she echoed, "darling. You go along back to bed. I'm putting Anna here on the couch for the night. She lives way out in Floridsdorf."

"There's not much left of the night, I'm afraid," he said. His words sounded lame. He felt awkward and inadequate as he turned to go.

He was still awake when Vania tiptoed into their bedroom.

"I'm awake," he said, relieving her of the necessity of being quiet.

"Oh, I'm so sorry, darling. I know you must be weary."

"No," he said. "But I'm sure you are."

"I'm frozen," she said, curling herself against him.

He encircled her slender body with his arms. "Vania darling, don't overdo it."

"Overdo what?"

"Whatever it is you are doing day and night now. I can see how tired you are."

"I'm doing nothing," she said in a voice that sounded unusually restrained and quiet. "Nothing really, compared to someone like Anna. She is so strong and so good."

"Is she good?" he said. "Yes, I suppose she is—though she does not look it."

"You mean because she is so ugly? . . . Perhaps that's why her heart is so big. It embraces the whole world. But she can hate too, and there are people whom we must hate. I'm beginning to see that—something new in my protected easy life."

Her voice had a sudden hard edge of pain and anger in it. Disturbed, anxious to quiet her, he began to stroke her forehead, her arms, her back and breasts. She began quietly to weep. . . .

Here memory became too painful for him. He tried to close the door on the questions, but they came anyway: How can it be possible for this body so beloved and so loving, this breast I have cupped in the tenderness and frenzy of love, these lips with which I have exchanged the slow sweet breaths of ecstasy, this hair I have braided with my fingers in the summer sunlight and beside a winter's fire—all this beauty and tenderness, still so rich and ripe when I last viewed it at the gate with upraised fingers in final salute—all this to be gone, and gone with violence, from the earth?

This is when the mind cracks, bursts open, splits apart and sends the cry hurtling up from the depths of being, the cry conceived in the brain and born within the moment out of the twisted bowel. If a man could howl like a beast trying to understand! But he cannot. He lays his head in his hands and locks up the scream, allowing only the groan to burst on his lips like the bloody foam-flecked bubble of some hidden mortal wound.

Why was I so blind? Why could I have neither guessed nor shared? That time when I was questioned, many months before they took her . . .

"Are you aware of your wife's activities?"

"I believe I know what my wife does with her time—yes."

"But you do not accompany her in the evenings when she goes out?"

"Naturally I do not attend my wife when she pays calls on patients. I have my own work."

"True, yes, but, Herr Doktor, we were not referring to paying calls on patients."

"Then to what were you referring?"

"To meetings—of a certain nature. Do you know that your wife belongs to a workers' organization in a district where, perhaps, Herr Doktor, you yourself have never been? Or perhaps you have?"

"Oh, I imagine I have been there all right. I know most of the slums of Vienna. After all, I took my internship here. I am quite aware that my wife works among the poor. She has a free clinic. I do not know what activities may, or may not, have grown out of her work, nor do I consider it any of my affair."

"Perhaps, Herr Doktor, you will sometime regret that you did not make it your affair."

He had told Vania of this interview in detail. She did not seem troubled. Shaking her head and smiling, "How little they have to do with their time," was all she said.

"But do be careful!" he had implored her. "I feel that there are no limits any more. . . ."

No limits! How lightly he had said it. There were certainly no limits to what he had imagined about her and her fate after the limping man with the broken face had come in the middle of the night bringing him the plain gold ring with the F.A. and the V.S. and the date of their marriage engraved on it. He would start up with a cry out of feverish sleep, drop a book as though it were charged with electricity at some word, some phrase: *lighted matches under the nails; the dentist's drill in the jaw* . . .

"They are never so hard on women," said the limping man. "You must believe it. Try to believe it for it is true. There are not so many women. That is one reason."

With the delivery of the ring at least one thing was certain —it was over for her. That was what the man's shattered jaws had told him. It was over. For the last time she had heard the heavy boots on the stone floors, the creak and clang of the doors, the key rasping in the lock, the screams that rose and died in the night.

A sudden wind struck the willow bush and it broke into a frenzy of joyous green movement. Franz turned away from the sight of it, heavy with the familiar weight of his impotence and despair. For I should have been the one, he told himself again. I should have been the one who was implicated and who was taken away and tortured. But I was not, because I had moved out of the concrete into the abstract world. I was a man in a study. A man who had not yet even published a book that could be burned. For three years I had taken no patients while I sat in my study trying to piece together some of my theories into a comprehensive whole. And so it was Vania who paid the price, protecting me to the last, even protecting me from her own thoughts and her own activities, lest the incursion of these alien ideas interrupt the measured pace of my own thinking.

Oh, he had had doubts—what man working alone is free of them? He doubted even while he was, with so much secret excitement and so much outward caution, developing his theme. All the while he was bolstering his ideas with proved facts, even with stories to excite the lay mind (the cure or development of warts under hypnosis by suggestion; the picture of the stomach of a person when enraged and when at rest; anything to lure readers to his volume—so bound on making converts was he); still his doubts persisted.

Eventually he took his doubts to Horvath in Budapest, sure that Horvath's answers would not be dictated—as Vania's might have been—by love, but by reason.

Was it, Franz asked him, an important task he had set himself, this proving by exact case histories, by example, and by premise that the body and the psyche are one, an indivisible unity; that only by believing this can we understand either disease on the one hand, or personality problems on the other?

"Yes," Horvath had said. "Yes, it is important."

"But lately," Franz had said, "this rising wave of barbarism—these new barbarians—sometimes they make one doubt all progress. Sometimes I question the—the timeliness of the task I've set myself."

He saw at once that he had said something disturbing. Horvath flipped the wide end of his soft silk tie out of his vest front and began to wipe his glasses methodically and slowly. He always used this gesture when differing with or correcting anyone.

"There will always be violence. Yes, always madness—barbarism, as you call it—until we come to know its cause. Until we know ourselves. We might start the cure with a more exact use of terms. These are not barbarians, my dear Franz. These men are, in part, too calculating for barbarians, in part too psychotic, too sadistic. In order to know how to deal with these men we must know what name to call them by; for the name will determine their guilt, their treatment, their possible cure."

"But," Franz had protested, "Vania has a friend, a doctor —she frequently says: 'We must not call them psychotic, for to call them that is to excuse them.'"

"But not they alone are on trial," said Horvath quietly. "Our society is on trial. These men have not sprung from the earth like Jason's warriors. They have grown up among us. They too are men."

*　　*　　*

. . . When Franz saw Horvath again, the year after Vania's disappearance, months after the gold ring on the callused palm of a nameless stranger had destroyed his hopes forever, he was abusive to Horvath about this memory of their last talk together.

"So it's important to find the right name!" Franz had scoffed. "Good God! What semantic quibbling! Try to find just the right word with which to address a steam roller, a juggernaut, a seven-headed monster? Words won't stop him. Ideas won't stop him. Only deeds will stop him."

"Deeds are ideas," said Horvath quietly, polishing the lens of his glasses on his silk tie. "And the reverse."

Franz had jumped up and left the room.

The next day Horvath sent around a note. It came just as Franz was leaving for the station to try to board a train for Switzerland.

Perhaps, my dear friend, it is not too much to insist that the right word may still save us. I am sure you will not accuse me of theological banality if I quote you an old line full of power and mystery: *In the beginning was the Word, and the Word was God.*

Crumbling the note in his hand Franz turned back into his room long enough to seize paper and write:

May I remind you of the medieval legend of the Golem? The man who created this monster-in-his-own-image was careful to hide the name of God under the creature's tongue for fear he would otherwise misuse his power. But one night he forgot to do so and the Golem went forth and did violence in the name of God and thus no one could resist him. . . . Today the Golem is loose again and he is raging and destroying in the name of God. He too has the word, the power of the word. That is why names, terms, words no longer avail us anything. There must be some other way, beyond the contradiction of words and terms—at least I can now only hope so.

And Horvath wrote again. The letter reached Franz long afterwards in France:

Yes, there are many paths. Each man has his own way of serving the world spirit, his own *daemon*, and his fellow man. You have your way. Vania had hers. I have mine. In theory we could all meet. In practice we may sometimes have seemed remote from one another. Perhaps you will still answer that the outer act is more than ever all that matters now. With this point of view—at the present time in world history—I cannot quarrel. Though should you say that it is all that *finally* matters I would most certainly contradict you.

Franz could write Horvath now—write him from the New World, from a town called Attica Center lying in a green cup among peaceful hills with white roads winding out to other names from classical antiquity—but Horvath was dead. He had been killed in the early bombing of Warsaw. He had gone from Budapest to try to save the manuscript of a professor at the university, a friend who had had to flee Poland for his life in the brief hours after midnight. Acting to save the Word, Horvath lost his life. He had thus, Franz said to himself, answered him adequately for all time.

He thought often of Horvath when he was preparing his lectures. Only last week, trying to make his students see the connection between the psychopathic personality of our time and the mass psychosis that seemed to be holding such power in its hands, he had written:

Man, economic and spiritual man (for I am not afraid to use that term), is everywhere today frustrated. Modern life makes this condition at present seemingly inescapable. Part of man's frustration springs from his growing hope that under some other "system" he might not need to accept all those frustrations. Disinherited, betrayed and bewildered, he is, individually, a clinical case—did we but have the clinics! In the mass there is danger of his becoming the Nazi Storm-trooper whose Leader has released his coiled-up, sick, repressed energies with a doctrine which says in effect: "Your antisocial primitive impulses, once considered to be retrogressive, are in truth progressive. They are strong and manly. Your brutal aggressions are virtues. Your inability to understand that others have rights is a source of great power. Your 'cure' will come when you have the world in the palm of your own hand, so do not be misled by any talk of acceptance, of limitation, or 'therapy.' The only therapy is brutal power. Don't look for doctors! Be yourself the doctor! Make the world your helpless patient on whom you experiment with your bold new theories."

Some students liked being challenged and puzzled; they sought him out later, questioning him:

"Did I understand you to say that Hitler is not entirely bad?"

"No, I did not say that—but I did imply that he has accomplished some good."

"Do you mind explaining how?"

"Well, he has brought into the open a lot of buried stuff in all of us. He is helping to explode a lot of half-formed, half-accepted ideas about a new so-called 'scientific' life for humanity, where the unfit and the sick are to be destroyed coldly in a wholesale fashion, where only selected people are allowed to reproduce, where children are conditioned in specified modes of conduct and ways of thought. It sounded pretty sensible in theory. In practice no civilized people like

t. . . . This is no inconsiderable balloon that Herr Hitler
has pricked."

In spite of all his brave words to his students he was not
able to keep his own faith at high tide. Over and over again
he questioned his own attitudes and motives. Was he merely
a man who, having survived a severe shattering blow, now
wanted only to rest? Was he now seeking an oasis in the great
desert of the century's despair? Did he want only to lie down
somewhere and sleep until the end?

But you cannot—even though you wish it—you cannot, his
inner voice told him. The easy sleep of one who has never
known primitive fear is forever denied you now. So you must
stay on your feet. You must fight. You must pretend to forget. You must try once more to believe. You must fight. Fight
for what? So that it does not happen again! Forget the day in
the 1930's when you saw the Stormtroopers parading near the
ruins of the ancient Roman wall in Trier. Forget that you
were assailed then with fearful half-formed thoughts of the
spiral in time which we call history, turning and turning again
on itself. Until you can believe again that the way lies ahead
and that the goal is sure, pretend at least to believe. For that is
why you came to America. You believed that here men might
still build—build again . . .

But in America he was a refugee. He knew the meaning of
the word at last—as he had never known it during the years
of hardship and wandering from one European country to
another. Here in America, he was something strange and
special. It was quite different from being an immigrant.

In other years men entered the New World with hope and
high vision. Today the man from Europe comes running,
looking back fearfully, or carefully not turning to see the
burning city. He comes with a mingling of despair and grati-

tude. He tries to throw off his suffering and his cynicism.
And this new country has its effect on him. It both invig-
orates him and wearies him—as older people are invigorated
by the sight of the tireless vitality of children, and at the same
time wearied because they feel by contrast the weight and
rigidity of their own bones. They long to cry out: If you
had seen what I have seen you would not be playing with
yo-yo's in the sun, or bouncing balls against a warm ivied
wall. And at the same time they want to say: Oh, stay this
way with the bright balls in the sun and make me believe that
I am only suffering from a bad dream, nothing more!

And now he knew why the impending visit to Wrenkill
was haunting and troubling him. He was about to be taken
into a warm and intimate place where old people were living out their fated span within a framework of family life,
almost as classically prescribed as that of the ancient Chinese.
This he knew from Louis Woodward's descriptions of his
home. He would see rooted people once more—people who
had never known collective fear. Not that this would be the
first home into which he had gone in the months he had been
in America, but that here, as part of its background, there
would always be Louis Woodward—Louis, his friend, who
chose to live his life in Europe where whole peoples and ideas,
not merely individuals like Louis's aging relatives, were
crumbling into obscurity.

"Why do you want to go to America?" Louis had asked
him. "There is nothing there for you."

"Have I something to give, to leave? . . . That is more
the question."

Louis had shrugged. "Hide it in a brown paper parcel and
bury it under a hedge. That's what my aunt Palm used to
suggest when anyone said, 'Listen, I've got an idea!' . . ."

The face of Fredericka Perry rose before Franz—the delicately pointed oval, the gray eyes with the play of flecked green in them, the mouth that was full with a curb to its fullness as though in some secret restraint echoed in the grave depths of her eyes. He was sure that he would inevitably know this woman better, and the thought filled him with apprehension. He would upset her. He would upset them all. It would happen merely by his presence among them, for he was the noise outside the bedroom, the insistent dim clangor rousing reluctant sleepers. They were all asleep. Their dreams might occasionally be troubled but they at least could still sleep. And in all likelihood they would not be asked to waken as he had been wakened, along with millions of others, only to die. Not this time anyway. In the next cataclysm . . . then perhaps . . .

Chapter Ten

FRANZ ALLERS SENT LOUIS'S NOTE TO Wrenkill in advance of his own visit. It was short, and mercifully written on the typewriter. Louis's hand was illegible.

Dear Flea—also Aunt Palm. How are you both? I'm sending a friend of mine to see you. He is a wise man and I think a good one, who has been through Hell. I'll let him tell you about it himself if he wants to sometime. Until then take him as you see him. He needs peace, affection, and optimism based on something more vital than the Chamber of Commerce statistics on summer tourists. I mean he needs Faith in Life. Got any to spare? I'm sure America is probably making it now in pellets—one-a-day brand. . . . He probably needs vitamins too, incidentally. I'm fine. So is Hedi. Love to all. . . . His name is Franz Allers. He is a doctor (medical) and a scholar. Also musician, critic, artist. You won't know the type. We don't have them in America.

Louis

"Let's make it a real party," Fredericka suggested to Aunt Palm, reading Louis's note aloud. "I'll get Owen and Bridgie and Father to drive over for dinner—they should for Louis's sake. And we'll invite Uncle Philander. He's such a wonderful American type for Dr. Allers to see. Besides, it will be a good chance to break down this bad feeling about the mountain goat horns."

"That's very thoughtful of you, lovie," Aunt Palm said, almost with enthusiasm. "I do miss seeing Philander. He is such an entertaining liar."

Philander had not been near the house since Uncle Caleb's will was read. This was because the will had left the two rams' heads locked in mortal combat, which Uncle Caleb had once got on a bad debt at the bank, to his son Robert for his Westchester ping-pong room, instead of to Philander who had always expected to inherit them for his museum. Uncle Philander was of the opinion that Aunt Palm could have averted this tragic loss to science.

Uncle Philander took his museum seriously. He had begun to collect material for it when still a very young man. He had been an ardent admirer of Teddy Roosevelt in Roosevelt's pre-Big Stick days and, with the help of some stock in the Erie Railroad and a third interest in a prosperous feed business, Philander had been able to follow his hero out west for a few years in his youth. During this time he learned to ride wild horses, permanently impaired his digestion with alkali water, cold baked beans, and half-cooked bacon, and amassed a large and eternally dusty collection of objects in natural history. This somewhat motley and depressing museum was responsible, Aunt Palm always declared, for the early deaths of his three wives.

Fredericka decided not to risk Uncle Philander's refusal by using the telephone. She drove over to the farmhouse at Sprague's Eddy to invite him. She found him where the old housekeeper said he would be, on the riverbank flat on his stomach with his binoculars to his eyes, and a flask of whisky beside him. He was plainly glad to see her. He rose, ran his long hands twice the length of his red-gray beard, made a pass at his muddy trousers and extended the whisky flask.

"Take a pull, Fredericka. It will keep the damp out of your bones."

Fredericka declined. He then offered her the binoculars. "There's a doe on that little island. Don't know what the hell she's doing there as early as this." He indicated a small patch of marshy green in the middle of the torpid stream.

Fredericka took the binoculars just to be polite.

They walked back up the hill. "Come on in," Uncle Philander said. "The gadfly will have some coffee ready." He referred to his housekeeper.

There were fresh cinnamon rolls with the coffee. Uncle Philander ate and drank what he pleased and relied heavily on bicarbonate of soda for relief later. He regularly overate on raisins and nuts between meals, claiming he needed their special food values. There were certain fattening substances that he did avoid, however, in wholly quixotic manner. Salad oil was one. He bought a low-calorie substitute from a Health Store in New York and always carried a small bottle with him when he went out to eat. This gave him the excuse to mix his own dressing at dinner and thus rivet all attention on himself.

"Pesky things, pine nuts," he said now, crushing the shells between his fingers. "But wholesome. Come and see the petrified clamshells someone sent me from Oregon."

Fredericka went into the main rooms of the museum, which had once been a downstairs bedroom and parlor. She walked along with Uncle Philander past the familiar rows of dusty objects: the prehistoric fish embedded in limestone, the stuffed birds, the mountain opals, the quartz, the jasper (orbicular and plain), the buffalo chips, the Indian baskets, the signed photographs of Buffalo Bill, Ezra Meeker, Theodore Roosevelt, and a nameless actress in black tights, puffed sleeves, and a frizzed bang. . . . They stopped as they always did before the pride of the collection, a dinosaur's track painstakingly chipped from the New Mexico desert while the Smithsonian's back was turned.

It was here, viewing the dinosaur track, that Fredericka dared to invite Uncle Philander for Sunday lunch. He accepted at once, with no bitter speeches. She stressed the fact that Franz Allers was a friend of Louis's. Uncle Philander was very fond of Louis.

"He'll come to no good end, however," he always said of him. "It's one thing to be a writer, and one thing to be a politician, but when you try mixing the two you're bound to come to grief."

"How's Palm?" he asked Fredericka finally at the door of the car, as she was leaving.

"Quite well. She sent her love."

Uncle Philander hesitated. "Greet her," he said formally, "for me. Until Sunday."

As she turned out the driveway he stood holding one arm upright in a theatrical gesture, like a figure on a mural, Fredericka thought, claiming a new land or crying, "We, the People!" She tapped the horn lightly to let him know she had seen him.

The thought of murals brought back memories of the ones Otto Schultz had painted for the main dining room of the Riverview Hotel: raftsmen guiding logs through a stiff white meringue, Indians lighting neatly constructed signal fires. Here Fredericka had gleaned her first knowledge of local history—rivermen, red men, early settlers—an erratic web of fact and legend woven by her elders on Thursday nights when they ate in the hotel dining room because the cook abandoned the kitchen then to go home and see her grown son.

"Very fine," Uncle Caleb always said about the murals to strangers. "Very fine."

"Very bad. Very dull," Aunt Palm would counter, though she usually defended Otto Schultz, who had done the large annually renewed sign for the Cascade Laundry showing a Broadway moon on the autumn Catskills.

She often followed her condemnation with a muttered recitation of melodramatic lines about a waterway, lines whose origin Fredericka never knew until she got to college and read *Moby Dick:*

". . . through the entire breadth of the state of New York; through numerous populous cities and most thriving villages; through long, dismal, uninhabited swamps . . ." (And there they were for Flea—as she was then called—the great trees, draped in shawls of white fuzz like the poll of Wrenkill's Uncle Tom, with a younger and more agile Uncle Tom dodging, slipping, now appearing, now dissolving in the dank mists, the dogs howling in the distance) ". . . and affluent, cultivated fields, unrivaled for fertility, by billiard room and bar-room; through the holy-of-holies of great forests . . ." (This was one of Uncle Philander's favorite lines. He always spoke it with solemn pleasure) ". . . on Roman arches over Indian rivers." (These words, too, woke echoes, evoked visions, for young Flea, listening rapt, with her eyes dilated and her mouth faintly smudged with the last spoonful of her food.) ". . . And especially," Aunt Palm would conclude, "by rows of snow-white chapels, whose spires stand almost like milestones, flows one continual stream of Venetianly corrupt and often lawless life. . . ."

"You are, of course, describing life on the Erie Canal," Uncle Philander reminded his sister at the end of this recital. "Not life on the river."

"Quite so, quite so, and every line of it might apply to the Delaware, and let Otto Schultz try painting the swamps and the barrooms and the Roman arches over Indian rivers."

"You should have painted them yourself," accused Uncle Philander. "Particularly the 'Venetianly corrupt and often lawless life.'"

Aunt Palm never replied to these charges. She might have said, I do paint them. I have painted them. But no one had ever seen the complete contents of her locked closets.

What had Louis told Dr. Allers about his quixotic aunt? Fredericka wondered. Had she imagined it or had he smiled when he spoke of "your aunt"? Would he see in her the charm, the talent, the rich layers of character that she, Fredericka, saw in this old woman, now gray and stooped, gnarled-fingered and dry-voiced?

Fredericka drove on from Sprague's Eddy to Thermopylae to invite Owen, Bridgie, and her father to Sunday lunch. She found Bridgie in the kitchen. She was making lemon pies with Florice, a pale and whiny local girl whom Bridgie, by the loan of smart magazines, was forever encouraging in discontent.

As Fredericka entered, Bridgie was just pinning her mane of brown hair on top of her head with a single comb, and although there was flour on her flushed cheeks she looked, as always, beautiful in an artless unmodern way. The big kitchen was alive with color and scent—spices, checked gingham, shiny pots. Fredericka would gladly have sat there but Bridgie, wiping her hands like a child on her flowered apron, took it off, hung it on the door, and pushed Fredericka before her into the long living room of the old Woodward house. She went straight to the fireplace, took some cones out of a

Mexican basket, threw on some small pieces of pitchy wood, and applied a match.

"I can only stay a minute," Fredericka protested. "I came to see Daddy."

"Let's be cozy even if it's only for a minute," Bridgie said, reaching for a cigarette. She dropped onto a hassock, pulled her striped dirndl up a bit so that the warmth could strike her sturdy bare legs.

Fredericka laughed. "That's so like you."

Bridgie laughed too. "Is it?" She didn't mind what Fredericka said to or about her. "How's Aunt Palm?"

"In a Cassandra mood lately."

"Cassandra?"

"You know—piercing the veil of the future."

"Oh, yes, I know. What about this time?"

Fredericka hesitated. "Us in general." And then trying to keep her voice casual, she added, "Christopher's gone to Washington to try to get into the Air Corps. Did you know?"

"No, how would I?" Bridgie looked at her in surprise.

"I thought he might have talked with Owen."

Bridgie shrugged. "Well, Owen's fairly close-mouthed."

Fredericka could not help smiling. She knew Owen told Bridgie everything.

Bridgie leaned over and threw another handful of pine cones on the fire. Pushing her plaid wool espadrilles toward the fire—"I think it's wonderful of Chris to want to go," she said, "but hard on you. With the children gone. Or will you bring them home from school?"

"What for?"

Bridgie looked astonished for the second time. "Why, for company."

Fredericka shook her head. "There's no place for them to

go to school in Wrenkill. The school's terrible now. The best thing about Uncle Caleb's long illness was that it forced us to send them off to get a decent education."

Bridgie sighed. "Well, I do admire you for being able to get along without them." She scrunched out her cigarette with a slow deliberate movement.

She doesn't mean that, Fredericka thought. She suspects me of being relieved to have them out of the house. She doesn't blame me for this, because she is so tolerant, but it disturbs her.

"I just pretend that our brood won't be permanently impaired by Thermopylae methods," Bridgie said with a little laugh.

"Their home life will save them," Fredericka assured her.

Bridgie laughed again, pleased; and then at once looked worried. "But, Flea, what will you do in that dead place with Aunt Palm getting dottier every day?"

Now that the moment had come to tell Bridgie her new plans, Fredericka hesitated. She knew that Bridgie admired her very much—she even admired her for being able to paint. But Bridgie was always a little baffled by what she thought of as "Flea's temperament." No one else in the family walked out alone for hours on a stormy day, not asking anyone to come along—except maybe Aunt Palm—mooned over strange poetry, lost track of time, disliked Christmas . . . Still, Fredericka concluded, sooner or later the family would have to know.

"Will you run the bank?" Bridgie asked in an excited voice, as though she had just had the most marvelous idea of all.

Fredericka recoiled. "Heavens, no!"

At the vehemence of her tone Bridgie looked a little taken aback. "I'd love it," she said.

"You're a heroine for a magazine serial, Bridgie," Fredericka told her. "I'm not, and never will be. No, I'm going to do something very selfish and probably useless. I'm going back to Attica Center and try to work with Farrell again on my painting."

"Why, I don't think that foolish, Flea," Bridgie said earnestly. "It will give you something to do."

There! It was out! Even from Bridgie. Painting was merely something to do, to while away the time, to occupy the dragging hours in a boring town like Wrenkill. Fredericka was astonished at her quick flash of resentment.

"And I've enrolled in a course in world history," she swept on hurriedly. "With a professor whom Dr. Cooper recommended. And—and this is the strange thing—he turns out to be a friend of Louis's and I've invited him for Sunday lunch. Next Sunday. He's coming, and I want you and Owen and Daddy to come to Wrenkill to meet him."

"If we can," Bridgie began hesitantly. "Daddy's not well, you know. . . . A friend of Louis's? You mean an American?"

"No, Austrian. I really don't know much about him. Louis sent a letter." She pulled it out of her pocket and handed it to Bridgie.

Bridgie read it through slowly. Handing it back, "It's funny Louis didn't write Daddy," she said. "Well, Aunt Palm always was his favorite . . . Of course we'd love to come. Owen will be interested particularly."

She rose. "Come along up and see Daddy," she suggested. She looked at herself in the mirror as she got up and put an indifferent hand to her careless pile of hair. "Heavens! I'm a sight," she exclaimed. Then feeling that she had been a little put out about Louis's letter and had shown it, she said with warm cordiality, "Why don't you stay for dinner, Freddy?"

"I'm afraid I can't, darling. Aunt Palm's alone. I think she may be a little broody about Chris's going, in spite of the way she seemed to take it."

"Going so soon after Uncle Caleb—I mean leaving," Bridgie corrected herself hastily. She began to rattle on to conceal the ineptitude of her suggestion that Christopher might be going to his death. "She never mentions Uncle Caleb, does she? I'm sure she's relieved he's gone, but I rather miss him. Owen is always saying he wishes he'd written down some of those clichés of his—'full of wrath and cabbage,' 'a dunghill gentleman,' 'jaybird jabber.' He'd collect them under the heading: Sayings of a Country Capitalist."

"Is Owen still collecting local lore?"

"Yes. Daddy's a big help. They're working on it now."

They walked into the front hall where another old gilt mirror occupied half of one wall space, with a marble shelf at its base on which there rested a tarnished silver dish carrying a few yellow cards.

"Your cards need dusting," Fredericka remarked.

They both laughed.

"It's a museum piece," Bridgie admitted as they started up the stairs. "I keep it here to illustrate the fashions of the past to the children."

Halfway up the stairs, they could hear Owen's voice. As they opened the door they found him sitting by his father-in-law's old mahogany bed reading aloud. The room was cheerful and cozy; every room in Bridgie's house managed to look like a colored illustration in a woman's magazine, Fredericka thought. There was a fire in the corner fireplace and above it one of Aunt Palm's paintings of the old Woodward house in the snow at night. It was done expressionistically, and it had a slanted, almost eerie, look, like a child's idea of a haunted house. Bridgie had always admitted it gave her the creeps. She insisted her father keep it in his room. He said he never saw it, so it didn't bother him. The rest of the room was serenely given over to the gentle nostalgia of the early American pictures of Messrs. Currier and Ives, with only one violent exception—the print of a burning river boat. Fredericka had sometimes pondered the fact that this old print was able to inspire more of a sense of the uncertainty and sudden tragedy of life than the most dramatic picture of a modern city burning in war.

Fredericka bent over her father's bed to kiss him. She had no chance to speak, for Owen had barely greeted her before he was asking in a loud voice: "What has happened to American names?" He lifted his eager snub-nosed face from the history of some county that lay ponderously in his lap, and went right on in his firm midwestern voice, reading aloud from the index:

"Where are the Erastus Twaddells, the Rit Apleys, and the Gilbert Walworths? Where are," he cried, tapping his finger down the list, wringing from each name its full antique and homely flavor, "the Ticknors, the Muckles, the Hazzards, the Birdsalls? Where are the Pollards and Pollocks, the Rigbys and Digbys?"

"Owen," Bridgie began, but he did not pause.

"Where are Cyrus and Serepta Salisbury," he inquired tenderly, rolling the names with loving attention on his tongue. "Where is Archimedes Sessions, born at Killawog, with parents Marcus and Celestia born at Lisle? And where," he concluded, approaching what appeared to be his climax with an expression of arch anguish, "I ask you, will you find a Saphronia Mix? Where lies Eutarpa Pickett Fairbrother? . . . "

"I believe she's buried up near Vestal," Jonathan Woodward put in quietly. "I remember taking some notes on her headstone when we were working on the graveyard inscriptions chapter."

"Mmm-huh," Owen said, not listening. "Seba Holcomb, Gideon Lownsberry, Ebenezer Crocker . . . "

He slammed shut the book. "We've lost our imaginations," he cried in his strong corn-country voice. "The American imagination is a dull business, a mass affair. You've only to read the childish names of movie stars, or any other flashy celebrities . . . Betty Grable, Clark Gable, Gene Tierney, Gene Tunney—see what I mean? Cheap, easy—no flavor, no dignity."

"Owen, please! Do let Flea at least speak to Father," Bridgie cried. "Mercy, darling!" But she spoke without rancor.

"Sorry!" Owen said, promptly putting the book aside. "It was rude of me. How are you, Freddy? No need to ask. You look great."

"You're a little thin, aren't you, dear?" her father asked in his usual tone of impersonal, faintly anxious affection.

"No, but you are." She knew that her father secretly enjoyed the role of pampered invalid (he was compensating for all the years he had attended his wife's sickbed) and she was willing at the moment to play up to it.

"Nonsense," he murmured deprecatingly. "Bridgie insists on putting me to bed every time I so much as sneeze."

"He's three pounds underweight," Bridgie stated positively.

It almost seemed as though Bridgie enjoyed having a semi-invalid to care for. You might have supposed she'd had enough of it from all the years of their mother's invalidism, Fredericka thought to herself.

Bridgie had come as a bride into a house dominated by chronic illness, but it had never daunted her seemingly inexhaustible cheerful strength. When death deprived her of her mother's care she promptly began to encourage her father in lazy ailing ways. Jonathan Woodward was happy to turn over to his son-in-law all responsibility for the Thermopylae *Clarion*, a newspaper he had inherited from a Woodward uncle who died young without issue, and become a hearthside figure. Bridgie and Owen lived on in the house of Bridgie's childhood, just as Fredericka had lived on with her aunt and uncle. There was only one difference. There had been a time when Fredericka and Christopher rebelled. For a few years they had talked of building a small house for themselves down near the birch grove. Aunt Palm had approved, but in one way or another Uncle Caleb always managed to postpone this move. Similar rebellions had never surged through Owen or Bridgie.

Bridget had met Owen Wright at a ski lodge in Vermont. He was a graduate of the Missouri School of Journalism who was taking a year of work at Columbia. Bridgie insisted that her initial interest in her future husband was aroused by hearing him talk of the importance of small-town newspapers. She knew how much her father needed an editor for the *Clarion*. Since it was unlikely Louis would ever return from the Paris *Herald* to rural New York, she invited Owen home for a family New Year's.

"Worked like a charm," Owen always admitted. "Why wouldn't it?"

Why not, indeed? Bridgie had been a luscious girl, competent and adorable. Owen had found all the Woodwards entertaining and charming. The various branches of the family scattered about the countryside were a rich source of the folk material in which he had begun even then to take great interest. Within a year of their first meeting he and Bridgie were married under the wisteria arbor of the Perry mansion, and now he ran the paper almost singlehanded while his father-in-law sank deeper and deeper into hardy perennials and a rereading of the classics.

The family were pleased that Bridgie's husband took such an interest in local history but they considered it just a little exaggerated. Sometimes Uncle Philander was unable to conceal his irritation when Owen, gesticulating with his pipe in one hand and a book in the other, would read aloud, or recite, or just blow his top.

For Owen was a great collector of homely expressions, tall tales, Indian legends, river ghost stories, and backwoods gossip grown with time to the impersonal and tragic dimensions of myth—all of which he intended eventually to present to a New York publisher.

The telephone in the upstairs hall rang and he jumped up now to answer it. "Yes, thanks," he said in his hearty voice. "Saito, the vegetable man, you mean? Well, thanks for calling but I don't believe a word of it. . . . Yes, I helped get him out. He's on a place in Connecticut. . . . No, not a word of truth in it. Sure I've seen the FBI. Well, thanks for calling anyway. . . ."

The three people in the bedroom listened openly.

"That's the fourth call in two days," Bridgie whispered to her father. He nodded.

"I noticed that Saito was gone," Fredericka said. "I was going to ask Owen about it."

"He got some threatening letters. Not Owen—Saito," Bridgie explained still whispering. "He's on a private estate now. I think it will be all right."

Owen had begun to argue some point on the telephone and as she went on idly listening Fredericka thought to herself with a certain surprise that Owen had a quality that was more like that of Aunt Palm and Uncle Philander, a quality of freshness and eccentricity, something that might crystallize with time into what was known as "character." That would never be said of Christopher, for Christopher was a type. The schools he had attended, the way he had learned to think, read, react, had made him a type. Was this, then, part of the difference between the University of Missouri and Princeton? Partly, yes, but not entirely, for Owen had had acquaintances visit him from the Middle West who were as much types as Christopher. That man from St. Joseph, Missouri, who was a Republican national committeeman and a manufacturer of turbines—he had gone to the University of Kansas, but manifestly he had found the Woodwards and Perrys astonishingly provincial, almost on the quaint side. . . .

"Owen!" Bridgie cried again, as soon as he reappeared. "Stop talking now! Freddy has some news." Then, not able to resist telling it herself, she finished in a dramatic voice, "Chris is going to war!"

"Why not let Freddy tell her own news?" Owen said, but fondly. "When?" he asked, turning to Fredericka, all attention.

When she finished telling him, Owen said, "Well, well, I think that's fine," but he looked a little worried. He'll feel now that he should volunteer too, I suppose, Fredericka thought. He wouldn't want to, for Owen was certainly not bored with life. He loved every minute of it. If he enlisted it would be from principle—from principle and nothing else.

"How does Palm feel about it?" Jonathan Woodward asked quietly, his faded eyes turned anxiously on Fredericka. He was fond of his sister, but he had never been close to her. She frightened him and he did not have with her the kind of bond that Philander had, permitting them to quarrel violently and recover rapidly from their ill will.

"She said she thought it was a good thing," Fredericka began. She caught herself up. "I mean she thought it was fine for Chris—he's in a sort of rut . . ." She did not continue with what she was saying, feeling suddenly that she might have said too much. And she was always constrained with her father, though she could not imagine why. He was gentle, interested, full of a quiet charm, yet she had never enjoyed being with him or ever felt really relaxed with him. She had sometimes wondered whether the embarrassment was mutual and whether it came from a shared unease springing from the fact that she, Fredericka, had never lived under his roof as his daughter, that he had acquiesced, apparently without a pang, in giving up his third child to his sister to raise.

Jonathan Woodward continued to look worried. "What about the bank?"

"Rusty Abbott can run it perfectly."

"I suppose so," Mr. Woodward murmured. "Still, Christopher may be gone a long time."

"Why, he may not even leave this country," Owen put in reassuringly. "There's not much risk involved in what he will do, I should guess—but a lot of boredom and that kind of hardship."

"He may end in Military Government," Fredericka said, "if he can't get in anywhere else."

"Wouldn't that be wonderful!" Bridgie cried. "I can just see Chris telling the people of Naples what to do . . ."

Suddenly the commonplace conversation took on a special tone to Fredericka. She had heard every word of it uttered sometime, some place before. This was not an unusual experience for her—she knew that it was supposed to indicate merely some slight maladjustment in brain action, that it was not conceivably a proof of the Eternal Now, or whatever you might wish to call it. Still, whenever it happened it gave her instantly a trapped sensation, as though everything were inevitable, had to be just the way it was. Thus her father had always been in bed, Owen always beside him with the frayed county history worn with time and handling, Bridgie fixed forever like the bride on the Greek vase, only with the faint smudge of flour and the careless hair; she, Fredericka, ready to depart, eternally ready to depart and never moving. . . .

It was significant that Bridgie said nothing about her sister's new plans; nothing about her enrollment at Attica Center; nothing about the new professor who had been invited to Sunday lunch. Fredericka's life was unimportant. It was set. No one expected it to change. Was it not she, herself, who was fixed like a figure on a Greek vase, much more so than any one of these other three people with their hobbies, activities, charities, civic interests? . . .

Her quick motion in getting to her feet startled them all. "Must you go?" Bridgie cried.

"I'm afraid so."

"Well, tell Chris we're very proud of him," her father said worriedly as she bent over to kiss him goodbye.

Bridgie walked downstairs, her arm linked warmly through Fredericka's.

In the side hall most frequently used by the family, in the

space nearest the door, hung Owen's cork bulletin board. It was here that he regularly posted facts and figures of an alarming, astounding, scientific, or civic nature in the hope that his children, his wife, his father-in-law, his servant, passing friends and acquaintances would read as they ran and thus keep their minds alive.

Since the country was now at war, this week's facts had to do with patriotic conservation. DO YOU KNOW appeared in big black letters accompanied by a red arrow which led the eye to the statement:

A half ounce of used fat will make enough smallpox vaccine for seventy-five injections; a single pound will process 260 quarts of life-giving blood plasma.

As Fredericka, responding to her sister's faint pressure on her arm, paused to read it, Bridgie said happily, "Owen has finally persuaded the high school to put up a bulletin board. He's provided them with a whole year of ideas."

"You all lead such useful lives," Fredericka remarked, opening the door, already ashamed of her feelings.

Bridgie looked astounded. "What do you mean?"

"Just that."

"But you do too," Bridgie hastened to say politely.

"I could hardly live a more useless one," Fredericka replied. "Goodbye, darling. See you Sunday."

"Goodness, I forgot to speak to Owen about Sunday lunch," Bridgie cried. "Shall I run up and ask him?"

"Don't bother," Fredericka said, getting into the car. "Just let me know tomorrow. Come if you can—but don't worry about it if you can't make it."

Her manner was unusually offhand and Bridgie noted it. She stood on the porch looking after her sister as she drove away, probably thinking, Fredericka's not acting herself to-day. Yes, she would go back upstairs and say to the two men, "Fredericka was really more upset about Christopher's going than she showed."

Well, that was all right. This notion, entertained by the family, Fredericka knew would provide her with more license to do as she chose, to get away oftener, to appear restless—the woman whose husband has gone to the wars. But why should she need an excuse for her conduct? What was this fear of being not misunderstood but understood, which ran through her thoughts continuously like an underground stream? She did not know the answer, or even how to look for it.

Chapter Eleven

ON SUNDAY MORNING AS SHE ARranged the greens in the sitting-room vases Fredericka found herself wondering how the house would look to an observant stranger. Would it seem cluttered and dark, more ugly than quaint? It did have a special atmosphere. She felt sure of that, but the atmosphere was not consistent. The sitting room—on the modern side—was perfectly ordinary; comfortable with chintzes and big well-made chairs. The parlor was entirely different—and it was the parlor where she wanted to see Franz Allers, among the fragments and tokens of dead people and forgotten ways of life.

Fredericka had always loved the parlor's stiff dark interior where every object had a history or a memory: the Civil War banner, the Javanese Buddha Aunt Palm cleaned seasonally with spittle on a man's linen handkerchief, the cabinets of old china, the landscapes and portraits, the hand-carved cherrywood chair made in the Perry furniture factory on the occasion of a special anniversary, with snakes for legs and swans for arms—"and who shall sit here, Leda or Eve?" Aunt Palm once asked after a Thanksgiving dinner at which she had taken three glasses of old port.

The portraits in the parlor were indifferent paintings, most of them deriving from a collateral Dutch grandmother born on the banks of the Hudson. The Van Tynes had been painted by one of the itinerant painters who traveled to the manor farms of colonial New York, coming with pose and garments painted in, with only the face to add from life. Stiff, high-colored, unimaginative, the Dutch Van Tynes looked down from the Perry wall with the same dispassion they had presumably shown in gazing on the romantic Hudson during the days when it was ablaze with brightly painted private sloops burning like great flowers on the blue water.

"Life was all stone crocks and butter tubs to them," Aunt Palm always said, dismissing the Van Tynes.

"Tulips too," Fredericka regularly reminded her.

"Only the bulbs," was Aunt Palm's opinion. "The Van Tynes were not the most cultivated Dutch—if there were any, and I suppose there must have been, judging from some of the stories. The De Windts, probably, and the Van Rensselaers. . . ."

The parlor invariably brought out family talk. For Owen's pleasure—though done with secret malice, Fredericka felt sure—Aunt Palm had put his carefully executed gold-leaf touched drawing of the Perry family tree (a Christmas present the third year after he and Bridgie were married) in the parlor cabinet with the lead flask of holy water from the river Jordan, the antique Chinese back-scratcher, the embroidered Persian hat, and the Algerian baby shoes that a remote cousin, with William H. Seward's circumnavigating party, had once brought home to prove where he had been.

Waiting in front of the bank for the noon bus from Attica Center, Fredericka, smoking nervously, could not remember at all what Franz Allers was like. Again she asked herself why she had been so insistent that he come immediately to visit them. Fiddling with the car's radio—which yielded nothing at the moment but the oily voices of clergymen selling the ancient truths in bumptious or dreary phrasing: "Remember the Lord will remember". . ."Repent ye, now"—she had again a feeling that had been mounting in her all the week, half anticipation, half qualm, as though her whole life were soon to be appraised and she held accountable for every action, even for the smallest, the most seemingly insignificant.

She looked down the empty ugly street of Wrenkill toward the corner where the bus would first appear, and it seemed to her very extraordinary that a great man from Vienna was soon to step out in front of the Citizens Bank and Trust Company and go up the hill for lunch. The last thing as exciting as this to happen to the family was Louis's visit with Hedi. . . . Yet our ancestors, Christopher's and mine, were adventurers, she thought, remembering that even the Perrys had come down along the Delaware, from Connecticut, in the period of unrest and migration following on the Revolutionary War; that it was a seafaring Perry, home on a visit, who had first pointed out to his brothers that they had a fortune on their tracts of land if they would cut and raft downriver to Trenton and Philadelphia trees for ships' masts and spars. The Perrys had moved, invariably a little ahead of their competitors, from pine into hemlock. They had, in time, their own tannery, a sawmill, a chair factory; finally, railroad stock and a bank—for three generations of mortgages and loans to fellows not quite so smart had set them up in the banking business. The Perry holdings were no longer immense by contemporary Big City standards, but since they did not measure themselves by these standards, and since the once-large clan had dwindled to Uncle Caleb's two sons, Robert and Christopher, there was plenty to ensure them all lives of comparative ease.

And so, Fredericka thought, waiting, looking down the deserted Sunday street, the restless forceful Perrys had grown static with prosperity. Their transplanted Yankee shrewdness had helped them to make money and placed them in a position of staid local eminence from which not even a genealogist could topple them.

When the bus lumbered into sight at last and Franz Allers stepped out, Fredericka was instantly relieved. He was younger and more distinguished-looking than she had remembered him, grave and dark; foreign-appearing too, in the topcoat with the round collar and the curious wooden buttons. His smile was unexpectedly warm.

"How nice of you to meet me."

They shook hands. She was glad he did not try to kiss hers. It was a gesture that made her feel awkward. Occasionally, of late years, visiting her brother-in-law, Robert and his wife Helen, in White Plains, she met foreigners. Their suave manners put her off.

"So here I am in Wrenkill," he said, looking about as she turned the car in front of the bank. "Citizens Bank and Trust Company," he read.

"The family bank," she said.

"Are you the leading family?"

"The Perrys? Indisputably. But I'm not a Perry, remember —except by marriage. I married a cousin . . ."

"Ah?" Up shot his brows in interest. "So?"

"It's rather confusing," Fredericka admitted. "As a matter of fact, I grew up in the home of my aunt and uncle from the time I was very young."

"So?" he said again. "And how did that happen?"

He sounded at once interested and entirely impersonal. She had the idea that you could tell this man anything without startling or shocking him. As to boring him—that might be another matter.

"It was all Louis's fault," she began.

"Ah, Louis!" He smiled. He shook his head as though at some amusing memory. It was plain he loved Louis. And understood him too, she was sure. "How did it happen?" he repeated.

Feeling completely at ease with him, although she had not expected to, Fredericka told him how she had come along ten months after her sister, Bridgie, when Louis was already six years old. There had been two children who had died in between. At Fredericka's arrival her frail mother felt unable to handle the baby Bridget, and the obstreperous little boy Louis, plus a newborn infant. So Aunt Palm had taken Fredericka off her mother's hands temporarily, saying that she had always wanted a girl. Her mother's invalidism had allowed Fredericka to stay on indefinitely. She had been like a daughter of the house and had made it definitely so by marrying her cousin Christopher.

Franz Allers listened attentively to all she said, as though the story were of particular interest, which of course it could not possibly be.

"So your mother-in-law has really been your mother."

"Yes." She nodded. "And we are unusually close to each other. It is a great bond."

"And you are alike?" He made a question of it.

"I'm not sure." Fredericka paused before adding, "Perhaps after today you will be able to tell me."

"Perhaps . . . Are you like Louis?"

She smiled at that, shaking her head.

"Oh, no, Louis is quite wild. We always called him Louis the Wild, you know. I think he inherited the blood of a mythical riverman who is supposed to have sired the d'Abbevilles from whom we Woodwards descend. Louis is the only adventurer we have now."

"You find him adventurous?"

"Yes, don't you? Of course I realize you probably know Louis better than I do."

He hesitated. "Everyone knows Louis, and no one knows him. I must admit he sometimes mystified me—or his motives for doing the things he did mystified me. But of course all Americans are mystifying to Europeans," he added at once. "And that's certainly too long a subject for a spring morning."

"What has Louis really been doing lately?" Fredericka asked, when she saw he did not intend to pursue the subject of Americans and Europeans. "No one in the family can quite figure it out."

She had deliberately taken the longer of the two ways home because she had it in her mind to pump Franz Allers about Louis. But she saw at once that he was not going to tell her anything.

"I told you Louis was mystifying," he said lightly. His smile was perfectly friendly and open, yet it seemed to guard something he was not willing to reveal. "Tell me more about this mythical riverman," he suggested, leading the talk away.

For a moment she did not follow Franz Allers; her thoughts were on Louis. She was seeing him as she often saw him in her imagination, sipping a small drink or a large glass of tea at a sidewalk café, with the daily papers spread about him. That was the "summer" Louis. The "winter" Louis was the same except that the setting was an interior—a paneled restaurant, more German than French. There was nothing particularly exciting about the atmosphere that surrounded this imaginary Louis, yet it was special, unlike anything American —more serene in rhythm, an easier pace, but without the stagnation, the death of a quiet spot like Wrenkill. . . . Louis moved about freely; he moved about fast, yet in Fredericka's mind she always saw him sitting at a little table with the daily papers and a drink. So, she supposed, men in Europe plan revolutions, shake the world . . . For somewhere, somehow she had come upon the idea that Louis was a secret fomenter of disturbance . . .

"Mythical riverman," she repeated now, in a vague voice, and then with more force: "Oh—of course—Philander Decatur Gleason. That was his name. Aunt Palm should really tell you about him. She makes him a sort of cross between Young Lochinvar and Mike Fink."

Driving slowly on the frost-torn road that circled the base of the Perrys' hill—prolonging their time together as much as possible—she told him some things about the d'Abbevilles, Henriette and Philippe, who had come north to the Delaware from New Orleans in the middle of the nineteenth century, fresh from France with a band of their own laborers and a plan for creating a great manorial estate. They, like the Perrys, had rafted on the river. When Philippe d'Abbeville died of the effects of falling in the water on an icy day in January, his wife Henriette carried on the business with the help of Philander Decatur Gleason, the most famous riverman of his day. With supreme contempt for public opinion—or as a subtle proof of innocence—she had named her second son (conceived while her husband was alive but invalided) for the riverman. This doubtful d'Abbeville, Philander Decatur Gleason d'Abbeville, was destined to carry on the family name in the New World, for the first-born of Henriette and Philippe died of a fever during adolescence.

"But he didn't carry the name far," Fredericka concluded. "He married a hearty-looking Dutch girl who only brought him one daughter. This daughter married one of the Woodwards, who were all quiet-spoken and easygoing, and this union produced my fabulous Aunt Palm, my equally fabulous Uncle Philander, and my quite ordinary father, Jonathan. In my opinion there is no way to account for Uncle Philander, Aunt Palm, and Brother Louis without accepting the blood of Philander Decatur Gleason."

"Maybe Henriette would account for it. She sounds quite a woman."

Fredericka smiled. "Perhaps."

"Is this a typical American story?" he wanted to know seriously.

"Typical? I really don't know."

They were winding up the drive to the house by this time and Franz Allers had begun to gaze about him with frank curiosity. Fredericka was glad he didn't pretend not to be looking.

"Everyone is so happy you could come," she said as she stopped the car at the door.

He gave her a grateful glance and thanked her formally.

She wondered why she had made such a point of his welcome just then; decided, getting out of the car, that she had had a sudden realization of the man's loneliness, a loneliness that the sight of this old house and these lovingly tended grounds might heighten.

All the family except Aunt Palm were in the sitting room. After Fredericka made the introductions Bridgie announced, "Aunt Palm's in the parlor. I'm afraid Owen has annoyed her. He insisted on correcting her again about the Big Pumpkin

Flood and about Philander Decatur's famous ride at Narrowsburg."

"Are there other stories about this—this hero?" Franz Allers asked. He appeared politely eager to hear more.

Fredericka glanced apprehensively at Owen. With the least encouragement he was quite prepared to take over and tell yarns all afternoon. Looking happy he removed his pipe and began to tell the story of Philander and the flood. Oh, how boring! thought Fredericka. They're going to begin by boring the visitor to death with silly stories. I've already told him enough about ancestors! . . . But there was no stopping Owen, and actually Franz Allers didn't look in the least bored as Owen told how Philander Decatur, anxious to get home, decided to swim the river near Narrowsburg though it was in full flood. No boatman would take him across. Everyone pleaded with him to restrain himself, but since his mind was made up he plunged his horse down the steep bank into the foaming current, crying, "What is to be will be! No man born to the gallows will ever drown!"

Fredericka never heard this tale without a thrill of excitement, a coldness down the spine and a light feeling in the head.

"When the torrent washed him from the horse's back," Bridgie cried, taking over excitedly, "he shouted, 'Gallows, claim your own!' He seized the horse by the tail and the horse carried Philander safely across."

No one could tell the story like Aunt Palm! . . . Fredericka could see her now, stooping among the drift of last year's leaves, searching for the early ginger flowers, exclaiming, "Here's one!" (for she always saw them first) and lifting to the light the pale-brown bloom with its spired petals and secret ornate heart. And then finishing the story of Philander and the flood: "When he reached the bank he turned and made the people on the opposite shore a deep bow and rode off, dripping wet."

"And so," Franz Allers asked Owen, apparently having enjoyed every word of it, "how does your version differ from your aunt's?"

"In one major respect." Owen returned his pipe to his lips and spoke around it in an annoying clenched-teeth manner. "I insist that this tale, apocryphal or otherwise, is a story about another man altogether."

"To which Aunt Palm replies," said Bridgie, "that she *knows* it was Philander Decatur Gleason because there is so much of him in Uncle Philander, and she brings out a snapshot of Uncle Philander riding a bucking broncho in Montana—and that seems to her to prove it."

"But what does it really matter?" Fredericka inquired with a mild irritation that she could not quite conceal.

"Even the minor facts of history are important," Owen replied sententiously.

"Well, for all this fuss you have to have sherry in the parlor," Fredericka stated firmly.

"Oh, dear, those dreadful chairs!" Bridgie complained.

"I know, but come along." Bridgie looked at her sister in amazement. Fredericka was seldom bossy. But Fredericka did not care. She was impatient to see the stranger with his head against the sad and spurious romanticism of the old landscapes. She felt that only in the parlor would she see him in all his essential difference, and know, at the same time, whether they could ever truly understand one another. "Coming, Uncle Philander?" she called.

Uncle Philander, in unpressed tweeds, his short bristle of

gray-red beard newly washed, his shock of strong iron-gray hair badly in need of a cut, had taken no part in the conversation about his progenitor. After greeting the visitor with his usual cordiality he had taken up his position in the window at the end of the room. He had brought his binoculars and he had them trained on the catbird's nest Aunt Palm had discovered in the cedar bush immediately under the window.

"Foolish, foolish creature," he was murmuring. "So low to the ground." Taking the binoculars from his eyes, "Thank you, my dear," he replied to Fredericka's invitation with dignity. "I'll stay here, if no one minds. There is more sun here."

"I.W.," whispered Bridgie, brushing past Fredericka. I.W. stood for Irish whisky—Uncle Philander's one conspicuous weakness. As soon as they left the sitting room for the parlor they knew he would hurry into the pantry and browbeat Eunice into giving him the bottle. Better not press him to join them, Fredericka decided quickly. The whisky would put him in a good humor. He had been rather silent so far and extremely distant to Aunt Palm. He was obviously determined not to relent too soon about the goat horns.

When Owen, Bridgie, Fredericka, and Dr. Allers entered the parlor, they found Aunt Palm in her stiff wine-colored faille, seated picking the dead leaves off the miscellany of plants in the old brassbound wine cooler that served as their container. She extended her wrinkled bony hand to the stranger and bent on him her dark intent gaze. There was something very impressive about her, Fredericka thought admiringly, and it was something more than dignity and a fine-boned face.

"This is the room where we keep our ghosts," Aunt Palm said to Franz Allers. She made a little gesture that included the Van Tynes, the Catskills in oil, the horsehair chairs, the cabinet of wedding china once the property of long-dead brides.

What a commanding first line! Fredericka was delighted. The shrewd old scene-stealer! She looked at her aunt with love.

"Ghosts!" Dr. Allers also appeared delighted. He looked about him with a quick bright glance. "Are there really ghosts in America?"

"Oh, my, yes," Aunt Palm said quickly. She moved away from the plants and seated herself on one end of a horsehair sofa near a table on which a collection of antique green glass paperweights caught the faint sun in their undersea depths. She lifted one and gazed into it as though it were a crystal. Was it an act? Was it unconscious? Fredericka could not say. "There are more ghosts here than anywhere else in the world," she concluded.

Everyone's eye was on her, astonished, waiting. Aunt Palm knew it. She did not return their glances but she put back the paperweight and with her left hand she brushed away imaginary dust. As she did so the opals in her ring glowed ominously. Opals are unlucky unless they are your birthstone, Fredericka caught herself thinking. And they were not Aunt Palm's. . . . "But nonsense," Uncle Philander had said once, in contradiction, "they are only considered unlucky because they are living stones which can sicken and die," and he had told the story of the man who put a bag of African opals in a San Francisco vault and opened it years later to find only a heap of opalescent powder.

"Do explain what you mean—about the ghosts." Dr. Allers went to sit beside Aunt Palm on the sofa.

"America," said Aunt Palm at once, continuing to surprise

Fredericka by appearing to want to talk, "hasn't buried its past yet, and so its dead are still earthbound. But they act like living people, and that is what causes all the trouble."

"All the trouble?" Dr. Allers pressed her. His voice had just the right amount of amused interest, just a faint underlining of compulsion.

But Bridgie intervened hastily. "Aunt Palm will tease you if you allow her to." There was a perceptible uneasiness under the sweetness of her voice. Experience had taught her never to count on Aunt Palm for strictly conventional behavior.

"I think I'd enjoy that." After a moment's silence, "As a haunted man," he began, and Fredericka, looking at him, caught Aunt Palm's quick eye also on him, "as a haunted man I cannot tell you how fresh and free from ghosts I find America. At least so far."

"Perhaps you have not seen America," Owen put in, getting out his pipe anticipating a discussion with some juice in it.

"That is possible. But still, don't you consider yourself here typically American? Is this not American?" His sherry glass, in a half circle, indicated the parlor.

"It's a memory of America," Fredericka said. "It's a stage-set for a comedy-drama laid in the past."

"So?" Up shot his brows. "Where would you really say America is to be found then?"

"California," said Fredericka and Bridgie together.

They all laughed.

"Tell me why," Dr. Allers turned politely to Bridgie.

"I don't think I can explain," she began, looking appealingly at Owen, who would not come to her aid because he did not agree with her as to where the center of America could be found. "But it's the kind of life lived out there—at least I think it's what most people think of as American—all the vitamins and the sunbathing, the open collars and no hats and the swimming pools and the drugstore soda fountains and the movie stars . . ."

"And the health groups and the religious cults," added Fredericka.

"Aimee Semple McPherson, Gerald Heard, and Shri Ya-Ya Pa-Pa Gadzooka," put in Owen, giving it a wry twist.

"Ah, hah! So that's it." Dr. Allers nodded gravely. "Perhaps you are saying that California is now living its own peculiar aspect of the American myth . . ."

"The *new* American myth," Owen corrected him.

"The new American myth," Dr. Allers repeated. "While the rest of America . . ."

"Is remembering its myths," finished Fredericka quickly. "Not living them, not creating them, but compiling them from records: The Flowering of New England; The Decline of the Old South; what happened on the Wabash, the Hudson, the Snake . . ." She saw Owen waiting to interrupt, but she swept on. This was something, she realized with surprise, that she had wanted to say for a long time. "We've had a deluge of remembrances of America these last years. It seems to me a sign of death. Maybe that's what Aunt Palm means about the earthbound ghosts."

Whether Aunt Palm had meant that or not, Owen gave her no chance to say. "I don't agree with you at all, Freddy," he put in a little stiffly, feeling that his own hobbies were being subtly attacked, "about signs of death, I mean. I feel rather that we are evaluating ourselves in this way, as a people, before the next step in our growth . . ."

Fredericka had to wait impatiently for a break in Owen's monologue in order to change the subject. The break was bound to come in time, she knew, because, sooner or later,

Owen would have to stop to light his pipe. He could almost puff and talk at the same time—but not quite.

When the inevitable break occurred she stepped in at once. "These paintings might interest you, Dr. Allers." She rose and crossed the room. "They're authentic Americana," she offered as bait. Dr. Allers came over and stood under the three landscapes.

These old parlor pictures had cast a spell upon Fredericka's imagination as a child, with their ruins in ghostly moonlight, their crumbling pillars seen through rising mists. The painters of the early Catskills could hardly have found them anything but fresh and glowing—still so close to Indian silence as they were—but on their untouched youth they could cast, none-theless, the current romantic shadow, a European shadow, with forms vaguely resembling the Coliseum, the Parthenon, Fountains Abbey. We too have suffered, hinted the paintings. We Americans also know death, decay, the glory that was Greece, the grandeur that was Rome. All, all passes! . . . It was like a high school presentation of *Macbeth*. You didn't believe a word of it, Fredericka thought.

"*Künstliche Ruinen*," Franz Allers murmured, amused. "So you had them too?"

"Had what?" Aunt Palm demanded from the sofa.

"Synthetic ruins. I'm surprised to find them in America."

"An elderly cousin of mine in Elmira," Aunt Palm said, "had some artificial ruined Doric pillars in her rose garden, made by a local headstone carver, after a photograph she found in an old book. People used to make long trips by surrey just to see them. She finally opened her garden every Thursday afternoon to visitors."

"Wasn't she the old girl with the Shakespeare corner garden?" Owen put in, sucking hard on the long stem of his pipe. "You know—'There's rosemary, that's for remembrance . . . and there is pansies, that's for thoughts.'"

"I have been told that she had the first one in America." Aunt Palm spoke almost with pride. "I'm not sure. There's one in Central Park, I know."

"A Shakespeare garden," said Bridgie, explaining patiently to Dr. Allers, "is a corner given over to plants that should instantly bring to mind lines of Shakespeare, if you have a literary memory."

"How perfectly extraordinary!" said Dr. Allers. "For instance, what?"

"Well, I'm not a literary scholar," Owen said. "I've done my quoting . . ."

"Violets," said Aunt Palm quickly, speaking it straight out and not like poetry, "Violets dim, but sweeter than the lids of Juno's eyes or Cytherea's breath. . . . Daffodils that take the winds of March with beauty. . . . Marigolds shall, as a carpet, hang upon thy grave, while summer-days doth last."

"Bravo, Aunt Palm," Owen cried. He was full of admiration. So was Franz Allers. He nodded with pleasure and approval.

Aunt Palm's color had risen becomingly. She was more animated than Fredericka had seen her for a long time. She likes this man, Fredericka thought, and she in turn interests him. Watching them side by side across the room—for he had gone back to the sofa—Fredericka tried to see him as he really was.

He carries about with him, she decided, his own atmosphere. It is special, indescribable, but nonetheless real. It does not come from his accent or the way he wears his clothes (with just a little too much preciseness for an American) but from something you feel that his eyes have seen, his body experienced, his brain remembered—something at once ancient and secure and at the same time very new and violent. He brings with him into any room, any gathering, all of Europe, the sum total, the Europe of the last five hundred years and the Europe of the last twenty. He carries with him memories more old and traditional than anything in all of America and at the same time visions more new and strange in the history of the world than anything America has ever known, even in the days of revolution, in the days of civil war. He has seen a thing of corruption and beauty, with its roots deep in the myths of poetry and time, uprooted and destroyed. He has felt on his very bones and flesh the cold-hot breath of destruction blowing from two mouths—the one that destroys for destruction's sake and the one that destroys to make room for life. Yet, unlike as they are, each in its blowing carries away all the familiar and the secure; the lamppost's shadow on the snow falls like a gallows, the postbox hints death, dust gathers on the pipe racks and the books; the yellow rose on the garden wall, from which the lice were pinched each spring, blooms now untouched, unseen. Those who opened the letters, filled the pipe, reached for the book, sprayed the roses are gone, and no one can say where or why.

Eunice thrust her expressionless tallowy face through the red portieres. In twenty-five years they had never been able to teach her to announce a meal properly. "Lunch!" she flung at them, scorning them all for their soft pampered lives, sherry in the parlor, Irish whisky in the pantry, and not a one of them out to church! Not a one of them!

Chapter Twelve

THE PERRYS HAD NEVER CHANGED the ritual of heavy Sunday mid-day dinner. Even Uncle Caleb's passing had not altered it, although while he was alive they had regularly complained about it and Christopher insisted it interfered with Sunday golf or fishing. The tableware was a part of the ritual. There were the elaborate cut-glass goblets for water and the cut-glass dishes—green pickles on the left, red jelly on the right—flanking the hothouse tulips in the incongruous modern bowl. Even the food was ritualized: the soup, the roast, the vegetables, the hot biscuits, the rich dessert, followed by the inescapable postdinner stupor. But somehow, today, Fredericka was glad of the way it was. She thought Franz Allers might derive pleasure from this air of substantial tradition.

Uncle Philander was waiting for them in the dining room. He had had his whisky. His eyes were shining with good will and appetite.

"Bless me!" he remarked, seating himself in his old place on Palm's left. "What an appetite I still get in spite of the lazy life I lead." He patted his sister's arm encouragingly.

Aunt Palm cast him a glance, half amused, half barbed, but she made no comment. This forbearance said to Fredericka, as clearly as words, how pleased she was to have Philander again at the family board. Uncle Philander, now that he had heated his stomach and his fancy with the old Irish, was ready to be his most expansive and charming self. Fredericka saw him preparing to enchant Dr. Allers, to establish himself as a unique personality not soon to be forgotten. Uncle Philander enjoyed meeting strangers. He often said that they were far too rare in his life and that is why he missed the Far West where "Howdy, stranger" was a part of the native tongue.

"Since you enjoy American yarns you must get Uncle Philander to tell you some of his," Fredericka suggested, dipping her soup spoon in Viney's reserved-for-Sunday-lunch clam bisque. "He and Louis have the adventures in our family."

"Adventures?" repeated Dr. Allers. (It is a form we are laying on our talk, Fredericka thought fleetingly. I say a word: "California," "haunted," "adventures," on the dead level; he picks it up, elevates it along with his eyebrows, puts a question mark after it: "California?" "Haunted?" "Adventures?". . .)

"Yes, for one thing Uncle Philander is a great hunter." She said it deliberately because she knew it was a sure way to get Uncle Philander started and she wanted to prevent Owen from monopolizing the conversation all during lunch, which, as a light eater, he was always prepared to do.

At her words Aunt Palm shot Fredericka a warning look. It said as plainly as it could: Careful! You are on dangerous ground. Fredericka could not imagine what she meant.

Uncle Philander began with his customary appearance of deprecation and modesty. "My niece exaggerates," he said, pleased and mild. "I hunt, but I am not a great hunter—not, at least, in the African safari sense, which is perhaps the proper association with a great hunter. Nor am I like an American hunter in the last century, like the mountainmen who did the trapping for the fur companies.

"No," said Uncle Philander, lifting his soup cup and drinking the contents in one easy gulp, "I am really not a great hunter. I have never collected trophies just to hang on my wall and boast about. There is something obscene to me about stuffing a fish—sailfish or brook trout, it is all the same—unless you stuff it for scientific reasons."

"What about all those moth-eaten birds of yours?" Aunt Palm asked tartly, her bony fingers linked above her untouched soup cup.

"Scientific specimens," said Uncle Philander with dignity, briefly massaging his beard with his napkin. "Take the whisky-jack, the venison bird of the Adirondacks—I admit he's fading and his feathers are falling out. But where can I get another? They don't appear any more, the old guides tell me. They used to materialize right out of the air," he explained, turning to the visitor. "When you were cutting up a deer's carcass in the deep woods, there they'd be, blue shadows, darting and murmuring—never saw them at any other times—not to be seen any more."

He made it sound like the mysterious disappearance of the pterodactyl, and, for the moment safe from interruption, he allowed the mystery of the whisky-jack to claim them all, as he spooned the fragments of clam out of his cup.

"I've never been able to endure the sight of a moose looking down upon me from a wall," he went on, enjoying to the full his easy monopoly of the table talk. "Its comment—the moose's—is much too acid. Particularly when seen on the walls of lodges: The Royal Order of the Double-Chested Canadian Moose, The Exalted Brotherhood of the Triple-Antlered Elk. For you know, Dr. Waller . . ."

"Allers," put in Bridgie hastily, in a low voice.

"Dr. Allers," he corrected himself loudly. "We have a great many unrobust organizations in this country bearing stout and hearty Wild West names whose membership is made up entirely of clerks in banks, bookkeepers, and haber-dashers who couldn't handle a flyswatter with assurance."

"Ah, yes," Dr. Allers said eagerly, breaking bread in his long right hand and popping it into his mouth with little quick gestures. "I have been interested for a long time in the role of the animal in the American unconscious. But go on. Do go on. Don't let me interrupt."

"The moose on the wall of the club above the pool table," continued Uncle Philander, taking his favorite second joint and a large helping of dressing, "says with a sad-eyed, long-nosed look of accusation: I have been betrayed! Who is guilty?" Holding the serving fork and spoon poised while he imitated the expression of the moose: "What have you done with the land you drove me from?" he inquired of them all.

"But mind you," he added quickly, before anyone could answer, accepting a biscuit, opening it at once, putting a spoonful of red jelly in its hot heart and closing it over to wait on his butter plate, "Mind you, the elk above the bar, the deer's head on the wall mirror in the hall with his feet mounted near by to hang a hat on, this is not a taste exclu-sively confined to Animal Clubs or to the bars of the Far West—as you, a European, might imagine, Doctor. No, it is in accepted usage in some of the finest Adirondack private lodges, even in private homes."

And now Aunt Palm's face set visibly. She was preparing for her brother's next remarks and suddenly Fredericka knew of what she had been guilty by introducing, in the beginning, the subject of hunting.

"There has been in all my life only one animal trophy that I was extremely anxious to have—other, that is, than the dinosaur tracks I picked up in New Mexico, or chiseled out of the solid stone, I should say, to be exact. This trophy of which I speak I wanted for purely scientific reasons for my museum."

He put extra weight on the word "museum." The dusty cabinets full of miscellaneous objects in the house at Sprague's Eddy assumed the scope and dimension of the Smithsonian.

"This trophy was the horns of two mountain goats locked in mortal combat . . . They went instead to a Westchester ping-pong room."

Scorn literally dripped from the two words "ping" and "pong," making them suddenly fresh to the ear and utterly absurd. Uncle Philander's color had risen slightly and he set his knife in the chicken with a sharp stab.

"These horns were found in a lake in Maine in very dry weather when the water was unusually low. My late brother-in-law had them in his possession at the time of his death, but he did not see fit to leave them to me. As I say, I wanted them for my museum—which I hope, my dear sir, you will sometime honor with a visit."

"I should be most happy."

Fredericka could see that, just as she had expected, Uncle Philander was fascinating Dr. Franz Allers.

Aunt Palm, using the thin flat voice she reserved for mild baiting of her male relatives now put in, "If you feel so superior about lodges what made you become a blood brother of the Sioux?"

"I did it as a favor," Uncle Philander replied, turning toward her with a look of wounded dignity. "They didn't ask anything special of me.

"I was invited," he explained to Dr. Allers, "to join this Indian tribe because I was a Harvard man. At least that's what I was told. I was the first Harvard man in that part of Montana."

"Where was it?" Owen asked, finally giving up hope of taking over the conversation, and conspiring with Fredericka to lead on Uncle Philander. "I've forgotten."

"Near Rosebud," replied Uncle Philander with an air of detachment from the subject. "Rosebud, Montana."

"Wasn't that the place where you saw the cave full of Indian mummies?"

Both Fredericka and Bridgie had to laugh seeing Dr. Allers' face at that one.

"Oh, but please!" he cried, delighted.

"No, no, it is too long a story for dinner, and my sister has heard it many times before and is already looking bored." Uncle Philander's tone was deceptively adamant.

"But please!" Dr. Allers repeated. He appealed to Aunt Palm. "Would you mind so much?"

She made no sign.

"Well, I can't tell it in detail," Uncle Philander insisted, yielding graciously. "Briefly I'll simply say that I heard about this cave full of dead Indians and I tried for six months to get an Indian to show it to me. No one would even talk about it. Scared! Bad medicine! Finally I got a sixteen-year-old boy to guide me there for ten dollars in cash—two five-dollar gold pieces. We rode ten miles, left our ponies, crawled like flies along the side of a mesa, and finally came to this cave. In it were about twenty Indians, upright like mummies in their bones, with their spears and trappings around them. How they died or why, no one would say. Someone told me it was a vow they took to go there and sit without food until the gods sent them game, and while they were sitting there the Blackfeet came in and massacred their whole tribe. They didn't get any message of success on their hunger strike, there being no one left to let them know what had happened, and since they were all too proud to be the first to quit they just sat there and died."

"Extraordinary!" said Dr. Allers.

> "Loosely on a snake-skin strung
> In the smoke his scalp-locks swung
> Grimly to and fro,"

recited Aunt Palm without looking up at anyone.

"*The Bridal of Pennacook* by John Greenleaf Whittier," said Uncle Philander, identifying it. "A man who may have known something about Indians but very little about poetry."

If Aunt Palm's quotation had been meant to stay Philander's recital it was not successful.

"One reason no one wanted to visit that cave was because it was guarded by rattlesnakes," he continued imperturbably. "I jumped down off the face of the cliff right into the biggest nest of 'em I've ever seen. Must have been two hundred. Fortunately they were just coming out of their winter hibernation. They sleep all rolled up in a big ball, you know, Doctor—and they were still too drugged to be vicious. But I got out of there fast, I can tell you!

"Strange thing about rattlesnakes," he mused, mixing his own salad dressing from the ingredients on a small special tray placed beside him by Eunice with a look of cold displeasure. "A rattlesnake, Doctor, if you throw him into a cholla bush will sting himself to death. Cholla is a kind of spiny cactus— the kind a rabbit can run right through without catching a hair."

"Born and bred in a briar patch, Br'er Fox, born and bred in a briar patch." It was Bridgie reciting now, in a dreamy voice. Then recollecting the stranger, "That's Uncle Remus," she explained. "American folk tales. You probably don't know them."

"I'm afraid I don't," Dr. Allers admitted. He seemed to be well out of his depth and willing to let the current carry him.

"We should read some of them aloud," Bridgie suggested. "I'm sure you'd love them."

"Is it *Burr* Rabbit?" asked Dr. Allers, tucking his brow up under his hairline again.

"No, Br'er—Negro for Brother," said Owen. "Another of those American folk animals of which you spoke. . . ."

"Ah, yes, Mickey the Mouse, Mr. Coyote . . ." He nodded happily.

Dinner was over. The family had scattered, Uncle Philander and Aunt Palm to take naps, Owen and Bridgie to return to Thermopylae. Franz Allers had refused to be driven home and it was decided that he would catch the seven-o'clock bus. Fredericka took him into the garden and they walked in the damp sweet air of the fading afternoon past the imitation antique Italian sundial, the old stone urns that held petunias every year, the lily pond that would soon have its fish again —the ones that were kept indoors all winter by Emmet Burns, the farmer.

As they strolled, "Are you exhausted?" she asked him.

"With what?"

"The family."

"They are amazing," he said. (*They*, why not *you?*) "Do they tire you?" he asked her.

"I'm used to them."

"But where do you live?" he demanded, stopping to look at the faint green feathery spray beginning to appear along the noduled brown twigs of the larch.

She repeated, "Where do I live?" She did not understand him. "Here, of course."

"No, I mean, where do you *live?*" And when he saw that she was unwilling to understand his meaning, still holding the larch bough with his hand, he nodded back toward the house they had left. "The house—it is hardly you, is it?"

"I have a room—a retreat," she said. "Upstairs. Would you like to see it?"

"Very much."

She turned and led him back into the hall, up the stairs, past the bright cushions of the window seat from which for so many springs she had watched the swallows fighting the wrens for the birdhouse. She opened the door to her little sitting room. He stepped inside and soberly considered it, detail by detail. And watching him, silent, observant, Fredericka also looked at the room, trying to see it as though for the first time.

Gray-white walls, crimson carpet, gray-blue draperies and couch, touches of Chinese yellow—all high, bright, light, gay, vigorous—obvious? Perhaps so. Not a very subtle choice of colors, she feared now.

"Extremely pleasant," he said. "Did you paint those?"

They were the portraits of Leslie and Forrest, the two blond heads, the sober eyes. Eight and six they had been when she did them.

"Yes. They are my children."

"Very arresting. And did you also paint that?"

It was the road leading down from Hungry Hollow—the

end of a barn, the forms of cows, the roily twisting turbulence of full spring.

"No," she said. "That was Aunt Palm."

"Ah!" His interest sharpened. "She has great talent too," he said.

Fredericka caught the word "too" to herself with a quick pang of happiness. He must mean it! It could not simply be mid-European politeness. Still you never knew.

"A little on the van Gogh side," he said. "Has she painted a great deal?"

"There is an attic—closets—full of her canvases." His remark about van Gogh gave her the courage to put to him the great question.

"Tell me," she said, unconsciously lowering her voice, sitting down, indicating that he too should sit. "Tell me honestly, how did you feel about my aunt?"

His brows moved up. "Feel?" He spoke in a puzzled tone.

"I mean, did you get any sense of her being—of her being not quite sane?"

He seemed genuinely surprised.

"Not at all. I found her most stimulating. Of course," he added more slowly, "she withdraws. You feel that. Perhaps she lives somewhat apart. But that might be very sane, not insane—no? But why do you ask me?"

"Because," Fredericka said, her voice dry with repressed emotion, "I know you have been a great doctor—and—and because I presume on your friendship with Louis to beg you to be quite honest. . . . The truth is that lately we—the family, that is, particularly since my uncle's long illness—we feel that Aunt Palm has been acting strange—unlike herself."

"Can you be clearer?"

"I'll try. I hesitate because I honestly don't believe it—not most of the time anyway. But it's as though she—she is only half here. As though she is—escaping—and yet when I use that word I don't know at all what I mean or what she would be escaping from."

He was listening attentively, his hands loosely clasped, his head a little bent forward. There was reassurance in his very posture, Fredericka felt. A warm wave of relief began to flow through her. She realized how much she had been worrying about her aunt.

"What was her life with your uncle like?" Franz Allers asked. "I mean, what was their relationship? Was he brutal to her?"

The word startled Fredericka. "Brutal? Uncle Caleb a brute? . . . Oh, I wouldn't say so. Not really. He was difficult at times, but certainly not brutal."

At her vehemence Franz Allers smiled faintly. "You mean —no beatings?"

"Oh, of course—nothing like that—but, well, perhaps he was brutal in an intangible way," she continued, beginning to amend her first strong denial. "For he was a tyrant, Uncle Caleb. He had insomnia and there's a family legend that when he couldn't sleep he would put his toes against Aunt Palm and wriggle them steadily to keep her awake. All night sometimes. I remember she was always very sensitive to touch, to pressures of any kind—maybe because of this . . . But she has been so good always—so wise, and gay, and original . . ."

Fredericka turned away, reached for the cigarettes as she felt the tears burning under her lids.

"You are very fond of your aunt," Franz Allers said, striking a match for her.

She nodded, wordless. After a moment: "She gave me such

a happy childhood. It was never dull, not for a moment . . ." She could not go on to explain about it. "She was so alive," she said. "She gave me my eyes and my ears."

And what have you done with them? Had he asked her that, or had she only imagined that he had? She looked at him quickly. It was plain that he had not spoken.

"I get the feeling that your aunt is a very remarkable woman," he said in his slow precise English, with its faint trace of accent. "She should have been—what is it you say?— a career woman. Yes, that is what I see in her—a career woman, without a career. She should have painted all the time, lived alone in a big room with a skylight, made herself one meal a day out of tin cans, walked alone in the fields and wept over sunsets . . ."

He had risen and stood looking, as he spoke, at Aunt Palm's scene of early spring.

"No," he said now, reflectively, "perhaps she should even have lived in a city, bought her plants from pushcarts, seen sunsets only two weeks out of a year, had no children of her own so that she could have really longed for them and maybe then painted them yearningly like . . ."

"Like Mary Cassatt?" Fredericka asked as he hesitated.

"Yes. If that is the one of whom I am thinking."

Fredericka was troubled. "You seem to be arguing for a life of frustration."

He lifted his shoulders slightly again, the characteristic gesture. "There is always frustration. It is only a choice of frustrations."

He did not speak cynically, but the words blew on her coldly. She did not like them. "Then you don't really think that my aunt is going mad?"

He raised his shoulders again, lowered them, lifted his brow, held it suspended, not superciliously but with the genuine air of one who seeks to weigh the imponderables—as though asking: Madness, sanity, good, evil, love, hate, who can say what they are, who can measure the opposites and name them correctly?

"When did you say you first got this feeling about her?"

When it was clear that Uncle Caleb was not long for this life Aunt Palm did what seemed to all of them a very shocking thing. She took a sketch pad and some crayons and went to sit by his bed to draw him as he lay dying.

The old man lay with his eyes closed, or, in turn, opened but glazed and sightless. He breathed in ugly gasps of sound, through the strong teeth that had sought the marrow in the heart of the toughest chicken bones and torn the succulent yellow kernels from the ears of Golden Bantam corn. He clutched at the sheet in paroxysms of pain and he did not once recognize the figure of the woman who sat beside him in the low chair, watching him die and recording his death with a gaze intent and cool, and a steady hand with the crayons.

The nurses were horrified. Fredericka saw that. Christopher tried to remonstrate, but the look his mother gave him— remote, scornful, silent—thrust his words back into his throat and he turned away outside his father's door and went on downstairs to Fredericka waiting in the sitting room.

"I wish you'd ask her why she's doing that?" he cried, angry and troubled. "I can't make her out. Not that I ever could."

"I can't ask her," Fredericka said, and she knew that she could not. It was the first time she admitted to herself that she was no longer able to ask Aunt Palm freely any question that rose in her mind. Why was this? When had the change begun? Was she afraid of Aunt Palm's possible questions in return?

The visits and the drawing continued until Uncle Caleb died.

On the day of his funeral, when Fredericka went into her aunt's room to help her with her hat and veil, three of the drawings were lying on the bed.

"What do you think of them?" Her aunt's tone was matter-of-fact on the surface but something played beneath it that Fredericka could not measure.

She tried not to show any surprise as she picked up the one nearest her. Under the sketch Aunt Palm had written: *"He was a man! The death of a man!"* The words in the clear Spencerian script leapt at Fredericka. Across the surface of her mind there ran a shock of fear.

"They're frightening!" But she did not know whether she meant the drawings or her thoughts. The drawings were coldly naturalistic. In one, all the contortion of pain; in another, the blankness of feature which can so curiously accompany extreme agony. The dying man's eyes stared sightlessly into time, and beyond it. Fredericka repeated the word "Frightening!"

"Death is frightening," Aunt Palm said shortly.

Fredericka put back the drawings on the quilted counterpane. The words were dimly familiar. They linked themselves with other words about death; echoes out of the half-submerged past: *People don't die smiling. It's a lie. If they seem to it's just a contraction of the lips. Quite often it's just the last puff of inner gases. Try to be rational, Fredericka. . . .*

Neither of them said any more, but a week later, sitting

· 187 ·

by the pool in the sun, lulled with the late bees and the afternoon languor, Fredericka asked Aunt Palm:

"What did you mean by the words you wrote under the drawings of Uncle Caleb . . . 'He was a man.' "

"Do you mean what do I mean by a *man?*"

"Yes, I guess that's what I mean."

There was a long pause. "There are very few left," Aunt Palm said. "I've noticed there are not many—not your age. Perhaps it is a blessing. On the other hand, it may be a loss. I suppose you never know what a woman is until you know what a man is . . ." She paused.

"You still haven't told me," Fredericka reminded her finally.

There was an even longer pause and in this pause the new fear began to trickle again into Fredericka's heart—the fear of what her aunt would say. She regretted having brought up the subject, hoped now her mind would wander and that she would not answer. But after a while:

"I think it is too bad that you should have to ask me," Aunt Palm said. "At your age you should know."

Fredericka's one wish was to keep the subject safely off herself. "Tell me another man," she said quickly. "Another man in this town, someone you knew."

Aunt Palm rocked, her hands folded in her lap.

"Otto Schultz. Though he painted, he was a man."

"Painted badly," Fredericka remarked, trying to keep it light.

"Otto Schultz had to earn a living," Aunt Palm corrected her. "To earn a living at painting in America you had to paint badly."

After a silence, "Dr. Hendricks was a man," she added, "a scholar and a theologian, but still a man."

"The Unitarian minister?" Fredericka asked, trying to remember him more clearly, trying to recall the warm full voice reading Emerson, tea in the parlor, Flora Tolley's shy flutings . . .

"You didn't have to be a weakling to be a preacher when I was young," Aunt Palm said, catching at something skeptical in Fredericka's tone. "Quite the opposite. People used to struggle then in a way they don't any more with something called the Religious Question. Did you believe in the divinity of Christ? Who, then, was Jesus? Was the Virgin Birth a possibility? Infant baptism, infant damnation—all these were ideas that could tear a human being into tatters."

Her nervous hands rested now quiet in her lap. There was a look of peace on her face, as though she were recalling something that gave her pleasure.

"To stand against the current religious prejudices took great courage. To have a real mind and to stand actively *for* religious principles took just as great courage, since people, the majority, believed blindly and automatically—as always—without thought or question. So in my day strong men and good men became either preachers or atheists, depending on their final convictions, but essentially they were very much alike. They had paid a price to acquire a true point of view."

"And that is what makes a man a man—to pay a price for a point of view?"

"Not always," said Aunt Palm perversely.

"Oh, Aunt Palm, you are an upstate sibyl," Fredericka cried.

Aunt Palm put on her quoting look. " 'Oh the difference of man and man,' as Goneril said."

She reached behind her back for a folded-up woolen scarf. Opening it she placed it over her bony shoulders. Often a quotation marked the end of speech. Fredericka did not want her to stop talking now.

"Do you remember a boy I brought home from college once? His name was Greg Davie."

"Yes," said Aunt Palm. "I do. I remember him."

"He could get very worked up about religion. What you said just now made me think of him."

"He seemed a fine wild boy." After a pause, "What became of him?" Her tone was genuinely curious.

"I don't know." Fredericka tried not to answer too quickly. "I'm sure he must be a very successful doctor somewhere. He was bound to be. He was very ambitious—and hard-working."

Aunt Palm seemed to show no further interest in Greg Davie. After a moment, "Neither of my sons is a man," she said positively. "I blame myself as much as I blame their father."

Here it was again! The little cold shock of fear. Fredericka tried hastily to turn the conversation away from—from what? From herself? From Christopher? Was that it? "But you said Uncle Caleb was a man and you haven't explained."

"Caleb had a point of view," Aunt Palm said. "It was his own. He was demanding and he did not understand me but he knew what he knew and he had to have it that way. Sometimes these are the traits only of stubbornness and immaturity. But sometimes it is the very substance of a man—for it is men who have, so far, made the world, and this is the way they had to be to do it."

Fredericka did not speak. She did not stir. She hoped for some interruption from outside—a flight of early geese honking high overhead, a sudden wind to make the woolen scarf inadequate—anything to prevent her aunt from saying what she felt sure she was now going to say, something that she could not listen to, could not answer. . . .

"You are upset, lovie." It was the old voice, the tender voice remembered from childhood, but now she was afraid of it, almost as afraid as she was of the other voice that spoke coolly even as it hinted at churnings in the depths and darts of sharp truth.

"Am I?" she asked. "Yes," she admitted. "I am."

"Why?"

Immediately there came the trapped feeling, the quiver of apprehension, the fear of tears. She gathered all her strength to answer. "You seem strange to me. I—perhaps it is I who . . ." She could not finish. The asters blurred, the maple was seen through a mist.

"Some years ago," Aunt Palm said, and her voice was the voice with which she concluded remarks, "when I ceased to be a female—physiologically—I said to myself: From now on I shall speak the truth. I can afford to. I shall speak the truth or remain silent. There are only two things to do."

Fredericka had stopped remembering out loud for Franz Allers. She looked intently now through the windowpane at the frail green worm of early April, caught on a spun thread of its own weaving, rising and falling under the budding maple tree in the golden evening light. . . . How much had she really told him? She had tried to skim off the safe sentences, detach from their deeper context only those which would not lead to troublesome questions, to his eyes' carefully avoiding or carefully plumbing hers.

"You said you had been unusually close to your aunt?"

Fredericka nodded. "Yes, very close."

She got up and crossed over to the fireplace, reached for the match in the glass dish on the mantel, lit the fire. When she returned to her chair they were silent. The window sash rattled faintly in a wind that had sprung up and looking out Fredericka saw that the light was waning.

"Today, earlier," Franz Allers said, "you told me you had been nowhere, done nothing. Why is that? If that is true, where have the years gone?"

She considered the question gravely. She tried to answer honestly. "It seems no time at all," she said, "in one way. In another it seems—a lifetime. First we were married, Christopher and I. Then there were the children. Then the Depression. Now this war . . ." She tapered off uncertainly.

She looked down into the palm of her right hand which lay open in her lap. She put the left one beside it, also open. "Do you believe in the mystery of the palm?" she asked irrelevantly. "I mean its lines. . . ?" She looked up.

He was looking directly at her, his gaze penetrating and still questioning. She felt her color rising—could not, dared not, answer his look in full. She dropped her eyes again as he said quietly, "Well, I believe in mysteries—I can safely say that."

She held her eyes down, still afraid to meet his, waiting. The sash rattled again warningly. When he spoke it was to say, "When will I see you again?"

She made herself look at him then, forced her voice into casualness. "But I'm your pupil," she said. "I'm coming to your classes. Don't you remember?"

"On Wednesday, then?" he asked.

"On Wednesday," she repeated.

Chapter Thirteen

. . . A FLUTTER, A MOVEMENT AND SIFT-ing of the air as though with the beating of small wings. Waking, Fredericka did not know whether it was rain, or moths on the screen. Then suddenly she knew it must be rain. It was too soon for moths and anyway there were no lights to draw them.

Lying in the stirring darkness, she began to ponder the mystery of moths and light. She imagined for a moment that she could feel what moths feel—a compulsion driving the delicate shaft of the body, agitating the soft wings, drawing and pulling, bringing the moth ever nearer and nearer the hot bright ecstasy of pain and death at the center of the burning nimbus.

Turning on her pillow, hearing the whisper of rain and leaves, she was surprised to feel—and to know that she was feeling—desire. It was the sensation she had had long ago in Attica Center, lying in the spring darkness, wanting to be taken, and afraid, and longing, yearning for she knew not what completion at the burning center of life itself.

"Oh, Greg," she said aloud. The wind entered the room to brush along the tabletop, under the rugs, over her bed, to finger her cheeks and hair as though searching something. "Greg." But the face she saw as she spoke was the face of Franz Allers, turning to her in the stirring spring garden asking her directly: "But where do you live?"

Every telling has a taling and that's the he and the she of it.
Aunt Palm's favorite lines from Joyce—they came now into
Fredericka's head—the lines from the expensive recording
with the Irish voice, all pucker and velvet moss, all bogs at
twilight and green taste of sour grass in late April: *Wait till
the honeying of the lune, love! We'll meet again, we'll part
once more. The spot I'll seek if the hour you'll find.*

"The spot . . . the hour . . ." The words turned and
turned in her head. Henley Hall, Room 21. The same remembered ugly room with the blackboards and the rigid
scarred chairs. Only now the figure was in front, lecturing,
not beside her, taking notes. "Your backgrounds are probably
very different," her father had remarked, speaking of Greg's
Buffalo grandmother. She had wanted then to understand,
to share, she had wanted to grow—that was it. Yet she had
chosen not to. Now it was not merely a different background,
it was an alien culture about which she must learn—for the
sleeping appetite, suddenly awakened, which had made her
say before lunch that she longed to travel and see the world,
made her crave now to hear, to share, whatever this man
from a dying world might be willing to tell her.

They had had a long wait together for the Attica Center
bus. It was thirty minutes late. Fredericka was delighted, for
Franz Allers had talked more in that half hour about himself
than he had talked all afternoon.

At sixteen, he told her, he had been in World War I. He
had a bullet scar on his right shoulder and a picture of himself young and frail in his uniform, the way he looked when
he was billeted in an old villa in northern Italy, a villa with
a library of English books.

"It's all I have of my boyhood," he said. "Indeed, it's almost my only personal possession—a picture of myself as a green young soldier."

"I'd like to see it sometime. May I?"

"Of course."

It was taken in Italy, he went on reminiscing in his quiet voice, with his friend Fritz, some months before that other hopeless war had ended. He and Fritz, arm in arm, looking pathetic, callow, and terribly solemn. Fritz died of an intestinal disorder brought on by bad food. He died just about the time the Armistice was signed. But in Italy, when they were together, they had practiced reading English aloud in the deserted villa where they were billeted. *Pickwick Papers*, on very thin Bible paper. What was it really all about, they had asked themselves. Was it tragic, was it comic? They did not know. *Oliver Twist* had been easier for them. Already, as the sons of Viennese doctors, they knew about crime and slums and the twisted characters produced by poverty.

After they finished reading a page of a book they would carefully tear it out and use it for starting the fire for their afternoon drink of stale tea from an old tin box in the pillaged kitchen. They would use the paper also for bathroom purposes. There was absolutely no other paper to be had anywhere.

"It must have pained you to tear up those beautiful books."

He lifted his brow. "Only the first few pages. . . . For that is always part of war—a terrible part—the unfeeling destruction of the records of man's thoughts, and the work of his hands. I have not remembered any of this for a long time —particularly that library of English books. Your house today reminded me of it. . . .

"I remember other things too. I can see our colonel, the day I crawled on my belly up the hillside under fire to carry the note that said we were to surrender. He was sick with dysentery and he was lying, pale and unshaved, on his cot in the sun when I got there. He took the note from me and without opening it he went into his tent and shaved, put on his dress coat and buttoned it up to the chin, came out and picked up the paper from the cot where he had laid it and read it. Then he sat down on the side of the cot and wrote a formal reply with a pen with the crest of his old regiment on it. I choked up so horribly I couldn't look at him or speak, and although I hated and have always hated military men, their training, their life, their aims, and ideas, I felt admiration for our colonel because I knew . . ."

"Knew what?" She was not following him.

He tried to explain: this officer, considering his training and his consciousness, would never be asked to face a more bitter personal defeat. Yet he took it with dignity; he even laid on it a certain ritual in order to keep it from being a low and shameful experience, the experience of defeat in a cause long known to be hopeless. He scraped his chin with his weak and trembling right hand, combed his neglected hair, put on his dress uniform, made an occasion of it so that a boy looking on, also sick and bewildered, would see a man meeting failure with dignity. . . .

"But wouldn't it have been better just to let the boy sense the full meaning of defeat?" She had asked him, glancing down the shabby street in the dim light, past Nate's vegetables, the Citizens Bank and Trust Company, praying the bus would be very late. "I mean, wouldn't it be better if everyone saw personally, young in life, how stupid and meaningless war is?"

"Ah, to be sure. But still . . ." He went on describing how, in the hills of a strange land, a sick man shaves, dresses, uses the last ink in the birthday present from his wife—the frail pale lady in the family house back in Christmas-card Vienna . . .

Fredericka lost him again. She said so.

He tried to make her see something. Here is one kind of man, here another—two creatures of different breed, hitched to a single common carriage that we call Human Life, the Spirit of Man, Progress, each trying to pull it in his own way, and the carriage is rocked and pitched about and racked with unlike motions and split aims, and still, somehow, miraculously, it manages to get ahead on the road.

"Ahead?" she questioned.

He repeated it. "Ahead? You mean you want me to question the word 'ahead'—to say life is only a treadmill? No, that I cannot. It moves—it moves ahead." He seemed to be arguing with himself, anxious to prove his point. "That I believe no one can deny," he insisted, "not even in the 1940's, and not even with all I know and remember to make me feel otherwise. . . ."

She saw his face with shock. It had withered before her eyes with the bitter pain that rose in it like a sudden tide. She thought he might groan, automatically, like a man torn unexpectedly with pain. "I am haunted," he had said in the parlor. Was this, then, his ghost visiting him now as they waited for the bus? She was sure of it. And the ghost was his wife, of whom he had said only, with hesitation, that she was dead. He does not want to forget her. He is struggling to hold on to her, and that means he has guilt—but why?

With difficulty he was continuing. "Not that it always *looks* like the path ahead. That I grant you. The challenge to a new consciousness may be too much for a given age, so that there is failure to meet it, and the failure often seems like retrogression. . . . But I conceive of it as a spiral . . ."

And there was the bus, turning the corner, lumbering toward them like some archaic monster from a prehistoric machine age—unstreamlined, gaseous, shapeless, creaking and quaking. Franz got out of the car, they said hasty goodbyes, and he boarded the bus. She watched him until it drove off. His face did not once lose its withered look. She could see his profile through the windows and it was frozen in exhausted despair.

The inner experience he had given her in those few moments was like nothing she could remember ever having had before. It was curiously compounded of gratitude and regret—gratitude that he had shared something with her, regret at her own inability to understand truly what it was he had endured.

He had, she decided, something of the quality of certain old friends of her uncle Philander's of whom it was always said they had lived "hard" in their youth. What they knew they knew finally. It had happened to them and it would die with them, for it was embedded in their bones and plasma. It lay—their life—like a great well of remembrance and experience, a bottomless reservoir of dream and fact. These were the people who created a country's legends, shaped its myths. . . .

As she drove home, Nothing has happened to me! she thought wildly, putting the car to the last hill like a horse to a fence. Nothing has happened to us—to Christopher or to me. Perhaps nothing ever will! She had seen the old Perry lantern in the bank's front window. Now, lying in her bed, seeing it again, her heart leaped once more in panic. Nothing changes!

She thought of Aunt Palm. Something did happen to her. It was Uncle Caleb. He was a "man"—so she had said—possessive, violent, demanding, eccentric. He did not understand the woman he married but the force of his ignorance was a living force; against it Aunt Palm could act with force herself, practice witty malice, and an almost surreal revenge. This is not the perfect life, but it has at least elements of living matter in it, she thought. It is not like us—like Christopher and me—two parts of a machine, moving near each other but never touching, never meshing . . .

She thought of Uncle Philander. Something had happened to Uncle Philander too, and it was more than Harvard. He had got the Far West in his bones. He had ridden bucking horses. He had dug up the tracks of dinosaurs from petrified primeval mud because his imagination was fired by these relics of a lost age. And he had slept with Indian girls probably, and worn out his three well-bred wives with his robust appetites. . . . Strange, when you stopped to think about it, that Uncle Philander had had no offspring from three young women.

Uncle Philander did not have life classified but its mystery and madness fascinated him. It would hold his interest down the dwindling years. He would be turning his binoculars on the May fly's mating flight, on deer in thickets and geese going north, until he was too feeble to get outdoors. Until the day of his death he would go on collecting fragments of meteorites and diorite, photographs of two-headed calves, Icelandic playing cards, Kwakiutul medicine-man rattles, and hinged hazelnut shells opening to reveal Mexican fleas dressed for operatic roles. All this activity made it possible for him to approach the trained individual in the fields of science and art with perfect aplomb, because he too accepted the wonder of life and, as far as he was able, assembled his examples of its beautiful, bewildering, and terrifying paradoxes.

I am nothing, Fredericka thought, hearing the rain beating

now more insistently on the roof. And I have done nothing, and this is true of Christopher also and may be true of our children. And I've seen nothing and been nowhere. Europe once, the tourist places, and California. . . . But in California it had been, of course, the prescribed place—the Mission Inn. Rooms high in the sun with your own little balcony and a "hostess" downstairs with a Massachusetts accent. Food rich in vitamins and balanced in calories, eaten in a patio; garden-fresh, frigidaire-crisp, tree-ripened fruit; melty green paste of avocado spooned from the paper-thin shell; lettuce, each leaf crackling with stiffness bouncing from the fork tines cool to the tongue; orange juice yellow as the advertised sunlight, sweet and tangy to the throat—everything sliced and iced, frappéed, gelatined, glacéed, hand-picked, hand-turned, by hands sun-clean and nimble from violet rays and vitamins. For we are all healthy here from Our Own Sun, Our Own Oranges, Our Own Lettuce, Avocados, Abalone, Clams, Crabs (from the coast daily by special express trains) . . . Did Americans really travel only to eat? Sometimes it seemed so.

The memory of the California winter came back to her now vividly, because of the afternoon's conversation in the parlor. They had worked on their sunburns every morning like patient neophytes. They had ridden horses up dry river beds. They had wandered sun-drunk and aimless through the cool dark rooms of the inn's immense gift shops where there were to look at and to buy Tibetan paintings, Mexican santos, Spanish prie-Dieu, faded Castilian damask, Japanese priests' robes, tin trays from Oaxaca, Chinese trees of jade—loot and plunder not torn from owners by war or power of arms, but taken quietly, stealthily, with the power of money; loot to be carried home self-consciously by tourists from

Iowa, Wisconsin, New Jersey, and Connecticut—the painted tin mirror, the grandee's worm-chewed chair, as mementos of a winter in the land of the golden myth. . . . She heard Franz Allers saying: ". . . *almost my only personal possession—a picture of myself as a green young soldier.*"

So he had nothing—and he had everything! She turned restlessly in her bed.

No, California was not what she meant that she had missed by not traveling. She tried to come closer to her meaning and her longing . . . . It was something more like life in the solitary cabin high in the Rockies, glimpsed from a train window (for she had raised the sash frequently to stare out as they flowed on the steel band across the black continent). Here where the nights were so wide, so high, so lonely that the stars, though nameless in their swing and dip and disappearance across the moving sky, must be known intimately as human beings are, and as no astronomer can ever know them through his great impersonal lens. . . . She lay now in her bed in Wrenkill longing for this mountain solitude, this remote and quiet isolation as she had longed for it in the lower berth of their Pullman compartment years before.

Or if not the rancher's cabin, she thought, then places across the oceans of the world—places that were not for tourists with guidebook and camera. She saw Greek children playing ball in old ruins at sunset; sheep cropping within the crumbling fragments of the legendary castle of King Arthur. She saw Carnac, the long plain with the mysterious menhirs, those broken teeth of stone, casting dark question marks on the moonlit plain, stating only: Man was here once, erecting shapes, making myths. . . . Guatemala, Peru, came into her mind. What was the mighty will that drove the human creature to carve the great stone faces of these now-neglected lands, faces gazing far beyond yesterday, remembering two-thousand years of civilization before the first blond, bearded men stood at their feet staring upwards stupidly?

The wind wrestling briefly with the tree outside Fredericka's window became her knife in the jungle undergrowth of Cambodia, cutting and hacking through the last tangle until she emerged into the green light and stood, speechless with awe, beholding the long row of stone figures supporting the body of the Great Serpent, trying to penetrate the stern detachment, the impersonal cold serenity of those mighty visages whose eyes still search all strangers approaching the Victory Gate of Angkor Wat: "There are," wrote the old Chinese Traveler, and Aunt Palm had read the words aloud from the travel book in a voice that was properly august, "fifty-four of these genii who look like gigantic and terrible generals turned to stone . . ."

Why did they seem to mean something special to Fredericka, to signal her in her bed in Wrenkill, pulling up under her chin the embroidered monogram of the sheet, hearing the rain strike the metal screen outside?

Is it because, she asked, I see myself sliding down the years without leaving a trace—no record of any kind to indicate that I have been here? My children? Ah, yes, the children—but the thought did not comfort her. There was a cramping tingle in her mind, like blood reaching a part of her body that had been asleep.

For years, she thought, suiting her mood to the rain's melancholy ticktack, I have not been deeply lonely, deeply sad or glad. My life has been lived in the middle of the road where the going was easy and I had only to follow the wheel tracks ahead of me. I've never struck out over the desert stretching from the train windows in all directions, flat, endless, yellow, blinding, without shade or water, tree or shelter, crossing it because it led to something I wanted—gold in the hills, or a green spot on the other side of it. I've never struck out ax in hand through the woods that pressed down on the last marked open place, pushing through the underbrush, chopping, lopping, blazing the trunks as I made a way for those behind me to follow.

I've been asleep, caught in a dream that I cannot yet read, but now I am beginning to wake up and, like a sleeper who is roused at dawn in wintertime and knows that the room is cold and he must light his own fire, I burrow back under the covers, seeking unconsciousness again, hoping that what I know to be true is in reality the dream, and that when I wake again the room will be warm and the day half gone.

Chapter Fourteen

WEDNESDAY MORNING FREDER-icka set off for Attica Cen-ter in the car with two canvases to show Farrell. It had been months since she had seen Farrell, and years since she had seriously shown anyone her work. In a state of mingled apprehension and excitement she had selected two paintings. One was called "Summer's Tide." She had painted it in July of the previous year—an explosion of full-blown roses, complicated dervish dance of thistledown and seed, riot of electric greens, a fury of color, a fume of bursting forms. The other she had been working on over the weekend. "High Wind," the action of a superior disembodied force on familiar objects: a bending tree, a running horse, a pond, its surface ruffling as the force struck; lines of energy scratched in with the pointed end of a brush making a great whirlpool of the landscape.

Farrell was in his studio at the college, working in a pair of faded overalls through which his ample belly—full of his wife Maria's famous arroz con pollo and lamb cooked in olive oil—showed like an overripe melon. He was plainly glad to see Fredericka, but when she said she was coming back to him for criticism he shook his head. "You don't want criticism, Fredericka. You just need to hear some shop talk. Isn't that it?"

She agreed.

"But it will be good to have you here," he added. "I'm sick of these dwarf talents. I'd say I've just one real painter in the whole lot now. A boy with only one kidney, so he won't have to go to war, which would certainly be the end of him. . . . What are you painting now?"

She tried to tell him, was vague and incoherent. She finally admitted that she had brought two canvases with her and together they went out to the car to bring them in.

"Why in hell didn't you just bring 'em in in the first place?" Farrell asked.

"I don't quite know," Fredericka said. She felt very much ashamed of herself.

"You're an odd one." He shook his head in bewilderment.

When they got her canvases into the studio, he put them up on easels and sat down with a cigarette to study them.

"They're good," he said finally. "I don't know why you don't take yourself seriously, Fredericka, and I never have known."

"I don't either," she admitted, her heart swelling almost painfully at his praise.

"I'll show you some of mine. I'd like your opinion." With his remembered air of half diffidence, half eagerness, he began to pull paintings from the racks.

His style had changed—was changing—she noted at once. From the somewhat sterile and tight semiabstractions involving factories, smokestacks, streets under lamplight that he had been painting when she was first his pupil, he was turning toward groups of suggestive figures, deliberately half-realized —in flight, in angry protest, collected like animals behind bars. Only occasionally did one of the sea of faces come into focus, sharply projected as though to say: The individual may still emerge from the great shapeless, worked-upon mass.

"How you are changing!" she cried.

"Am I? Yes, of course I am." He was pleased.

"Do you know Franz Allers?"

He looked at her with a quick smile. The association was clear to him.

"The wanderer from Europe? You are very astute, Fredericka. Yes, I have heard him talk. And you are right. He set me thinking, feeling . . . seeing the great migrations. And" —reaching for another canvas—"man's inhumanity to man."

He turned toward the light a curious canvas, still incomplete, too pictorial, too literary, and yet the most moving of all to Fredericka, partly because of the further change it indicated in Farrell.

In an underground room with bars at the window a broken man was seated at a table. Across from him there appeared in the cold light from the window the effete gloved hand of another man with a cigarette in a long holder. Only the hand. The rest of the figure was lost in shadow. But the hand was enough. Set opposite the whole suffering broken skeleton of a human creature it was stronger than a fully delineated figure would ever have been. For that gloved hand was a symbol, a symbol of ugly decadence and cruel power.

"I don't know why you want to come back here to Attica Center," Farrell said, standing off and looking at his canvas with impersonal eyes. "We seem more and more like a backwater to me. Strangely enough, all these boys in uniform just increase the feeling. Unthinking kids, caught in a great impersonal fate, they go around whistling and laughing, getting ready for death and horror. And we go on teaching Old and Middle English, General Economic Geology, History of Coins . . ."

"Oh, come now!" Fredericka said, laughing. "History of Coins!"

"It's the God's literal truth. Open to students by special permission."

"Well, I don't mind that so much."

"I don't either, honestly," he admitted. "I learned a lot from coins when I was young. And those seals from Ur in Philadelphia—everyone ought to take a look at them once a year—at least once a year just to keep a perspective on progress."

"The truth is," he went on, putting back his canvases, "there's too little talk around here about art and associated topics and too much about Electrical Measurements, Measures and Integrals, Determinants and Matrices. . . . But these courses will certainly increase, not decrease, with radar and all the other new stuff coming up in the world. . . . Either of your kids artistic? You've got two, haven't you?"

"Yes, two, and the answer is no. Not in the least. Leslie cares only for horses and wants to study veterinary medicine. Forrest—well, Forrest is interested in being a good shot and in knowing all models of airplanes."

"My gosh," Farrell said sympathetically. "Well, my oldest boy is a genius in music, I'm told. His head is as large as mine right now and he's just twelve and God knows I pity him—though it's better to be a musician than a painter, because music is something more of a science, and this is an age for science. . . ."

After she left Farrell, Fredericka went to Franz Allers' afternoon lecture. She tried to listen to what he was saying but her mind refused to rest. It kept wandering off, back and forth, through her life, onto Christopher and off, onto the children and off, onto Aunt Palm and off . . .

Allers' subject, so he said, was the ancien régime in France. Once the class's sudden focusing of attention and scattered laughter fixed in Fredericka's memory a remark that did not seem at all related to the subject he had announced.

"Women dislike their husbands' mothers so intensely because they live with the older woman's mistakes. The immaturity and lack of discipline of the husband seems a direct result of his upbringing. The mother hasn't paid the full price for her mistakes. It is left to the wife to do that, hence the resentment."

I missed all that, by marrying Christopher, Fredericka thought to herself. It had never occurred to her in any domestic crises that Aunt Palm was her "mother-in-law."

She intended to ask Franz Allers what had led to his remark, though it meant confessing that she had not been paying attention, but as soon as she was with him she forgot it.

"Can you stay and have dinner with me?" he asked her when she came down front to speak to him.

"I'm afraid I can't," she began, and then, "but I don't really know why not. Yes, I'll telephone home."

"Not that there is any place to take you to dine," he said.

"It doesn't matter."

They were walking out together into the shabby hall of the building, echoing now with heavy shoes and young laughter.

"Where do you eat usually?" she asked him. She remembered Louis's remark about vitamins, and was sure that he took no proper care of himself.

"In the cafeteria in the Domestic Science Building."

"Balanced meals?"

"They must be." His face grew surprisingly young with a certain smile he had. "Will you come and see my apartment? My landlady has made it very pleasant for me."

"I'd love to."

As they were going up the side path between the dwarfed cedars to the conventional shingled house, she thought briefly: How protected my life has been, shut off, without incident, so that going to strange rooms even in Attica Center is in itself an adventure. Yet if I lived in a big city I would probably see unfamiliar rooms every week of my life—if, that is, I was out in life, with a job . . . And her mind racketed away to New York and established her in a walk-up in the Sixties from which she flew out every morning at 8:45 to tap her heels swiftly to the Madison Avenue bus and make her way to some high cool advertising office, or a book-lined cubbyhole at some publisher's, with pipe smoke seeping under the door and hearty cultivated male voices settling literary futures in the adjoining room. . . .

"How nice!" she said, feeling a slight pang as she stepped into Franz Allers' sitting room and saw some early daffodils in a Toby jug on the table. "Who is she?"

"Who is who?"

"The woman who fixed this room."

He was amused. "Mrs. Adams. Her husband is a dentist."

"Oh." She felt ridiculously relieved. There seemed nothing challenging about a dentist's wife—a singular point of view that she tried to examine in passing, deciding that it sprang probably from her opinion of dentists as little men of limited destiny.

"This is the best chair." He offered the wing chair by the

fireplace. "Mrs. Adams collects what she calls antiques. I'm afraid they're just that, most of them."

His face was growing steadily younger.

"How were you ever lucky enough to find two pleasant rooms—and a fireplace?"

"It was good luck, wasn't it? I got here just after her mother died. The rooms came on the market late. It was purest luck. . . . Look, I've some sherry here, not bad, and even some Scotch a friend gave me."

"Scotch, if you please," Fredericka said, though she thought instantly that it might shock him, a European, to drink hard liquor at four-thirty in the afternoon. She rarely did it at home.

He poured them each a glass, went into the bathroom to draw tap water. "To my new pupil," he said, lifting his glass.

Fredericka flushed with mingled emotions—guilt, for she had not listened to his lecture; embarrassment at a teasing quality she imagined in his voice; the bright alarming thread of excitement running through her nerve ends.

After drinking the Scotch she called Wrenkill and left the message with Eunice.

It was nine o'clock before she started home. Where had the hours gone? Looking back she could not say. They had talked steadily.

"Will you go on teaching?" she had asked him near the end.

The shadow fell immediately on his face. "I don't know. Right now I have no plans."

With the dropping of the shadow a world of shadows appeared dimly behind him—wasteland, ruins, broken forms, broken bodies, lost faces. . . . She regretted her question, hating herself for stupidity. She managed to force her way out of the paralysis that the sight of emotion in another always created in her, and said haltingly, "You have been through a great deal, I know. I—I wish I could help."

At first he had not tried to reassure her with a lightened expression, or a lifted voice. He had sat quite rigid and dark-browed, but after a moment, "You do help me," he said.

"I do?" It was genuine surprise.

"And I don't know how—or why. But you do help me. I have looked forward to today since Sunday. Now I shall look forward to Friday."

He had turned then and looked at her, a look of deliberate intensity and directness. The look made her afraid, and she was sure her fear showed in her eyes. She could not return his glance. "I'm glad," she stammered. A moment later she rose to go.

When she got home there was a wire from Christopher.

FIXED UP FOR THE AIR TRANSPORT STOP MIAMI TRAINING IN A MONTH'S TIME THEN WASHINGTON AND POSSIBLY LONDON STOP LOOKS FINE STOP WILL BE HOME THURSDAY.

Christopher came home elated. The nervous irritability that had marked the days before his trip to Washington was quite gone. He walked already with a new air, a springing tread, shoulders back. His manner, Fredericka thought, is already faintly military.

"Of course the Air Transport isn't real war," he was careful to explain to everybody. "I mean to say, it isn't a combat unit, but they're doing a damned important job. They carry everything from jeeps to plasma, and they carry them everywhere. . . ."

His assignment was in the supply end. After his training he would commute between Washington and London. His horizons were suddenly unbounded and he was in turn very generous about Fredericka's new plans. He thought classes in Attica Center a good notion, he assured her. He urged her to get away oftener—go down to New York, see some shows, take Aunt Palm along. He even suggested that the gas allowance for the farm tractor should give her enough to go back and forth to her lessons twice a week, particularly since he wouldn't be there to drive twice daily to the bank.

He wanted to spend his last weeks at the lake place to have some fishing. It was early to open the house, but as it was unusually warm for the season Fredericka agreed to make the effort of getting the place in order six weeks ahead of schedule.

For ten days she did not have a chance to go to Attica Center. There was no extra help to be found in the countryside. Viney, the old cook, was beyond any extra effort; Eunice had rheumatism. Alone, Fredericka attacked dust, cobwebs, mice nests, squirrels' caches in the great rambling barn of a house. She did not actually mind the hard physical work. It relieved her tension, more psychological than physical. The sight of her in such furious unaccustomed domestic activity seemed pleasing to Christopher. She wanted to ask him about this peculiarly male response to women working, but because she was sure he would not believe it, or be able to explain it if he did, she said nothing.

When she got to Attica Center again Farrell was very short with her.

"Where in God's sweet name have you been?" he wanted to know.

She told him.

"Look here," he said sternly, "get this into your head, Fredericka. Either you work at your painting or you don't work. Half measures are no good. If you ask me, that's why women fail as artists. They're always dropping out to have babies, clean house, can strawberries, or something. They always seem to feel guilty if they don't. I don't blame them. It's probably society making them feel guilty. . . . But I just want to say this to you: If you're going to be a painter, then for Christ's sake get somebody else to scrub the woodwork."

"But I told you," she said. "There isn't anybody else. They're all making chemicals at Spartanville."

"Then let the damned woodwork go," he cried.

"That's what Aunt Palm said."

"Your aunt has sense. She probably doesn't want to see you throw away your talent the way she has hers."

"I suppose you're right," Fredericka agreed feebly.

When she saw Franz Allers, "I wondered where you were," he told her after she had explained. "I missed you."

Her heart leaped.

"I'd like to have you meet my husband before he goes. Could you come on Sunday?"

"If you wish."

"I do. Everyone would like to see you again."

"I've thought of them so often." He smiled as though remembering something pleasant. "Your aunt and uncle . . ."

"Are you happy here?" she asked him abruptly. She surprised herself by the question.

"Happy?" He repeated the word as though it was unfamiliar, as though it was astounding for anyone to use the word at all. It was after his class and she had driven him out —at her suggestion—to a famous "view" of the lake and distant hills, because she felt he looked worn and disheartened. After a long minute of silence he spoke in a remote voice, dead and weary: "I am resting here, like a swimmer who has been in the sea too long. I've got my breath back, but not my strength. I don't feel anything yet really, not even relief, except in momentary flashes."

It was the most personal speech she had heard him make. His tone was not emotional, he did not invite pity, but she felt such pain for him that it struck her with physical force. He looked at her and saw her tears.

"My dear Fredericka." It was the first time he had used her name. He put out his hand and covered hers.

They were both silent. After a moment he withdrew his hand and said quietly, with measured dispassion, "I do not understand it but in certain moments with you—the other night waiting for the bus, in my room the other afternoon, today here—I feel the numbness going a little. Please do not misunderstand my telling you this. There is great human warmth in it for me—the telling of it, I mean. . . ."

He was strangely agitated. He pulled out the ash tray in the dashboard and pushed it back in with an impatient grating noise. "God help me," he said almost angrily. "I cannot utter directly the simplest words of human feeling any more . . . I walk around feeling like an animal around a trap."

Fredericka wished desperately to know what to say or do but was paralyzed. She sat silent, her hands resting on the sides of the wheel.

"I have a long way to go yet," he added.

After another silence she asked him, "To get where?"

He answered slowly. "To get back to pure belief, to faith in life, in human creatures."

"Then you don't really believe what you said that first

day—man the measure, and the postage stamp and Cleopatra's needle and all the rest of it?"

He lit the cigarette she offered him, looking out at the lake and the blue sky. Two students on bicycles, talking at the top of their voices, whizzed past down the hill. When their voices died in the distance, "Yes, somewhere I believe all that," he said finally.

"Do you believe it with your head or your heart?"

He smiled faintly. "That's a good question—oh, pupil."

He was quiet a long time. The wind came over the grass smelling of moss, and mud, of sap and blossoms. There was a flutter and chitter of birds in the willows. "I've asked myself that many times. I think I believe it with my head. It is a reasonable belief, that man has meaning. My heart is now not so sure. I hope someday my heart will be sure again."

Oh, she wanted to cry out. You may be sad and discouraged, full of despair even, but to me you give life meaning, you prove its meaning to me; just by questioning it, you make it alive and meaningful.

"I'm dead too—somewhere," she said abruptly. "I didn't know until—until recently. I know it now."

The speech cost her great effort. She trembled as she spoke. It seemed a confession far more weighty than the mere words themselves. She felt that Franz Allers accepted it as a serious speech, and that they had come very close in those few minutes by the lake.

"Until Sunday," he said when she dropped him by the dwarfed cedar hedge.

She was again afraid to look into his eyes. "I'll call you about how to get there."

*   *   *

The next night at the lake, while Christopher was cooking the fish he had caught, she broke the news about Franz Allers' Sunday visit.

"Fish," Christopher was explaining as he always did, holding back the campfire with a little green wood, "must be cooked slowly. Like eggs, they are spoiled if cooked too fast."

"I've asked Franz Allers for Sunday lunch," Fredericka said abruptly. "I hope you don't mind. It's a family picnic, except for him."

Christopher, poking gently at a trout, inquired in a flat voice, "Who the devil is Franz Allers?"

"Don't you remember? I told you about him—that friend of Louis's who is teaching at Attica Center."

"Oh, yes . . . Do you have to ask him, my last Sunday?" He sounded faintly put out.

"No, of course not, but I—I thought you'd enjoy him and you really should meet him before you go off."

"Why?" He was cold. He turned his large gray eyes on her with an opaque stare. They were beautiful eyes, without life.

"Because of Louis. They're great friends. Louis sent a letter about him. I do think you should meet him." She did not add what lay in her mind: Because I plan to invite him again, when you are gone, and this way is more proper.

Christopher grunted. "Is he as crazy as Louis?"

"No, quite different," she hastened to reassure him. "He—Dr. Allers—has had a very great personal tragedy. His wife was murdered—a political murder—in Vienna. He has never mentioned it. Dr. Cooper told me."

"Oh, yes—I remember your saying something about it . . ." He looked a little ashamed of his inhospitality. "Is he a Jew?"

"No. Why should he be?"

He shrugged. "Most refugees are, aren't they?"

"I don't believe so."

He shrugged again. "It doesn't matter anyway. I've nothing against Jews. Sure, ask him!"

She remembered something Franz Allers had said to her: that he thought Americans tended more than any people to make lump judgments, a strange characteristic for a nation which made so much of individualism.

Christopher was saying, as he put the fish on the platter and cut the lemon in slices. "I want Joe and Merry to come Saturday, and ask the Keynes too, and the whole crowd. It'll be the last get-together for us."

"Remember the children are coming for the weekend," she reminded him.

"I haven't forgotten. It won't be a drunken brawl. Anyway, the kids will be in bed before anyone gets going."

Chapter Fifteen

FREDERICKA HAD ASKED BRIDGIE AND Owen to pick up Franz Allers at the Thermopylae bus and bring him along to the lake on Sunday morning.

Last night's guests had gone. Sitting on the porch alone in the gentle sweet air of the May morning Fredericka heard the shouts of the three young Wrights a quarter of a mile away as they turned into the last stretch of the bumpy road that led to the back door of the sprawling old house. The top was down on the ancient Ford touring car Owen had brought out of hiding when the gas shortage threatened. The three noisy children in the back seat with Franz had entwined him like vines with their spindly legs and arms. They had been playing "One, Two, Three, Hit Me!"

"He won! He won! He's really awfully quick," Mopsie announced. "For a man with glasses," she added. She fell out of the car and both her brothers plunged after her.

"Whew!" Franz Allers said. He leaned back a moment, shaking his head, laughing. In that moment Fredericka saw him as he must once have been—gay, warm, wholly alive. She saw him in a dark-green hat, one with shaving-brush feathers, carrying a stick, wearing lederhosen and socks to the bare knees—that sensible and attractive male attire which photographs of Hermann Goering at play had made forever repellent.

"You've been a martyr," Owen said, turning around to him at the wheel. "I apologize."

"You've been an angel," Bridgie told him, getting out of the front seat, giving her hand to her father, who was stepping down, leaning heavily on a stick.

"Gout," Bridgie announced, shaking her head at Fredericka coming forward from the steps. "I don't know which ancestor is responsible. Certainly it has nothing to do with Daddy's diet now."

She talked of him in the third person as though he were not present. He winked tolerantly at Fredericka before he kissed her. "Bridgie's bound to make me an invalid."

Leslie and Forrest, who had been politely and somewhat restively waiting for their cousins before starting any of the day's activities, came running up at once from the dock. Fredericka called her children over to present them to Franz. She saw how intently he looked at them, and observing them herself with a critical eye she felt pride and at the same time a certain misgiving. They were beautiful children, but a little cold and reserved, she had to admit. They did not have the free and easy bounce of Bridgie's lot. She did not understand it. No restraint that she could think of had ever been laid upon them. They had been brought up very much as she and Christopher had been brought up. They too had had the benefit of Aunt Palm's eye and ear, her stories and her fancies, yet it had not stimulated either of them to liveliness or imaginative flights. Perhaps, as Uncle Philander said, they had dipped into the Dutch genes.

The two young Perrys did not appear to look at Franz with very much attention but Fredericka was sure that they would have a definite opinion to offer later. Briefly she wondered, looking at her daughter, whether Leslie had read—

was now at the age to read—*Little Women*. Thirteen. That must be about right. She could not remember at what age she had read it herself, although she did remember that it was around the same time that she had plowed laboriously through Tolstoi's *Resurrection* (for she had heard this book alluringly discussed in lowered tones by her aunt and Flora Tolley from the library). At fourteen, or thereabout, she had certainly found Katyusha's involved baffling troubles much less moving than Jo March's, and she could still remember vividly how she and Bridgie had cried together when Amy got Laurie and Jo married the "professor."

She was thinking of all this as Christopher came out onto the steps and Owen presented him to Franz. As they shook hands she looked at them together—Christopher with his soft conventionally handsome boyishness, the flat stomach he was so proud of, the hair still thick enough, although thinning faintly on the crown. Franz Allers was lean too. He had known hunger probably—prolonged hunger. And he knew the nervous creative tensions that drive away the appetite.

He did look foreign, though it was hard to define the quality that made him so—something in the expression, the way of standing. As one who paints portraits you should be able to define it, she told herself, but she could not. She thought again of the professor in *Little Women*. German also, as she remembered him. She had seen the movie years ago at Radio City in New York, with Hepburn as Jo; had thought to herself with relief at the end: But, of course, Laurie, the eternal adolescent, would never do for Jo.

"What are you thinking of, dreamer?" Bridgie asked, linking her arm through Fredericka's.

"*Little Women*," Fredericka replied. She laughed at Bridgie's expression.

"What about it?"

"That it really is a classic."

Bridgie did not pursue the subject.

The party was dividing up into separate groups. Christopher and Owen were going to fish. Forrest wanted to come along but Owen Junior, who had a sprained wrist and was feeling grumpy, said he would rather stay behind and read. He was finally persuaded to go out in the old flat-bottomed scow with the girls. Uncle Philander saw with delight that the visitor was going to be left to him. "Come into the living room, Doctor," he said with a faintly conspiratorial air. "There's something I'd like to discuss with you."

Franz Allers cast Fredericka an amused glance. "Delighted," he said, following Uncle Philander's broad back into the long living room with the floor of wide oak boards, the great stone fireplace, the wicker chairs, the stuffed heads of bear and deer, the bodies of prize trout.

Bridgie sat down beside Fredericka on the steps. She gazed after the departing children.

"Leslie and Forrest look very well."

She spoke in astonishment, as though she had expected them to return from their boarding schools gaunt and undernourished.

"They seem to be unusually well."

"Leslie's going to be a beauty," Bridgie said appraisingly. "Blond and leggy. . . . I'm afraid Mopsie is going to be a butterball." She spoke regretfully.

"Maillol masses are returning," Fredericka assured her. "So Farrell told me the other day. The war will do it, he says. Dreams of lonely men on desert islands begin to take actual shape."

"That sounds like Farrell as I remember him. Do you see him often?"

"I'm working with him in Attica Center—getting criticism on my painting."

"Oh, of course—you told me. . . . Where's Aunt Palm?"

"Upstairs in the front bedroom—working on her baseball scrapbook. I think it's a bit musty up there but she said she wanted to be quiet."

"How is she?"

"Broody."

"I'll go up and see her in a minute. Worse than usual?"

"Not any better. Restrained, as though she wants to say something and can't find the words." Fredericka was surprised at herself for speaking so frankly to Bridgie, but Bridgie did not appear to give it any special attention.

Peeling off her sweater, "Peace," Bridgie said. "Heavenly, delicious peace." She lay back and closed her eyes. "I'll just stay here a minute."

After a long silence in the humming warmth, "I think Dr. Allers is awfully attractive, don't you?"

"Yes," Fredericka said honestly, "I do."

"It's nice to see a new face," Bridgie said. "I was telling Merry and Joe about him. I hope we can get him to speak to the Current Events Club sometime."

"Oh, don't pester him," Fredericka said. "I really think he would hate it."

"Why?" Bridgie asked, a little defensively.

Fredericka retreated. "Well, maybe he wouldn't," she said. "Why don't you ask him?"

They were both silent.

"Was it a big party last night?" Bridgie asked. . . . "I was sorry we couldn't get here but I couldn't get a sitter for love or money."

"Oh, the same crowd," Fredericka said indifferently. "You know." She didn't list them. Bridgie knew them all anyway. The group never varied—the Terrys, the Joneses, the Barretts, the Keynes. . . . The party had been like a hundred others. Somebody had managed to find steaks, in spite of the meat shortage. It was Joe Barrett. He had a story about a little butcher he had discovered at some crossroads "doing a land-office business." Joe didn't know how, couldn't explain it. "Didn't seem to be black market, but you can never tell . . . Don't get Merry started," he pleaded with everyone. "You'd think the OPA paid her to do their checking."

Christopher had done his act with the salad dressing—an act complete with cloves of garlic and a crust of bread tossed with the greens. This was a performance reserved for picnics at the lake when the men took over with a great flurry of asbestos gloves, chefs' hats worn at a dashing angle, aprons reading *Mamma's Helper*, and other useless equipment. Everybody drank old-fashioneds and "dago red" and Joe spoke his piece on the California wine business and how we'd show those Froggies yet, and what was all this stuff about wine temperatures and colors and all the rest of it, anyway. He and Charlie Jones, whose uncle in Boston contributed articles to *Gourmet* magazines, got into an overheated argument on this subject which ended in Charlie's drinking more than he should—as usual.

The women had grown shrill, a little sharp. They had employed pet names constantly in addressing one another; barbed darts had been thrust through the word "darling" like hatpins concealed in a silk envelope. They talked of children, the Book-of-the-Month, the coming fall hats, and their Current Events Club—but not about any current events. They told Fredericka they thought she was being perfectly wonderful about Christopher and they didn't know how she did it. They asked her guardedly about Aunt Palm's health. Before the evening was half over Fredericka realized that she was merely enduring the gathering, and that this had been (for a longer time than she cared to admit) her feeling about getting together with their friends.

"I suppose Charlie got drunk," Bridgie was saying.

"Plastered, as usual," Fredericka said dryly. "Joe took him home."

"Good old steady Joe," Bridgie murmured.

Fredericka had the impulse to counter this appraisal of Joe but she checked it.

"How was Merry?"

"Much as usual."

"Why don't you like Merry, Flea?"

"I like her all right. She just doesn't interest me much."

"But she has such a good mind."

"I know. Maybe it's her personality that seems to be minus something."

Bridgie did not press her friend's virtues on her sister. She acted a little hurt. Why do I bother? Fredericka thought. I shouldn't bother to say what I think. It doesn't matter. I seem to be growing argumentative. It's probably a thoroughly bad sign.

"I'll just run in and see Aunt Palm for a tick," Bridgie said, sitting upright and running her fingers through her hair, "and then we can start the lunch and get it off our minds."

She rose lightly and went into the house. Fredericka remained where she was, thinking of Aunt Palm with her paste pot and her shears upstairs in the musty old room with the straw matting and the flowered pitcher and bowl, the golden-oak bed, the dreadful pictures of "The End of the Trail," "The Moose in the Sunset," "The Old Mill in the Snow," which Uncle Caleb would never allow her to take down. Now that he was gone she no longer seemed to care. Either she did not see them or perhaps they even amused her as they amused Fredericka and Bridgie.

When Bridgie returned she came by way of the kitchen and she had the ingredients for the salad and the sandwiches with her on a huge tray. Sitting down again on the top step and beginning to spread the things about her, Bridgie recited in a set voice, "Skeeter Skat sliding safely into third on Splinter Shank's single to right in the third inning. Skinny Whoosis is awaiting the throw while umpire Joe Booboo calls the play. . . . It's a masterpiece."

Fredericka laughed. "Comparable only to 'The Annunciation' by Raphael."

"Right."

"She's fabulous," Fredericka said.

"She's balmy too," Bridgie remarked, but without meanness.

"I wonder."

For a moment Fredericka considered confiding in Bridgie about her talk with Franz Allers on the subject of Aunt Palm. Then she decided not to. Bridgie would probably not approve of taking a stranger into family confidences.

"She's definitely acting odd," Bridgie was continuing. "Maybe it's just old age—or is there a streak of something in the family?"

"A streak!" Fredericka said. "It's a yard wide!"

They both laughed.

"No, seriously," Fredericka went on, sitting up to help Bridgie. "Maybe we're the strange ones, not Aunt Palm or Uncle Philander."

"We seem dully normal to me," Bridgie commented.

"That's just it. Maybe that's a worse symptom than Aunt Palm's—eccentricity."

"Well, maybe. I see what you mean, though I don't believe I agree. . . . You make the salad dressing, Flea, and I'll do the rest."

"I think every generation gets duller in this country." Fredericka pulled toward her the mustard, salt, pepper, paprika, and sugar. "I think my children will be duller than Christopher or me—and that is really quite a sobering thought."

"Mercy, I can't call mine dull," Bridgie insisted.

"It's just because they're full of vitamins and less disciplined and repressed than we were," Fredericka said. "I'm sure they'll never have the marvelous qualities of Aunt Palm or Uncle Philander . . . At least I'm sure mine won't. They're going to be conformists of the first order."

"You never know." Bridgie was determined to be blithe about it. She began to cut up tomatoes for the salad. Her knees were spread wide apart and her full turkey-red peasant skirt looked like an ample canopy under which stray dogs and children might find shelter from sun or wind. Her bosom stood out firm and round in the starched white blouse with the ruffles at the neck which gave her an absurdly Victorian air.

"I must really paint you someday, Bridgie," Fredericka said, looking at her with pleasure.

"I wish you would," Bridgie cried, kicking off her sandals. Her bare feet were surprisingly dusty, like a child's. The pink nail polish which she had applied in slapdash style after a bath some days before, when she had had a few minutes to spare, was already peeling. She tossed back her dark hair and began to hum to herself, slightly off key, "Shine on, shine on, harvest moon."

She is a harvest moon, Fredericka thought, glancing again at her tenderly, and almost at once in despair, asking herself: Why can't I be more like Bridgie, quietly seated in the center of life, at ease, undemanding, outgoing, free, gay, and generous? Happy? Yes, because Bridgie does not question. She accepts. How can we share the same blood, the same ancestors, she and I? How can there be less than a year between us in age? Is it indeed Aunt Palm who has given me my quirks and bias—as I know Bridgie herself thinks, fond as she is of Aunt Palm—or did Aunt Palm choose me from the brood because she felt, as she used to say, that we were alike? Did my mother's illness from the day of my birth really so profoundly affect my life and bring me, by all the by-passes and side paths that we call fate, to Franz Allers?

The startling end of these meandering thoughts pulled her up short. So that was the way her mind was working! But why should the discovery startle her? Franz Allers had given her consciousness a good jolt; he would probably give it more. That was all there was to it.

"Watch the mustard," Bridgie said, stopping her humming. "I think you've put in twice what you need."

"Have I? Mercy! Maybe I'd better start again."

With Bridgie's interruption she became aware that she had been crushing the salt, pepper, and mustard in the bowl for a long time. Had Bridgie observed her abstraction? Bridgie was very quick.

"Mum," cried Jeb, Bridgie's youngest, coming just then around the end of the sagging porch carrying a can of worms. "The loons are down by the rocks. Come and call them, will you?"

"Just let me finish with these four tomatoes, then I will." Bridgie cut up the four tomatoes with quick movements of her knife.

"What are you doing, Aunty Flea?" asked Jeb.

"I'm feeding salt, pepper, and mustard to the pine needles," she said, scraping it out of the bowl beside the steps.

"What for?"

"To baffle them." It was Uncle Philander coming out of the door with a section of the Sunday paper extended before him. Franz Allers followed, pipe in hand, his face relaxed and amused. Uncle Philander sat down on the porch steps and Franz perched on the rail.

"Mind that railing," Bridgie warned him. "It's getting awfully rotten. Some winter I expect this whole place will fall into the lake."

"It is so pleasant here," Franz said. He looked out at the water and sighed. "Such peace!"

"I have just been saying to the Herr Doktor," said Uncle Philander, waving the newspaper to indicate that he was about to refer to it. "That there may be some great cosmic plan but I find it hard to see its workings. Why moths, the kind that eat clothing? Why tent caterpillars, locusts? Why ants, except as aids in framing moral precepts for the young —the industrious ant improving each shining hour and so on."

"That's the bee," Bridgie put in.

"No matter. It's all the same." Uncle Philander dismissed the interruption with an impatient gesture.

"Here, for instance," he continued, tapping the paper with the wet end of his cigar, "is an account of the sugar-cane leafhopper coming over from Australia to plague and bedevil the sugar-cane growers of the Pacific islands. No damn use to anyone, that kind of creature. Did immense damage. Only way to check it was to import another parasite that laid its eggs in the hopper's eggs and thus slowed him up considerably in his mass activity."

Jeb began to bounce a ball on the bottom step. Uncle Philander raised his voice a pitch to overcome this annoyance.

"By God!" he intoned. "No sooner do they check the leaf-hopper with this parasite that lays its eggs in the hopper's eggs than a species of borer is on them, one whose grubs keep themselves alive by eating their way up the sugar-cane stalks. So then they have to go out to New Guinea and find this borer's enemy and it turns out to be a special devil of a fly."

Jeb began to recite as he bounced the ball:

> "Knife and fork!
> Bottle and cork!
> That's the way to
> Spell New York!"

"Stop it," Bridgie said firmly. "Listen to Uncle Philander. It's fascinating!"

Uncle Philander, frowning at the interruption but softened by the word "fascinating," boomed on. "All right, so much for the borer's enemy, imported from New Guinea. Can we rest there? Not a bit of it. Next in line is another pest called the *Anomala* beetle—quite a name at that—and it goes after the cane *roots*. So then what do the growers have to do but bring in a wasp from the Philippines which lays its eggs *in* the young beetle. Round three! How many to go? Nobody knows—and I'm just talking about the sugar-cane world, that's all."

"Come on, Mum," said Jeb, openly bored with Uncle Philander and the sugar-cane pests.

"Coming, my chick." Bridgie put the salad bowl on the top step. "Though you've been very rude. . . . Don't drop ashes into the bowl, Uncle Philander."

He grunted. "Tiresome creatures, modern children," he commented, watching Bridgie and Jeb depart. "At that boy's age I had the finest collection of birds' eggs in all upstate New York."

"Jeb likes moths," Fredericka said. She felt she must defend him.

"Modern children have no imaginations," Uncle Philander continued sourly. "Too much radio."

Bridgie had gone with her son to the rocky point that jutted into the lake.

"Ah-ooo, Ah-ooo!" The thin chilling secret cry blew out of her mouth and came faintly back to them on the steps—first from the opposite shore as an echo, then from the unseen loons around the point, near the little island with its three spires of pines.

"They are floating down there," Bridgie said, her voice carrying clearly to them, "and the little babies are riding on their backs." Her hair blew back in a great red-brown mane and her eyes became as mysterious and pure as a clear pool in the forest. She looked rooted in the earth and in earth rhythms—tides and seasons, bud and bloom, wax and wane.

Oh, thought Fredericka, dropping her eyes again to the mustard, the salt, pepper, and vinegar, to be as simple, as bosomy and good as Bridgie—a woman to whom you could still give the kind of trusting hug you might, as a child, have bestowed on a doll, or a pillow, or a tree trunk. . . .

Uncle Philander got up from the porch rail and walked

down to the shore. Fredericka was alone with Franz Allers. His eye was traveling with pleasure over the scene: the shining water rocking gently between the walls of green, the sky with its feathers of cloud shredding and gathering in the high blue arch, the sprawling ramshackle house, graying slowly with neglect to the tone and color of the lichen and the rocks."

"I cannot tell you how it restores me to be here."

She looked up at him, her eyes shining. "I'm glad. So glad."

"I shall write Louis," he went on. After a moment, "How far away Louis seems!" he said in a low voice. He had been swinging his leg gently over the rail and now he stopped its movement and grew very still. Fredericka felt him leave the porch. His body remained, but he had gone. His face lengthened, grew stern and tired. The youth she had seen in him when he got out of the car an hour before, the air of casualness and ease that he had been wearing, entirely dropped away. He was a middle-aged man, desperately tired and somewhere sick and hopeless.

She felt she must speak, must talk to divert him. "Yes," she began quickly, "Louis does seem far away. He always has. He never lived here among us. He was always a visitor. . . . I'm sure he must seem more at home in France. I've thought about what you said about Henriette d'Abbeville. Louis probably is very like his French grandmother."

Franz Allers made no reply. After a few moments, "Tell me about this place," he said in his ordinary voice. "How can you own a spot so lonely so near to towns? . . . But I suppose that is America."

"I suppose so. It is also Uncle Caleb's father who is responsible. He bought the surrounding land long ago for timber. He cut off the big trees and—"

"But the woods look untouched!" he cried in surprise.

"That is because they were cut so long ago." She went on with the simple narrative, feeling that there was something soothing in its commonplaceness. "Cyrus Perry kept the lake for fishing. He was a great fisherman. Christopher takes after him. And so, now, does my son."

"Your children are very beautiful."

"Thank you. Yes, they are, aren't they?" She continued hurriedly with the story of the lake place. "We came here a lot when we were children. My own family and my aunt and uncle—my adopted family, that is. We came late in June and stayed until early autumn. It really is quite wild to be so accessible. We often see deer and foxes. I once even heard a panther scream, right outside the house."

"A panther!" He looked startled.

"Yes, a kind of mountain lion. I suppose it wandered from the Catskills. It was late in autumn. Aunt Palm and I were alone in the house. It frightened us almost out of our senses. They have a terrible scream, like a maniacal woman. Uncle Philander reported it to the Museum of Natural History."

She laughed, but she heard again the panther's cry in her memory and a chill passed across her body.

"When you said panther," Franz Allers said, "I thought of the big black cat of the zoos."

"Oh, no, this is yellow, I believe. I've never seen one. Ask Uncle Philander to describe it. He'll give you all the details." She laughed again.

"How beautiful you are!" he said abruptly. "So beautiful! Here in this clear light, with the green behind you."

She looked down. He said nothing more but between them hung for a moment a shimmering canopy like a water-jeweled web in early morning grass. . . . I must be careful. I must be careful. Surely my face will reveal what I feel, she warned herself.

"Here they are now!" cried Uncle Philander, reappearing at the path leading to the little dock.

Fredericka looked up expecting loons. It was Christopher, Forrest, and Owen in the boat, coming around the point.

"Three!" Christopher cried as soon as he was within ear-shot. "Beauties!" he added. He held up the fish to view, looking pleased and proud. "Forrest caught one."

"The family talent," Franz Allers murmured behind Fredericka.

"Heavens!" Bridgie cried, also appearing near the dock. "The sandwiches!" She came running lightly up the path to the porch.

Franz left the rail and went to join the men on the dock. Aunt Palm emerged from the house into the sunshine and sat down on the steps, drawing a little white shawl around her shoulders. It was one of her few old-lady gestures, this drawing of a scarf or shawl about her when she changed temperatures.

"What's all the excitement?" she wanted to know tartly.

"Three fish," Fredericka told her.

"Is that all?" She began to turn with her bony fingers Philander's cache of stones, which he had placed on the top step. "There's a new kind of lichen up here now," she said. "I never used to see it."

The men were coming up the path from the dock and Owen was talking. When they got to the steps he stopped to fill his pipe before continuing. "Call me any name you please . . ."

All three women pricked up their ears.

"Call me any name you please," he repeated, sucking

fiercely on his pipestem to get it started, "but the present war means just this to me. It is either the last dying gasp—or a new chance at life—of the Anglo-Saxon, democratic, individual way of living. It is that tradition, that way of life, set against all systems, all collective ideas, whether Soviet Communism or Fascism. And when I say that don't jump to the conclusion that I am an enemy of Soviet Russia. For I'm not."

He stressed his position with his pipe, pointing its stem at them all as though it were a pedagogue's ruler.

"I do feel, though, that I can see this conflict in its historical perspective, and I have a feeling that the history books will, in time, bear me out. We, people like ourselves, are fighting for our way of life—the democratic, individual way of life—against some new, and, I think, less fulfilling, system."

"Are we going to win?" Franz Allers asked quietly.

He was bending over taking a stone that Aunt Palm was offering him as a greeting.

"Personally I think we are," Owen said. "I have to think so—to sleep nights, with three kids growing up . . ."

"Don't *you* think so, Dr. Allers?" It was Christopher. Did she imagine it, or was his tone faintly hostile? Fredericka asked herself.

"We must win," Franz Allers said quietly, turning the small round stone in the palm of his closed right hand. He hesitated for a moment and then, as no one spoke, he added, "We must also change. We must get clearer about some things like collective security." He tossed the stone once, closed his fingers on it with sudden firmness. "We must not go on confusing these big new ideas in the world with—with closed systems, with serfdom, absence of individual freedom." He spoke like one who, though interested, plainly does not wish to precipitate an argument.

"Well," Christopher said, somewhat patly, shaking a cigarette out of a pack, "I guess there's a job to be done, to win this war—and that's about as far as my mind will carry me right now. Let's get that over with first, and then take the next things as they come."

"Don't for God's sake say, First things first," said Uncle Philander irritably. "I know of no phrase more meaningless . . ."

"I'm sure this is going to be fascinating," Bridgie put in sweetly at this point, "but Flea and I will have to excuse ourselves or you will get no lunch."

Fredericka rose reluctantly and went with Bridgie into the kitchen.

"Women's work," she said to herself, out loud. Bridgie did not take it up.

When Fredericka emerged onto the porch some time later she sensed tension immediately. Even the children, who had appeared scrubbed and ready for lunch, seemed aware of it. Christopher was looking stubborn, flushed, and faintly annoyed. Franz Allers was speaking to him, quite calmly, but with a quality in his voice that betrayed emotion.

"Mind you, I think the same rule should apply to Europeans. Less criticism, less differentiation. For Europeans are as sharp about Americans as Americans are about Europeans. But this present situation—it isn't America going once more to the relief of poor old inept and doddering Europe, as I feel you just now implied. We are all of us—all humanity—in it together.

"I am sure," he went on, leaning against one of the cracked and peeling pillars, speaking with slow deliberation, "from certain—well, straws that I observe in the wind, that before long we shall see this even more clearly to be true. Within our time, I believe, we will see finally, without argument, that we, human beings, are one body."

He paused here, his hands in his pockets, his eyes on the porch boards. His accent deepened as it did in his classroom when his emotions were touched. "Within our time," he repeated, "we shall see that when we make wars we, in effect, decide to destroy a part of our own organism, that war is a kind of psychotic compulsion, a collective will-to-death that is truly sick."

He raised his head, looked around the circle of their intent faces. "Yes, I believe we, all men, will have—no, now have, *already* have—the choice of collective life or collective death."

There was a silence. Owen cleared his throat. "Do you mean to imply that some revelation, some specific—well, discovery, will show us this?" he asked. Fredericka could imagine him framing his weekly editorial from the material of this Sunday conversation.

Franz Allers hesitated a moment. "Yes," he said, "it seems to me very likely."

"Could you give me a little more on that?" With difficulty Owen restrained himself from reaching in a pocket for pencil and paper.

Franz Allers' tone lightened. It was almost as though he was preparing himself to meet their scornful laughter. Either that, or it was so serious that he felt he must deal with it indifferently. "Well, who knows? It has long been speculated that we shall control the atom. A lot of pseudo-scientific writing has been done on the subject, and certainly there is now a great deal of secret research."

"Stupendous!" Uncle Philander murmured, twitching in his tweeds with suppressed excitement, making the snake-taming gestures with his straggle of reddish beard. "Stupendous!"

"Are you a pacifist?" Christopher asked. The irrelevance of the remark was surprisingly rude. He seemed almost deliberately to wish to misunderstand Franz Allers or to put him in an awkward position.

Franz Allers looked at him in surprise. "Not at all," he said quietly.

"Dr. Allers worked for the Underground in Europe," Fredericka heard herself saying in a tone that was plainly defensive. She came forward. "You never told me," she went on, looking at Franz Allers, her color rising, "not directly, but I knew somehow. I—I hope it doesn't matter, my saying it," she finished lamely. All their eyes were on her. She had created something of a stir.

Franz Allers' glance was warm, his voice reassuring. "No, of course not. It is quite all right, of course."

"Isn't it about time the Underground showed what it can do?" Christopher demanded. "It seems to me this whole infernal mess is dragging on a good while. If the Underground is going to do any stabbing in the back, isn't it about time they got at it?"

"It's harder than you can imagine," Franz Allers said slowly. His tone was kind, patient. "Here, so far away, it seems like a match between equal opponents, like a great game, a contest, a struggle of wits . . . Actually, close at hand, it is very different."

He paused. After a short silence. "You are so far away," he said, "it is difficult for Americans to grasp the whole situation, to see the almost insuperable dangers and obstacles . . ."

"It isn't like the movies where the right side always wins," Fredericka suggested.

"That's it." Again he gave her his warm grateful glance.

Bridgie appeared suddenly in the doorway. "Lunch, lunch," she cried, clapping her hands lightly as though she were about to organize square dances. With one quick glance around the group she too caught the tension as Fredericka had. "Now, no arguing at lunch," she stated firmly. "Not about anything. It's such a beautiful day. Too beautiful for arguments. Don't let's spoil it."

"That's right, honey." Owen went to put his arm around her, giving her a hug of appreciation. "You're absolutely right."

"But were we arguing?" Franz Allers asked. His surprise was genuine. "Wouldn't you call this a discussion, not an argument?"

"I would," Uncle Philander said, glowering at Christopher. "That would be my word for it."

Christopher said nothing. He looked annoyed and acted detached all during lunch. It troubled Fredericka. Why has Franz Allers rubbed him the wrong way? she asked herself. Is it merely that old dusty prejudice of Uncle Caleb's about "foreigners" raising its head again? For Uncle Caleb, try as he would, had never been able to consider anyone with an accent as an American, or even as potential American material. It was a deep-rooted prejudice that no facts could ever shake.

Just as they were finishing their coffee the true explanation came to Fredericka: Christopher's nose was a little out of joint. He had enlisted like a hero. It was his last weekend at home before his training began. He had wanted, unconsciously perhaps, to be the center, and the attention had been stolen from him by a stranger. No matter what the stranger had been through, no matter how he might need care and kindness, Christopher could not relinquish the spotlight graciously.

Chapter Sixteen

WHEN CHRISTOPHER LEFT FOR Washington Fredericka went with him as far as New York. They had both tried to persuade Aunt Palm to come along for the trip. She stubbornly refused.

"I'll be glad to be alone in the house," she had said. She spoke almost irritably. Fredericka understood, but Christopher stiffened visibly. After all, Fredericka could imagine him thinking, the house was his, left to him by his father. He did not care for the tacit implication that he was in his mother's way.

But he was determined to be kind. "You're going to have a lot of time alone," he protested. He turned to Fredericka, including her. "Both of you. I'm afraid you'll start living like a pair of hermits."

A number of times in his last days at home he spoke solicitously to Fredericka of her possible loneliness—the isolation of Wrenkill and their lives on the Perry hilltop. His new attitude sprang, Fredericka felt sure, from his inner rejoicing at his own escape, and the shame he felt at recognizing his relief over getting away from the cramped Wrenkill life and its prescribed round of small duties.

"What you cannot seem to understand," Aunt Palm had replied emphatically at the last of these conversations, "is this: I do not have enough time alone. I have never had enough. Every human creature needs more time alone."

Christopher said nothing more.

He and Fredericka went out to White Plains to spend the night with Helen and Robert. Christopher wanted to settle some business matters with his brother, who still had an interest in the family bank in Wrenkill, along with a wide net of other investments in everything from cosmetics to real estate. Robert's financial interests were being boomed by the war and he was in the happiest frame of mind since the pre-crash days of the twenties.

His wife, Helen, who was mildly neurotic in a chic way, who had no children and spent her days in a round of social activities as far-flung as her husband's business interests, had also been helped by the war. "I'm feeling so useful," she told Fredericka, describing her work as a nurse's aide, an ambulance driver for the Red Cross, an assistant at the Blood Bank. She insisted on taking Fredericka to the tailor with her to see the fit and cut of a new uniform, to the Red Cross to give a pint of blood, and to visit the children's home of which she was a board member. On the way back, without an apparent qualm, she picked up her black market butter and bacon. She said she felt, with all that she and Robert were doing for the war effort, they "deserved" some of the creature comforts to which they were accustomed.

Helen was a continuous source of astonishment to Fredericka, for she read every new book, saw every new play, went to any concert that commanded unusual critical attention, and to all the openings at the Museum of Modern Art where she regularly collected autographs from stage and screen celebrities for her orphans. In spite of—or because of

—all she saw, read, heard, and did, she was a woman without a point of view, without a single solid opinion. Although she had a lot of information she had nothing that could pass for knowledge. Her friends in Westchester seemed, to Fredericka, to be cut on the same pattern. They were not unlike the circle to which Bridgie belonged upstate, only they were more knowing, because nearer the Big City, and certainly more smart. Why these women frightened Fredericka she could not say, but in the presence of Helen's acquaintances she was invariably tongue-tied.

Helen could even outtalk Fredericka on her own subject, painting. She was more glib with all the new patter and with the little stories that regularly circulate about the more unconventional characters among artists. She had little conversational tidbits on Picasso, Tchelichew, Dali, Sandy Calder, and the Diego Riveras. Two of her classmates from Brearley had opened, some years before, a gallery which had sold modern reproductions, "matched" to your carpets and draperies. Helen had made a small investment in the business and this had brought her into what she thought of as the world of art. When the war made it difficult to get new materials the girls had had to start selling originals by modestly priced beginners who could imitate a Braque, a Klee, a Matisse quite creditably.

Fredericka had gone once with Helen to a sherry-drinking opening in the two large sunny rooms of this gallery in a 57th Street building. There she had witnessed the spectacle of a young man, whose name was something lyrical and alliterative like Bevin Bede, circulating haggardly among the mink coats, replying in flutelike monosyllables to the questions timidly or aggressively put to him by his possible patrons.

Helen had had it in her mind to get Fredericka "started" as

a promising unknown. Fredericka's very palms had sweated in terror at the thought that she might find herself trapped into declaring a wish to be shown sometime in this gallery. She had managed in the end to evade it quite easily. There had obviously been nothing about her manner, appearance, remarks, to make either of these shrewd-eyed women in their late thirties consider her a good financial risk.

"I still think you could be a *succès fou* if you played it the right way," Helen had said on their way to the Blood Bank Fredericka's first morning in White Plains.

Fredericka let this pass with a vague murmur of "*Succès fou?*"

Helen spattered her small talk with the more commonplace French phrases: *pas de tout, bon mot, pied-à-terre, merveilleuse, tant pis, tant mieux*. She was always the first person to take up any new phrase and the first to drop it. Some years back she had gone through the "making" period: "sick-making," "blush-making . . ." This had been followed by the "but" period: "but definitely," "but divine." People of her acquaintance were "dream men" "he men" "wolf men," "glamour pusses," "witch-bitches," and the "mother type." They were "monstrous," "shocking," "fabulous" and "dreary." Without a quiver she would introduce into the simplest conversation such a word as "panache." She had just picked up a new adjective from someone. It was "lamentable." Fredericka counted thirty uses of it in a day and a half and then stopped counting.

In spite of Helen's scattered wits, her lack of a fixed center, Fredericka did not dislike her. She was warmhearted and generous. When, since Robert was in such an expansive mood, Fredericka dared bring up the subject of the mountain goat horns Uncle Philander wanted so much, it was

Helen who cried at once, "Oh, let the old dear have them! Everyone here has seen them." Biting the finger on which he wore the ring with the d'Abbeville seal, Robert, who hated to relinquish anything in his possession, reluctantly agreed to send the goats' horns to Sprague's Eddy for Uncle Philander's birthday surprise.

The picture of reluctant Robert biting the finger with the seal ring came back to Fredericka the next day when she stood at the train gates waiting for Christopher to tell the porter how to carry his bags. Caution! A Perry trait. When Christopher had made certain that the bag with the liquor was on top, he turned to Fredericka to kiss her goodbye.

"Goodbye, darling. I don't think they'll keep me long in Florida. But you never know. Wish me luck."

"Oh, I do. Take care of yourself, darling."

"And you. Don't let Mother get out of hand. Tell the kids to write me."

"Don't worry about Aunt Palm . . . I'll remind them . . . Goodbye, darling."

They embraced. He went through the gates, turning once to wave, walking off down the grimy platform in his fresh tropical worsted. Fredericka stood and watched him until he disappeared into the train. Then she turned squarely around from the gates and took a long deliberate breath. Christopher was gone! She walked slowly through the vast crowded and noisy rooms of the Pennsylvania Station, so full of accelerated life, of greeting and farewell, of coming and going, sleeping and eating, meeting and waiting to the rhythm of war—a new community consciousness. As she moved through the knots of people—joyful, tender, sad, or desperate—she had the sensation that something was dropping from her, falling away, moving backwards from her in time, disappearing as definitely as Christopher had disappeared into the door of the train moving now through the hidden tunnels below, carrying her husband to an unfamiliar life that she was not to share.

Now she too might create something new. It was stirring within her—a growing sense of release. The mood quickened to elation as she stood alone in the middle of her small hotel room and tried to touch the walls on both sides—and almost succeeded. She felt concentrated and contained within this limited space, and at the same time boundlessly free. What more does one want than this? she thought, stretching her arms out again, then above her head as far as she could, a long free and full stretch.

She would have liked to stop and abandon herself to this unaccustomed sensation of freedom, but she had a shopping list several inches long. She left her bags untouched and went out again into the bright hurrying streets that now seemed to her full of fresh excitements and adventures.

On her shopping list, at the top, was written: *Uncle Philander's salad oil*. It was the least important item but she decided arbitrarily to get it first, since it might lead her into unfamiliar places. "Any health food shop will do," he had said when he telephoned her about it from Sprague's Eddy. "There's one every other block."

As she came along the street near lunchtime her eye was caught by a sign: VITAMIN BAR AND HEALTH FOODS. She turned and entered. People were eating at a counter that ran the length of the small room. Fredericka took the one vacant stool, thinking to herself, "It will make a story for Aunt Palm."

"What will it be?" asked the thin woman behind the "bar"

with the blotchy skin, the determinedly happy expression, girlish air, and ravaged face of a fanatic. Her yellow red-brown hair was worn to the shoulders (Mary Pickford in *The Little Sweetheart*, thought Fredericka) and held behind with her mother's old tortoise-shell barrette (practically an heirloom).

"What will it be?" she repeated a little testily.

"I don't know yet," Fredericka said timidly. "Have you a menu?"

At this question all the occupants of the other stools cast her a collective glance of suspicion and amazement. Ordering the cream cheese on date-nut bread, the coffee substitute, Fredericka wondered why. It did not take her long to discover. Everyone who entered here came for a specific purpose. They had the passwords.

"Juice," the devotees said immediately on entering. Or, "Stewed apricots and wheat germ." Or, "Any strawberry yogurt today?"

"Juice," though the menu must have listed ten, seemed to mean just one thing to the patrons of the Vitamin Bar. At the utterance of this magic word the proprietress—or priestess—drew on a large rubber glove, which made Fredericka think of doctors' offices, opened an icebox below the counter and took out of it a large bunch of parsley, two stalks of celery, some beets and carrots. These vegetables she fed into the open maw of an electric grinder, after which there issued, from a hole in its side, the most unpleasant-looking liquid Fredericka had ever seen. She had, indeed, to avert her gaze from its bile-green and blood-red drool. The woman on the next stool drank a glass of this life-giving fluid, accompanied by three unappetizing corn-plaster wafers, and spooned down with loving attention a double helping of yogurt with honey and cinnamon, all the time gazing fixedly at a sign propped against two small jars, filled with what appeared to be eye salve, reading AVOID CONSTIPATION.

It was a little like neurotic children playing at keeping store, Fredericka thought. The priestess, or First Voice, passed on her order to the Second Voice, a very old woman with a palsied hand who slowly made her way to the rear and repeated the order in a genteel whisper behind a partition—for this was the Nonvital, or Less Vital, department, hidden back in the darkness. Eventually there emerged from this secret chamber a sullen Negress (allowed to play with the other children by special privilege) bearing Fredericka's sandwich on a large plate. She clumped the length of the room and flung it down on the counter as though she were ringing a suspect silver dollar in a far-western gambling dive.

Oh, Fredericka thought, paying her lunch check and buying Uncle Philander's salad oil, how good to be out again in the pleasantly germ-filled air! How wonderful a big city is, how beautiful, terrible, depressing, and wonderful! And I wish I were twenty-two again, she thought, seeing the three WAVES swinging past in their trim dark blue, with their over-shoulder bags and jaunty hats. Twenty-two, and just beginning. Beginning what?

She looked at everyone she passed until she was tired from using her eyes. She studied especially the fashionable women with their pointed faces gaunt with hunger, lean as laths under dotted veils of deceptive feminity; their hips deprived of middle-aged bulge by forms of discipline and rites of denial comparable only to medieval saints and early Christian ascetics. . . . How do I look to them? she wondered, and laughed at herself, realizing that since they were city people they would not look, would not see. For no eye meets another in the hurrying crowds of Fifth Avenue, of Madison, Lexington, or Park, because everyone is hording his little stock of energy against all subtle tricks of depletion. Eyes meet eyes only near the end of day, over two dry Martinis in a darkened room; then the eyes search and wander, furtively, fervently seeking the lost life, the life unspent or misspent. . . .

"You're looking particularly fit," Robert told her when they met at five-thirty in what he called his "favorite saloon." They were waiting for Helen, due in from White Plains at six for more drinks, a dinner in an air-cooled restaurant, a show in an air-cooled theater.

"I was wondering today how I looked to city people," Fredericka began.

"Look to city people?" he asked, amused, popping salted nuts one after another into his open mouth. "You mean would they notice the hay sticking out of your hair?"

"Something like that."

"The only difference any more between a smart city woman and a smart woman from a small town is that the small-town woman has more natural color in her face," said Robert authoritatively, wiping his soft white hands on his oversized linen handkerchief.

"Is that the only difference?"

"Positively."

"Hello, hello." It was Helen, lean as a stick, sharp as a needle, got up to look like a Vertes drawing, all line, no mass . . . At once Fredericka felt like the southern heroine of nameless novels, in her flowered print dress with lace at the neck and a hat with flowers on it.

"How garden partyish you look," Helen remarked. But

she said it without any sting. "You're the prettiest of the lot, Fredericka."

"The lot?" Fredericka said. "There were only two girls, remember—unless you mean to include the boys."

"I mean prettier than Bridgie, though she has her points too. It's Palm who has the face, though. My God, what a face! She looks like something that should hang in the Frick —I mean, you know, like a famous portrait. . . . Double Martini, please, and extra dry, no olive—just a squeeze of lemon rind, but don't put in any peel . . . No, wait a minute. Is that a Daiquiri, Flea?"

"Yes."

"Is it good?"

"It tastes all right to me."

"Then make it a double Daiquiri."

As the waiter left, "You needn't ask 'Is it good?' about any drinks here," Robert said disapprovingly. "It's the best liquor in town."

"I know," Helen said. "But it doesn't do any harm to inquire."

Robert was constantly nodding and speaking to the people who groped their way into the dark interior from the bright street outside. It was something like a club, Fredericka decided, or like an English pub where the men of the neighborhood drop in for their liquor. These nodding acquaintances of Robert's were all men with the same kind of faces—tense, concentrated forcibly at the front of the skull, and yet curiously without strength or true masculinity. They seemed to Fredericka to be faces without profile, as empty as though they had been frozen at one time in a permanent expression of attentiveness, after which the animating spirit had departed, leaving behind only the mask to rule the life of its owner. With liquor these faces grew looser, without acquiring animation. The lips merely slackened, the planes of the faces dropped, the eyes dilated, the lids drooped.

"What *are* you looking at?" Helen demanded, challenging Fredericka's abstracted and distant air.

"Faces," Fredericka said, starting slightly. "I wish I could do faces better."

"It must be fascinating," Helen murmured indifferently. "Painting, I mean. I still think you could—with the right start—make a place for yourself in this town. You know, maybe through someone on *Town and Country* or *Vogue* or some other smart magazine, you could get some publicity. We might persuade someone to go up and take pictures of Uncle Caleb's monstrosity in Wrenkill. It's such a fabulous bit of Gothic horror, and that kind of thing is the vogue now. Pratty Leon, the composer—you know he's the one that did that incredible score for that long poem of Auden's—I think it was Auden's—anyway, he has his whole house done in Victorian. And he's started collecting the Hudson River school. You know how they've been neglected. *Fortune* had a piece on it—the neglect, I mean. It's incredible! The effect of an Eakins alongside a Morris Graves. You wouldn't believe it. Pratty has a little room he calls a Snuggery. It's all done in lime and cerise, with blue satin drapes. You may think it sounds awful but I can tell you it looks like a set for a ballet, on the small scale. You know I told you, Robbo, what Gertrude Vance said—Freudian slip—when she saw the snuggery. 'Snuggery-buggery.' She said he pretended not to notice and she just pretended she was feeling her liquor. . . . You know the more I think about you, Flea, the clearer I can see it. No one has ever discovered 'upstate' and it's something pretty special, I think—all that perverted classicism. . . ."

Her own phrase stopped the torrent. "Perverted classicism. My God!" she cried. "That's precisely what it is. *Precisely!* And you've painted it yourself. Or Aunt Palm has. One of you has a painting of that front porch and that watchtower . . ."

"That's Aunt Palm," Fredericka said. "I think Aunt Palm would be your *succès fou* if only you could pry her out of Wrenkill."

But Helen had exhausted her interest in the subject of Fredericka's career in painting. She pushed her bony left arm under the little lamp on their table and nearsightedly gazed at the crystal watch, one of the numerous dangles she always wore. These dangles and bangles, depending from a series of gold chains on her left wrist, were constantly clanking and smiting one another with nervous disharmony as she moved.

"Drink up!" she cried in horror. "Drink up! Or we're going to have to rush with dinner, and I loathe missing the curtain on a serious play. It doesn't matter with a musical comedy, but with a Barry play . . ."

The Museum of Modern Art was having a show of its own possessions—room after room of the dreams and fancies, the memories and anticipations, the fears and aspirations of modern men. Fredericka spent her second morning wandering slowly through the rooms, half looking at the paintings, half watching the people who, drawn by honest interest, by curiosity, by love of art, by wish to scoff, shuffled through the galleries. They pointed, they thrust elbows, they murmured, exclaimed, giggled . . .

She herself was affected by the miscellaneous paintings in a fresh way, like one who returns to familiar haunts after a long absence. In the room with the early works of Cubists not many people lingered. The once controversial abstractions hanging there seemed now to Fredericka remote and dead, as though they belonged to a world much further removed in feeling than it actually was in time. Strange, she thought, that serene dismemberments of fruit, machines, guitars, and plaster casts from antiquity, composed together, could ever have been so angering and upsetting to the public.

For now emotional response, like a hidden dark river, flowed through other rooms where a new type of violence was most cunningly and terribly set forth. People paused to gaze, compelled, at paintings which displayed the naked vulnerable world of human flesh, blood and bone.

Little knots of troubled people stood, silent, before a painting called "Hide and Seek." What did the title mean? Who could say? Perhaps the artist and perhaps not. It did not matter. Its effect was that of an ancient true tale of horror told in a language vague and poetic, at the same time as exact as the language of science and nature. Here was a tree. The tree of life? Behind and through the veil of artery, muscle, and entrail, of vein, leaf, wing, and web, there appeared and disappeared to Fredericka—now dimly, now strongly, sometimes as horrible as decay and mutilation, again as beautiful as butterflies or flowers—the bloody head of death and the bloody head of birth. Children, babies—dead ones with swollen bellies, great skulls, and shriveled legs, fetal ones with the same dominant skull and frail extremities . . .

"Echo of a Scream," another canvas, and the baby in his blood-red shift emerges screaming with furrowed brow from his own great screaming head swollen to gigantic proportions, huge, monstrous, against the leaden sky of death. Today, thought Fredericka, the artist uses the child as a symbol of death. Once it had been the Divine Child, cradled in straw, surrounded by light—the symbol of eternal life. Now it is the human child howling in terror, bleeding, dying unborn, dying with violence, ripped from his mother with the demoniac strength of unseen nameless forces. . . .

Death. Everywhere death. "Collective Suicide," a painting from as long ago as 1936, with the little separate semiattached paintings at the bottom of the canvas showing, as in old tales, death by men with lances and helmets, tumbling idols in the legendary lands of the American South. The large main canvas above these semiseparate painted tales was merely a formless wash of strong colors, red and black, as from burning volcanoes, with a sickly central wash, sulphurous and vaporous— a great whirling, spiraling, moving shapelessness in which you expected to see appearing the wraiths of things recently alive.

Standing before this canvas Fredericka thought of Franz's words at the lake that sunny Sunday. . . . "We, all men, will have the choice, of collective life or collective death." And she heard Aunt Palm saying, as she so frequently did, "Art is prophecy."

Fredericka turned away feeling suddenly cold and sick. Wandering, aimlessly looking, she passed a canvas called "Time Is a River without Banks." A fish with flaming wings flew in a bright blue sky, above an old wooden clock with a long swinging pendulum of gold. From the fish's belly depended an arm with a fiddle. On the blue banks of the river a boy and a girl lay together, and little houses faded in the blue distance.

Fredericka's imagination began to stir. She decided that she would do a painting and call it by the name of some daring new formula in physics. She would ask Franz for a formula—one that stood for the mystery of the x force in living things. She would paint the three-legged dog outside the Wrenkill bank, and the skeleton of a leaf with a Buddhist prayer inked on it. She would show the Egyptian pyramids rising into the air as though by magic, as Aunt Palm had implied they did, and twentieth century rockets propelled by robots into a sky from which the bodies of young men dropped as unheeded as the body of Icarus in the old painting by Breughel. In this same sky, minute formulae from chemistry and physics would float about like the little insects, the fantastic beetles, of Bosch. . . .

The imaginary canvas grew to gigantic size, and although she knew that she would never paint it, she wished suddenly to be at home and at her work again.

Her impatience was so strong that she left the museum, packed her bags, and took the afternoon train to Wrenkill. As she traveled slowly up the green valleys of New York State everything out the windows seemed to her to be paintable, everything from the green hillsides with their strong-rumped horses, white fences, gracious houses, bright figures moving through the middle distance, to the grimy depots and the gray streets thinning off into cramped neighborhoods with ugly airless dwellings in which, she knew so well, only the ceaseless voice of the radio would ever stir the static atoms.

How alive I feel! she thought to herself as she rode along, looking out the windows. She saw Franz Allers lifting up his foot before his class in Attica Center that first day, regarding it with a look of mingled wonder and delight. "I am alive!" he had said.

Chapter Seventeen

IN THE NEXT WEEKS FREDERICKA'S life filled gently like a cup held in a spring. She could not remember ever before when she had been so happy and so full of energy. She had returned to painting with a joy and concentration that amazed her, for it came so easily, this return, though she had expected she would find it necessary to lay disciplines upon herself in order to keep her resolve to work every day without fail.

She went twice a week to Attica Center, eager for Farrell's word, eager also for Franz Allers' eye upon her canvases, and for his comment, which she had discovered to be invariably perceptive, original, pertinent.

"You must work, work, work," he said to her on his second Sunday visit to Wrenkill, three weeks after Christopher left. They were in the attic going through her old paintings—some that dated back as far as her teens when she had first bought expensive canvases and paints and spoken haltingly of a "career."

You must work, work, work, she would repeat to herself in the mornings after that, rushing through her errands and the small household tasks that fell to her, eager to be at her canvas. You must work, work, work!

"But for what?" she had nonetheless asked Franz when he said it, for she still believed that you must work *for* something. "For a show?" she had asked him. "For a New York show?"

The look he had given her was blended of faint amusement, patience, sadness. "Just work," he said, "work, and 'what for' will become apparent—if, that is, the work springs out of your true nature."

"Your true nature." These were the casual phrases to which Fredericka's ear never grew quite accustomed. There appeared always a challenge in them, a ring of some special awareness. This was the quality his lectures held for her also. Perhaps she was not learning much about what was called, in the textbooks, history, but she had begun to perceive certain truths about human creatures, about man who has made the thing called history.

She found herself reading the daily papers with unusual attention and concentration. Parts of the European world that had seemed dim to her, remote, without reality, took on meaning because Franz Allers had been there, or knew someone who was still there. On the days that she went to Attica Center she either lunched with him or stayed to have dinner. They drove out frequently just a short distance to the view of the lake, and sat there on the hill smoking and talking. They had drifted tacitly into these arrangements. Without being committed to the pattern they found it suddenly there, taken for granted by them both.

Time became for Fredericka a new experience. When looked at in one way the period during which she had known Franz Allers seemed to stretch to phenomenal length, like a lifetime. Viewed in another way it contracted to a flash, a breath. Actually it was not quite three months. At moments it seemed to her that they were both waiting for some outside force that would propel into the open the unexpressed emotion existing between them. She was sure Franz felt as committed as she to this power which lay outside their own wills.

With different shades of emphasis, curiosity, and question, her family and her friends observed the change in Fredericka. Bridgie was all warm interest.

"What's happened to you, Flea? You look as though you'd found a secret formula for health and happiness?"

"Little pink pills," Fredericka managed to say lightly.

"No, honestly, what is it?" Bridgie persisted. Her persistence meant that she had no real clue. Had she suspected she would have been silent, or else more direct.

"I'm painting again," Fredericka said. "I'm at work."

"Then you should certainly keep at it," Owen put in. "Bridgie's right—you do look as though you'd found some special hormone."

"Mercy!" Fredericka felt herself growing red.

"Your color is improved," her father said, looking up from his newspaper at just that moment. "I thought you were looking a little pale this winter."

"You are all embarrassing me," Fredericka protested. "I must have been looking fearfully seedy. I thought you told me early this spring right in this room, Bridgie, how well I looked."

"I did, but that was different. That was smart—this is revitalized, like having a baby."

"Painting is having a baby with me," Fredericka said. "That's what only Aunt Palm has ever understood."

Bridgie gave her a long solemn look. "I know. I do think maybe you should have done more of it, Flea darling."

"I'm sure of it."

Even that phrase shows the change in me, Fredericka thought, driving on from Thermopylae to Wrenkill through the slow twilight. She could not remember when—if ever—she had spoken so aggressively.

The family were not alone in their comments.

"Widowhood is certainly agreeing with you," Cliff Keynes said, meeting her one morning in the bank. "Never saw you looking better." He gave her elbow a warm lingering squeeze.

The gesture, and similar ones, were quite automatic with Cliff. Fredericka, personally, had never believed that his constant tacit invitation to secret embraces was more than an unconscious gesture, born of a frustrated life with his cold wife Laura. Fredericka had always been able to treat these stereotyped advances with the accepted blending of good humor and indifference. But this morning his dog's eyes, moistly protuberant as though they had been recently poached, affected her unpleasantly. She withdrew her elbow with unusual firmness.

"Don't be sore, Freddy," he said instantly, looking as though he had been struck. "I meant it as a compliment."

"I'm not sore," Fredericka said quickly. She regretted that she had revealed any feeling. But what were her feelings? And why had she responded so quickly to an intimation that she was looking improved in Christopher's absence? I acted guilty, she thought after she had left him. And actually there is nothing at all to be guilty about. Certainly I can have a friendship with an interesting man without having to explain to everyone I know that it is quite innocent, can't I?

She was unreasonably annoyed; resentful of the inevitable intrusion of Christopher's friends into her new life.

The fourth time Franz came to Wrenkill for Sunday the Gilberts dropped in from Spartanville late in the afternoon and found him in the garden alone with Fredericka. They were the first of the local group to meet him. They seemed to accept his presence with perfect casualness, but three days later, down in the town, Fredericka ran into Joe and Merry Barrett in the bank and Joe at once began:

"Say, Freddy, who's this long-hair I hear you've been entertaining?"

"Long-hair?" Fredericka asked. She knew instantly whom he meant but she pretended not to.

"A long-haired refugee from Attica Center."

"Oh, you mean Dr. Franz Allers."

"Yeah, that's the name. Big-shot intellectual, I understand. Going highbrow on us during Chris's absence?" His tone was teasing and light, but there was something in his eyes that denied the tone—a look that was ugly, venomous, envious.

Although she saw the look plainly, Fredericka tried to assure herself that good-natured little Joe could mean nothing wrong. He had always liked to tease. She tried to reply with friendly casualness.

"Dr. Allers is an old friend of Louis's. I hope you'll meet him sometime." Her look included Merry who was standing with her hands in her coat pockets, aggressively, a little challengingly.

"Yes, I'd like to," Merry said coolly. "Bridgie says he's fascinating," she added pointedly.

"You know it's not fair to keep a bona fide intellectual in hiding," Joe went on. "Not from Merry's club members. You know—the Girls with Ideas."

"That's right," Fredericka said, determined to keep it light. "I hadn't thought of that. They represent the local intelligentsia, not I."

"Well, ask us around," Joe suggested.

"Yes, do," Merry pressed. "We all enjoy a change of face from time to time."

"We are an incestuous lot, aren't we?" Fredericka remarked. She regretted the word at once. It was almost too true when she thought of Christopher and herself—first cousins. . . .

"The truth is, Flea," Joe said in a lowered voice after Merry had gone over to the cashier's cage to draw out some money, "I don't give a damn about the long-hair, but I do miss seeing you. We never see you any more with Chris gone."

"Why, Joe," Fredericka began. She was embarrassed by his voice, which had grown a shade too intimate. Her immediate discomfiture was not lost on Joe. In a heartier and more impersonal tone he went on:

"Had a letter from the old boy a few days ago—Chris. He seems to be having a whale of a time—new-lease-on-life department. Wish to heck I could make the break. I need a change of scene myself."

After she had left them Fredericka was troubled and annoyed. She felt that she should ask these old friends to meet Franz Allers and she did not want to. There was something about their sudden interest that seemed to her furtive and prying.

"Shall I have Dr. Allers over to meet Christopher's friends?" she asked Aunt Palm that afternoon.

"What for?"

"Well, I see him quite frequently, and they might wonder why—why I never introduced them." She was being very lame.

"Rubbish and rot!" said Aunt Palm. "Why bore the man any more than he is already bored?"

"Oh, I hoped you'd say that," Fredericka cried happily.

Aunt Palm gave her a long penetrating look.

"Do you really depend on my advice, lovie?" she asked.

She used the old pet name but her voice was not gentle. It was troubled and faintly stern.

"A great deal," Fredericka said at once.

"That is too bad," Aunt Palm said. She looked grave and concerned. "Too bad," she repeated.

"Why?" Fredericka asked. "Why shouldn't I? I've depended on you all my life . . ."

Aunt Palm rose and went out of the room as though she did not care to hear the rest of it.

Although Fredericka could not face a meeting between Franz Allers and her Wrenkill friends, she found no hesitation in inviting him, at Farrell's request, to dine with Farrell and his wife one night just after the beginning of the summer session.

The Farrells lived in a built-over barn several miles from the campus. The house was charming in a slapdash untidy style that would once have been called Bohemian.

The Farrells enjoyed with shameless gusto such simple pleasures of living as good wine and good food. Maria Farrell's culinary triumphs appeared on the table in ample earthenware casseroles, unfamiliar enticing confusions of chicken, rice, garlic, saffron, onions, chilies, tomatoes, parsley. You washed down the spicy mouthfuls with swallows of claret while Maria, ladling out more pollo, tossing the salad, would minimize her efforts with a shrug of the shoulders. "Very easy! Only be sure the spoon is wooden, and only a charcoal fire, of course, and not more than a half-inch piece of saffron . . ."

Since gas rationing Maria seldom got out, except by bicycle, and she was full of pent-up Spanish energy. After supper, when the wine and the chilies had begun to have their enlivening effect, she took down her high-piled black hair and danced flamenco dances to the music from scratched and cracked imported phonograph records that, like every object in the Farrell household, had been much lived with and seldom dusted.

Farrell enjoyed seeing his wife yielding to her emotions. "Bravo!" he cried, applauding the spectacle of Maria stamping, arching, looking alternately cruel and tender. "We'll get José," he cried, and went to telephone the local teacher of Spanish who, in a surprisingly short time, appeared in the doorway carrying a guitar almost as big as he was. José Bardo, dusky and bright-eyed as a Goya, played steadily for an hour —Spanish songs high and thin as a reedy wind, lonely as a sunset in the desert. Then he moved eastward across Europe, singing as he moved, until he came at last to the green Germanic forests where he paused and politely asked Franz to make a suggestion. They sang a duet together: "Grün ist die Heide."

The faces of the two men came close together in the candle-light as they harmonized. Fredericka studied them, wishing they might be painted, naturalistically but without banality, for it was a strangely moving sight: two men of different blood and impulse, of different history and fate, sitting together in a dimly lighted room, their heads close together, singing two parts of the same song. Their faces were very unlike—the Spaniard's dark, round, full-cheeked, liquid-eyed, the glance warm yet veiled; the Austrian's fair-skinned, lean, angular, the eyes guarded, yet the glance paradoxically direct and penetrating. One was like a ripe fruit, the other like the prow of a ship, the wing of a bird, any outgoing form in motion. . . .

The slow-swinging yearning phrases of the song brought

Fredericka close to tears. She could see even Franz Allers struggling not to show his emotion.

"I remember the beggars singing it, outside the windows in the winter, the young boys out of work," he said when they had finished. It was almost as though he spoke of the beggars to break other associations, memories of green earth, of sweet wild places in a landscape from which he was now exiled.

"I want you to look at a painting of mine," Farrell cried abruptly, jumping up. "I've shown Fredericka. She was good enough to say . . . Just a minute. I'd like your opinion."

He rushed out of the room. Fredericka turned her face away so that no one would see how moved she was. Farrell had spoken of her opinion as though he valued it!

He was back in a moment with his painting, the one of the gloved hand and the broken man opposite.

At her first glimpse of this canvas Maria jumped to her feet and rushed at her husband. "No, no, no!" she cried vehemently. "Not that! Positively not that! We must not look at that picture. It will change all the evening. No, no, no!" She seized Farrell's arm and held it in a firm grip. He looked down at her astonished, for a moment indecisive, then half laughing, with a shrug, "All right, conchita! Don't work yourself up."

"We are singing tonight," Maria cried with passion. "Only singing! That is what we do tonight. What shall we sing, Fredericka? It is your turn to say."

"I love 'Shenandoah,'" Fredericka said. She hummed a bar or two. "Do you know it?" she asked José Bardo.

"But of course." He began to play and sing it.

"I must learn that one," Franz cried. He was eager, relaxed, showing a side of his nature which Fredericka had not seen before. They taught him the song, all of them singing together. He had a quick ear and a good voice, deep, rich, and melodious.

"I thought it was 'Shanandore,' " said the Spanish teacher, when they sang it together for the last time.

Fredericka laughed. "There's been many an argument about that song at our house. Uncle Philander insists it's called 'The Wide Mizzoura.' "

"The Wide Mizzoura," Franz Allers repeated. "The Great Open Spaces, The Lone Star Trail . . . What a country! This summer I mean to go west."

It was his first mention of leaving. Fredericka's heart did a sudden jump.

"Oh, you must!" Maria Farrell cried. "To the Southwest, eh, Farrell? That he must surely see."

"It's a painter's country," Farrell began.

"A poet's country," Maria added.

"Then, perhaps," Franz said, "it may be the country for a tired—philosopher."

Fredericka was seated next to him on one of the wide soft couches that appeared to be everywhere in the Farrell house, couches that made upright positions impossible, so that you found yourself lolling on pillows whether you wanted to or not. ("Half-reclining people act themselves," Farrell had said once. "The theory is perfectly sound really. Don't analysts put their patients flat on their backs? It stirs up the subconscious." "People always say here with us, I talked too much," Maria had added laughing. "It is partly the wine, partly the couches.")

To her own surprise Fredericka heard herself announcing, "I will now say that I am mildly tippled."

"Oh, how lovely!" cried Maria, clasping her hands together

joyfully as though she had heard some long-awaited good news. "How lovely! For now I shall no longer be afraid of you."

"Afraid of me?" Fredericka asked in astonishment.

Franz Allers turned to look at her, smiling.

"Yes," Maria rushed on, "afraid of you. You were always so—so stiff, so well brought up."

"Don't pay any attention to Maria," Farrell said, lazily. "She's a gypsy. How about some Mexican songs, José?"

José began to play "Cielito Lindo." Maria rose and put out all the lights except the candles that stood on the long table where they had eaten supper. Half reclining next to Franz Allers, who was humming almost below his breath as he tried to learn the melodies, Fredericka, with her eyes closed, saw them all—Farrell, Maria, José, Franz, herself—dressed like conquistadors, kneeling to drink from a fountain among rocks, in a distant pink desert, a fountain of new life. These are my people, she thought. Here I belong. Why have I not lived among them all my life? She thought back, through the cloud of the wine and the music, to the feelings she had had long ago as an undergraduate when Farrell first brought his Spanish bride to the campus, with her untidy hair, her exuberant ways, and her extravagant speech. People had laughed at her, then avoided her.

"They're a touch on the Greenwich Village side, aren't they?" Christopher had remarked, the one time she invited the Farrells to Sunday lunch at the lake, years ago. "A little too Left Bank for my taste," he had added.

She remembered how annoyed she had been.

"Just because they weren't interested in your talk with Robert about the stock market . . ." (For Robert and Helen had been there that weekend. It was just before the crash.

Robert had said it wasn't going to happen. There was nothing to stop the market going on and on, climbing. They had all argued about it—Uncle Caleb, Robert, Christopher, even Philander. The Farrells, who obviously had no investments of any kind, had looked bewildered and amused. Feeling distinctly out of it, they had both drunk a little too much. Aunt Palm, who liked Farrell, had asked to be excused from the table, pleading a headache. Envying her with all her being Fredericka had shot her an accusing look. Deserter! . . . Well, it had been a social fiasco of the first order. She never had the Farrells again when Christopher was at home.)

"Don't forget," he had replied cuttingly to her remark about the stock market, "that it is businessmen who endow that chair at Attica Center that Farrell parks his behind on. And it's Business with a capital B that lets him teach useless daubing to a bunch of undergraduates . . ."

"Useless?" Fredericka had begun hotly. But she had not continued. "Useless!" she repeated in another key. She meant to convey: Useless to discuss the subject with the prejudiced. And Christopher was prejudiced. He disliked painting. He considered it a waste of time.

The wine was having a curious effect; her head seemed woolly on top but clear underneath, exceptionally clear, as though she were seeing far far down into her mind. I did not openly oppose Christopher's attitude on painting because I felt guilty. I felt guilty because—because I had married him. Was that really it? And the only way to make up for what I had done was to subtly pretend to accept the life that was natural to him.

The shock of this discovery sobered her for a moment, until the swinging sensual melodies carried her off again into vague longings.

If only she could move without delay into a new world, a world of painters, poets, philosophers; *this* world, where even old songs, folk songs, sung of a Sunday evening in childhood, were a part of an ever-growing, ever-expanding consciousness of—of what? Again, as so often, she was stopped short in her idle thinking, and could not find the word for which she groped.

Now José had finally put away the guitar and they were all talking. About Soviet Russia. How strong was she, they were asking. Franz thought, very. (Christopher, Fredericka remembered, thought Russia was a big bluff.) She sat up on the pillows. Maria, making coffee with the door to the kitchen wide open, so that she could put in remarks from time to time, did not seem to mind this discussion, serious though it was. She did not interfere to stop it as she had interfered to prevent the showing of the canvas. This was wisdom, Fredericka decided, analyzing it. Maria had realized that the emotional impact of the painting would sadden them, perhaps bring painful memories to Franz. But this subject, the subject of Russia, though solemn, touched only the mind. It would not really depress them. A wise woman, Fredericka admitted humbly, a truly wise woman; and the sense of her own inadequacy washed over her. She felt that she was nothing—a neuter. Not truly a woman, yet certainly not a man. Not a wife, not a mother . . . Nothing.

The wish to pour out the story of her wasted years, along with the new and growing feeling of life and promise, thrust sharply into her consciousness. It was Franz Allers in whom she wished to confide. She longed to be driving with him alone into the night, for hours, moving through dark space as she talked and talked . . . But she was spending the night with the Farrells and he would soon be leaving. . . .

"You are very quiet."

His grave voice spoke beside her. The conversation had momentarily died. Farrell had gone upstairs to take a child to the bathroom. He could be heard crashing about overhead. Maria and José were singing in the kitchen. The water in the sink was running and Maria was holding the dinner dishes under the tap as she sang. Coffee was beginning to fill the living room with its strong dark scent.

"I think I was half asleep," Fredericka answered. She added impulsively, "I'm afraid I'm always half asleep."

He looked at her quietly, as though trying to decide if this was true. He put out his hand and covered hers briefly, gave it a reassuring warm grasp. He said nothing.

I love him, she thought to herself. I really love him. She remembered that he was going west.

"I envy you going west. I didn't know you were planning to go."

"I only just made up my mind."

"I do envy you," she repeated.

"Why not come along?"

She looked up, startled.

"Why not?" he repeated. He seemed quite serious. His eyes were perfectly calm and sure. Did he really mean it?

"I'd like nothing better," she was able to say lightly. "But I'm afraid I couldn't."

Maria was coming in with the coffee, calling to Farrell upstairs. Their moment together was over.

When he left, Franz took Maria's hand, held it a moment, bent over it and kissed it. "A beautiful evening!" he said. It was the first time Fredericka had seen him kiss anyone's hand. So he did not do it automatically.

He came next to Fredericka and as the Farrells were talk-

· 268 ·

ing and laughing with José he was able to say, taking Fredericka's hand, "Beautiful!" He meant that she was. His eyes
were warm, ardent . . . She saw him in that moment again
as a young man, as a man he might be again—strong, vital,
passionate, full of fire, of will and energy.

Chapter Eighteen

ON A SUNDAY IN JUNE, FRANZ was to come to Wrenkill for his last visit before going west. In the middle of that week Merry Barrett had called Fredericka to invite her to a dance at the country club in Spartanville on Saturday night. They had an extra man, a naval commander, a friend of Joe's. Bridgie and Owen were both coming. Fredericka simply couldn't say no!

Fredericka, in spite of Merry's protests that a negative reply was impossible, could have managed very easily to refuse, but because Franz Allers was coming on Sunday she agreed to come. When she hung up the receiver she tried to analyze her reaction. It seemed to her she had begun to practice some subtle form of deception that she did not understand herself.

It had been months, even years, since she had gone to a Saturday night dance. While Uncle Caleb lay ill for so long she had found an ever-ready excuse for not accepting. Christopher did not mind. He had never cared for these affairs. He preferred a good game of poker with a few of the boys in somebody's library.

Fredericka was surprised to find how little the country club pattern had changed from the first years of her marriage. There was the same elaborate pairing off of husbands and wives with other husbands and wives, as though it were an unforgivable breach of etiquette if anyone rode to or from the party with his life's partner. Drinking was heavy. There was the usual small talk, the usual "kidding." Fredericka came in for her full share.

"Flea's gone highbrow," Joe Barrett announced over cocktails. "She's joined the long-hairs in Attica Center."

"What's more she keeps them to herself," Merry put in with a falsely hearty air and a voice of good will but with cold and resentful eyes. She had come up to join Joe's baiting, carrying a tray of canapés. She made Fredericka think of a hunter closing in for the kill.

"I've been longing to meet Franz Allers ever since Bridgie told me about him," Merry added, offering the elaborate bits of olive, bacon, cheese, domestic caviar, and "baby franks" impaled on separate toothpicks. "But he wears an invisible cloak when he comes to Wrenkill, I guess." Her voice was thin and tinny.

"Heavens, what's so special about Dr. Allers?" Fredericka said, trying not to show her resentment. "He doesn't see many people, that's all. I mean he's very tired when he comes. I never plan anything. He always says he only wants to sit around and—"

"How does your aunt like him?" Merry asked. Her voice, her intonation indicated instead: What does he think of the mad relative?

"Very much," Fredericka said shortly.

"Now, Merry, don't be silly," Cliff Keynes put in. "What have we got to offer a European highbrow anyway? Hell, we're a bunch of lowbrows if ever I met any."

"You can speak for yourself, Cliff," his wife Laura said tartly. "I don't care to be called a lowbrow."

"That's right, Cliff. You're dead wrong!" Joe winked

elaborately through his shining lenses. "We married blue-stockings, don't you remember?" He pinched Merry's arm good-naturedly to let her know he was only kidding Cliff, the lunkhead, that he was actually proud of his wife's reputation as a local intellectual. And, hell, he could understand why she was sore at Fredericka Perry who had never even pretended to be interested in ideas, or the new books, or what was happening in Cuba, tracking down a bona fide European scholar and then never sharing him with the people who made up the community intelligentsia.

Bridgie and Owen had contributed nothing to the scene so far. Owen, as a matter of fact, was deep in conversation about something quite different. But Bridgie, Fredericka was aware, had been listening to every word. Now loyally she turned around to protect her sister.

"Flea's being absolutely candid. It's the truth. Franz Allers is sort of—well, remote in a way, you might say. He's not unfriendly or anything like that, but he just isn't much of a mixer, I don't believe. I really think he might even bore you unless you could really get him to talking. And of course he would never have come to Wrenkill in the first place if it hadn't been for knowing Louis so well in Europe."

"Well, it can't be Louis that keeps him coming," Joe whispered to Fredericka. He pinched her arm as he had just pinched Merry's, only furtively this time, trying to give Fredericka a special look through his glasses, a look archly accusing, as though saying, Don't try to fool me, old girl. I know you've got what it takes. You can't fool a sly old dog like Joe Barrett who has known you all your life.

Fredericka's boredom turned abruptly into sharp distaste. She felt she could not wait for the party to be over and cursed herself for not having brought her own car so that she could leave when she wished to.

Bridgie and Owen departed early without telling her. When she went to look for them and found them gone she was furious. She told herself it was all a part of a conspiracy to make her take part in local life. By eleven o'clock she could stand no more and she told Joe, who had hardly left her side all evening, she would have to go home, that she had not said anything about it but Aunt Palm was not well and she didn't like her alone in the house with only Eunice, in case she was really ill.

"Hell, the party's just warming up," Joe protested.

"I know. I hate doing it, Joe. Let me take your car," she suggested, "and you can drive home with Commander O'Brien. I'll pay you back the gas tomorrow."

"I'll speak to Merry," Joe said, hesitating.

"Don't urge her to leave," Fredericka begged. "I don't want to break up the party. I can go alone perfectly well. Please, Joe!"

Merry didn't want to go and said so. But she insisted that Joe take Fredericka home, and then come back.

"But the gas . . ." Fredericka began in protest.

"I don't have any gas worries," Joe said pointedly.

She was longing to be able to drive off by herself into the darkness, with the top down, the air blowing in her face, dispelling from her mind and her spirit the uncongenial atmosphere in which she had spent the last five hours. But instead here was Joe, slightly tippled, getting in, insisting on driving—and driving slowly—through the warm soft blanket of the June night.

As soon as they had turned out of the country club drive

he pulled her over nearer him with a rough gesture that he managed to make so offhand she could not openly resent it, though within her she stiffened in protest.

"Don't sit clear over there in the next county. I want to talk without making myself hoarse."

He began at once to reminisce about the "old days." "Do you remember?" he asked from time to time, but he didn't stop to find out whether she did or not. She let her thoughts drift, imagining—with an almost desperate longing to be there—her cool quiet room, the open windows, the night air coming in over the honeysuckle . . . But suddenly she was remembering a moment in childhood with Joe. She could smell the sour-sweet scent of crushed fern, in the jungle gloom under some low-growing willow where they had once played "house." She saw Joe beside her, panting. They had been running. They were hiding together as a part of some game. His eyes were pinned on her. It was before he wore glasses. There was a slight cast in his left eye. She could see it now as plainly as she had seen it then. And the pupils were mottled like the pebbles in a trout pool. There was something unfamiliar in his stare—and frightening. His breathing was not coming fast because he had been running. . . . The next thing she knew she had risen and bolted from the hiding place. At once Christopher, who was It, spied her. She hadn't thought of the incident from that day to this.

"And do you remember . . . Cripes!" Joe was saying, rolling his laugh a little tipsily on his tongue. "I was thinking about it just the other day, that time we went down to somebody's house in Wrenkill—what was the postmaster's name? Redding, wasn't it?—he had that big-busty blonde daughter who—well, anyway, I'm sure it was their place. It was her birthday party and her mother turned the whole thing over to the kids to run as I recall it, and that sexy little blonde—she was only fourteen but she started early—suggested post office. She meant business! Well, you and the other girls from our crowd had been told at home, no kissing games! But the boys were all set and Christopher was delegated to go and twist your arm and talk you into it. Remember?"

"Dimly," Fredericka answered, as distantly as she dared.

"But we played it anyway," Joe cried. "Ha! Ha! And I got you. I can still remember it."

They were pulling under the porte-cochere now and he stopped the car abruptly. At once the swelling chorus of the summer night came to them; rich, dark, secret, a song of the earth in full bloom.

"Flea," Joe said hoarsely. He turned and seized her awkwardly in his arms. For a moment she was too startled to move. "Flea," he repeated in the same unnatural voice. "I've always had a sneaker for you, and you know it. God, there's something about you—not like anyone else." He tried to pull her toward him again on the car seat. She pulled back violently.

"Joe!" she cried sharply. "Joe! Stop it!" She freed herself with a jerking movement. "Really, Joe," she said angrily, "what in the world has come over you?"

He was not at all abashed. He kept his face turned toward her in the pale light, grinning fatuously. "Nothing's come over me. I'm trying to tell you how I've felt about you for almost forty years."

"You mean you began in the cradle?" Fredericka asked acidly. She opened the door of the car.

"As soon as I was conscious of a girl, you were it," he said with drunken solemnity.

"You've been drinking too much! It's stimulating your

imagination." She got out of the car and started firmly to close the door.

"No, you don't!" Joe said roughly. He pushed his feet hard against the door so that Fredericka, leaning forward, was thrust back with such force that she stumbled and fell back on the steps.

At once Joe was out of the car, trying to help her up. "Freddy, my God, I didn't mean to—Christ, Freddy, are you hurt? You aren't hurt, are you?"

"Not at all," she said in a cold angry voice, getting to her feet, pushing his hands away.

"God, Freddy, honestly—don't be angry with me, Freddy. This has sobered me up. Honestly, I'm all right now. Forgive me, will you? Can you?"

He looked suddenly so ridiculous that Fredericka's anger left her. She felt like laughing.

"I forgive you," she said. It was only silly little bouncy comic-strip Joe Barrett with his glasses and his growing girth. "Though you certainly don't deserve it."

He was humble with gratitude. "Gosh, thanks, Freddy. I know I don't deserve it. Don't go away angry. Please." He touched her arm timidly. "Let me come in for a drink. Just one. I'll show you I can behave. Please! Otherwise I'll go away feeling a heel—I won't sleep all night. Please, Flea, be a sport. Come on, let me!"

She hesitated a moment. "All right," she said indifferently. "But only one—and a short one."

He followed her into the hall. The night light was burning on a side table but she switched on the old Italian lantern at once and flooded the hall with radiance. Preceding Joe into the library she turned on all the lights. There was a tray with liquor and ice laid out by Eunice. She poured him a thin one, took some soda for herself. They both sat down. She could think of nothing to say. In the silence she again heard the sound of the night, rhythmic, sensual, the breathing of the earth, the faint murmur of a thousand insects. The vases full of garden flowers filled the room with sweet languor. If she could feel all this, then Joe must too. She regretted having allowed him to come in.

He took his drink quickly, rose and without permission poured another. She said nothing. When he seated himself he began again in the voice he had used at cocktail time, teasing, suggestive.

"Come clean, Freddy. What is this guy from Attica Center to you?"

"What's he to me?" Fredericka asked icily. She felt herself coloring. "What would he be?" She sounded flatly contemptuous but Joe was not in the least affected.

"That's what I'm interested in finding out," he said with sly inference. "You know, Flea, you can't fool people. You've looked like a different girl ever since Christopher went away. You must be getting it somewhere."

For a moment Fredericka did not understand the full implication of his last phrase. When she did she had a sudden wild impulse to pick up the fire tongs and hit over the head this offensive little man with his lascivious eyes peering damply through his glasses, his little paunch quivering with the rising of suppressed desire, his pudgy hands holding the glass of whisky as though he had them clasped around some full white throat.

"You dirty little sap," she heard herself saying in a deadly voice. "Get out of here!"

He did not move. His expression did not change. He looked amused and sly.

"Get out!" she said in a louder tone, rising to her feet. Still he did not stir. He leaned back, his face drawn into something horrible—between a leer and a sneer, she thought, and wondered briefly if she could ever laugh over this episode with anyone in the years to come.

"Now don't try to scare me, Fredericka, because you can't do it. We're both adults. We both think like adults. We both know something about life. You can't upstage me into stopping observing and thinking. I'm as smart as you or anybody else."

His voice thickened. He spoke slowly, deliberately: "When a friend of mine goes to war and his wife, after a suitable period, begins to look as though she had been taking shots in the—arm—it doesn't take much imagination to figure it out. The only thing that makes me sore is, as you can readily surmise, I'm not the lucky man. Don't imagine I blame you, Freddy. Why should I? Nature is nature, isn't she? I'm just sorry it had to be some lousy foreigner, sneaking in when the husband's back is turned . . ."

His voice had grown abruptly harsh and evil. Fredericka stood for a long moment looking down at him with loathing. Then she turned and walked out of the library and upstairs to her room. She locked the door and stood just inside it, tense and trembling. It was ten minutes before she heard Joe's car start and storm out of the drive. Then she walked over and dropped weakly on the bed. She lay there, sick and faint, while the swelling voice of the night rose about her and beat on her reluctant ears. Finally she got up, took a wrap from the closet and went back down the stairs into the garden as far as the fishpond, where she sat down. She felt entirely out of relationship with the sweet murmurous night, with the season, its scents and sounds. It was as though her body— heavy, clumsy, inert—had crudely pierced a delicate veil of otherworldliness as she sank onto the old stone bench; as though she, a human being, was inescapably corrupt and polluted and thus might never lose herself again in the world of nature. . . . Nature! Joe's word. Used sickly, used accusingly. She buried her face in her cold hands. She began to cry.

Her friendship for Franz Allers seemed now like some pure and fresh experience to which she could never return because suspicion had been cast on it by sick minds. She sat for a long time without moving until there came the magic shift in the air that signals the change from fading night to rising day. Then she admitted once more in her secret heart that she loved this man; and she saw that she could not expect anyone she knew to understand this, or, if they did, to admit their understanding, or to help her with any of the joy or anguish through which she must inevitably pass. From now on she was alone with her secret. Even when it was no longer a secret she would still be alone. Yet underneath the fear, the wish to avoid what had come upon her unsought, there began to stir a new sensation. Thinking of Joe, of Merry, of the rest of the local group, pity rose surprisingly in her. She pitied them all because they would not admit—would not dare to—what they must know within them to be true: the wonderful and terrifying unpredictability of life.

When at last she turned toward the house she saw with a start that the light was on in Aunt Palm's room. She walked back quickly. Outside her aunt's door she asked quietly, "Are you all right, darling?"

The familiar voice came back reassuring, steady. "Yes, lovie, quite. Why?"

"I was walking in the garden and I saw your light."

"Can't you sleep?"

"No."

"Nor can I. Come in."

Fredericka turned the knob and entered. Her aunt lay propped up on her pillows, surrounded by books and pictures.

> "O sleep! it is a gentle thing,
>   Revered from pole to pole . . .

Coleridge, and not very good at that," Aunt Palm said. She gave Fredericka a sharp but guarded glance.

"I've been crying," Fredericka admitted quickly, "but not about anything much."

Aunt Palm said only, "Well, there's plenty to cry about in this world."

"What are you doing?" Fredericka asked after a moment.

"Living other people's lives," Aunt Palm said dryly. She waved her wrinkled old hand above the scattered pictures on the blanket cover: Rembrandt, Manet, Watteau, Delacroix . . . "How was the party?"

"Awful," Fredericka said brokenly. "Stupid and ugly and degrading—and everyone there was all those things too."

"Humph," said Aunt Palm. She reached under the pile of books and drew out a thin volume. "Take a glass of warm milk and some Giottos and go to bed," she said, dismissing Fredericka.

Fredericka leaned over to kiss the old withered cheek, took the book in her hand obediently and left the room.

The next day when Bridgie arrived early for lunch Fredericka debated whether to tell her about Joe or not. She decided not to. But she did bring up the subject of the general baiting to which she had been subjected the night before. "I suppose I'm going to have to introduce Franz to all of them sooner or later," she said. "They're getting pretty rude and insistent about it."

"Well, I do think you could," Bridgie said soothingly. "Maybe even should."

Instantly Fredericka bridled. "Oh, should, should!" she cried angrily. "Why should? They're all a lot of stupid prying idiots, and I hate every one of them."

"Oh, come," Bridgie said smoothly. "They mean well."

"I doubt it," Fredericka said, still angry. "I think they mean badly—and one might as well see the truth. They're small-spirited, envious, greedy, gossipy, and bad-intentioned. I really dislike every one of them, and always have, and at last I admit it."

"You don't mean that," Bridgie said with perfect composure.

Fredericka said nothing more.

Later in the parlor Fredericka, who had been silent all during lunch, could not bring herself to enter the conversation. She was still feeling sick from the experience of the night before. Aunt Palm had not appeared all day. This too was troubling. She saw herself infinitely removed from everyone —even now from Franz Allers, who had taken a Lowestoft teapot out of one of the cabinets and was commenting on the quality of its glaze.

"It's my pet," Bridgie told him. "I believe I'm supposed to inherit it someday."

"It reminds me," Franz said, turning it carefully in his hands, "of an old lady in England who couldn't be parted from her teapot. The spout was broken and it had a crack, but she would never let go of it. It was her one link with the past."

They were all looking at him, listening, but not following his meaning.

"She was an evacuee. I worked with evacuees and refugees for a while—at one time."

Whenever he spoke of his former life Fredericka was aware that everyone grew very quiet. It was almost as though the pressure of their expectation acted as a curb, for he seldom said more than a sentence or two, and always reluctantly.

"And she kept her teapot?" Bridgie asked encouragingly. "I think that's sweet—I mean, I think the authorities must have been very understanding to allow it."

Franz smiled at Bridgie. "They were." He hesitated, as though debating in his own mind whether he should say any more. The windows were open and the sweet air of early summer stirred the dark-red damask draperies and the matching roses in the crystal vases. The parlor, heavily shaded by the trees outside, was like a cool quiet cave in the midst of the glitter and murmur of the June afternoon beyond the windows.

After a moment Franz went on. "They didn't realize at first, the authorities—no one did, for that matter—how important a small familiar object can be to someone who has lost everything. Very often the whole loss gets pinned to one particular thing of no intrinsic value—a workbasket, a favorite chair, the picture of a child . . ."

"How far away it seems," Bridgie said. "Far far away and remote."

A bee came in through the open windows and his sleepy murmur as he lingered over the roses heightened the contrast between this world of summer peace and that other world of violence and disruption.

Franz nodded. "Sometimes, even to me, it can seem like a bad dream."

Again there came the weight of their collective anticipation. This time he did not disappoint them. He went on speaking, as though he were thinking out loud, following with his eyes the murmurous suspension of the bee above the flowers.

"There is a new disease in the world—who can cure it? The shock of uprooting, the shock of forever broken bonds with home, family, country . . . It will take more than canned milk and blankets, cast-off winter coats and dehydrated eggs . . ." He tapered into silence.

Owen cleared his throat and remarked a little sententiously, "I suppose displaced people do develop certain similar symptoms—I mean, due to loss and so on." He bit into his pipestem and resolutely pushed on. "I'd like to run a piece about this whole—er—psychosis in the *Clarion*—simple terms of course. As Bridgie says, we are so shut off . . . Just what are the symptoms?"

Shut off and soft! Fredericka thought in shame and anger. Soft and stupid! But Franz Allers, who was putting back the teapot, seemed to feel no anger as he repeated Owen's word.

"Symptoms?" he said, closing the door of the china cabinet. "What symptoms follow sudden and violent loss of everything? . . . Well, lack of initiative. General anxiety. Bitterness. Deep feelings of inferiority, as though somehow the individual himself was to blame for his plight. Above all—or so it seemed to me in studying refugees—complete inability to accept any routine."

"Now, that's very interesting. Why?" Owen demanded.

Franz began patiently to explain, a little like a lecturer,

· 283 ·

as though intentionally, to keep it impersonal: how, for the refugee, all the social criteria with which he has been familiar during his lifetime are suddenly gone. He has been victimized and he wishes revenge. This hidden unconscious wish for revenge appears in a desire to defeat authority—any and all authority. The refugee's one bond with other human beings becomes too often the bond of common bitterness and complaint, the aim to cheat those who now control his destiny, regardless of their attitude toward him.

"Mass hunger isn't the only problem we'll have to face when this whole abominable business is concluded," he said with a bitter sadness. "The psychological problems seem sometimes beyond solution. Our wise men are too few. We've only come to the place where we recognize occasional symptoms; we're still groping for the cures."

"Oh, could you, would you come and speak to a group?" Bridgie asked eagerly. "Fredericka says I shouldn't pester you —but couldn't you? Wouldn't you? Maybe you could help us *not* to be so stupid."

Why should he? Fredericka wanted to cry out angrily. Why should he? She saw Bridgie and Merry and the earnest ladies of the Current Events Club closing in like cultural vultures. But Franz Allers seemed unruffled at the prospect. He said only, "Perhaps, sometime—next year, when I come back."

He turned then to Fredericka and changed the subject. "How about a walk?" He quite obviously and openly meant only the two of them.

"I'd like it," Fredericka said, but she did not have the courage to leave Owen and Bridgie behind. "Will you come?"

"We must be nipping home," Bridgie said with perfect composure. "The children are alone with Daddy."

As soon as they were in the garden, walking beside her without looking at her, "What is troubling you?" Franz asked. "You're not yourself at all."

Fredericka began to cry. She could not speak. They walked on silently beyond the cedar hedge out of sight of the house. "My dear, what is it?" He put his hand on her arm and turned her toward him. She did not want him to look at her while she cried, and she tried to cover her face with her hands. Instead he pulled her against him and let her hide her face in his shoulder. She stood there for a moment weeping brokenly. But only for a moment. She felt as though the garden, the hidden house, the very sky, had a thousand prying eyes. She released herself from Franz's arms. He did not try to hold her.

"Forgive me," she said weakly. "I hate to cry."

She began to walk on. He took her arm and linked it strongly through his, and they went on down the garden to the bench at the edge of the birch grove, where they sat down.

After he had lit a cigarette for her and taken one himself he said authoritatively, "Tell me."

She told him then about the episode of the night before with Joe.

When she had finished he took her hand and held it in both of his. "I'm sorry. I had no idea this would happen."

"Well, I might have known," Fredericka said bitterly. "Little lives—little rodent minds . . ."

They were both silent.

"The thing I hate most about it," she said, trying to make clear to herself her own feeling, "is the cheapness of it. It makes everything seem sick and ugly . . ."

"Don't let it do that," he said quietly.

She did not continue.

"We must talk together," he said out of their silence, "before I go away. Somewhere, where we can really be alone. I'm going to New York next week before I go west. Could you manage to come down?"

"I think so."

"When would you know?"

"I know now," Fredericka said. "I'll come."

"Only if you want to."

"I do want to."

They looked at each other then.

"You are afraid," he said softly.

She nodded.

"Don't be afraid," he said. "Not of this. There are so many other things one *has* to be afraid of."

Chapter Nineteen

IN NEW YORK FRANZ WENT FIRST TO see his old friend Carl Reuter, the fashionable psychiatrist.

It had been months since Franz had seen him, when he first came to America. Reuter had been very kind then, offering him two rooms at the top of his luxurious house, a key to the front door, a typewriter, solitude and peace. Franz had stayed with the Reuters for two weeks and then he had finally decided on the position at the college in Attica Center and had gone off to take it, with Reuter looking dubious over his shell-rimmed glasses at his decision.

Franz had known Carl Reuter in Vienna as a young man. They had been students together. Reuter was not a refugee in America, although he said now people tended to classify him as one, because of his accent, and all people with accents were, since the war, considered newcomers. Actually he had been in America almost twenty years—long enough to have built up a flourishing practice and to own the fine house in the upper Sixties where he received his patients and lived with his wife and half-grown children.

Years of psychiatric work had given him a tired, faintly bored expression, the expression of a man who has heard everything and found it all surprisingly similar. Dispassion and compassion seemed to fight for mastery in his face. Although his manners were indifferent almost to the point of heartlessness, they did not deceive Franz. He understood how a man as sensitive as Reuter would find it necessary to simulate cold detachment in order to face, day after day, the record of human mistakes and human pain. And Franz knew a good deal about Reuter's secret generosity, and what share of his income he gave away to help people in Europe.

Reuter was alone for dinner Franz's first night. His wife had gone to the theater with a woman friend. While Franz was staying with them before, he had had the strong impression that the Reuters saw little of each other, that they had decided amiably to keep up a front for the sake of the children, and within that arrangement each of them lived quite independently. It seemed, on the whole, to agree better with Reuter than with his wife. Mrs. Reuter wore a permanently harassed expression, like a woman who is insecure or unhappy, or both. She had been quite beautiful in her youth, largely because of the extraordinary placing and color of her eyes. But years (and secret tears, so Franz suspected) had darkened the flesh around them and given her face in middle age a faintly sinister air.

Franz was glad to sit at table without her high-keyed presence. He was fond of Reuter and although their talk was not of home, nor of any of the few memories they had in common, still there was something intangibly comforting about sharing in a foreign land the sense of a common birthplace and a common heritage.

"So how is it really going in the New Greece?" Reuter asked. His tone was the rather mannered and cynical one that had become his nonprofessional voice—a deliberate relief from the solicitous and intimate inflection he had to use with his patients.

Franz smiled. "You mean Attica Center? Quite well, thanks."

"Not absorbing?"

"Not completely."

"Wouldn't you rather be doing something in research?" Reuter carefully did not look at him as he put this question. "Medical research?"

"Not now—not yet," Franz answered. He added quietly, "I'm contented enough."

Reuter did not press it.

"The world is one great tossing groaning invalid," he said, spraying seltzer into his white wine. He looked fixedly at the wall opposite, as though the sick world could be seen there by television. "The question is: Does it need a midwife or an undertaker?"

"What do you think?" Franz asked him.

"The undertaker, of course. The mortician in black suede gloves with a black orchid in his buttonhole. The cosmic cremator. Let it burn!" He spoke in a voice that was disproportionately harsh, almost crudely so.

Franz said nothing.

"Do you remember Bob Goodwin?" Reuter asked, after a little silence in which a crystal clock on a side table shrilled eight times. "You met him when you were staying here before."

"The chemist? Of course."

"He's dropping in tonight." Reuter stuffed his mouth with a large leaf of lettuce from his salad plate. He spoke around it: "He's a sick man. You'll see it the moment you see him. He's at work on something that's killing him. I've watched it coming on."

"What do you mean—something that's killing him?"

"I mean some secret discovery—top-priority secret. Atom-smashing, I suspect. He was always after that." Reuter took up a wooden pepper grinder that stood in front of his plate and with a faint squeak he sprayed the pale-green leaves of the lettuce with the coarsely ground spice.

"But how's that making him sick?"

"Fear. . . . They're going to discover it—that's my hunch. Goodwin sees they are, and he's afraid of the consequences."

"Good God!" Franz said. "The control of the atom?" But the astounding statement from Reuter did not, he realized, seem too fanciful to him. "I've always thought it would happen in our time," he said aloud, musingly. "Vania and I used to speak of it—try to imagine what it would be like."

"Well, when *that* breaks on human consciousness," Reuter said gloomily, "God knows what kind of psychoneurotics I'll have to deal with. It's bad enough now."

"Maybe the discovery will cure them," Franz suggested. "Can't fear act as a bracer—a big enough fear?"

"Not permanently," Reuter said, even more morosely, "not when you live with it day after day."

They were both silent.

The servant came in to remove their salad plates. She returned with a bowl of fruit for dessert. As she put it down Reuter said, "Bring the coffee here, Anna. I'll get some brandy."

Anna! There was always for Franz a little sharp prick in this commonplace name. It brought back Dr. Anna Weissberg, the kitchen of the Vienna flat, the ugly woman worn with exhaustion, indifferent to his presence; the smell of coffee, Vania's pale face . . . He shook off the memory.

Reuter was unlocking a small cabinet and bringing out a

bottle of old Armagnac. Franz looked about him at the room, so unlike that other house to which he was no longer a stranger —the one in Wrenkill. Here at Reuter's the dining chairs and table were modern—or so he supposed you would call it— *Chinois Moderne* or some fancy decorator's phrase like that (for in form the furniture was cut like the old solid teak pieces from China, only less dignified, less elegant, curiously bastard, and light green in color). The room was deliberately cold, done in tones of green and cream, lime and silver. An early Masson of the wars of insects hung above the fireplace; a later one, its theme less easily discernible, hung above the buffet which held a formal arrangement of silver candelabra and celadon vases containing giant gladioli. The flowers were flame-colored; they, and the paintings, were the only things in the room that seemed real. The furniture, Franz thought, must surely be Mrs. Reuter's taste. . . .

"I see you studying the room," Reuter remarked, bringing the brandy to the table. He inclined his head like a bird about to peck. It was the attitude of a man who leans forward in order to hear better. The posture had become an unconscious physical attribute. "What do you think of it?"

Before Franz could speak, "Early Metro-Goldwyn-Mayer, my daughter says. I suppose it is pretty Hollywood. It's Maida's idea. I'm not sure, however, but what modern furniture is the only proper thing for a psychiatrist's house, at that. No associations—or no deep-rooted ones, anyway. Perhaps I find it self-protective myself. . . . How do you like the Massons?"

"I think they might take some studying," Franz said, looking at the paintings.

"I'm going to take the new one"—he nodded toward it— "out of here and hang it in my office. Should stir up the patient's sexual fancies, don't you think? You can see almost anything in it that you want to."

How American he has become! Franz thought to himself. He is terrified of showing any feeling, and abruptly, as he reached over to take a peach from the bowl the maid had left, "Carl, I'm in love," he said.

Reuter did not speak, he did not even glance up. He carefully poured the Armagnac into two small glasses.

"I suppose you are going to ask me: What do you mean 'in love'?" Franz continued.

Reuter twisted his face into a wry grin. "No, I won't ask you that. Is she an American?"

"Yes. The sister of a man I knew in Europe."

"Beautiful, of course." Reuter came around by Franz to put down the glass in front of him.

"Yes, and talented—a painter, who has neglected her work."

Reuter, back in his chair, took a sip of brandy. "Therapy?" he asked, rolling his tongue around his teeth.

"You mean on my part for her? Oh, no—but therapy for me, though I can't say why, or how."

"The mysteries," Reuter remarked, taking another sip. His voice was suddenly relaxed and gentle.

Franz pretended to appear surprised. "You still grant the mysteries?"

"Oh, to be sure. More than ever. More every day." His tone had become again wry and acid. "Well, here's to the Atomic age." He lifted his glass. "About to dawn on us."

Somewhere distantly a chime rang announcing a visitor. There were steps and movement in the hall and the door opened and Robert Goodwin, the chemist, came into the room.

He blinked as he entered, although the room was not

brightly lighted. He was thin and round-shouldered. His dark-blue suit was shabby and shiny. He wore glasses with heavy lenses. His strawlike hair was growing thin, and what there was of it was in disarray, his whole appearance a perfect caricature of the absent-minded scientist.

He sank into one of the bastard pieces of Chinoiserie; refused the brandy, refused fruit, asked if he could have a bottle of Coca-Cola.

"It's fine to see you." Although he spoke warmly to Franz his face remained unchanged.

"Bring my adolescent friend a bottle of Coca-Cola," Reuter said to the maid. Goodwin paid no attention.

"How's it going?" he asked Franz. "What made you decide on teaching?"

"I was too lonely for anything else."

Goodwin shot him a quick glance. "What do you mean by that?"

"I was too lonely for research. I'd had too much solitude. I just didn't want to work alone for a time."

"He'll go back to it." Reuter spoke with cool assurance. "He'll find what all developed people find to be true—young people are too depressing. They're finally much more depressing than solitude."

"Some people find youth hopeful," Goodwin remarked, but without much conviction.

"It's the repetition that destroys you," Reuter went on, pouring more brandy for himself. "The pattern never varies. The faces change, the theme remains the same. People are incredibly repetitious. They're all alike. At twenty-seven they cry: What is it? At thirty-seven they cry: Whatever it is I want all of it. At forty-seven they cry: Whatever it is I don't want any of it. At fifty-seven they cry: Whatever it *was* I want more of it. At sixty-seven they cry: Whatever it is I don't want to lose it."

"The past tense only once?" Franz inquired idly.

"That's right," Reuter said, nodding. "At fifty-seven. Then they think 'it' had exclusively to do with the body and the glands, and they think they're through. By sixty-seven they know better. Second wind. They return then to the present tense."

"You Freudians!" Goodwin said carelessly.

"Why are they so negative at forty-seven—'I don't want any more of it'?" Franz asked.

"That's the mental menopause—general feeling of what's-the-use."

"It's all glands," Goodwin declared, still wearing his abstracted air. He did not appear to be at all interested in the subject.

Reuter looked at him and gave a short laugh with no mirth in it. "You have all the dogmatic ignorance of a great scientist in one field who is a perfect booby in every other," he said rudely.

"Reuter, I wish you'd go to work on me," Goodwin pleaded suddenly. "I need help. I'm not myself. My dreams . . ."

"I told you," Reuter interrupted, nodding at Franz. "He's a sick man." He spoke ironically, but his eyes were worried. "I can't help you, Bob. You're too busy cooking up universal destruction to have time for your eternal soul."

"I don't want you to work on my soul," Goodwin protested in a voice that was almost whining. "To hell with my soul—I want to sleep nights, that's all! I want you to work on my dreams. They're growing constantly more horrible. Excuse me . . ."

He got up and abruptly left the room.

Reuter looked after him, turning his glass slowly in his fingers. "Weak bladder," was his comment. "All a part of his general breakup. I suspect he's impotent now too. . . ."

He uttered these intimate facts about his friend in a voice as without feeling as that of a man who comments on a chart in a medical textbook. Again Franz felt the shock of recognizing in Reuter this new, deliberate, and, he felt—and so could forgive it—self-protective callousness.

"He's too delicately made for what he's doing, just as I told you," Reuter was continuing. "Scientists in our century are all working for Death in one way or another. And Goodwin's sensitive. He's a musician—did you know it? Plays the violin. We used to try to play together every week. Now we're lucky if we get together once a month. It's harder and harder to find any time to live. . . ."

Goodwin reappeared in the dining-room door. As he came back to the table and took up his glass of Coca-Cola, Reuter, watching him, said devilishly, "When are you going to get rid of your secret? It had better be soon. You look like Sindbad carrying the Old Man of the Sea."

"Secret?" Goodwin asked evasively. Then he shrugged. "You're the man with secrets. I often think of the burden you carry."

"Thanks," Reuter said dryly. After a moment in which no one said anything he asked abruptly, "Did you bring your fiddle?"

Goodwin nodded. "In the hall."

Reuter got to his feet. "Good. We'll have a little Mozart." He took the brandy bottle, his glass, and the box of cigars and preceded his two guests out of the dining room across the hall and into another coldly impressive room running the full length of the house with a grand piano at one end and walls of books at the other. Here the atmosphere was faintly terrifying, owing largely, Franz decided, to a case of African carvings: pale masks of female ghosts, dark fierce bodies of conjure men. There were two enormous modern paintings, geometric and mechanistic, showing wheels and turbines, bolts and pistons, along with the human creature—reduced also to geometry and mechanics, with knee joints, elbows, toes, and fingers like machine parts being assembled for some great robot ballet. There was a sculpture of twisted copper wire and brass, and another that appeared to be a large well-eroded stone from the shore. The chairs were all square and looked as though they had been constructed for people of exceptional stature. The extra-long yellow rectangle that was one sofa faced another identical yellow rectangle. This last effect was a little like a European railway carriage in its chilly formality.

Franz stretched out full length on a divan that stood before the two open windows giving on the small city garden. While the other two played, he lay with his eyes closed, the brandy warming his veins and mind. And as the music rose and fell and looped and whirled, softly and incongruously in this aggressively contemporary room, he saw Fredericka's face in the Wrenkill garden, wet with tears. He looked at the face long and lovingly and then he brought up from his memory the face of Vania, and he found that he could gaze at it at last without pain.

He opened his eyes and regarded the two men at the end of the room in the light from the indirect chromium lamp, shaped like a tulip. Though they were concentrated on the music, they were more in repose than they had been in the dining room. Franz lay studying them, thinking of the way each of them had appraised the other's burden. It seemed to him that certain modern men, working in the special sciences, investigating the new and limitless boundaries of the mind, of space and time, of chemistry and physics, were being asked to carry a load of knowledge, a burden of responsibility almost too much for any single human creature to endure.

One thing he knew: in the company of these two men his forever-present sense of loneliness grew less heavy. And more than ever he felt blessed, particularly blessed, because he had had the privilege—granted most often only to the young—to fall in love; to wish once again for a woman's presence, in the same room, beside him on a windy path, opposite at table. He wanted Fredericka near him now, in this moment. He could imagine her sitting beside him with her head bowed, drinking in the music. He thought of the deep quiet, the air of repose that she habitually carried with her, and he realized how much sustainment there had been for him in just this quality in the weeks since he had first come to know her.

The music had stopped.

"*Genug!*" Reuter was saying, rising from the piano.

Goodwin stood for a moment putting away his violin, then he too crossed the room and sank down into one of the chrome-yellow squares. The three men were silent for a few seconds, quite peaceful, feeling no need of words. They could hear voices in a garden below, laughter, a distant radio metallically setting forth the latest news of the war in Europe. As they sat there, not speaking, relaxed and soothed by the music, the hall door opened and Maida Reuter entered with her friend.

"I'm so glad you didn't go, Carl," she began at once, dropping her light wrap over the back of a chair. "It was abominable. Really! You can't believe it. A barbarian production—and it is the greatest hit of the spring season."

"But why are you surprised?" her companion asked. "Americans have no taste." She spoke with simple finality. "I'm one, and I should know." She stripped the long black silk gloves from her arms, took a mirror from her bag and looked into it fixedly as she ran a small tortoise-shell comb through her short black hair. Then she reached for a gold cigarette case, a gold lighter. Out of her bag she pulled a little jeweled box for vitamin pills (she identified it as she dropped it onto the cushion beside her), a compact in a suede case, a little red-leather notebook, lipstick, eyeshadow, mascara—a collection of the most charming small objects designed to embellish beauty and sustain health.

They all sat watching her as, after tipping out the contents of her bag in her search for a cigarette holder, she calmly returned them one by one. "The drawstring bag," she remarked with perfect composure, aware that she had their full attention, "is quaint but impractical. One of Valentina's ideas that is *really* unfunctional." She spoke to no one in particular but with the air of making an important pronouncement.

"Daddy, I want it!" Reuter said in a mocking voice when she had finally placed the bag of antique velvet beside her light furs.

"What do you mean?"

"That's where Americans are—in the Daddy-I-want-it stage . . . You can't blame them. They don't know any better."

Reuter's wife looked at him suspiciously. Neither woman seemed to understand what had prompted his remark.

"Papa, I'm afraid," Goodwin said suddenly in a surprisingly eager voice. "Do you know that story?" He showed more animation than he had shown all evening.

"What story?" asked Mrs. Reuter without much interest.

"Do tell it," begged her friend indifferently, placing a cigarette in her long jade holder.

"You must know it, Allers," Goodwin said, turning to Franz. "It's Turgenev. You're something of a literary man, aren't you?"

"Thank you—but I don't believe I know the story you refer to."

"Go on, Bob, for God's sake, what *are* you talking about?" Reuter cried impatiently.

Goodwin got to his feet and moved toward the bookshelves. "Have you any Turgenev?"

"We must have." Mrs. Reuter rose also and went directly to the section of the library where the hand-tooled, gold-touched sets of books were housed.

"It's in *Prose Poems*," Goodwin said, his voice still eager.

She handed him a dark leather volume and he took it to the nearest light and turned to the index. "Page 154," he murmured. When he tried to turn the pages the volume proved to be uncut.

Reuter gave his mirthless laugh. "Uncut! Hah! That's good. And it was bought at an auction. Book lovers all!"

Mrs. Reuter looked faintly annoyed as she went to the desk for a silver paper knife which she brought to Goodwin. He stooped over the book in the light from the metal lamp, carefully cutting the pages. When he had finished he handed the book to Franz.

"You read it. I can't. You've a professor's voice—or should have."

Franz took the volume without protest. "The Destruction of the World," he read aloud. The words fell with shocking finality into the softly lighted atmosphere of this luxurious modern room, open to the warm airs of summer, so recently stirred with the waves of noble music.

As Franz read he felt the silence among the four people deepening until it was as loud, as deafening, as a sustained roar:

I dream that I am in a peasant's hut in some remote corner in Russia.

The room is large and low, with three windows: the walls are whitewashed: there is no furniture. In front of the house stretches a broad plain, sloping gradually and losing itself in the distance: a monotonous sky hangs over it, like a roof.

I am not alone. About ten men are in the room with me. They are very simple people, and are dressed simply; they pace back and forth, and regard each other furtively. They avoid one another, but are constantly exchanging anxious glances.

Not one of them knows how he came to be in this house, and what sort of people are there with him. Anxiety and weariness are on their faces . . . they all step in turn to the windows and look out intently, as if expecting something.

Then they turn again and wander restlessly up and down. A small boy walks among them. From time to time he whimpers in a thin, monotonous voice: 'Papa, I'm afraid!' This whimpering fairly makes me sick, and I too am beginning to be afraid . . . but of what? I don't know. I merely feel that some great terrible misfortune is approaching.

The small boy goes on whimpering. Oh, if we could only get away from here. How suffocating it is! How sultry! How oppressive! . . . But escape is impossible.

The sky is like a pall. There is no breeze . . . the air seems dead.

Suddenly the boy runs to the window and cries out in

the same piteous voice: 'Look! Look! The earth has fallen away!'

What! Fallen away? . . . It is a fact. There had been a plain in front of the house, and now it stands on the summit of an immense mountain. The horizon has fallen, and close to the house there yawns a steep, black, gaping abyss.

We all press round the window . . . Terror makes our hearts cold.

'Look there . . . look there!' whispers my neighbor.

There, over the whole wide boundless waste something stirs, something rises and falls in tiny little round hills.

'The sea!' we all thought in one and the same instant.

'It will engulf us! . . . But how can it grow and rise to the height of this lofty summit?'

Meanwhile, it rises higher and higher . . . Now there are not merely little hills visible, moving in the distance . . . a single powerful monstrous wave sweeps across the whole circle of the horizon.

It is flying toward us. Like an icy whirlwind, it approaches, circling like hellish darkness. Everything around us begins to tremble, and there, in that flying chaos, is heard a crash, and thunder, and a thousand-voiced iron clamor.

What a howling and moaning! It is the earth giving voice to its terror.

It is the end! The end of everything!

"Great God!" Reuter said when Franz closed the book. The story had obviously moved him.

"You read it beautifully," the woman with the jade cigarette holder said to Franz. It was, he supposed, her way of saying that she too had been affected.

"I've never heard it before." Maida Reuter's voice, thinner and higher pitched than usual. She took the volume of

· 301 ·

Turgenev from Franz and marked it with a cerise cord from a desk drawer. "It's terribly powerful."

"Papa, I'm afraid," Goodwin repeated. He was sitting with his eyes closed. He looked quite pale under the light, Franz thought. He had taken off his glasses and when he opened the opaque gray pools of his eyes he looked even more white and drawn. "Quite a yarn," he said. "Written in the 1870's . . . I've had it in mind a lot lately. . . ." He got exhaustedly to his feet.

"Thanks for the music, Reuter." He walked over to the piano to get his violin. Lifting it off the orange and red skirt from India, "I'll not be seeing you again for a while. I'm going out west."

"Out west!" Reuter cried in amazement. And then, as though determined never to reveal anything as natural and simple as surprise, he added matter-of-factly, "I hope you're going to a dude ranch. You need a change of pace!"

"A dude ranch!" This idea seemed to amuse Goodwin very much. He showed his long irregular teeth in a mocking grin. "I always wanted to learn to ride bareback. I'll let you know when I master it. I'll send a picture postcard."

"Don't forget," Reuter said lightly, but he followed Goodwin into the hall and their voices could be heard murmuring there for some moments. When he returned he looked subdued and weary.

"What a strange man," Maida's friend remarked, reaching for her furs and gloves, preparing also to leave. "Is he a genius?"

"Yes, God help him!" Reuter said. "Well, I'm for bed. Sweet dreams, all!" he added mockingly and walked from the room.

Franz remained behind for a few moments talking to Maida

and her guest. When the woman left he went downstairs with her to help find a cab. Luckily, one had just stopped next door. He claimed it, put the woman in, and returned to the house.

He went up to his room at once, but he was not sleepy. He undressed and closed his eyes determined to rest, but he could only see Goodwin's pale face under the metal lamp, and the expression with which he had repeated, "Papa, I'm afraid!"

Finally Franz got up, dressed, and went out into the hot summer night. The streets were quiet, almost deserted. A long way off he could hear the echo of his own footsteps sounding hollowly under the dim lights. He passed only one policeman. They did not speak. The policeman did not so much as glance at him. What a country! Franz thought.

In the dark of the dimout the sky had a light of its own and the stars were cool and quiet. He was glad of the occasional block with trees. Walking under them he felt a pleasure more intense and concentrated than his pleasure among the abundant trees of Attica Center, for these were city trees and seemed to him worthy of a special respect and attention because of their powers of endurance.

The lingering terror of Turgenev's vision dimmed here in the sleeping streets. He thought again of Fredericka and of Vania, as he had earlier in the evening. I will take it, he thought, meaning love. Not as a hedonist, not "If there is to be more terror let me have heartease while I may" but because love is an affirmation in the face of the great negations of our day. And I choose to affirm. . . .

I must talk to my class about the Russians, he thought as he walked. Not just of today's Russian, but of the eternal Russian. Suddenly he felt like a father thinking of his children . . . I must talk to them of Tolstoi's *Confession*, of the act of faith, the vision with which his long mental torture was finally ended. I must help, if I can, to strengthen them for the great ordeals ahead—and he stifled the feeling that threatened to engulf him with the word "ordeal," that feeling of despair, of ultimate weariness and doubt, to which he had so often in the past fallen prey.

Chapter Twenty

FRANZ AND FREDERICKA HAD AGREED to meet in New York at a restaurant Fredericka suggested. She had been in this particular restaurant once before with Robert and Helen. It was conveniently located and she remembered the bar as dimly lit and large enough to be reassuringly impersonal.

Fredericka had come down on the night train from Wrenkill, had spent the morning at the hairdresser's and the afternoon at the movies, because she was too keyed up to do anything else.

She arrived early at the bar and although she had never conquered her embarrassment at entering this kind of place alone, she forced herself to wait in the anteroom, looking about her with a false air of composure.

It was, she decided, a public boudoir to which she had summoned Franz. Here men and women, intimate strangers, were meeting out of separate environments for a drink together, prelude perhaps to another meeting, more secret but less exciting, because well beyond the reach of the measuring eyes that went slipping along the walls, recognizing, avoiding, appraising, knowingly or uneasily. And she was not without qualms herself. What if Robert or Helen should enter, find her here with a stranger? What would she say—what excuse would she give for not having telephoned them? She had even lied to Aunt Palm and Bridgie—had said she was going down to try to arrange for a show sometime in the autumn. Nothing was further from her mind.

Franz was late and her nervousness mounted in this unfamiliar atmosphere, in these artfully darkened rooms. It's the return to the cave, she thought, wondering about the lives of the people who walked past her with such brusque city assurance, into the twilight beyond, claiming tables, summoning waiters; from the steps, surveying the scene with the predatory eye of bright sleek birds. What was the room's power?—for it had a power, she could feel it. Was it that it had successfully created an atmosphere designed to avoid all familiar domestic associations for those who frequented it?— the radio executives, advertising men, editors, department heads, Powers models, Long Island matrons. . . . Was this the bridge of heightened pulse beat and unraveled nerves by which men got themselves from the reality of their work-world over to the unreality of their home-worlds lying somewhere at the end of a suburban train ride?

All these ideas, if she told them to Robert and Helen in White Plains, would make them laugh heartily. They would cry: My dear Flea, you make it sound like something from the Fall of Rome! And perhaps it is the Fall of Rome, she would say—or rather she would not say—for she would utter none of this; to do so would mark her a provincial, the little cousin from upstate. For if you lived in New York you took these things for granted: the five-o'clock tête-à-têtes, the loud continuous drop of nickels and dimes into the boxes of telephone booths, as the calls went out to White Plains, Morristown, Garden City, and Greenwich, the call announcing that the six-ten had been missed, and the seven-five, and "Don't wait dinner! I'll grab a bite when I get through at the office. . . ."

Franz came at last and they found a table. He spoke little at first. He seemed tired again, although his face had lifted and lost some of its age when he saw her waiting for him in the outer room.

After the clarity and exhilaration of the night before, Franz found himself, because of the people he had seen during the day, struggling again with the familiar feeling of aloneness, that bleak and terrible aloneness that sent his mind ranging out into the darkness, searching the world for a face or name to hearten him.

Often at these times, when his need was greatest, his mind would perversely supply him with examples of life's eternal paradoxes: of man's high thoughts and low deeds, his potential nobility and daily pettiness. As he came along the street he had been thinking of his friend Stanov, the eminent critic and admirer of Dostoevski. Stanov's inspiring monograph on The Great Invalid, dealing with Dostoevski's "sacred" disease of epilepsy, had set a new critical precedent. It had lifted Stanov at once to the top rank of contemporary critics, to those writing with a new literary insight born of profound psychological acumen. But Stanov's monograph preceded by just three years his discovery that his only son and namesake was also an epileptic. There had followed Stanov's bottomless despair, his inability to find any comfort in the thought that his son also might leave behind magnificent records of the flights of the spirit, the descents into hell and emergence from it, to which a gifted epileptic is subject. . . . Why should the story of Stanov return again and again to plague him?

Against his memory of Stanov, Franz strove to put other memories, in an attempt to maintain the balance of some private imponderable scale of human values. He reminded himself of Peter Heimbrich's years in prison—the devices he had used to keep from going insane in the long silence. Peter had forced his mind back and back into the labyrinthine days of childhood, recalling, with all the assiduousness of one who seeks a clue to misconduct, the minutest details of his early life. He had dragged up from the dark well of memory old verses to speak aloud to the walls. Week after week he dredged for half-lost lines from Hölderlin, Goethe. He reviewed the plots, analyzed the characters of every novel he had ever read. He added long columns of figures in his head, invented problems in algebra. And thus, by all these methods, he saved himself. By his will, his intelligence, he was able to emerge from enforced solitude—though gray as a potato sprout, sixty pounds underweight, and with white hair, nonetheless unbroken, and with a mind that was still a useful instrument. . . .

Franz had spent the day among Europeans, all comparatively recent arrivals like himself. It was they who had depressed him. Their failure, for the most part, to adjust to the country that was harboring them distressed and annoyed him, though he could understand and even share their anger, their criticism, often justified enough, of the behavior patterns of a protected and unconscious people.

"I have trouble swallowing," Erich von Abetz had confided in him, standing in the little room of the cramped 57th Street gallery where he sold his own and his friends' family possessions—paintings, sculpture, china and even antique jewels. "The doctors say there's nothing wrong with me. But I simply can't swallow. Or, if I wake in the night, then I *must* swallow, swallow and swallow . . . What is it?"

"You have swallowed too much," Franz said. "We have all swallowed too much."

"This awful country," Erich had groaned. "It makes me

sick. I feel sick every time I go into the delicatessen on the corner to get my supper; all those hot and cold dishes, meat and salad and hams stuck full of spice, and beef with blood coming out of it, and cakes with nuts sprinkled on them. It is obscene. While the rest of the world starves."

"You can't blame them for not knowing," Franz began.

"Father forgive them, for they know not what they do," Julia Kranz said exaggeratedly. She laughed. She shrugged. "Franz is right, Erich, we should pity them."

"What are you doing now, Julia?" Franz asked gently.

"Turning up hems, taking out shoulder pads, kneeling on the floor all day with my mouth full of pins . . . Someday I think I shall just open my throat and let the pins go down. . . ."

But she tried not to speak too bitterly, though it was hard. He could understand how hard. She had been a leading stage designer in Vienna. To become in her late forties a dressmaker's assistant in a strange land—that was not easy.

"The thing I simply cannot bear is their assumption that we—that refugees—are special cases," she cried, her voice suddenly angry. "That there must be some reason *why* it had to happen to us—I mean something *wrong* with us to make it happen. They just can't see that it might have happened to them—that we are people just like them."

She pulled off her little knitted cap and Franz saw with a start how white her hair had become.

"I know," he said, still gently. He had often felt this way himself. No matter what the sympathy, what the wish and will to understand and help, the unconscious belief endured among Americans that your particular case must be exceptional; that surely, *surely*, not many Europeans could have come to such a pass.

Still for all his agreement he found himself, in justice, resenting his friends' bitter criticism of the generous strangers who had given them shelter. He tried, with these acquaintances out of that other world from which he was now so totally severed, to defend America. In the end, this afternoon, there had been sharp words.

"When even those who have suffered the most can't agree among themselves, the outlook for world peace is a dark one," he had said as he took his leave. He was sorry for his words before the elevator had deposited him on the ground floor. But he did not go back. He was already late in meeting Fredericka.

And now the subtle decadence in the restaurant's scene affected him in an exaggerated way. He studied the room coldly, observing the artfulness of its effects—the contrived undersea gloom, the tide of formless sound obliterating the individual, inviting easy death by simulated drowning.

"There is a deadly familiarity in all these places," he said to Fredericka, after he had ordered. She had never heard him speak in a tone so flatly critical. She flushed, feeling responsible because she had suggested this meeting place. Before she could speak he added, as though talking out loud to himself, "the escape, the public hide-out. Berlin, Vienna, Paris—now here—they're all alike."

The blank cold mask that had so haunted her, on the few occasions when it had dropped over his face, appeared now.

"We can leave," she said nervously. "I'd just as soon go. It looks an awful place to me too."

"No, no, they're all alike," he repeated. He tried to throw off his mood. "It's all right." He drank quickly and when his glass was empty he asked at once, "Shall we order another?"

She was surprised. He always drank sparingly. "If you wish."

When the second drink came he began to talk, turning the glass in his hand, beginning without preamble to describe Vienna as it had been in the 1930's, as it was on the very day Dollfuss was murdered. Fredericka could see it plainly: midsummer in an old and charming European capital. Park benches and sidewalk cafés crowded. A nation on the verge of internal collapse, yet its people drank wine and beer, coffee with whipped cream; its children ran with hoops in the park; its women bought hats and pastries. It was a modern city with radios, telephones, newspapers, yet for hours no one on the streets or in the parks guessed that Dollfuss had been shot, that he was dying, bleeding slowly to death in a small room in the Chancellery. . . .

"There were no signs of violence," Franz was saying. "Only a few cars with armed men, a common enough sight in those days, yet there it was! Another nail in the casket of Europe —and few saw it for what it was. Don't misunderstand me— Dollfuss could not have saved Austria. He was a little man. But he was the head of the state, done away with violently —the gangsters' solution, like a Hollywood feature. . . ."

He went on turning and turning the glass in his tense hands. Three women entered to take the table next theirs. Though they had the skin tone and eyes proper to brunettes, they were all wearing blonde hair, assertively goldenly yellow, up in front in a whirl as fixed as Hokusai's forever frozen wave, down behind in a great sack, in a mesh bag dangling to their shoulders. High-pitched, excitable, they took their seats in a flurry of gloves, furs, pocketbooks as large and shiny, as gleaming with metal, as showcases in a medical laboratory. Their deep insecurity came through strongly in the very pitch of their voices, the nervous darting glances of their eyes, in their bleached hair, their exaggerated attire.

Franz watched them expressionlessly until they had settled to their orders, then he went on in the same quiet, almost monotonous voice:

"When the workers' houses were fired on in Vienna those men died unattended, too. They also bled slowly to death, in the courtyard of those model dwellings, those bright, light twentieth-century workers' apartments which students of architecture all over the world were studying as a symbol of a new order . . . Here also was one of the signs of the eleventh hour in Europe—but who heard the clock striking?"

He finished his drink before he spoke again. "I too was deaf and blind," he said, gazing vacantly above the heads of the people in the room before him, like a man who looks across a dark and troubled sea hoping for a landmark, a sail, a sign that there is another life like his own in the great waste of waters. "Blind and stupid! I could not see. I refused to look. It was my wife, Vania, who . . ."

His voice died in his throat. Fredericka felt that he was drowning before her very eyes and she powerless to save him.

After a long silence, which she made no attempt to break, he said, "All these terrible memories! And yet I find myself homesick. Can it be? I ask myself. Am I still a man who longs for his country? And it is true. I suffer from *heimweh*."

As he uttered this word *heimweh*, there rose in him the aching wish that he had held so firmly in check since coming to the New World, the wish to see again the steep pitch of the roofs of an Austrian village sharp against the sky—an old village like the villages of Dürer and Holbein, built for gray winters, designed to resist the pelting slant of rain and the weight of wet snow.

His longing centered around a dimly remembered Dürer of a farmyard with pigs and a kneeling man, barefoot . . . Was he praying? The prodigal son returned—returned quaintly to a northern scene familiar to the artist. His hair to his shoulders, his face drawn with remembered misery, the wanderer looks again on the barnyard of his father, the discarded wagon wheels, the haystacks, the rooks and swallows high in the eaves. Franz could not remember where he had seen the painting or where it hung, but in his mind he identified himself with the kneeling man.

And always following this image there came another, and again he could not say on what gallery wall it had hung. But this remembered painting belonged *beyond* the returned wanderer; it lay the other side of pain and nostalgia. It showed an island in a tranquil sea with six trees growing out of it and cliffs and shores guarding the sky lines. Lazy boats with vertical sails set the mood of dream. A watchful bird hovered near the solitary figure of a man who, with down-dropped eyes, serenely read the book that was propped on his knee. The dark robe about the man's shoulders, the guardian rocks and shore line held the whole scene within a magic circle.

Here lay, in two images, certain states of Franz Allers' own mind: the wanderer who longs for his home place, the man who knows there is now no rest except on the island within—and only there, at rare intervals, when the fury of conflicting outer forces dies down. So distant indeed is this island, though it lies within and as close as the heart, that to imagine being there rests more in the realm of wish than reality. . . .

When Franz looked about him again at this actual scene

of which his body was a part, he could not find himself. The two strong drinks, the unfamiliar bizarre setting, the clarity of his inner visions, had disoriented him. Without warning he was seized by the sensations of his nightmares, and Fredericka, watching apprehensively, saw panic and uncertainty flash up into his eyes.

"Let's get out of here," he said thickly.

"Yes, of course." His expression frightened her terribly. She summoned the waiter. "Let me pay it"—for she had the feeling that Franz would not, in his agitation, be able to make change. She took his arm then and led him out of the noisy glass aquarium.

In the taxi she took his hands in hers. He pressed one of her palms hard against his cold cheek and with his eyes closed rode the few blocks to her hotel. When they drew up in front he too got out without question. As they walked together through the crowded lobby, into the noisy elevator, Fredericka began to feel increasingly weak and afraid.

At last the door of her room closed behind them. They stood just inside, locked together blindly and dumbly, like creatures clinging for warmth in the midst of a whirling storm. Standing there in a long silent embrace she felt strength begin slowly to flow back into his body, until finally he murmured in his familiar voice, "You are trembling."

She could only whisper, "Yes."

"Are you afraid?"

With her face against him she shook her head. "It's only . . ."

He loosed his arms from about her, took her hand, and led her across the room to the bed. They sat down together on the edge of it, her hand still in his.

"Only?"

"Only that I feel that everything is slipping from me, all my careful structures, my little dams and walls and storm doors, all going down in a flood. What if I'm never able again to build them? What if I'm just carried on this flood all the rest of my life, thrown here and there, washed up onto banks, and off banks . . . ?"

"I know."

He abruptly released her hand, rose and walked to the one window.

"I've upset you," she cried. "I didn't mean to. It's wrong of me. I should just go *with* my feeling, instead of forever questioning, weighing, measuring, half-doing . . ."

"You are not to blame for that," he said after a moment. "Partly it's your temperament, partly it is—" He broke off, turning the cord of the window curtain in his fingers, gazing out at nothing.

"Partly what?" she pressed him.

"Partly the times in which we find ourselves. When there is so much tragedy, insecurity, destruction, loss, separation . . ." He spoke slowly and deliberately as though each word summoned before his inner vision a picture that he had to study. "How can one add to it, you ask yourself. Yes, it is a grave question. I understand it. I understand it even though now I no longer have anything to lose, no one to hurt, nothing to cling to."

As he spoke he heard himself inside crying: Vania! Vania! in terrible pain and it seemed as though his whole being was caught into the silent utterance of the name of his dead wife. How can I? How can I? he cried wordlessly in anguish. "Oh, my God!" he said aloud and his voice was so hollow and so full of desperate misery as he turned away from the window, blindly now, that Fredericka jumped up from the bed and ran to him and put her arms about him.

"Oh, my dearest, don't despair!"

Then he clung to her. He let fall the terrible burden of his misery and his guilt, allowing her to feel his need and his pain, sobbing out all the old unexorcised dark pain of childhood and adolescence, and the more recent, more conscious and personal pain that had come to him as a man.

She could feel that she had ceased to be herself to him; she was both less and more, for she was a woman, a woman who loved him and on whom he could rest. Even as she supported him, murmuring formless words of reassurance, cupping the back of his head with her palm, she was somewhere protesting and afraid, somewhere in flight: For who will support and succor me? she cried, thinking prophetically of Christopher, of Forrest perhaps, also leaning, asking for help, demanding, needing. . . . Am I alone then and must I bear it, keep on enfolding with my arms and murmuring and stroking while somewhere within me, below the deep welling pity and sympathy, is the wish to run and run and run? From what? From life, then—if this is it.

She helped him at last to the bed and he lay back exhausted, without speaking, his eyes closed. He was very pale and she saw him old and ill and weary of existence. She got a towel from the bathroom, wrung it out in cold water, and put it across his forehead. She lay down beside him then, holding his arm against her side.

Lying there with the rhythm of their breathing shared between them she, too, closed her eyes and was at the shore with the waves rocking far out, plucking softly at the sand, sliding up and back up and back. She was reading "Dover Beach" long ago at the lake and it was plucking softly at her senses like the sea that prompted its writing: *Begin, and cease, and then again begin with tremulous cadence slow, and bring the eternal note of sadness in.* Note of sadness. Was that the full meaning? Note of sadness, heard by *Sophocles long ago . . . on the Aegean.* She could not have been more than twenty-three but even then she heard it, far out beyond the watery horizon, the *melancholy, long, withdrawing roar* which is the sound of *the sea of faith . . . retreating, to the breath of the night-wind;* the very sea that once was *at the full, and round earth's shore lay like the fold . . . of a bright girdle furled. . . .* Oh, was that true? Had it ever been true? Had not people always desperately turned, clinging even on a *moon-blanched land,* to cry: *Ah, love, let us be true to one another!* Why? Because the world which once seemed *to lie before us like a land of dreams* (When? At six years? Seven? Eleven? Twenty-one?), *so various, so beautiful, so new, hath really neither joy, nor love . . .* Nor love? Could the poet have meant that? For why then had he cried: Ah, love, let us be true to one another? Was it only because of the darkling plain, the ignorant armies clashing in the night? The darkling plain, the darkling plain . . .

Together they turned in the unlit room and their lips met on the pillow.

When later, much later, they spoke together, he told her the story of the murder of his wife.

He took Vania's picture from his wallet and put it in Fredericka's hand. It was a small snapshot, but clear—a woman with a wide fine brow, eager eyes, light soft hair, sturdy slender body, sitting on a garden bench, half turned, smiling, in repose . . . Dead? Murdered brutally? It was not possible.

He spoke then slowly of himself. Of the guilt he had felt

to have been no part of the life that cost Vania her life; the fear he had had of being hunted himself; the period of wandering rootless and without deep inner purpose watching Europe sink below the waves; the slow revival within him of a real focal point of interest again—personal interest—which she had so mysteriously brought into his life.

"It was also your brother, as you have long suspected," he said. "It was Louis, in Paris, who helped show me how, for a time, I could help by . . ."

He hesitated.

"By what?" Fredericka asked him at last.

"By risking my life also. It meant nothing to me then. It was nothing to ask, so I count it nothing . . . This is something about which there is not much to say. I only mention it in passing because of you . . . You and your brother . . . Life is strange . . ." He tapered off.

After a long silence, without looking at her or touching her, he said quietly, "I have nothing to offer you. At times with my body I feel like a foolish boy, but my mind says to me even then, Tired old man, what are you doing? What can you give this woman? You cannot give security, peace of mind, stability of any kind . . ."

She was silent, lying on the pillow listening, looking at him on the edge of the bed, holding his hands slackly between his knees, his eyes bent on the floor.

"The wish to be with you has grown steadily from the first day . . . You have much more to give me than I have to give you."

"No," Fredericka said.

She stretched out her hand and he took it, pressed it.

After a silence, "Any strong emotion creates the illusion of permanence. . . ." Turning to her with his faint half-grin, "I am now the professor," he said. "This will last forever, we feel, we think, though dimly at the same time we fear that it will not. . . ."

He seemed to lose the thread of what he was saying. Finally, "Neither is true," he said. "Both are true. The complete truth is that human relationships are organic. They live and die by their own laws."

And my relationship to Christopher long since died by its own law, Fredericka said to herself. She did not say it aloud.

"To break with the past is not easy," Franz was continuing. "It is the hardest of all things to do. My past was broken for me, in one great blow. It seemed a death. For a time it was just that—a living death. Now at moments—rare, but still they come to me—I can see it almost as a resurrection. Because I can see this for myself personally, I can hope it for the world, that the death of so much beauty and truth, along with so much of horror and stupidity, may still result in a resurrection—a renaissance for humanity.

"Yes," he added after a silence, as though reassuring himself. "There is still a chance. For a long time I did not believe this, but looking back, remembering, I do now. . . ."

"Once," Fredericka said, "you began to say something to me about a spiral, and then the bus came for Attica Center and you didn't finish."

"Yes, I remember: History as a spiral, experience as a spiral," he said half dreamily. "Seeming to wind away, down, back, actually perhaps winding up; coming near again, seeming to repeat, the same kind of experience—only at another place in time."

He was speaking quietly, disconnectedly, as though feeling his way into ideas he had not expressed in just this way before.

"Today is like the Middle Ages. You can see it in art. You have spoken of it. Medieval symbols of man's dark unconscious, his dreams and nightmares, spewed forth in his art forms. Today's fantasies, collective and individual, appearing in the work of surrealists. . . . In this century, because of psychology, we can interpret what a past century could only express. . . . In both periods, war and turbulence, and the travail of birth—birth which always approaches death."

He lay on his back looking at the ceiling. "Cyclic and spiral," he murmured, "eternal motion. . . . Perhaps it is a law of life, an unread law, the spiral—progressive even when it is seemingly retrogressive. . . ."

"Eternal motion!" Fredericka repeated. It seemed to her a thought gloomy to the point of terror. "Never any peace?" she asked him. "Never any rest?"

"In the dark night of Brahma," he mused, as though quoting something from an old book, letting his thoughts carry him where they would.

She could not follow him here. She knew only that her terror began to assume a form. She saw herself a part of cosmic impulses faintly glimpsed, never named, following laws of which only fragments, never wholes, were known. Turning and spinning, in dark and in light, out of knowledge and into knowledge—where, then, was there ever repose, the fixed place? It became too big for her, out of reach, completely unreal. Groping back to find herself, she returned to the room and the moment through the dark mist of the present, thinking: How black and evil and without direction the very times are! And suffering! Everywhere suffering. Were there no cures? There must be cures. At least one thing was cured with me, she thought—the wound of Greg. But even in the curing must I be wounded again, and must I wound again?

"Why did the spiral interest you?" he asked suddenly, out of their silence.

"Because of something that happened fifteen years ago."

She began then to tell him slowly and quietly, still lying beside him, the story of Greg Davie. At last she could see the experience for what it was. She understood and could describe her fear, her flight, the complete submergence afterwards of even the memory, until just before Christopher's departure to war, when it had come back as vividly as opening a closed door and seeing a cinema playing.

"Then you see," she said, "right after that I met you, in the same room, in the same place where I first met Greg. It was like fate, like something I couldn't evade—a man to stir me to life. As a girl it was Greg Davie, as a woman it was you. The spiral. . . . Do you see?"

He put out his hand to take hers without answering.

She sat up. "Can it be really true that it took fifteen years to recover from that shock—a shock I seemed to weather without betrayal to a living soul?"

"It is possible not to recover at all from shocks of the most seemingly trivial kind," he said gravely.

"Then suddenly, mysteriously, the hidden festering wound can be healed?"

"These are the miracles."

"But when you know that—about pain, shocks, how they may perhaps never be recovered from—you said it yourself just now—" she was thinking of Aunt Palm, Christopher, the children—"how can you ever bear to shock or wound anyone for whom you care at all?"

"Aha," he said sadly. "There you come to the hard core; there is where you must have more faith in life than most people manage to acquire in a lifetime of shocks and knocks of their own."

"Is it protection, then, for oneself, this refusal to cause pain? Is it a wish, somewhere, not to have to grow up?"

"I believe that is part of it," he said.

There was a long silence. The roar of the city came up to them dimly, muffled and diffused, like the breathing of a distant monster. Finally Fredericka turned her face toward the man beside her. The lamp by the bed shed its guarded glow into the stiff conventional hotel room. By its light Fredericka looked deeply into the eyes of Franz Allers.

"Am I to marry you, then?"

He looked back quietly, steadily. "If you wish it—and I hope so."

It was she then who clung to him, pushing out of the room the face of Aunt Palm, the voice of Bridgie, Christopher's eyes, and the lean childish faces of Leslie and Forrest.

In the morning, before she left for the train, she had tried to speak of plans; she felt she should. Actually she was always so fearful of the positive that now, in a combination of guilt and nerves, she forced herself to bring out into the open many things that might better have been left unsaid. Earlier, lying in her tub in the faint scent of her white lilac bath oil, she had been swept with waves of happiness. Examining herself for regrets she found none. Her only fear was the fear of discovery. But later at breakfast she felt that she should speak of "what to do," of "when" and "how." His calmness had astounded her.

"Don't worry it," he said. (She saw herself like a dog with a bone.) "Let it be. It *is*. Let it grow."

When still she went on with her halting phrases and questions, he said only, "Live with it. You'll know what to do when the time comes, what is right."

"What makes you so sure?" she cried. "*I'm* not sure!"

"Because I know you. You're wiser than you care to believe."

"I wish I had your faith in me," she cried, near to tears.

She left on the afternoon train in a mood of serene fulfilled happiness. As she traveled slowly up the familiar countryside in the crowded and gritty train full of sprawling holiday-makers, she believed, with Franz, that she could take care of whatever situation arose.

When she got home, safe within the accustomed surroundings, she had a moment in which she was less sure of herself. She wondered if there was any significance in the fact that Aunt Palm asked her no questions at all. But in the evening, by the time Bridgie had telephoned to ask her about the trip to New York and the possibilities of an exhibition next winter, she was able to frame lies with perfect composure.

Chapter Twenty-One

FRANZ WENT TO NEW MEXICO FOR HIS holidays; Christopher was still in Miami, complaining bitterly about the delay in his orders, about the debilitating damp heat, the dull mess fare, the routine of his work. Fredericka's spirits dropped like a stone with every letter from him. She had hoped to break her news at a time when he would be exhilarated over his own expanding life. And now here he was caught in Florida, like a bored and disgruntled tourist forcibly detained out of season.

The children had come home for a month and were now away at separate summer camps. While they were in Wrenkill Fredericka had suffered beyond expression. Every night she lay in her bed crying, wishing one moment that she was closer to them, wondering the next if it wasn't better this way, without a bond as deep as many mothers, she was sure, had with their children. Bridgie had it with Jeb and Mopsie, though not with Owen Junior. Owen Junior walked alone. Children! she thought. How they are invariably lumped as creatures of single dimension, of common aspect! Actually they are as different, as baffling and complex, as adults. Perhaps even more so, for she realized that she had no notion at all how either Leslie or Forrest would take the news that sometime within the next few months they were going to hear. It was far easier to imagine Christopher's reaction, though she would not allow herself to picture it.

When she saw the children off on the train to camp their clear untroubled eyes in farewell stabbed her. She had an impulse to cling to them at the last, to cry, Wait! Don't go! Don't leave me, because while you are gone I am going to act on your destiny, alter your futures! She saw herself like some dark goddess of fate as she stood gazing up at their narrow sloping shoulders, their shy poised heads in the train window. They would never find their home the same again —not if Christopher came on leave in early September as he planned and she broke the news to him then. For children lived by their intuitive antennae. They would sense immediately the atmosphere of dissolution and change.

After the train left she returned to the car and drove it as far as the old Wrenkill cemetery. The rusty iron gates stood open and she drove inside and parked under one of the tall dark firs on the edge of the family burial plot. She got out, for the day was stifling, and sat down on the edge of the iron coping that bounded the Perry domain, setting the clan apart even in death.

The formally planted plot appeared neglected and unkempt in the merciless sun of July. The old caretaker was growing increasingly feeble. He had never been one to trim the dwarf trees, cut back the myrtle, weed around the perennials, unless his worn ledger of funeral dates hinted that some relative might appear to lay a flower-token on one of the graves. During the last year his neglect had even allowed moss to form on the headstones.

Sitting there with the weight of her secret heavy in her breast, Fredericka's eye traveled over the familiar carvings: "Devoted wife of . . ." "Faithful wife to . . ." "Candace, Hope, Elizabeth, Clara". . . She would never lie here under these words of simple dignity.

The hot sun drew the breath from the wallflower border, pressing the blossoms lustily back against the stones until their very stems were limp. Theirs was the scent of all scents to melt the heart, Fredericka thought, feeling her own heart go soft like butter in summer. The tears began to fall weakly down her face as the breath of the wallflowers floated toward her—that breath of muted spice, that velvet evanescence, indescribable, impossible ever to recapture in a small glass vial with a nonleaking stopper, impossible even to recall in a rainy season when you might wish for all the sensations of wallflower weather, and hope by recalling its scent to summon a mood of July languor. . . . She checked herself firmly. Weeping in a graveyard! This was altogether too Victorian. Even the visit itself might be considered morbid, though Aunt Palm maintained that visiting graveyards was a salutary thing to do. If you allowed your mind to wander at will, she said, you could quickly banish all thoughts of the "good old days" and be thankful you were alive now. So Aunt Palm, if she saw Fredericka reading, through a mist of tears, through the breath of the wallflowers, "Candace, devoted wife of. . . ." would probably have facts to contribute on Candace: how she died at thirty of too many childbirths; or was crippled badly with rheumatism from her damp house; or that she drove her husband to sleep and eat in the woodshed. . . . There was no end to Aunt Palm's supply of family stories. And now she, Fredericka, would be a story, a legend. In another time, someone would tell it, someone listen: the first of the Perrys or Woodwards to be divorced. The very word made her shudder. When you read it in a book it sounded commonplace, taken-for-granted. "She divorced him." "A divorce was granted to . . ." Now she would never be able to see the word again without acute awareness of the suffering that had probably lain around it.

With the children gone she knew that there had begun for her the long wait. She recognized quite consciously the meaning of this pause in her life. It was the pause before the actual break in the pattern of her existence. In one sense the break had already occurred; within her the decision had been made, but she knew, with an interior quaking and sickness at the realization, that the outer break would be far different, that it was going to take a kind of courage and simple faith that she was not at all sure she possessed.

She lived for the letters from Franz in the Southwest. The day began, and ended, with their arrival or nonarrival. Sometimes after reading one a sense of even greater unreality took hold of her at the thought that this was the man to whom her life was now joined—no longer Christopher, to whom she also wrote faithfully twice a week.

Franz tried generously to bridge the space between them with detailed pictures of the mighty western land that was having its inevitable effect on him, both vitalizing and relaxing.

"How you would paint this country!" he wrote. "(How you will, for we will come here together!) I must confess that for one of my reserved tastes it is almost overwhelming . . ."

And he went on with his vivid descriptions until through his eyes she saw the hot, high, lazy and stimulating country of the Southwest with its blazing days, and nights made for blankets. She exulted in the pinks, the blues, violets, and sharp whites of hills, skies, shirts and houses, the shrill green cry of strings of peppers drying on sun-bleached walls. She smelled the mingled scent of adobe, juniper, and piñon smoke hanging in the bright air. . . . The moon shot up as the sun shot down on the road from the cliff-village of Acoma, quite alone, without a star to keep it company; like a celestial plate released by a hidden hand, it sailed into the sky to stare down upon the empty purple, gray, and golden land. . . . Fat Indian women with braids down their backs, working hand looms at Chimayo, sold her root beer from a cool room at the rear. . . . A Navajo model in a sculptor's studio gently beat on his drum, singing a chant that was like an uncertain wind, rising and falling as it passed across his memories of sheep and hills, of squaw and children and remote mysterious ancestors. . . . She stood in the open square of Taos watching the life of the pueblo—women carrying water, walking with their awkward fat wide-apart walk in their white buckskin boots, touching up the walls of their dwellings with a trowel and their hands; women and men on the roof-tops against the sky, strangely foreign, bringing thoughts of the Near East.

The same magic power that permitted Fredericka to hack her way through the Cambodian jungle and see through the enraptured eyes of a French naturalist the first outlines of the lost city of Angkor, enabled her now to enter with Franz into the little hidden hill towns of Truchas and Cordova where a laughing boy steered his straw-loaded burro straight at the camera; where a family with twenty goats and six little girls, with switches and straw hats, walked around and around a heap of grain until, seeing the camera, papa made the little girls run and hide, and a boy in a neighboring garden—unconsciously posing himself for a garish penny postcard, in a pink shirt, oversize hat and tattered pants, with his hand on an upright stalk of magnificent Chamber of Commerce corn—also ran and hid in fear.

Fredericka did not attempt to conceal from Aunt Palm the fact that she heard regularly from Franz. In one of his first letters he had asked her to tell her aunt about the little Mexican woman who had come up to "exercise her English" as he stood taking a photograph of the intricate stamped-tin façade of a mountain village general store. Holding on an outthrust hip her round-eyed baby in his absurd cerise hat, she revealed herself as a thoroughgoing feminist who thought three children were quite enough, if you planned to send them to school. She had begged for magazines with "pictures of American señoras."

Stimulated by Franz's descriptions of a distant desert landscape, of the Indians and Mexicans who inhabited it, Fredericka and Aunt Palm decided to reread *Death Comes for the Archbishop*. Eunice, bringing the pitcher of cold tea with the pale-yellow disks of lemon and the sprigs of mint into the garden where they sat waiting for the day to cool, little suspected that she was serving Padre Baltazar and a traveling friar among the whispering vine leaves on the rock at Acoma.

After *Death Comes for the Archbishop* they read, for the first time, *The Delight Makers* and *Ancient Life in the American Southwest*.

Then Aunt Palm began to paint. She painted first an abstraction that she called "Dark Echo." Using only red clay color, black, white, and gray, she produced a canvas that had all the haunting charm of the prehistoric pottery by which Uncle Philander set such store. She seemed happier than she had been in many months and Fredericka felt that somehow this was a good omen, though Aunt Palm still kept unopened the inner door she had closed at the time of Uncle Caleb's death.

But Fredericka could do no painting herself. It was as

though she did not have the patience, or the powers of concentration. She went about like one waiting to be summoned away at a moment's notice and so wishing to have nothing on hand that could not be instantly abandoned.

There was nothing to rouse her from her somnolence. They had given Bridgie and Owen the lake place for several weeks. The village of Wrenkill slept its dusty sleep. It was only a little quickened by the tide of people passing through to livelier places—a tide that not even the war could stem entirely during the month of August.

Fredericka went on one picnic with "the gang," following a letter from Christopher in which he said, "Joe complains that no one sees you. I warned you you'd become a hermit. Why not go out more?". . . How could she tell him that far from being a hermit during his absence she had . . . She would not phrase it to herself, but these were the intimations of the coming agony that pounced on her without warning and chilled her blood in a flash at the most ordinary moments—as she spooned up the red quiver of madrilene at lunchtime, as she threw out the faded phlox, bent over her herb garden . . .

The picnic had been marked, so she felt, by a definite restraint on everyone's part. In the opinion of all their friends, Fredericka had finally made herself plain. Christopher's departure had established her as a recluse—by choice. Joe made no allusion to the scene of that unhappy night in June. She had run into him before, down in the town, and they had acted with guarded politeness to each other. The subject of "Fredericka's refugee" did not come up at the picnic either. This might in itself be an ominous sign, but worrying would not help a situation that was now beyond help.

So the days inched past, pinned to this or that small routine event—the paper at morning and at evening; the turning dial on the radio regularly bringing war and destruction into the flower-filled rooms; burning cities, sinking ships, and tooth powders that are cleansing but not abrasive. . . . Tooth powders . . . Powders . . . Sleeping powders—that was what she craved, to do away with the heavy weight of this endless August. . . .

There was a gangster's moll dying soon in a prison. The newspapers and the radio kept the people posted hour by hour as her death approached. The eyes of the nation were on her, all ears bent to catch her last words. The identification was complete, and when, as collective mouthpiece, she finally spoke, it was with the voice of the Great Audience itself. Waiting for the Final Mysterious Nothing, of what did the condemned woman think? "The radio programs—particularly the Goldbergs, my favorite—will still be going on." And her ear not there to receive them! Thus the gangster's moll recognized death and had a faint chilling intimation of what it meant to cease to be. . . .

As for me, Fredericka thought, I too am waiting for something; but this is something to strengthen me to act. Everything seemed suspended. She thought of the word "limbo," coming out of the Middle Ages. It carried a meaning intimately personal to her at this moment in her life. There was nothing in the papers, on the air, anywhere, but the end of things: breakup, downbeat, destruction, death, like a reflection on a world scale of her own state, of what lay immediately before her, lay in the way of a new life.

Chapter Twenty-Two

FRANZ RENTED A HOUSE JUST OUT-side Santa Fe for a month—a house which in outer form and interior appearance was unlike anything with which he had ever been familiar. The thick adobe walls, slightly curved, with the padded look of some warmer substance than clay, had been painted a soft white with the faintest trace of gray. There were deep windows and a plain fireplace, bright Indian rugs—not too many—a few old Mexican carvings, wooden beams overhead. The house inside and out had all the uncluttered simplicity of what he thought of posses-sively as his "view"—that vast eye-stretching scene, stripped, treeless, but not at all cold, with simple basic forms of rec-tangle, cone, triangle, in mesa, peak, and distant mountain, lying serenely under an eternally blue sky. In this abstract and impersonal atmosphere he sat down quietly for the first time since Vania's death to look at himself and the road im-mediately ahead.

On Fredericka's urging he had taken with him the manu-script about which he had once told her. He had believed he would never seriously work on it again, but one bright morn-ing, as he sat under a piñon tree behind his house, he was moved to rise and get it from the bottom of his traveling bag. He returned to the shade of the tree and began to read, hap-pily conscious that there would be no interruptions. The air carried the faint singing tone that comes with altitude, purity, and wide empty distances. Occasionally an airplane, high in the swept blue sky, deepened the tone, but it was no more intrusive than the brief solo of some insect close at hand. The sun fell warmly around him. A few of his neighbor's chickens picked at the dry soil. A Mexican on a donkey plodded by in the soft dust of the road. Everything was peaceful, serene, lazy, warm, unchallenging—and yet. . . .

"I have been dodging my responsibilities," Franz found himself saying aloud, accusingly.

A fly resting on his sandal took off, feeling the vibration from his words. A chicken stopped for a moment, transfixed, its beady eye alert for danger. When the figure continued to be silent it went back without alarm to its pecking.

As he spoke the word "responsibilities" Franz saw the ancient Indian remains at Puyé and Canyon de Chelly to which he had been taken by an anthropologist. There seemed in his mind some connection between these remains and his thought of "responsibility" and he tried now to trace the association, remembering particularly the mixture of awe and gratitude which he had experienced in looking at the spectacular white ruin of the "apartment house" of legendary people set in the red cliff. His emotion had sprung, he believed, from an overpowering sense of the mysterious flux and flow of civilizations, the courage of man in the face of the great ocean of time and change, continuing to leave his frail records—pots and baskets, pictographs, jewelry for braves and brides. . . .

He had been reading, in the small but select library of his rented house, stories of the early priests who came into this beautiful and terrible land of Nueva España centuries before— cultivated men from Europe, to die here in loneliness and often in spiritual despair, faced with the timeless, tideless, unchanging culture of the Indians on their cloud-hung mesas, or in their villages among the sandy hills, villages that could hardly be seen for their similarity to the landscape; might indeed, to this day, be passed like a mirage in the glitter of sun on sand. There was comfort to Franz in the thought of these other pilgrims from a foreign shore cast up, solitaries, in a strange and often hostile world. They, the more sensitive among them, had found themselves moved, sometimes even troubled, by a pagan wisdom among the Indians, by powers of meditation, forms of art, worthy of any spiritual man's respect. Whatever the motives that prompted their voluntary exile, Franz felt a certain kinship with these European wayfarers. He did not choose to examine this kinship too closely. He was content merely to feel it—did not seek for the flaws and inconsistencies that a comparison between his outlook and the outlook of these proselytes of the Catholic faith might uncover to him.

An unexpected wind ruffled the papers on his knee as though drawing his attention to the long-neglected manuscript. He let his eye move in and out of the typewritten pages with the legible small notations in purple ink above the lines. He had not looked at it for so long that it held for him the freshness of a stranger's work. The almost forgotten pulse of mental excitement began again to beat in him as he read:

> The human being is a unity. When he is less than that he is not well. . . .
>
> Disease: a disturbance in two dynamic equilibria—the equilibrium by which the organism relates to its environment, the equilibrium between all parts of the organism itself.
>
> . . . When the organism as a whole loses its power over

its component elements, or when any of these elements, without reference to the whole, acts independently of the good of the whole, then we have sickness which may range from deterioration of the personality to actual alterations in the physiological structure. . . .

He saw himself in his study in Vienna, the tight cozy room with its porcelain stove, warm walls of well-handled books, easy chairs, dark-red carpet. That room belonged to another world, a dead world of material security, a contained and prescribed way of life. Now he sat out in the open, in the vastest landscape he had ever seen, with his back against a familiar tree, reading the words he had written down years before in that warm sheltered room across two continents and an ocean.

And again, as long ago in that other life with Vania, he saw the parallel between the organism of man and the organism of the world itself—man's total organism.

The whole world, he said to himself, is now like a patient undergoing a psychoanalytic treatment. During this treatment, as so often happens, organic symptoms are produced when repressed material rises to the surface. And just as the human creature often *chooses* (if that perhaps too conscious word may be used) to solve his personal conflict through disease, rather than face reality, thus making his own physical body the battleground for the new consciousness trying to emerge, so man in toto also does this: he *chooses* war, destruction, universal sickness, rather than face the necessity for creating a new way of life which would permit all his forces to operate in balanced equilibrium.

"Horvath," he said aloud. It was an appeal for support. He looked far out to the blue mesas breasting the heat waves like the prows of steady ships. He could almost hear Horvath speaking, reassuring him: This material is more than ever important. The very destruction of the war, the despair and negativism that will follow, make it so. What if much of what you found so novel, so advanced, ten years or more ago, is no longer new? It is still not known to many. So go on. Write. Talk. Put before simpler minds, younger minds, any small gleanings you may have on the unsolved mystery of man and his universe.

Franz was as moved by this moment in which he again accepted his life's work as he had been in the sleeping streets of New York, earlier in the summer, when he had determined not to turn his back on his love for Fredericka. He drew a sheet of paper from the bottom of the pile and began to write to Fredericka. He could imagine her carrying the letter in her pocket down to the antique Italian well, or to the fishpond, and reading it there alone in the midst of all the sounds and scents of the August garden.

I know now that I shall be able to go back to what I once considered my life's work. Where this will take me I cannot say. You are now included in this uncertainty, which is, paradoxically, not uncertain at all. . . . I probably should not write this but I must: between us at times there will have to be, my dear one, the closed door of my study. This will not matter if you are also in your own work, living in the center of your own life. . . .

He put aside his pen for a moment, disturbed by a vision of her face, anguished, tightly drawn, torn with conflict in the hotel room in New York when she asked, "Am I to marry you, then?"

Now he asked himself: Had he realized fully what she must give up, what it would cost her to come to him?

He wrote again:

I know you will have to suffer to come to me. I feel that you are suffering already more than you say, in your wish to spare me. This sense of your suffering pains me inexpressibly even—perhaps most—in the moments when I enter completely into the serene beauty of this fabulous landscape.

He again put down his pen and sat for a long time in the humming warmth, with the enormous sky—more enormous here than anywhere else in the world—folding down around the land like an inverted blue cup. He added another line:

I miss you more than I can possibly say and need you so much that I fear to tell you how much . . .

When he had finished, Franz folded the letter and decided to go into town to mail it. It seemed to him—and he smiled at himself for his foolish thought—that this act would bring her nearer. Getting the bicycle that went with the rent on the place and mounting it, he told himself half humorously that his sensations of vague restlessness and longing were the sensations of a much younger man.

After Franz had posted the letter he decided to go into the bar of the hotel and have a beer and a sandwich. When his eyes, blinded from the bright sun outside, became accustomed to the darkened interior he looked about to see if any of the few people he had met in Santa Fe were in the bar at this hour. He almost hoped so. Over in one corner he saw a slouched figure that seemed in the first glimpse to be vaguely familiar. He looked more closely at it. Where had he seen this unkempt head of strawlike hair, the heavy glasses, the stooping shoulders? . . . It was Robert Goodwin, Reuter's friend, the scientist.

Franz rose at once and walked across the room to where

Goodwin sat with his head in his hands above an untouched Tom Collins.

"Hello," Franz began. "This is a surprise!"

Goodwin started, half rose, fell back, his face astonished almost to the point of terror. He acted like a man who is awakened too suddenly from deep sleep. He seemed so shaken and unsteady that Franz put his hand on his arm to reassure him.

"What's that?" Goodwin cried tremulously. "What do you want?"

For a moment Franz thought he was drunk. "Don't you remember me? It's Franz Allers. I'm a friend of Carl Reuter's."

A look of suspicion, a guarded look, crossed Goodwin's strained face, but only briefly. Then pulling himself together, he said, in a dry, absent-minded manner:

"Oh, Allers, of course. Yes, of course I remember you. Didn't recognize you at first." He rose irresolutely to his feet. Although he seemed weak in his legs, Franz was now certain that he was not drunk.

"Sit down, won't you?" Goodwin went on indifferently. "I wasn't expecting you—I mean, this is a surprise! What are you doing here?"

"I'm loafing—that's all," Franz said. "Don't let me intrude. I'm having a sandwich and a beer. Will you join me?"

But the waiter had already come in with Franz's order, and seeing that his customer had moved to a new table he quietly brought the tray to Goodwin's corner.

"Fine!" Goodwin said with empty politeness.

Franz felt very much unwanted, but he did not wish to make the situation any more awkward, so he sat down opposite Goodwin.

"I remember you were going to the Southwest when we

last met," he remarked, pouring his beer. "Are you living here now?"

"In Sante Fe? Oh, no," Goodwin said quickly. After a moment he added guardedly, "I live quite a ways from here."

His reluctance at giving information was so marked that the idea came into Franz's head that the man might be what the local residents called a "lunger," and that he had kept the secret of his disease from all his friends.

"Do you hear from Reuter?" Franz asked after another silence which Goodwin showed no inclination to break.

"Reuter?" Goodwin spoke the name as though he could hardly put a face to it. "No, never." Then after a moment he grinned—the sudden, sharp-toothed, mocking grin that Franz remembered in New York. "That's right: I promised Carl a picture postcard, didn't I? Must put that down." He drew a small notebook from his pocket and elaborately jotted something in it with the same mocking air.

"What are you doing here?" he asked Franz abruptly. His face sharpened, his eyes behind his glasses narrowed as he asked the question.

Franz replied in the offhand manner with which he had first spoken, "Well, I said loafing, but, actually, I believe I'm working—somewhere in the basement. Anyway, I feel some ferment."

Goodwin's attention was quite obviously drawn by this remark. He studied Franz's face gravely. He seemed to consider the statement one that required special attention on his part. After a moment, "You're living here—in this town?" he asked.

"Just outside it. I've rented a house for a month."

"Haven't got an extra room I could have for a couple of nights?"

"As a matter of fact I have. Would you like to use it?"

"If I could, it would be a big favor. I can't get a room in the town—all filled up. It would only be for a night or two. It would certainly be a help to me."

"Of course," Franz said. "Delighted." He wanted to ask Goodwin what business had brought him to Santa Fe but he decided not to prod, to wait and let the answer appear in due course.

As though something had been settled that they had been discussing for a long time, Goodwin immediately summoned the waiter. "My bill," he said impatiently, "and this gentleman's—oh, I'm sorry, Allers, finish your beer."

"I've finished," Franz said, draining his glass in a gulp.

As they emerged from the dark room into the hot bright day, Goodwin said, "I've got a car. Any place you'd like to drive?—or have you something else to do?"

"Not a thing," Franz said. "And as a matter of fact you can do me a favor. I want to go out to some Indian remains near here—about an hour's ride. I went once and I want to go again. If you wouldn't mind taking me."

"Sure thing," Goodwin said. He showed no surprise as he climbed into the car. The car was a conventional closed model, with two seats, the car of a suburban family man.

"Are you married?" Franz asked casually as he opened the door and got in beside Goodwin.

"Yes." Goodwin was opening his window to let some air into the stifling interior.

"Is your wife in New Mexico, too?"

"No, she's in Los Angeles." He answered briefly, coldly, obviously not wishing to discuss his personal life. He started the car with all the gear-grinding and general ineptitude of the brilliant technician who cannot function with simple mechanics. Again Franz thought of his likeness to the stereotype of the absent-minded scientist.

"I'll drive if you like," Franz offered in the offhand voice he was careful to continue to use. "I know the way."

"Would you? Good! I hate driving." As he spoke Goodwin pulled the car to the curb. They rolled up on it, jounced off. "Sorry!" For the first time he seemed embarrassed. He stopped the car with a jerk. Before getting out to change seats with Franz he said, in the most natural voice he had yet used, "Look, Allers—I've had a couple of drinks, but I'm not drunk."

"No, I know you aren't," Franz said. "But I think you're tired. Maybe you'd rather not take this ride."

"No, I'd like to. I'm not tired, I'm just—well . . ." Finding no word he shrugged and let it go.

They rode a long way in silence. As they drove they began to pass open land in which wildly tossed fantastic and tumbled shapes of stone stood and lay about on the ground as though some giant had come along to interrupt and half destroy his labors.

"I find this landscape very stimulating," Franz said, nodding at it in passing.

"You do? Why?" Goodwin seemed more relaxed now and genuinely interested in the question.

"All these half-forms, like things becoming."

"Or like things destroyed," Goodwin said angrily. "I don't like it. I'm surprised that you do, after Europe—and what you must have seen there."

"Strange that it doesn't have any associations of destruction. . . . Maybe the mesas soothe me. They seem so out of it all —as though if you could just get up there and lie down, with nothing above you but the clouds, you'd see everything clearly, and forever. They're like great beds. . . ."

"Are you looking for a bed?" Goodwin asked harshly.

The pertinence of the question took Franz aback. "I was once, not so long ago," he said. "I don't think I am now."

Goodwin made no answer but after they had ridden another mile or so he asked, "Is your wife with you?"

"My wife has been dead for several years," Franz said quietly.

At once something in Goodwin's stillness told him that he remembered the story of Vania's death. "Oh, yes, I recall now . . . Reuter told me." He stopped. After another silence, "Men like ourselves should live alone," he said in a harsh voice. "Cut off from normal life—in the end it's better, less suffering for all—not that any life is normal any more, only some lives are less so. . . ." Before Franz could speak, he added, "My wife wants another child."

When he had recovered from the surprise of this intimate announcement Franz said quietly, "Well, why not?"

"I'm sorry we have the one we've got now," Goodwin said bluntly.

Since he had broken down to this extent, Franz felt free to question further. "My dear fellow, is there some reason . . . are you sick—or no longer in love with your wife, or . . . ?"

"Oh, love!" Goodwin said. He turned the mocking mirthless grin on Franz. "Love! In the 1940's—you still talk of love? Does no one *see* it, except a few mad Russians? You speak like a schoolboy," he finished scornfully.

"Maybe it's because I feel like a schoolboy at times lately," Franz said. "For I'm in love myself. And I can't doubt it—love —because I feel it."

Goodwin was silent. "Well," he said, "enjoy it while you can."

They drove on again in silence. Within a mile they passed

a rock on which the words Prepare to Meet Thy God had been printed in white paint. Without a word, with his mirthless grin, Goodwin pointed a long, uncared-for finger at it.

When they came to Puyé they got out of the car and climbed up through the scattered pines to the top of the high rocky plateau where an ancient nameless people had lived in some remote forgotten day. They stood together in silence looking down into one of the kivas—the ceremonial holes in the ground which were the living heart of these ancient communities, the deep dark subterranean room close to the ear and lips of the Earth Mother.

"What do you get out of these places?" Goodwin asked finally when, before leaving, they stood again on the top of the great rock gazing out across the far-stretching landscape. His voice had lost its guarded note of hostility.

Franz took his time about answering. "So much," he said finally.

He tried to describe the country as his anthropologist friend had done for him, to explain to Goodwin that they were standing on one of the many geological islands, some circular, some mere strips, that lay in the landscape below them. Centuries of erosion had reduced a thick tufa blanket covering the plateau to these irregular fragments. In all directions from this rooftop of the world mountains stretched into the farthest distance, their nearer slopes dark with forests, the farthest peaks seen only as outlines and tones of color. The Rio Grande River lay here in the bed of a Miocene lake. In the foreground were towers and turrets and heaven-pointing fingers of marl sculptured by the wind. On the nearest slopes, among the junipers, beds of bright yellow bloom marked the once-cultivated fields of a vanished people. . . .

"Where could you go to find a mightier record of the

action of time and the elements upon the natural world?"

"What's uplifting about that?" Goodwin demanded gloomily.

"Well, I only know that the sight of it lifts me out of myself—and then, when I look nearer at hand, I'm returned squarely to myself. For here, on this mesa, all around us, are records of a vanished race, remains that tell us about human creatures who came into this mighty impersonal land and built here, in a time outside reckoning, a good way of life and a distinct culture."

Franz was silent a moment and then he added: "I can't say why, but this challenges me—brings up my own sense of responsibility to life."

"But *meaning!*" Goodwin cried impatiently. "Where's the meaning?"

Franz did not attempt to answer. But when, halfway down from the plateau, they stopped again to rest and smoke, he began to talk, as much to himself as to Goodwin, trying to say how he had come to feel that each person has something to give, to leave—*unique*—and that this is an imperative. He spoke hesitantly about his own determination to return to his work on the union of the mind and the body. He touched briefly on the research he had done in Vienna on the human organism as a whole, and how he knew this organism could not be split into separate parts if it was ever to be fully understood.

Goodwin was silent until they rose to continue down the slope. Then he spoke quietly:

"Some Russian mystic said this: It is impossible to save half a man. It is possible to save only the whole man. It is equally impossible to save half of humanity. It is possible to save only the whole of humanity."

Franz nodded. "You read the Russians a lot?"

"I did at one time," Goodwin said. His voice suddenly assumed the bitterness it had had earlier in the day. "They helped prepare me for my fate—man's fate," he corrected himself.

Franz did not press him to explain. They drove home slowly through the almost painful beauty of the sunset, the color of the mesas and mountains running from pink to purple into deepest blue. The stars came out in a green sky, clear and sharp and close at hand. Franz saw that Goodwin was nodding in his seat, like a man momentarily numb after some unusual strain.

They stopped for supper in the town, a Mexican meal of frijoles, tortillas, green salad, wine, before riding home to Franz's house. Goodwin said he was exhausted and he went straight to bed. Franz lit a fire; one of the great joys of New Mexico was the warmth of the days and the sharp relief of cool nights. He sat by the sweet smoke of the piñon logs reading his manuscript with a rising sense of relief and determination.

It was well after midnight when he heard Goodwin stirring in his room. After a few moments the door opened and Goodwin came out. He was wrapped in a bright blanket of Indian design. His haggard face and pale hair rose with a somber incongruity from the bold primitive pattern. Without a word he crossed the room, lifted Franz's hand from the pile of papers on which it rested, opened the palm and laid in it three white pellets. Franz knew instantly what they were, knew with some extra sense for which later he was at a loss to account.

Yet he asked: "What are they?"

"You know what they are," Goodwin said. He spoke defiantly, and then in a voice abruptly sad and weak, added, "They are poison."

Franz continued to hold the pellets, looking down at them, curiously.

"And what am I to do with them?"

"Anything you like," Goodwin said indifferently. He dropped down into the chair on the opposite side of the fire, hooking one of his long legs over the arm. He seemed suddenly to Franz, with his untidy hair, long lean frame, the blanket around his shoulders, like some unruly or troubled boy coming in for a late-night talk with a parent, or a professor.

Franz put the pellets carefully beside him on the little table and rose to place a fresh log on the fire. When the blaze caught it, and the added warmth began to fill the room, Goodwin started to talk.

"I had made up my mind to die. I can't tell you why. I know I can trust your discretion this far: it has to do with some experiments I've been working on. . . . I haven't been able to sleep well for a long time. . . . I understand what you meant today when you spoke of responsibility to life—to yourself and humanity. I have—or I had—the same ideas. That's why I've been sick for almost a year. I didn't think I could stand any more. I think now, after today, maybe I can. I'll see it through. I'll try to do what I can to keep it—what we're at work on—from being—disastrous . . ."

Still Franz said nothing.

"I know I must be sounding like page two hundred of a mystery novel," Goodwin said a little sheepishly. "I'm sorry. I can't explain. Maybe you have some idea why. I imagine you have, from all I know about you."

"And you were killing yourself to escape universal death?" Franz asked.

Goodwin shot him a quick glance. He laughed, a forced hard laugh that would have sounded brutal in a more virile man. "Maybe," he said. "Though maybe I was really afraid I —afraid I might live," he finished.

Franz reached for the pellets and again held them in his hand. "Do you know," he said quietly, "there was a time, not so long ago, when I would have given anything I had (but I had nothing to give) for such a way out, lying easily in the palm of my hand. Now I no longer want it, and here I am given it."

Chapter Twenty-Three

THE LONG LETTER FROM FRANZ in which he said that he now knew he would be able to return to his life's work, the letter in which he spoke of the possibility of there being, at times, the closed door of his study between them, reached Fredericka on a day when she had awakened tremulous and fearful of the future. It was her weekly day at the Red Cross Center in the town and she had no real chance to read his letter quietly until late afternoon. Then she took it with her into the garden and there, in the fragrant warmth in which Franz had imagined her, she read and reread his words.

As she read, the meaning of what he had written seemed alternately to retreat from her and then again to come very close. One moment the lines seemed reassuring, the next upsetting. The remark about the door of his study drew her attention particularly. She would be with him—yes, of course, but alone, on her own—was that what Franz was saying? "This will not matter if you are also in your own work, living in the center of your life." Was she to prepare herself to be more alone than ever? Was that it? She reread the paragraph again feverishly: "I want you to be free—freed—to realize your own gifts—gifts which I believe are considerable, and which I also believe you must no longer bury in that figurative napkin." (Where do I live? she thought hysterically. Or rather, where do I lie buried? In Wrenkill, the Figurative Napkin.)

Was Franz weakening, wondering, now that he had space and leisure about him, whether he was not making a mistake: "I can, I do question, what we are doing . . . I have always admitted that. Yet there is a place beyond which one does not question. It is! So be it! One must act upon it. Live it out. It has to be."

The final effect of the letter was to frighten her, although she told herself that she was reading into it more than it contained, infusing it with her own qualms and trepidations, based on her immaturity, springing from the deep unconscious wish never to grow up, never to have to face the cruel anomalies of adult life.

What am I planning to do? she asked herself, looking distractedly about the garden in the uprush of her fear. Leave this place forever? The pain began immediately. It was a pain she now knew well, associated as it was with pictures and memories that passed swiftly across her vision—the catbird's nest in the cedars; the death of Oliver Goldsmith, king of the goldfish; Aunt Palm ahead of her on the rocky path up Hungry Hollow; the sagging gray porch at the lake with the golden scallops of the water moving on the ceiling as she lay in the porch swing reading to the children, waiting for the creak of the oarlocks, the watery halloo . . . "Mum, can you get this out?" Leslie impossibly heroic with the fishhook through her thumb. Forrest burying a penny bank in the orchard, making maps, pinpricking page three hundred in *Prince Otto* when the gold-seeking rage was on him after he first read *Treasure Island*. The time Christopher's beard caught on fire when he was playing Santa Claus. . . . Christopher! She saw his face, so familiar, so soft and unaware. No, it is impossible! she thought. What am I doing? I don't hate him. It would be easy if I did, but I do not.

Suddenly it was all impossible, and Franz Allers and his letters from the Southwest became as unreal as a dream. She could not even call up his face before her, she could not remember their hours in New York together—it was all gone and she felt only tired, half dead. She put her head back against the chair and passed into a semisleep, a trancelike state that she realized, with a trickle of apprehension, had been growing on her—the "cocoon death," she called it in her unwilling mind.

After a while she felt the heavy throbbing air shift and sharpen a little. It was evening. She rose and walked slowly into the house. The silence in the darkened rooms was oppressive. Aunt Palm had not been well for several days. She had lain in bed, uncommunicative, white-faced, surrounded by books, eating little, speaking less.

No wonder I want to escape, Fredericka thought; this house is a tomb, a crypt; and she went up to her own sitting room. On the stairs, "But *who* wants to escape?" she said aloud. She walked to her window and looked at the view she had so often turned to for comfort. But something ominous seemed to be reaching toward her out of the garden this evening. Was it the night, or the creeping years, signaled from the vine on the distant wall, the writhing possessive vine which extended its greedy length along the bricks and even thrust out aggressively into the air as though it would claim empty space too and fasten its parasitic tendrils upon it? The vine, the lurking mist beneath the trees, thickening with the shadows, creeping upon the pane, under the door; breathing the breath of damp and mold, decay and the long, long cold. . . . Suddenly there was in an August garden more of terror, more of death, than she had ever found in the empty frozen fields of winter.

She turned from the window and hurried downstairs again. She must light a fire, must have something alive! When it was lit she crouched down in the corner of the big sofa, waiting —she did not know for what. The dusk flowed into the room through the five windows. Like a slow wave it washed down the hillslope, past the fir trees and the russet of the willow fringe, across the lawn and into the room where she sat. She felt it come like a living presence and, as it washed over her and into her own heart, she was for a moment serene and at peace again.

The fire was slowly brightening, beginning to push its glow against the green wave of the twilight. Dimly from the kitchen end of the house she heard the homely sounds of footsteps. A faint pleasant scent of food in preparation began to drift through the halls, mingling with the smell of the early asters she had just picked on her way inside.

Why isn't this enough? she asked herself. It should be for anyone, in dark chaotic days like these. Why would anyone wish to leave a refuge? It *is* enough! I need no more. I do not have to go. I can stay right here in this house and grow old and die in one of the rooms upstairs, as Aunt Palm will. . . .

The undercurrent of tension, fear, worry, with which she had been living for months, mysteriously departed. She let her head fall back against the couch, and she floated once more, without guilt, without challenge or question, in the warm apprehension of familiar shapes, familiar sounds and scents, the cozy and beloved world of childhood, the world of pure feeling existing before there were decisions to be made, plans to be followed.

Almost as though this change of mood was a genie that had

summoned her, Aunt Palm came abruptly into the room. She was dressed for dinner in a long, old-fashioned green chiffon tea gown and she was carrying several portfolios. Fredericka jumped up joyfully at sight of her.

"How wonderful!" she cried. "You're better! I was hoping for company at dinner."

Aunt Palm made no direct reply. She opened the top portfolio. She thrust abruptly at Fredericka a picture of Leonardo da Vinci's St. John, the sensual half-naked pagan saint with his summoning enigmatic gesture—invitation to some secret, transcendent tryst.

"Not for nothing was Leonardo's right hand paralyzed when he painted the St. John," Aunt Palm began, as if merely continuing a conversation already started. "Of course there are those who say he was left-handed. I don't believe it. But certainly this was done with the left hand. . . ." Her voice was authoritative.

"What makes you believe that?"

Aunt Palm closed the first portfolio, as though closing this phase of her subject. "The right hand is the doer, the left hand the dreamer. The St. John was painted out of something Leonardo knew but dared not say too openly."

Fredericka put up her guard. She had to ask the next question, but she tried to make it casual. "What things daren't one say, Aunt Palm?"

Her aunt regarded her with eyes that were like closed doors, a face that said nothing. Yet her voice was passionate as she answered: "You might better ask, What things dare one say? Almost nothing real, lasting, strange, or true dare be uttered in all one's life."

"Aunt Palm, you frighten me," Fredericka murmured uneasily.

"Why?"

"You sound so—so cynical. Were you always cynical?"

Aunt Palm shrugged as though to say: Cynical—what does the word mean? Then deliberately changing her manner, producing another print from another portfolio (almost like a traveling salesman with samples, Fredericka thought), "Renoir," she said, in a voice that was both admiring and amused, "as an old man, had them tie a brush to his paralyzed hand, and he painted too—bosoms and buttocks and big cabbage roses. He was more normal perhaps."

"And what will you paint . . . ?" Fredericka caught herself up. She had been going to say, "in your last years."

Aunt Palm finished the sentence for her quite calmly. "When I am blind and paralyzed? Faces, as I remember them. Until then I shall paint leaves, stones, fungus, and kinds of bark."

Fredericka made no reply. She is really mad, she thought. Her aunt sat down near the fire and closed the second portfolio.

"Are you feeling better?" Fredericka asked.

"I haven't been ill," Aunt Palm said shortly. After a moment, "I have been studying."

"Studying?" A fresh wave of pain and meaninglessness passed over Fredericka. Her aunt's lined face, the wasted years . . .

"I'm sure you want to ask me what for," Aunt Palm said, reading her mind. "It's a fair question. For myself, is the answer. I am studying only for myself. But only for myself because there is no one else—and that is the penalty of wasting one's gifts and one's life. . . . Women!" she muttered with apparent irrelevance. "Women, women, women! . . . Let us have a look!"

And opening the third portfolio she handed Fredericka, with quick nervous gestures, four prints.

Fredericka began to look at them, trying to separate her critical faculties, her mind, her head, from the churning malaise of her midsection where all the varied emotions of this day, of the last weeks, lay uneasy. . . . So this was what Aunt Palm was doing in the nights when her light burned late, so that Fredericka, sleeping fitfully, would see its reflection come on in the maple trees long after they had said good night? She could imagine her lying in the narrow bed—the one she insisted on moving into her room with what Christopher thought had been shocking haste after his father's death —and there, propped up on pillows, she lay looking at pictures like an invalid child. And what was she seeking as she looked —a clue to some elusive mystery of character? of technique of representation? of a lost way of seeing, feeling, living?

Whatever it was, Fredericka now wanted to understand what Aunt Palm was trying to say to her, for she knew by her aunt's manner that this was an important message she was about to convey. She knew, from experience, that her aunt often used pictures as parables. Something Aunt Palm desired passionately to say to her niece and daughter-in-law—something for which she could not find the proper words—she would attempt to say now with her long gnarled index finger pointing, with a few terse and cryptic phrases. So Fredericka looked, willing to see, to understand—and yet somehow also afraid.

The first painting showed two courtesans of fifteenth-century Venice, caught by the painter Carpaccio in a balanced and formal tableau of eternal ennui, a trance unrelieved by the pigeons, or by the dogs, one listlessly pulling on his mistress' stick, the other balanced on his hind legs questioning the painter's arbitrary will as he alone gazed sadly out of the canvas. . . . There they sat, the two heterae, together but alone, forever waiting in unrelieved boredom with their frizzed hair and embroidered sleeves, waiting without anticipation. Not even the page, approaching through the columns against which they rested, could rouse them to look or speak.

"Women, women, women!" repeated Aunt Palm, as though saying, Woe, woe, woe!

"Agnes Sorel, and who might she be?" she asked, pulling forth the next one, a portrait by a nameless artist of the school of Jean Fouquet, a woman worldly and individualized, with one breast deliberately offered like a flower, like a jewel, and no child to excuse its display; instead, though this was the fifteenth century, a book held in the long, cultivated, and tense left hand. A figure without emotion but studiedly, compellingly sensual, made so by the dark restraint of the robe covering the arms entirely, the contrast of the exposed flesh, so insisted upon in shoulder, cheek, forehead, down-dropped wide eyelids, and single breast cupped in a fold of turned-back white satin.

"If you don't know who Agnes Sorel is, then probably no one does," said Fredericka, humoring her.

"Nonsense," said Aunt Palm, making light of her knowledge.

The third print was Cranach's painting of Luther's wife. "She looks like a smart woman executive," was Fredericka's comment. "Very modern." She indicated the hair in a snood, the half-exposed ears, the starched collar of sheer white.

"She got out of Luther, the ex-monk," remarked Aunt Palm dryly, "after he wrote *The Vindication of Marriage*, three boys and two girls. There is a lot in that face."

With the tip of her finger she touched the mouth, the two

shrewd and humorous points of the upper lip, the lower one full but disciplined.

How had Aunt Palm learned all she knew? Where had she acquired this sum of information? By what thieving of time, what mouselike furtive nibbles in the ever-watchful tyrannical presence of Uncle Caleb the Cat, had she managed to put away this secret horde of material—material which was for her as living, as vital as the lives of those around her—perhaps even more so?

"Art really lives for you," Fredericka began, but Aunt Palm was not listening. She was thrusting at Fredericka the fourth print. It was another Leonardo: the Virgin and St. Anne with the Christ child.

"I gave you one of these when Forrest was born," said Aunt Palm, tapping it significantly. Clearly she spoke with special emphasis. Remembering back, Fredericka had a feeling that when Aunt Palm gave her the print, many years ago, she had presented it then with a special air of attaching great importance to it.

They both looked at it now intently.

It was for Fredericka, as ever, compelling in its deceptive simplicity, its indefinable air of mystery, this otherworldly pyramid of two women and two children: the Virgin, a grown woman, seated on her mother's lap—though with nothing awkward or uncouth in the strange position—bending slightly toward her child, the child bending toward the St. John, who in turn looks down dreamily. The Virgin is remote, her babe a part of her tranced state, her inviolate enchantment. It is the St. Anne, the Virgin's mother, who dominates. She dominates by her expression, by a look at once intimate and open, innocent and clandestine, bland with the blandness of the nonmoral deities of the Orient, a look which seems to wish to convey a secret message, verify a bond, express a sympathy, sound a warning, a look timeless and transcendent, given by an older woman to a younger, sharing an experience that is both human and eternal, and certainly more than mortal. . . . What was it Aunt Palm wished to convey? Did she see herself as the St. Anne? Fredericka as Mary?

"The church scholars had a bad time with St. Anne," Aunt Palm was saying. She made a sound like a sardonic chuckle. "Was the Virgin her child, or not her child? Was she too— the Virgin—immaculately conceived? Born not of man? How the brows puckered, furrowed! How the voices rose! The pens flew! . . . Ah, leave the mysteries alone, gentlemen! Leave them! Leave them! For you will never understand them. You can know only one mystery, and do not feel it when it happens—the mystery of death. But women also know the mystery of birth, and only divine hermaphrodites like Leonardo dare approach the painting of these last of all the mysteries. . . ."

Yes, she is mad, wonderfully mad, and since she is mad I need not fear her, Fredericka said to herself, keeping her eyes pinned on the print. Her aunt's voice reminded her dimly of a voice in a play, something classic, something not understood, but nonetheless moving, out of distant reading. Was it Hecuba? Medea?

"Fredericka," said Aunt Palm, calling her name out of a prolonged silence. "I have always felt that you were my child. You mean more to me than any one of my sons ever did. I understand you. I warn you! Do not throw away your life!" She spoke in her gentlest, most impressive voice.

"But which way is throwing it away?" Fredericka cried, raising her face, twisting her hands in her lap as she let the prints fall to the floor, beginning suddenly to weep.

Aunt Palm looked back without expression. "But surely you know that," she said.

In the hall a door opened and closed. There was a cheerful whistle. Fredericka startled, began to dry her eyes. "Who is it?" she whispered, like a conspirator.

"Philander," said Aunt Palm loudly. "I invited him to dinner."

Uncle Philander came tramping in full of vigor.

"A fire already? Good idea!" he said. "Early autumn this year! I predict it! Had a letter from your friend Allers today. Ever hear from him?"

"Yes," said Fredericka faintly, trying to pull herself together. "He writes to me."

"Writes well for a foreigner," said Uncle Philander, producing the letter. "In fact he writes exceptionally well for anyone. Should be a literary man, not a doctor—if he is a doctor. He is, or was, wasn't he?"

"Yes," Fredericka said, still weakly.

Uncle Philander was unfolding the letter. "The thing that beats me," he said, wagging his red beard, "is why it takes a foreigner to appreciate the Indians. Never could get Christopher or Robert to take any interest. Even Owen acts bored—will look at anything in my collection except my baskets and the medicine-man rattles and fetishes. Best things I have. Should be in the Heye museum. But Allers writes: 'I very much want to look at your collection of Indian things when I get back. I'll understand them better now.' "

Uncle Philander's face shone with simple happiness.

"And he's been to the cliff dwellings. I told him to go. He said he was 'profoundly moved.' His own phrase for it— 'profoundly moved.' . . . What does he write to you, Fredericka?"

"Much the same kind of thing," Fredericka said. She added, "I think the country is helping him."

At once Uncle Philander focused. "Helping him what?"

She regretted her remark. "Helping him grow stronger. He's had a lot of shocks."

"Oh, yes, of course." Uncle Philander nodded. "You're looking rather peaked, Fredericka. Anything wrong?"

"How tactful you are, Philander," Aunt Palm remarked tartly. "You must surely see that she has been crying—and when you see that you should know better than to speak. I'd say you learned very little from three wives."

"I am perhaps the best judge of that," said Uncle Philander.

They began to quarrel in the amiable, slightly theatrical style they had used from childhood to hide their deep affection for each other. Under the protection of their banter Fredericka got out of the room to put on powder and make-up. Dinner passed off without any further strain.

Later, after Aunt Palm had gone to bed, and she and Uncle Philander were enjoying a frappé of white mint in the breathless night that was now brewing a thunderstorm, Fredericka asked her uncle:

"Do you think Aunt Palm is really touched in the head?"

Uncle Philander looked at his niece with a long measuring look. He laid his finger to one side of his nose in a quaint gesture he occasionally used. "Palm's up to something," he said.

There was no use to ask him what he meant, for he would never explain.

Chapter Twenty-Four

THE NEXT DAY THERE CAME news from Christopher. He was coming home for a week's leave before his first trip to England. It seemed that finally the shuttling back and forth between Washington and London on which he had counted when he entered the Air Transport Command was about to begin. His arrival at just this time seemed to Fredericka, in her nervous overwrought state, a sign, a symbol. She could not read it yet, but she felt she would be able to when she saw Christopher.

But when she saw him nothing happened. Nothing had changed. It was all the same. She was the same. He was the same. He seemed glad to see her, although he told her at once that she was getting too thin. "Dieting?" he asked her. She told him no. "God, this place is really a dump," he commented, looking with distaste at the unpainted houses, the hot and dusty streets of Wrenkill, as they drove from the station to the Perry hill.

Helen and Robert came for two days. There was a party on Saturday night and once again Fredericka found herself in the midst of the familiar group. So much secretly happened to her between these now infrequent meetings with their local friends that she felt more and more a stranger and was surprised to find no one treated her as one. Even the coolness on the part of the Barretts, which she was afraid Christopher might feel, he did not seem to notice. He appeared to enjoy himself. Plainly he was set up by the program immediately ahead of him. A new assurance and ease shone in his manner. "It does a fellow good to get out of the rut," he said frequently.

"Not but what the army can be a rut too," he admitted finally. "The routine is pretty deadly. Particularly around offices."

"So war is boring," Helen cried, jangling her bracelets, knitting a winter jacket for her dachshund.

"Everything gets to be boring in time," was Robert's considered opinion.

It was after Sunday lunch. They were in the living room waiting for the effects of overeating to subside. They were all nobly resisting the impulse to go upstairs and take naps. The yawns, the scattered newspapers, the open windows admitting the heavy breath of a hot day at the end of summer. . . . This is it! Forever! Fredericka thought. Somehow, without knowing it, I have killed the albatross and now the ship will never move again. . . .

"Don't you feel well?" Bridgie asked her in a whisper with real concern.

Then it had shown in her face, the panic, the fear and uncertainty? . . .

Fredericka did a vague pantomime intended to convey to Bridgie: Moon rhythms or what have you—the female cycle. . . . This alone would satisfy Bridgie as to why her sister's face was pale, her manner abstracted, her hand cold, her voice remote. Bridgie appeared to accept the explanation in good faith.

Fredericka lay awake most of Sunday night, having managed to evade sharing her bed with Christopher by the same device she had used to satisfy Bridgie's curiosity as to why she seemed distrait at lunchtime. Lying there listening to all the familiar sounds—the moths on the screen, the rubbing of the maple on the roof in the occasional stirrings of air, toward morning the Burns's roosters far away, a mournful signal with ancient associations of betrayal—she knew that she could not continue this way any longer; she would have to end the impasse.

They were going to the lake place on Monday, the two of them. Christopher had four days more before he would have to leave. She counted up the hours and there were ninety-six in all. Could she live through ninety-six hours of hell and ever be the same again? Could she endure this prescribed length of torture and keep her mind clear and her purposes steady? She was not at all sure.

She got up at dawn and dressed and went out into the garden. The moisture of the night was drying already on the flowers. It was going to be a hot day—a day that would be preparing another thunderstorm probably, so that the air would be heavy and ominous and press on her aching temples with a throbbing heat, as she faced the ordeal of changing forever her life and Christopher's. Once again, in the slowly rising tide of the day, she asked herself dully: Why do I do it? Why? But this time the question had less force. She knew it was here at last—the final decision. She had known it very definitely when Christopher put his arms around her in the bedroom and she had eased herself gently out of his embrace. It had not been distaste, not at all the feeling she had had with Joe, but quite simply a feeling of inability. She knew, having been with Franz, that she could never again be with Christopher.

As she walked, catching and recognizing the morning notes of each bird—the distinctive calls, trills, runs, and chirrups that Uncle Philander had taught her to hear and name—she thought it unlikely that this instinctual purity (for so it seemed to her) could be a universal trait. Surely not everyone found it so impossible to share more than one bed at a time. Wasn't one of the problems of every period of war precisely this: that men and women had again to come to grips with the old problem of married infidelity?

She found herself wondering about Christopher and realized, though a year ago she would not have thought it, that she had no notion what he might do in months of separation from her. Nor did she care. And she should care! To be possessively jealous was one thing, but to have no feeling of the oneness of a union was another. This latter she had never had with Christopher. Yet she had always been true to him. So far as she knew he had been true to her. And now, in the clarity of the early morning light, this seemed to her but another proof of the lifelessness, the inertia, of their existence in Wrenkill. They had been too sleepy, too drugged with monotony, to even be aware of their condition. Their coming together in the act of sexual union was merely another habit, fixed and regulated, timed in relationship to the prescribed schedule of the week's activities.

She turned back to the house and, since it was still too early for breakfast and no one seemed stirring, she took her bicycle and rode down the hill to the post office. The night train was likely to have brought a letter from Franz and she wanted to read it before she faced the day.

There was one in the box and she stopped just outside the door to open it. As she tore the envelope Nate Frisch came around the corner and started to pass her without recognizing her. "Nate! Good morning."

He looked at her absently for a moment through his old-fashioned glasses. "Oh, Miss Fredericka!" He had not called her that in years—not since she used to roller-skate past his open door.

She saw that something was very wrong. "Nate, what is it?" Immediately she knew. "Your boy!"

He nodded.

"Oh, Nate, how dreadful! Is he . . . ?" She could not bear to say the irrevocable word. She did not need to. He nodded slowly, his face broken, bewildered, sad beyond bearing. They stood together in the warming day in front of the old red-stone post office. She had given him her hand spontaneously and he held it in his calloused palms. He did not seem to want to move on. She had the feeling that he wished even to talk about his boy, but could not find the words. At last he said:

"They say what he did was beyond the call of duty—that was the phrase they used. He'll have a medal. You'll read about it in the papers. It'll be nice for his son."

"He had a son? I didn't know."

"Born a month ago."

"I remember the day when I came in for the ointment—it seems so long ago—it was only a few months really. . . . You said then, how the war would reach all of us, even in sleepy Wrenkill, sooner than we thought. Now it has. . . ."

Suddenly she had the impulse to confide in Nate. "I may be going away, Nate. If I do I want you to know—I'll never forget you." She looked at him through a film of tears. The first step had been taken! She had told someone what was in her mind. Strange that it should have been Nate Frisch to whom she spoke first—the village barber, the kindly anarchist who had lent her *Equality*, *Looking Backward*. But no, perhaps it was not strange at all to have confided first in the one philosopher she had ever known until she met Franz Allers.

Nate showed no surprise at her news. "I'll always remember you too, Miss Fredericka. And I'll always keep the painting you made of my window with the plants in it."

She had forgotten the painting. "One of my first oils. I remember. I did it my junior year at Attica Center."

She did not try to read Franz's letter again until she was almost home. She had to walk the bicycle up the last stretch anyway, and she got off and sat on the stone wall and took the letter from her pocket and read about Robert Goodwin and the poison. When at the end of the letter Franz told her what he had told Goodwin—that once he had wished for this way out and had not been able to have it, and now when he no longer wanted the escape of death, it was placed in the palm of his hand—for the first time she had some sense of what she meant to him. The letter gave her a feeling of strength and she went on up the hill to breakfast with a stouter heart.

After breakfast Christopher went to town to attend to some business matters at the bank and Fredericka strolled out into the garden with Aunt Palm. The supplies for the lake were already packed. She had only to wait for Christopher. Aunt Palm was silent, as she was so much of the time lately. This morning, however, she did not seem unhappy or abstracted; she seemed to be in deep thought. Because of her own secret wish to unburden her mind, Fredericka was afraid to speak at all. She felt that she must tell Christopher first.

After they had sat by the pond in silence for a long time Aunt Palm spoke in a voice that was strong and calm. "I once thought I would live to be a very old lady, but now I think not. I may, however, live some years yet. I've never resided in a big city and I believe I would like to end my days in one. New York would be my choice. I want to ask you, Fredericka, to give me your support when I put this idea to Christopher, which I intend to do in writing before he leaves."

Did Aunt Palm suspect? Who could tell? The eyes were the same closed doors they had been when she brought the portfolio of selected paintings to Fredericka only a few days before. Fredericka felt as though her heart was splitting in half with love and sadness. She wanted to cry out: Aunt Palm, don't sacrifice yourself. Not for me anyway. It will be all right. You needn't try to help me—to make it easier. . . . But she could not speak. Aunt Palm had closed the inner doors and she alone could open them.

"I promise," was all Fredericka could say, chokingly. .

"That's good of you, lovie," Aunt Palm said gratefully. "I do hate a fuss."

Nothing more was said. At noon Christopher came with the car and they went off. At the last minute Aunt Palm handed him an envelope.

"What's this?" he asked absent-mindedly, pocketing it.

"A matter for you to attend to when you've the time," Aunt Palm said quite blandly.

From the turn in the driveway, as they wound down the hill, Fredericka looked back. Aunt Palm was standing under the wooden eyelet embroidery of the hand-carved porch, a small figure, bony, erect, with something distinctive and special about her even at this distance. She did not wave her hand in farewell like Uncle Philander posing for an imaginary mural. She stood quite still. Fredericka put her hand out of the car. She extended it as though she were reaching for Aunt Palm's hand. Although she was sure Aunt Palm's fingers twitched under the little shawl she was wearing, she did not move them. Very slowly, very deliberately, she nodded her head three times. No. Distinctly, she was not mad; she was saner, wiser, stronger than any of them.

"Why are you crying?" Christopher asked, a few minutes later.

"The war," Fredericka said brokenly, "Nate's boy—I feel so badly."

"Nate's boy? God, that's a shame. But it's hardly something for you to cry over, is it?"

"I don't know . . . I suppose not." Now, something said to her, Now! Now! Tell him! Begin!

"I see a good deal of Jack Pearson and his wife in Washington," Christopher said. His intention was obviously to divert her. He began a running conversation through which Fredericka could not break. Later! she told herself. Later! It can wait.

They got to the lake early in the afternoon and when they had eaten the sandwiches and the hard-boiled eggs Eunice had given them, Christopher took a nap and afterwards went out in the boat to fish. He would be gone until after dark.

With the coming of evening all nature seemed to Fredericka to conspire to intensify her pain. The moon had never seemed more mysterious, more beautiful, than it did rising over Sprucetop, tossing the great silver coin of its image on the quiet lake, welcomed in rising by tree toad, cricket, heron, and owl, with a swelling chorus, faint murmurs and low cries of surprise and joy. The warm night began to pulse to the sounds of insects hidden in grass and tree, weaving a canopy, a counterpane of soft and easy dreaming through which one dared not break with shuddering force.

Before the moon came, as she sat waiting, looking out across the twilight where the blue was creeping slowly into the green, she had thought about fireworks on long-ago Fourths of July. Now she imagined them across the lake between the veiled and misty maples and a dark cone of fir where the shore trees met the hill trees. There they would be most effective. Nothing elaborate or spectacular—only shooting stars, perhaps, dropping in multicolored dying falls against the growing night. . . . And so, thinking of fireworks, she began thinking of the princes and dukes of little European principalities who could once, with a clap of the hand, a pointed finger, cry: There! Right there! A fountain with a thousand sprays, or Roman candles, or a tableau of live maidens holding jars of wine, bowls of grapes. . . . Or a string quartet, or a quintet, at suppertime in the balcony any night you might care to summon the musical serfs. . . . Yes, this life must have undeniably had its special theatrical charm—for those who commanded it. What charm anywhere today for anyone? No charm—only fixed dull patterns, or challenge, not loud, perhaps, not clear and ringing (no bugle notes—they too were the past) but something subterranean, persistent, gnawing and pricking in the watches of the night. Up! There is work to do! The world stands in peril! Mankind too! But how could you believe it on this gently sagging porch with the water lapping the old stones?

Charm! Gaiety! "Let us be gay!" Maria Farrell had cried, taking the combs out of her hair and whirling on one heel, tapping and stamping with the other. This was not escape, only respite—valid enough, for Maria's eyes were open, her eyes beheld. "No, no, no," she had exclaimed. "Do not show that painting tonight!" And she had been quite right. It said too much. Let us try to find a moment to sing together around a fire—friends in a half circle in the firelight, singing, "Oh, Shenandoah, I love your daughter, Hi-oh, you rolling river."

La Cucaracha, Cielito Lindo, sang the Spanish teacher and Maria together. Franz Allers bent his dark head nearer to them to catch the melodies. "The Mexican cowboys sing only love songs," said Maria, "only love songs all day long."

But all this was long ago, very distant, before the break, before the great decision. The days were growing darker, the news blacker, life more uncertain and tense, and she too, Fredericka Perry, was no longer to escape, was caught into it and asked at last to do something which produced in her at the mere thought of it a feeling of terror, a pounding of the heart, and cold perspiration all over her body.

If Christopher were going away actually to fight, could I do it? she asked herself. She could imagine Bridgie's shocked face. But you can't, Flea. Not possibly. Not just now when he's going away. Put it off! Postpone it! Maybe you'll change. . . . But, Bridgie, don't you see, can't you see? This is like asking him not to go and do what he's doing, change his life, alter his pattern, move to another level of experience. . . . Was the argument a good one? She no longer knew. She had gone back and forth over it too often in the long stretches of sleepless nights. She was certain of only one thing: that behind Christopher's back she could not, would not, live any longer in a way that he did not know.

She heard the boat and she watched it approach, a dark form through the dark waters. There was the homely creak of the oarlocks, the grinding noise where the keel struck the beach. Christopher got out, pulled the boat farther onto the stones. His feet on the path, on the wooden planks, on the kitchen linoleum . . . Already these sounds were an echo in her memory. How often would they break into the quiet of sleepless nights ahead?

"No luck!" Christopher said glumly. This meant his mood

would be bad. She heard him put his tackle behind the door. He came in, reaching automatically for the evening paper as he passed the table.

"Any news?"

"I haven't had the radio on."

He sat down under the lamp. Any news? What a strange phrase, she thought . . . I suppose he means: What is the last report on Europe, the dying patient?

I must do it now, she thought. Right now before he gets sleepy. Now, this minute, I am finally going to live out that awful nightmare toward which I have been deliberately walking for six months—or is it for fifteen years? For a lifetime? His back was toward her, the paper was held in front of him. She crossed the room and sat down opposite him on the old faded chintz couch.

"Chris," she began.

"Mmm," he did not lower the paper. She waited. She began silently to count—an old habit. Fifty-four. He lowered the paper.

"Yes."

"Chris, I—I want to talk to you."

He lowered the paper a little more—did not fold it, just held it tentatively to one side as though sure that what she had to say would be brief.

"Yes."

"It's about us. I—our life doesn't have much meaning together any more. I think you know it!"

She took a great breath and almost hurled the rest of it at him, fearing if she did not she would never utter it: "I think we should divorce each other and start again."

Instantly his face became a complete mask. Only his eyes stayed alive—those eyes of a beautiful forest creature that had always, she realized in this moment, baffled her with their empty striking beauty, a beauty that promised so much and had never given it.

"What do you mean?" His voice was quite normal.

She clasped her hands together, hoping that the palms would at least lend each other warmth. But they were cold—dry and cold. She felt as though the whole middle part of her body were packed solidly in ice.

"Help me," she began quietly.

"What do you mean?"

"I mean help me," she repeated with sudden passion. "Help me to be honest. Let's help each other to be honest."

"Fredericka," he said, "I don't understand you." He spoke quietly, flatly, yet with an edge to it.

"Have you ever?" She asked it as a simple question. She really wondered.

He made a gesture that was almost a shrug. "Of course."

"I really don't believe you have."

"That's not true," he said, "and you know it. Think of our childhood together."

"I have thought of it," she said. "And I know we didn't understand each other, even then. We were just near the same age, and grew up in the same way. That fooled us."

"Fooled us!" he repeated.

But she was going on. "You never understood your mother. You've admitted it a hundred times. But I always understood her. If you didn't understand her you can't possibly have ever understood me."

"What is this?" he said sarcastically. "A you-don't-understand-me session?"

He began to fold the paper precisely in half. It was a gesture very like Uncle Caleb's in time of domestic stress. Yet she saw how his hands were shaking and a stab of such unexpected pain went through her that she was tempted to jump up, throw her arms around him and cry: Oh, forget it! Forget I said it! It's just that I'm not myself today—this war, your going. . . . But she knew she could not change any of it now.

"What is it you really want to tell me?" he asked her coldly.

His face was angry. She wondered, briefly, how she looked to him—uncertain? frightened? She tried to quiet the trembling deep inside her. She waited a long moment before saying:

"I want to tell you that I don't really love you as a wife should love her husband. I never have. It is a terrible truth, but it is a truth. And I don't believe that you have ever really loved me either . . ."

"Just leave me out of it," he said coldly. "This is your story, not mine."

"But I can't leave you out of it!" she cried.

"Well, try anyway."

She waited a moment before continuing. "I've gone over and over how we happened to get married. All of it. I have finally faced it. Don't think I'm blaming you. I'm blaming myself. Believe me . . ." She clasped her hands more tightly together, then thrust her hair behind her ears with an old nervous gesture that she used when she came to a tough place in her painting. Her voice rose a little. "Believe me. Please believe me, when I tell you that I blame myself more than you will ever believe or know. In the nights . . ."

She choked, the tears rushed forward. She tried to keep them back, determined not to cry before it was all out.

"In the nights I've gone over it and over it, trying to understand what happened to us that made us take the easy way. . . ."

"The easy way," he interrupted. "What do you mean by the easy way?"

"I'll try to explain. I mean there we were, both of us, ready for love—for *mating*, that's nearer it. Both of us. And we fell right into—into nature's booby trap." It was an unfortunate phrase. She didn't know where it had come from. It sounded like Owen. She hurried on, determined now to bring out first the facts about Greg Davie. "The truth is, I fell into—into the trap—because I wasn't afraid of you and I was afraid of another man. I wanted to be with him far more than I ever wanted to be with you, but—oh, forgive me for telling you all this, Chris, but I have to. . . . You see, to have gone with him would have been unlike anything I knew, strange, and so—frightening to me. I would have been unprotected, on my own completely—and although I loved him, wanted only to be with him—I just didn't have the guts. I couldn't make the break. . . ."

"Who was this other man?"

He spoke as though he were being strangled.

"Greg Davie."

"Greg Davie." He repeated the name, and then in amazement, "Not that guy from Attica Center?"

"Yes."

"That guy?" He couldn't believe his ears. She could see how shocked he was. The skin shows shock, she observed almost clinically to herself. It goes gray—even though the face registers nothing.

"You ask me not to include you," she hurried on, "but I have to. I don't know what was working in you that—that first night long ago in the boathouse." (She felt the color rushing into her face. How could she feel this embarrassment after fourteen years of marriage?) "Probably just—spring juices—but it—it looked like fate to me, and it seemed so—so natural, so simple and easy—so *easy*, the whole thing. That was it! So we could just go jogging along in the same familiar rut for all our days. You must have wanted it as much as I—only, life doesn't let it happen that way apparently."

She felt the strength suddenly deserting her. She would have to rest before she spoke of Franz. She put her head back and closed her eyes.

Christopher's voice, stony, angry, broke the silence: "If you've felt this way for fourteen years why has it taken you so long to tell me?"

She opened her eyes and looked at him, trying to reach through the stone to the flesh it encased.

"Yes," she said, "that is the question." His eyes did not flicker, his expression did not alter. "Because I didn't know I felt that way," she went on simply, almost humbly. "I was just living along in a fog, in a dream, half alive. I don't think I even knew I was only half alive until—until Aunt Palm began to act strange, began to shut me out—or so it seemed—anyway, to detach herself from me, and then I knew that it was really she, not you—not ever you really—who had held me to Wrenkill and to this way of life.

"Somewhere in me I always knew that—and yet I didn't know it—because I didn't really admit it. But somewhere I was guilty about it all—and that's why I never painted more—because I had something worked out somewhere in my head that if I gave up *that* I'd pay off some of the guilt . . ."

"You're not making much sense," he said coldly.

And yet as he spoke she saw, looking at him, that she had made sense. That somewhere, down deep inside him, he was understanding her better than he himself knew. His face darkened abruptly.

"I blame Mother for all this," he said. "She's been a dissatisfied woman all her life, and a dissatisfied woman is just a slow-working poison in any setup. We should have left Wrenkill long ago—you and I. I knew it. I even talked to Dad about it once or twice, but he—he made it so worth while to stay that I always gave in. I knew it was a mistake with Mother the way she was."

"Oh, don't blame your mother," Fredericka cried. "Blame me—blame us—or don't blame *anyone*, for maybe even we aren't to blame—unless we go on living in this fog. Then we are blamable, I think, and that's why I had to tell you. Now that I've really seen our life as it is I had to tell you, or I'd be more dishonest than even I can bear to be, and apparently I've been so unconscious most of my life that I could live a lie and not even know that I was doing it."

"Why can't you be like Bridgie?" Christopher cried with abrupt irrelevance. "I can't believe you're sisters . . . It's all Mother's influence," he repeated bitterly.

"I wish I *could* be like Bridgie," Fredericka cried. "I really do, but I'm not—and that's that!"

"But how are you different?" he asked unreasonably. "I mean, what is it you want? Do you want a career? Do you want to be a painter? You can paint all you please right at home. Mother always has."

"No," she said, "it's not that—not really—not all of it, anyway. I just want to live before I die. Really live!"

"Live!" he repeated, and now he was baffled.

Somewhere strength came back into her. She felt it like a second wind. "I know it seems obscene just now," she said, "to insist on it, to even put so much emphasis on living when everywhere everyone is dying. But perhaps that's just why the feeling rises so strongly, the necessity to live when everywhere all one sees is the end of things—death, destruction . . ."

To her astonishment she saw that this had registered on him. She could feel his response. She pressed on quickly.

"Actually, your going away, joining up when you didn't have to, is a part of it—it's seeking life, even though to find it you have to put on the uniform of death. Oh, you do see what I mean!" she cried. "Please admit it. Please let's try to help each other."

"I'm not asking for help," he said coldly. "I never have."

And now she saw that he was going to get rid of an old bitterness. She was amazed to feel the depth and acridness of this stored-up bitterness in Christopher. It came tumbling out, a stream of words, deep anger at the bond between her and his mother, perhaps never really suspected until now. He began to take his father's side. Father suffered over Mother all his life, he cried. Mother's selfishness, indifference, the way she went to her room and locked it. "Only in the daytime," Fredericka put in. But he did not seem to hear. How she went walking without a word, came home drenched to the skin, kept canaries in the room off the dining room until Father poisoned them. "So he did it! I always wondered." On and on Christopher went. The words were a rushing torrent. She thought of Niagara Falls, the man who went over safely in a barrel. It was a symbol to cling to. She would just let the angry torrent wash over her; she would keep the barrel around her and eventually be washed up, battered and bruised but still alive, still breathing.

She had never heard Christopher speak at such length. She would never have believed that he could. It made her sick to hear him. Perhaps there isn't ever long enough to live through, live out, get rid of, the bad behavior patterns that people set up between them. Perhaps they can never live through, completely finish with, their mistakes. Life is not long enough, the years go too fast. How people grow apart, storing bitterness, making little secret hoards of it that they put away and try to forget, or that they cherish and nourish in the quiet times, in the night, wakeful—the wife, shedding warm tears of self-pity into the pillow: "He'll be sorry." The husband, driving from home to the office: "She'll never understand." Then there was anger too, anger hard and solid, a wedge of something edible like a too-rich pudding, full of all sorts of unrecognizable oddments and elements, good as it goes down but indigestible—ah, finally, so completely indigestible.

"And the children? What about them?" He was crying. She thought to herself: The possibility of another man hasn't yet occurred to him. That will come tomorrow. After this long night is spent. . . . I've ruined his fishing, she thought, stupidly.

"I know," she said. "The children. I've thought and thought about them." Cried too, over and over again; but she would not speak of her tears, would not angle for any sympathy from him. "And yet," she said, "they aren't my life, our life —they never have been."

He was stunned. "What do you mean?"

"Just what I said. They aren't my life. Children never are their parents' lives, though they may seem to be, for a time, when they're little and need you constantly. It doesn't last —shouldn't last. If it does—the feeling that they're your reason for being alive—then you're—you're sick."

"Sick?" He was growing furious.

"Yes, because it's their life you're leading, not your own."

She had a strong feeling that she was saying all the wrong things, none of the right. She was sounding hard, indifferent, callous to the fate of her children.

"I know how they'll probably suffer," she cried. "You certainly can't believe that I don't think of that. I can only comfort myself with the thought that the war will make it easier . . . All around them homes are breaking up. It's in the picture of our times. Actually our home was broken anyway—the fixed pattern. They've gone away to school, you've gone to war. . . . Oh, don't look at me so accusingly! I know how responsible I'll feel! But we're both responsible. We were responsible before we ever had them. Before they were born we were responsible. We should never have had them."

The terrible words were uttered at last.

"I always knew you didn't care for them," he said, thrusting in the knife. She simply looked at him without words. "Why shouldn't we have had them?" he demanded.

"Because our reasons for marrying each other weren't right."

"Rot!" he said. "I asked you to speak for yourself. These are your confessions, not mine."

She said nothing.

"I can't believe it's you," he went on, "this absolutely hardhearted attitude about your own children. You don't give a damn about loading them down with problems of insecurity, a broken home—"

"Stop!" she cried. She could not stand it. "Stop!" She stood facing him, her hands clenched. "Don't talk that way to me! You don't know anything about how I feel inside. And you never have . . . But let me ask you this: what children anywhere in the world today have security? Where are they?

In England? In China? In France, Russia, Holland, Austria, Japan, Germany? . . . Where? Do you ever think of that? And perhaps security isn't, after all, the biggest thing, the most important thing. We had it. Did it work for us? Or did it simply make us soft and unconscious and unwilling to grow up and face the tough life of adults?"

"I'm going to bed," Christopher said stonily. He rose, dark with rage. He marched to the sideboard and Fredericka heard the liquor flowing into his glass. He went off into his bedroom and banged the door. After a long time she lay down on the couch and pulled a blanket over her, but she did not sleep.

It was the first of the three days.

In the morning as soon as she heard him stirring Fredericka got up and put on the coffee. She knew he had slept. Toward morning she had heard him snoring. The sound had heartened her. The blow cannot have been too terrible, she told herself.

They breakfasted almost in silence. As soon as he had eaten, Christopher, lighting his first cigarette, began abruptly, his tone still hard and without feeling.

"Are you going to marry someone else?"

"I am in love with someone else."

"Who is it?"

"Franz Allers."

He was stupefied. "Allers! That refugee!"

"Yes."

For a moment he said nothing. "Allers!" he repeated. "I can't believe it."

"Why not?"

"Because," he began falteringly, "he's—he's broken, he's—he's a tired-out European. What has he got to offer you?"

"Life," Fredericka said.

"Oh, rot!" He was not so much angry now as disgusted. He simply could not credit his ears. "You certainly don't mean to marry him." He made it sound as though her choice of a European refugee offered him some personal affront.

"Yes." She had never been more sure than at this moment.

"Why? Try to tell me why."

"Because I love him. Because for the first time in years and years, since knowing him, I've felt alive, and like painting, like moving fast and doing things and seeing new people, talking and reading and—for the first time since I was a child—" (and now her own words astonished her) "I feel really free of Aunt Palm and—and of nature too."

"*Nature!*"

"Yes, nature. I mean, I'm not so fastened to things like—like the garden, and the woods, and birds and the seasons. I seem to feel them more, and yet they aren't so important. Once they were everything, like a substitute for something I was missing. Now . . . I can't explain." She was silent.

"Apparently not."

"I know," she cried as he rose, "how hard it must be for you to understand. It would have been for me a year ago. Even more so five years ago. But this—this action of mine, which almost everyone will call a sin, doesn't seem to me a sin at all, but something quite different. Like an awakening, as though for the first time I am really linked with life—all life."

He was staring at her coldly.

She forced herself to hurry on against the stony wall of his disbelief, his growing distaste.

"I even feel that in losing this—this easy bond in which I've lived with you, I'm able to understand—to feel some of the troubled confusion, the loss and homelessness of the whole world. I really share it."

He assumed an expression that was very like a sneer. "I suppose you're saying that everyone should get divorced—share the world's mess . . ."

"Of course not." She was angry but she held back the coldness. "Only those who are living without . . ." She did not finish.

"Without what?"

She saw Aunt Palm with her portfolio of pictures. Yes, pictures were an easier way! Words were inadequate, words were hard to get at. They lay buried under habits of expression, clichés, dead timber of meaningless talk.

"Without any real relatedness," she said. Oh, God! It sounded awful. She felt it sincerely—knew just what she meant, but it sounded stuffy. She hurried on. "People just pretending they belong together because they *are* together—and it's so hard to break things when there's no outer trouble. It's hard to believe enough in life—at our age—to break a pattern. Everyone feels: What's the use! Things don't change! People don't change!"

Christopher had used up his supply of words. It was plain from the way he stood, glowering, in the middle of the room, baffled and angry. Yet somewhere, Fredericka felt convinced, since she told him that Franz Allers was the man, he took it all less seriously. For what did this middle-aged refugee possibly have to offer Fredericka Woodward Perry?

"I'm going out in the boat," he said.

He stomped out with his tackle and left her alone. She forced herself automatically through the housework. She did the dishes, made the bed with extra care. She wanted desperately to cry, but even when she summoned the faces of Leslie and Forrest—their baby faces in their prams blinking into the sunlight—the tears would not come.

Christopher came back early. He had no fish. He flung himself down in the porch swing with a bottle of beer. "Let's have this out," he said harshly.

"It is out," she said tremulously.

"Not by a damn sight." He spoke angrily but he looked so sick and broken that her heart failed her. How can I do this—how can I?

His bitterness welled up again. It began pouring out: she too was as selfish as his mother. She was unnatural. Again he spoke of Bridgie, of Merry Barrett. Why couldn't she be like them? She didn't like the town. Didn't do what other women did. If she hadn't lived there all her life people would call her a snob. Looking back he blamed his mother—yes, but also he blamed her, Fredericka. A mature woman can make her own life what she wants it to be.

"But I was never mature. That's what I've tried to tell you."

He did not pause to listen. She made no further attempt to explain. She sat letting the torrent beat on the barrel in which she had again enclosed herself. Not that she did not listen. She heard every word. She knew that she would hear them again many times as she would hear Christopher's footsteps on the dock, on the path, on the steps, approaching her for the last time as her husband. For now the bond was severed. It had been severed since the evening before.

"But the thing that really beats me," he said at last, "is this guy Allers. That you can ever take him seriously—consider for a moment joining up with that—that *cynic*."

"Cynic?" The word astounded her. But she considered it. Was Franz a cynic? Perhaps in a way he was, for he had admitted that it was hard for him to keep his faith alive in the modern world.

"No matter what you do," Christopher was imploring her, "for God's sake, Flea, don't take on a broken man. These Europeans flocking here now—I've seen dozens of 'em—they're all alike. They're tired, they're *through*, I tell you."

"I think you're wrong," Fredericka denied. "Maybe they're stronger than you know. Some of them are broken, but I don't think they all are . . ."

But he was not listening.

"I tell you that guy is through. He'll just be a second-rate professor here, all his days, or go back to Europe and try to find his place again—a place that's gone for good. Sure, he was probably a big shot in Vienna. But that won't make him a big shot here, not by a darned sight. They think different, act different—they've a whole different set of values."

"He's got a job to do here—and I think he'll do it," Fredericka said quietly. "And I don't happen to agree with you about refugees. This country could use them—needs them. We're so untouched here, so young . . ."

"Young!" He caught quickly at the word. "You're right!" he cried hotly. "Young and strong. America doesn't need anybody. This war is proving it. We're the strongest nation in the world today and every nation—*every other nation in the world*—is depending on us."

He spoke as though he were speaking of himself, a personal dependence of the world on Christopher Perry. She was tempted to say, You're identifying yourself with America. Big stuff! Easy arrogance born of never being tested. You've had it easy, all your life . . . But I must keep my temper, she thought. She said nothing. He drove on and on until finally she could again stand no more.

Then she said: "If nothing else proves the gap between us, this does, Chris. You've no idea what I mean, and what you are saying sounds to me like nonsense. I never have this feeling with Franz—and I don't believe he has it with me."

He gave her a long stupefied look. Then he got up and left the house. In an hour he was back. The day dragged by in argument, upbraidings, a long slow-grinding torture. Twice Christopher flung out of the house, returned, began again. He stomped into his room at one point, emerged, began again. They both grew gray and drawn with the strain. It seemed to Fredericka that a week had passed since they left the Wrenkill driveway. She shed no tears, she held herself steady, while back and forth he began to run the cruel machine of his accusations, his reminders, over the bodies of Aunt Palm and the children: "How can you do it? . . . Leave me out of it, if you want, but think of them. What will Mother do without you?" . . . "We'll have to meet these problems when the time comes . . ." Then suddenly she thought of the letter. It must contain Aunt Palm's newly hatched plan— her life in New York. Should she mention the letter to Christopher? Would his anger be worse now than later? Would he accuse them of conspiring together? She decided she had to risk it.

"Anyway," she began with a trembling voice, "Aunt Palm wants to live alone. She told me so. She wants to go to New York and live there. She told me that too."

He stared at her stupefied. "Leave Wrenkill? I don't believe it. It's just a whim."

"I don't think so. I believe it's what she put in that letter she handed you the day we came up here."

He got up after a moment and went to his coat for the letter. He read it through in silence. It was brief. He threw it

· 384 ·

on the floor. "You've told her, of course," he said in an ugly voice.

"No, no, I swear it."

"Well, she knows, anyway. The letter begins: 'Fredericka will have told you her news.' "

"I never told her," Fredericka reiterated.

"Well, I suppose it's been plain enough—plain enough to everybody. I suppose the whole town knows it. This is probably what Joe meant by saying they never saw you while I was gone."

For a moment Fredericka had the impulse to betray Joe to his old friend—but only for a moment. She did not wish to upset Christopher any more than he was. She let her thoughts rest on Aunt Palm. The sly old witch! Forcing her hand! What if she hadn't already told Christopher? Then she would have had to. . . .

That night she was so exhausted that she took sleeping tablets in order to rest.

She did not know how long she had been asleep when the scream hurtled her out of unconsciousness. After she was awake the murderous cry lingered in her head with frightful clarity. She was so terrified that she felt as though her whole body were held rigidly in a vise. She could not move, could not even shift her eyes to identify the room or to find herself; her very eyeballs felt frozen in their sockets. She waited without moving or breathing. There was only the sound of her own blood pouring through her heart. But the night still seemed to echo faintly, dimly to the terrible cry. What had it been? What could make a noise like that?

At the question it came again, across the lake, on the shore, a cry like a maniacal woman, like someone screaming in violent death, loud and terrible beyond all imagining. And with the second cry her brain supplied the answer: Panther! Panther on the shore. At the thought her body burst instantly into a warm bath of sweat and she remembered Christopher.

She got up at once, reaching for her robe, putting it on as she groped her way down the hall, for she was afraid for some reason to turn on any of the lights. She spoke outside his door, "Chris."

"Yes," his voice was rigid with terror, like a child's.

"It's a panther," she said.

"Is that it?"

His fear communicated itself to her through the wall. She opened the door and went over to his bed. He looked like a frightened child lying there on his back, like Forrest, and she could not resist putting her hand to his face. It was icy under her fingers.

"It frightened me horribly, too," she said, as though to reassure him.

"How do you know it's a panther?" His voice was still unreal with his fear.

"Because I heard one here years ago—don't you remember? Uncle Philander wrote the Museum of Natural History."

She could feel him begin to tremble under the covers. "I was dreaming," he said hoarsely. "I—I thought I'd made the noise myself."

O God! She felt stabbed in her vitals, weak with the sudden sharp stab, and the feeling: I can't stand it! There's no use thinking I can, because I can't. It's beyond bearing! Outside this moment everything became blurred and unreal. There seemed no reason for any of her actions of the past days. What am I doing causing such pain—such pain that the cry of a

· 386 ·

wild animal sounds to a man like a cry sucked up out of his own guts by his terrible confusion and anguish?

"Oh, Chris—God!" She buried her face in her hands. She began to sway with weakness, felt her knees begin to beat together.

After a moment, "Get into bed," he said, "you're shaking." She hesitated, trying to control her weakness.

"It may come again," he said, still hoarsely. "The cry."

He is so terribly afraid, she thought, and I am too. Afraid because of my own heart, my dread of pain, of conflict and uncertainty. She opened the covers and crawled in, lay down flat on her back. Side by side they lay then, waiting for the cry to approach or grow distant. She thought of old statues of medieval ladies and their knights, laid out in stone effigy on their tombs, hands clasped across the breast, long-toed shoes pointed heavenward, cold and still in death. Why, then, do I sever this bond? Why not go down to death preserving it, for it must have a meaning, even though it is only a symbolic one—the sharing of a life with one man, the father of your children, the possessor of your body.

Christopher reached toward her, his hands groping, tremulous and beseeching. They were not the hands of habit, of taken-for-granted custom. These hands asked again, like a stranger, like one unsure of himself. No, no, she cried, racked in her bowels with her fear and resistance. No, no! And she lay rigid under his touch. Yet out of his suffering and shock she knew that something more than he had ever been able to give he could give her now.

"Flea, darling, oh, darling, God, don't! Let's forget it. Let's—Flea, I don't think I can stand it. Don't do this to me. Don't! Don't!"

She heard herself groaning, somewhere deep inside her. But no sounds emerged.

Christopher was going on:

"I've thought about what you've said, these two days. There's a lot of truth in it. Maybe I have been half dead . . . I admit I never understood you—or Mother. I—I even believe maybe I—wanted to marry you because of Mother. At least I think it might have some truth in it. I—maybe I felt I could have something then that you two had never had together . . ."

He began to sob, his face pressed against her shoulder. She felt his tears on her flesh, on her breast, wetting her gown, running under her armpit, but she could not move, could not turn and touch him.

"I can't go on alone," he was saying. "I can't face it—when I get back . . . What is there for me? That town—I hate it really. The children . . . No, Flea, don't! Don't! For God's sake—let's try again . . ."

"Don't go back," she forced herself to say. "Why go back? Go on yourself. Live some other place. Live your own life. You never have. You lived your father's. Lots of sons do, in one way or another."

It was no use. There were no words. Words were no good. They served no purpose. It was all beyond the reach of help. To try to explain—useless. Words did not reach, did not touch. "Let's try again?" Try what? What was there to try? It was gone and could not be recalled. It was gone because it had never been. Their life had not been a life. It had simply been the acceptance of a design into which they had both fitted for a time as neatly as inanimate matter. They had been the knight in effigy and his lady, laid out in cold stone, side by side on their tomb; in life already laid out for death.

"Let's leave it the way it is . . . until I come back. Let's see if we can't make it work . . ."

Why do you want it left the way it was? Is it merely to serve unconsciousness? While I was unconscious I could do it. Now I am no longer unconscious, so I cannot. . . . Suffering! This was it at last! Without bottom, without shape or dimension, or limited extension . . . All-consuming! His had just begun—the awareness of it. It seemed to her that she had been suffering for so long now that she could not measure the time. Have pity! Had he cried that? Had she cried it? Let us pity ourselves . . . But who are we to demand pity? Think of the people of the world, of Europe—of men who have lost their beloved wives to brothels for enemy officers, to firing squads, to prison camps. Think of women losing their unborn babes from their tortured wombs, their fathers shot before their eyes, their husbands hanged in the village square, lying unburied in a communal ditch. This, then, is suffering! Let us not speak of suffering! . . . Yes, but these also were only words. For they *were* suffering. That he was suffering was all too plain. His sobbing, growing weaker, was like the sharp edges of a hundred knives cutting into her shrinking flesh. How could she ever condone or excuse herself for causing this? Was some curse now being laid upon her; had she committed a sin that she could never expiate, this forcing another to unwilling anguish? She shuddered with cold and fear, longed for the comfort of arms, but would not, could not, turn to him. For there was no comfort in these arms except the comfort of long association. She dared not turn to him and make it appear that he might hope, that they might turn around and walk back along the turning spiral, back through the spiral of the day before yesterday.

So she could only lie and wait for dawn, saying to herself

with the first signs of light: There must surely be something that we learn from this sharing of pain, of a world's pain, pain born of not seeing, not knowing, not daring in the given hour. The price of unconsciousness, of cowardice—that is what I am now paying. The price of not growing up, of not wishing to enter maturity years ago . . .

The birds began, only faintly, a few of them, the satisfied and gentle songs of dying summer. The cicadas were strumming already; they promised, so Aunt Palm had always said, a golden day.